MOONLIGHT'S AMBASSADOR

T.A. WHITE

To my family and friends—your unwavering support means the world to me.

CHAPTER ONE

SLIME. OR SO close to it that the description fit. It was everywhere. In my hair. Covering my body. Oozing from my shoes with every step. I grimaced as my skin pulled and a patch started to itch. The only thing worse than slime was slime as it hardened.

I held my bike at arm's length, with as few fingers as possible, to prevent the slime from adhering to it. Bad enough that it was going to take me hours to get this stuff off me. At least I could stand in a shower to loosen it up. No way was I subjecting my bike to the same treatment. Bikes were expensive. Good bikes even more so. Mine may not have been top of the line, but I had no intention of letting a hundred-dollar job destroy it. If it meant I had to walk four miles home rather than risk getting this stuff all over my bike seat, then so be it.

This was the last time I accepted a run for a kappa. I didn't turn down paying work often, but I think I had finally found my line in the sand. The damn thing had thought it was funny when its pet covered me in this sticky gunk after I startled it.

A creature straight out of Japanese folklore, the kappa was about the size of a child and had made the sewers under the city its home. It wasn't on my normal route, so I'd never dealt with one before—much less known how easy it would be to freak out its pet, which was the size of a small truck and had teeth as long as my arm. Evidently, that over-sized worm had a thing about phones, the sight of which sent it into a sliming, vomiting tizzy.

Normally, Tom, a gnome and my arch nemesis at Hermes Courier Service, was the one responsible for running messages for the kappa and others in the Fey community, but since his involvement in trying to fix the vampire selection, he had been MIA. That left the rest of the Hermes couriers to pick up his slack.

No more. Jerry could find someone else to deal with the kappas. I was done. Those aquatic pranksters could go pick on someone else from now on. I didn't need the headache.

I turned the corner onto my street and frowned. Something was different.

It took me·a moment before I realized what it was. The lights. Someone had gotten all the street lamps working, making the small stretch almost seem like a legitimate neighborhood for once. It was a nice change, since the lights had been out since I moved in several years ago. The city got around to replacing them every once in a while, but they were always broken again before the night was through, leaving the street in shadows until the next time the city's budget accommodated new bulbs or someone's parents complained.

1

It was almost more surprising that they were still working. It might be the wee hours of the morning, but college kids never slept—at least in my experience. Most nights someone would have knocked them out by now.

A street without light didn't really bother me. As a vampire, my night vision was better than anything technology could create. Even on a moonless, cloudy night, I could see as clearly as I had during the day when I'd been human.

The only sound in the night was the whirring of my bicycle wheels as I headed for my apartment building. An old duplex just outside of campus, it had seen better days. The new lights cast sharp shadows on my home, giving it an almost sinister look and highlighting the fact that it was one step above a slum. It looked like it had been built around the turn of the nineteenth century, but not in a cute, 'look at how historical this is' way. It was more of a 'please don't fall down on my head' style.

The stoops tilted at odd angles and drooped forward like a drunken sailor on shore leave. All the windows were slightly off kilter, a side effect of settling that had never been mitigated.

My place was a second floor walk-up. I was ninety percent sure the wooden stairs on the outside of the building leading up to my apartment weren't up to code. They always shook and trembled like they were in the midst of an earthquake when anything bigger than a cat stepped onto them. One of these days they were going to collapse. Knowing my luck, I'd be standing on them at the time.

The postage stamp parking lot was looking a little rougher than usual. The weeds that had grown through the numerous cracks were gone. The pavement itself looked like someone had taken a jackhammer to it and huge chunks were now missing or had been pulverized into a million pieces. The only untouched spot surrounded the black Escalade sitting on the far side. Maybe someone had finally decided to demolish the old lot.

The urge to stop and make sure the vehicle remained unmarked was brief. I waved it away almost as soon as it occurred. Though I was technically the owner, I had not decided whether to accept it. There were strings attached to anything vampire related, and since it was a gift from my sire, the man who turned me into what I am today and then subsequently abandoned me, I was pretty determined to steer clear of those strings. It didn't matter if he didn't remember changing me because of some curse. His problems had destroyed the life I'd planned. A fifty-thousand-dollar SUV wasn't going to make up for that.

I continued past the Escalade toward the stairs that would take me to my apartment and the wonderfully hot shower waiting for me there.

Stepping onto the rickety stairs, I froze as a figure moved at the top of the landing.

"Caroline."

Her jaw had a pugnacious tilt to it that practically dared me to give her grief. At odds with the defiance in her expression was the uncertainty and hint of fear hiding in her eyes. It was that uncertainty and fear that kept my first reaction locked inside. It had been months since I'd last seen her. Months, since her life had been upended when she was kidnapped by a demon and bitten by a werewolf. She'd cut me out of her life after that. Turns out lying, even by omission, pretty much kills a relationship—especially when the part of your life you tried to keep secret tears hers apart. We hadn't been on good turns before the unveiling of my new condition, and that had worsened when Caroline found herself donning a coat of fur every month.

Besides the lack of the black rimmed glasses she'd worn since we were kids, Caroline looked normal. Maybe with more of a glow than usual, but anyone looking at her would never guess she was werewolf. She was the typical girl next door. Pretty, with wavy blond hair and blue eyes.

After a moment of hesitation, I continued up the steps.

Her expression turned uncertain before her mask slid into place, and she watched me with a cool sense of poise.

"Aileen, I've been waiting for hours."

I paused my ascent as I processed that statement. "I'm sorry. I had a job to finish before I could quit for the night. Had I known you were waiting, I would have perhaps expedited things."

Her expression flickered. She seemed to just take note of the state of me, her nose crinkling. "What happened to you?"

"Kappa's pet. We had a bit of a disagreement over a phone. I lost."

"That's a myth from Japanese folklore, right?" she asked.

I made a sound of agreement as I gained the top of the stairs and set my bike down on the narrow landing. Caroline stepped to the side, giving me room. Her eyes were searching as they examined my face. I kept my expression neutral. It hurt when she cut me out and refused to talk to me. I'd be lying if I said there wasn't a small, petty part of me that held onto a heaping dose of anger. The rest of me understood.

She'd just been trying to do an old friend a favor, not knowing all the shit that friend was going through, and that simple act of kindness destroyed life as she knew it. I understood. I'd faced some of the same anger and played a similar blame game when I'd been turned. I didn't fault her for her reaction, but it had still hurt to be told my best friend since childhood didn't want to speak to me.

"I forgot you worked nights," Caroline said, her voice stilted.

I nodded and looked at my door and then back to her. Did I invite her in? Send her on her way? I hated this awkwardness between us.

I decided to be direct. Caroline had never been good with subtext. I doubted that had changed now that she was a werewolf. At least, I assumed she was a werewolf. I didn't really know, since Brax had stopped providing me with updates when she made it clear she wanted nothing to do with me. As the alpha of the wolves, Brax's loyalty was to them first. It meant he did what was best for her; my feelings be damned. It was the right call, but it still stung.

"What are you doing here?"

She fiddled with a rubber band on her wrist, snapping it against her skin three times before her hands dropped to her side. Caroline had never been fidgety. Now, she looked like she was sitting on a rocket blaster of energy and barely keeping it contained.

She took a deep breath, her gaze coming up to meet mine before wandering away again as she looked anywhere but at me. Another difference from the old Caroline who could stare down even hardened criminals.

"I need your help." Her shoulders slumped as if a great weight had been added to them.

I studied her for a long moment. Caroline had never been one to ask for help, even when she so clearly needed it. It was a trait both of us shared. I fished my keys out of my pocket and turned to my door.

"Aileen, please. I have nowhere else to go."

I unlocked the door and stepped inside, holding it open. "Come in. I have a feeling that whatever this is, I'm going to need alcohol."

"You don't want to know what I need first?"

I snorted, the sound containing little in the way of humor. "You've only ever had to ask. You know that."

Her eyes softened as they held mine for the first time since I'd stepped onto the landing. She gave a small nod, stepping past me and into my home.

While the outside might suggest a drug dealer lived here—or a college student without much money—the inside was a different story. It said I cared. Sourced from garage sales and thrift stores, the furniture looked well-loved and cozy. It invited you to sit down and put your feet up after a hard day's work. It was bright and cheery and everything my life was not. It'd never be featured in a magazine—unless that magazine was Thrifter's Anonymous—but it suited my personality, which was as tattered and cobbled together as the place I called home.

"Can vampires even drink alcohol?" Caroline asked.

I propped my bike against the wall, tossed my keys onto my kitchen table—really just a catch-all table—and headed to the kitchen.

"This vampire does," I said, pulling open the fridge and reaching for a bottle of red wine. Real wine. Not the stuff I hid my blood in to prevent nosey family members from figuring out my secret.

I took another look at the bottle. At least I thought it was the real stuff. I tilted the top towards me. Yup. It was unopened. Should be safe enough.

I pulled the bottle from the fridge, grabbed some wine glasses from the upper cabinets and fished around in one of the drawers for the bottle opener. I came up empty. Those damn pixies had better not be fucking with me again. We had a deal. They didn't play pranks on me, and I didn't figure out a way to evict them from my apartment.

Ah, found it. The opener had been wedged at the very back under a pair of tongs and a mallet, neither of which I knew I owned.

Popping the cork off the bottle, I poured both of us a generous glass. I had a feeling I was going to need it for this conversation.

"So, what brings you to my part of the city? I thought for sure Brax would have you sequestered in some remote part of the wilderness for a few more months."

Caroline accepted the glass I handed her and took two big gulps of the wine. I watched her chug it before taking a small sip of mine.

"You're closer than you think," Caroline said when she had finished draining the wine. She held her glass out for more. So, it was going to be that kind of conversation. I set mine down and retrieved the bottle, pouring her an even larger portion than I had last time. "He has a piece of property down in Kentucky. Over one hundred acres of untouched land that his pack has owned for several decades. It's where they send their pups."

"Pups?"

"It's what they call the newly bitten." This time she sipped her wine.

"Ah, the vampires call the newly fanged yearlings." I started to lean against the cabinets at my back before straightening at the last minute when I remembered what I was covered in.

"Sounds better than pups. As if we're children needing to be told what to do."

Sounded familiar.

"They expected me to stay there a year. Longer if I couldn't control my wolf." She set the glass down hard. I winced as the glass stem cracked, enough that I suspected it would be going into the garbage once she was done. "I have a life. I have a career—one I worked my ass off for. Do you have any idea what it's like to deal with an entirely male teaching staff? The comments? The snide jabs at my gender or intelligence?"

I took another sip of my wine. "I may have some idea."

Being in the military meant getting used to being one of the few females in any unit I joined. For combat camera, whose specialty oftentimes demanded we go out on patrol with the infantry, it meant even less women. During a mission outside the wire, it was relatively normal to be the only American female around; sometimes for weeks.

Caroline's shoulders relaxed, and her lips loosened, some of the anger that had been brewing sliding away. "I imagine you would. I couldn't take it anymore. I needed to get back, to remind myself that everything wasn't about this." She waved her hand in the air as if to indicate everything. I could only assume she meant the supernatural detour her life had taken.

"How did Brax and Sondra feel about that?"

Caroline's face darkened at the mention of the woman who'd turned her. At the time, Sondra was being controlled by a demon, but that didn't change the fact that Caroline's entire existence had been upturned as a result. I'd guess that even though Brax had made Sondra Caroline's mentor, the relationship was off to a rocky start. I didn't blame Caroline. My own relationship with my sire could be categorized as nonexistent—not for lack of trying on his part.

"They don't know."

I blinked. Then I blinked again.

Caroline's expression was set.

"Wait. What do you mean they don't know?" I set my glass of wine down hard, barely flinching at the sound of a crack.

Caroline drummed her fingers against the chipped counter and looked away. "I may not have had permission to leave."

My mouth dropped open. The sound that escaped was closer to sputtering then actual words. "Explain."

"I found a way off the farm and then stole a car."

"Please stop explaining."

Caroline watched me as I ran through all the awful scenarios that could result from what she'd just revealed. It didn't really surprise me she had stolen a car. We'd done that a time or two in our misspent youth, and Caroline had never been one to let pesky details like ownership get in the way when she needed something.

"What did you do with the car?" I asked. I hadn't seen it when I came in.

"I ditched it on the other side of the city and then caught a ride here."

Smart. This way she wasn't leading them directly to my doorstep once they figured out she had stolen a car.

Brax and the wolves were not going to take this well. If there was one thing my experiences have taught me, it was that they took one of the newly turned bucking the system very personally.

"We need to call Brax and explain," I told her, heading for my phone.

"No, you said you'd help!"

"I am helping. He's going to show up looking for you, angry and ready to blow my house down. It's best to take care of this now. Manage expectations and head it off before it gets blown out of proportion. We'll just tell him you don't want to stay on the farm and get him to work with us."

"That won't work," Caroline snapped.

"Did you already try?"

Her expression made it clear she had.

"Perhaps it'll go over better coming from me." Caroline wasn't good at arguing with people. She was too autocratic—and given Brax was an alpha, unused to doing as other people ordered, that probably hadn't gone over well.

She huffed. "I'm not as bad at communicating as you make it sound."

I arched an eyebrow. Did she not remember the time when we got detention in high school because she pissed off the chemistry teacher while trying to convince him to let us perform an advanced experiment? Caroline was a great liar. Butter wouldn't melt in her mouth, but when it came to persuasion or the truth, it was better she not be involved.

"I've somehow managed to stumble through the last few years without you," she said.

What lingered in the air was the thought that she would probably have continued to be just fine if I hadn't involved her in my problems.

"Caroline, I understand your frustration and the instinct to hide. Believe me, I went through many of the same things when I was first turned. Hiding just makes things worse. It's better to meet this head on. Eventually, he'll catch up to you, and you'll lose all leverage. It's best to be proactive, so you can control the agenda."

"I said no!" Caroline shouted, her voice deepening by several decibels and carrying distinct notes of a growl. Her eyes flashed amber and for just a minute I saw a weird overlay of a wolf's head through one of my eyes.

I went very still, my instincts telling me this was no longer my friend but a predator seconds from ripping out my throat.

"Okay, Caroline. If that's what you want," I soothed.

Jeweled wings fluttered in my periphery and one of my pixie roommates landed on the far end of the counter, watching Caroline with thoughtful eyes. Inara had wings of iridescent green and yellow that had a spidery network of veins made of every color green imaginable. When she fluttered her wings, it looked like a tree rustling in the wind.

Caroline's growls continued as she remained focused on me, not noticing the pixie.

"I need you to calm down, Caroline. This isn't helping matters." I took a step back and made myself look away from her eyes. Meeting a wolf's eyes in the wild meant you were challenging their dominance. Werewolves should have some of the same instincts. Right?

The growl grew in volume, and she took a small step forward. A burnt umber light, tangled with inky blackness, coalesced around her. It was only visible with my left eye, the one the sorcerer had taken from me so he could use it as an ingredient in a spell. Ever since it grew back, I could see weird things. At first, I thought I was crazy, before I realized what I was seeing was magic. Or something close to it.

7

She took another step forward. A blur of green and yellow darted toward her eyes.

"Bad dog." Inara fluttered around Caroline's head, evading the swats aimed her way.

The growling stopped, and the light faded bit by bit. The pixie's distraction worked.

Caroline looked shaken and upset. "Aileen."

"It's fine. I had more than one episode myself when I was first turned. I even almost chowed down on Jenna once."

"I'm so sorry. You've got to know I would never hurt you."

My smile was sad. "That's just it. You don't know what you're capable of anymore. It's like being a teenager—only about a thousand times worse. You've got all these hormones and new urges running roughshod through your body, only it won't just be shouting matches when you lose it. People will get hurt. Best case, you change them into what you are. Worst case, they die."

"How did you do this? Alone? Without help?"

I lifted one shoulder. "Very carefully. I had some help in the beginning, but every day is an exercise in self-restraint. You'll get there; it'll just take time."

She nodded even though she didn't look convinced. The loss of control seemed to have taken the wind out of her sails. "I know you're probably right, but please don't call him just yet."

I hesitated, knowing the best thing would be to take care of this while we had the chance. It would have taken her hours to drive from Kentucky; longer if she had to walk out of the farm. If they hadn't already, they would learn of her disappearing act very shortly, and it wouldn't take much of a leap to guess she'd head here.

She didn't say anything else, just looked at me as if her entire world was falling down around her. She was begging me for a respite, even if it was for just a few hours. I knew that feeling. I knew it intimately.

I sighed, the sound heavy and resigned. "How 'bout you go get a shower. You can have my bed for the night; I'll sleep out here on the couch."

She started to turn and then looked me over. "Shouldn't you get a shower first? I can't imagine it's comfortable covered in whatever that is."

I looked down at myself and grimaced. No, it wasn't. I was afraid to move for fear of getting more of it all over my kitchen.

"I'll be fine," I said. "Just maybe don't take all night."

She looked unsure but accepted the offer. "Thank you, Aileen."

I nodded. I doubt she'd be thanking me when Brax broke down my door in the middle of the day to drag her away with me lying dead to the world on the couch.

Inara landed next to my hand on the counter as we watched Caroline head for my room to get a change of clothes for the night. "You look and smell disgusting."

I drained my glass of wine. "I do try."

Inara waited until the water had turned on before she said, "It was a mistake to let her stay here."

"I know."

"They sequester their pups for a reason. A newly turned wolf is stronger than normal and has little control of the change." She flicked a look my way. "She could probably tear apart a baby vamp very easily."

"Great."

Inara wasn't telling me anything I didn't know or suspect.

"I'll call him when I wake. That should give her time to calm down." And for me to think of an excuse for why I hadn't called him sooner.

"And if she flips out again?"

"We'll cross that bridge when we come to it."

I collected Caroline's glass and deposited it in the sink. While Inara kept an eye on the hallway, I opened the fridge and pulled out another bottle of wine, this time one created for me and my needs. Anybody taking a sip out of it would find themselves in for an unpleasant surprise.

I tilted it over my glass, watching the dark red liquid collect in the bottom. The smell of death and rot reached me, and I curled a lip. Ever since I'd tapped Liam's vein earlier in the year, my stored blood hadn't tasted quite the same—the flavors lackluster and nasty, like a powdered protein shake and not the good kind. Whereas before I couldn't get enough of it, now I could barely stomach gulping it down. Worse, I could feel the difference between it and live blood. Now that I'd had the premium, grade A stuff from tall, dark and handsome, I could tell how inadequate it was in meeting my needs, barely abating the hunger these days.

I turned to find Inara regarding me with a dour look. "What?"

"I forgot. Your friend isn't the only one with troubles."

"I don't know what you're talking about." My voice was defensive despite my best efforts.

For such a small being, Inara could throw skepticism better than anyone I knew. Including my mother. She shook her head and leapt off the encounter. "This should end well. It's like the blind leading the blind."

"You don't know what you're talking about," I called after her retreating figure. I grumbled into my glass, "I'm perfectly fine with bagged blood."

Finishing a sip, I held the glass away from me and grimaced. It was like drinking that fermented stuff that was the newest fad. The kombucha or whatever. I'd tried it once as a human and had sworn never to step near the nasty drink ever again.

"Inara is just looking out for you," a tiny voice said near my ear.

I started and then turned my head, careful not to disrupt the pixie's perch. I'd done that once; it had not ended well. Lowen sat on my shoulder, having found one small spot unmarred by the gunk covering me. His tiny little feet kicked back and forth as he looked up at me. His purple and blue wings glittered as the light caught them. Unlike Inara, who was pale with a slight green tinge, his skin was a burnished copper. He wore tiny trousers that ended at his knees and a sleeveless white tunic.

"I'm pretty sure Inara only tolerates me," I told him.

He leaned back on his hands and peered up at me. "True, but she doesn't want you to die. We'd have to find a new home then."

"You could always just remain to torment the next inhabitants."

His face was thoughtful before he gave a noncommittal shrug. "There's something odd about your friend."

I snorted. "Yeah, she was just turned into a werewolf after learning there's a whole supernatural world out there. Anybody is bound to be a little off after that."

He shook his head, his large eyes looking reserved. "No, it's more than that. Something's wrong with her. You should be careful not to get torn apart."

With that he took off, leaving me to stare after him in frustration.

CHAPTER TWO

A KNOCK AT the door summoned me from my deathlike slumber. Really, it was more of a pounding that caused my door to shimmy and quake. I lifted my head without opening my eyes and then let it drop. It was too much effort to get up. Whoever it was would go away eventually.

The knocking paused. Moments later it resumed, louder than before. I pried my eyes open and blinked at the purple and blue wings filling my vision. Lowen leaned forward. "You have company."

I turned on my side and buried my head in the couch I'd ended up on last night. "I can hear that. Tell them to go away."

Between one breath and the next, I drifted off. A sharp pain on the rim of my ear brought me back to the land of the living.

"Take care of it before they break the door," Inara ordered. She released the abused appendage and flitted out of range before I could swat her.

"I'll be fast enough one day, pixie," I said, giving her a dead stare even as I lumbered to an upright position. When had sitting gotten so hard?

"Not even in your prolonged life," she returned in a scathing voice.

"Yeah, yeah." I yawned, my eyes falling shut. Couldn't this wait? I thought it could. I started to lean back against the couch. I was just so frickin' tired.

One of the pixies dive bombed my face. "Get up and answer the door, you worthless blood sucker."

With a long groan, I made it to standing and with the help of the pixies swooping at me whenever I veered off course, I made it to the front door. I leaned against the wall for stability and unlocked the first lock, then the second. I'd barely finished with the last lock when the door thrust itself open and a very angry pair of werewolves stalked inside.

"Please. Come right in," I said in a dry voice as I squinted against the bright light. Well, that answered the question of why I was so exhausted when I normally woke up bright eyed and bushy tailed. As a new vampire, I still struggled to stay awake when the sun was in the sky. Most of the time I could only manage a few minutes at sunrise and sunset. At the moment, the sun was shining bright and cheerily in the sky. This had to be a new record for me.

"Where is she?" Brax rounded on me as Sondra moved through my small apartment, her head up and face alert. A pair of ice blue eyes glared at me with a fierceness that would have taken my breath away if I'd been able to summon enough energy to feel fear. His power, that thing that only he as alpha had, filled the room with heat. It felt like standing next to a raging wildfire. You just knew if the wind shifted in the wrong direction, your ticket was up, and it would be an unpleasant way to go.

I shut the door and shuffled back to my couch. I collapsed onto it. "Who are you talking about?"

"Don't try to lie to me. I smelled her on your landing. I know she came here."

I made a whimpering sound. Why couldn't the big, bad werewolf just shut up and leave me in peace? Couldn't he see that I was in no shape to deal with his shenanigans?

"She's not here," Sondra said, appearing from the hall that led to my bedroom. She moved with an almost feline grace through my apartment, which was funny since she was a wolf. Her hair was a curly mess around the feral beauty of her face.

Brax leaned down, trying to use his standing position and general badassery to intimidate me. Most days that would work. Today, I was just too tired to feel anything beyond the smallest spurt of concern. Then that too was gone. Even now, I could feel the allure of sleep sucking me back down.

"Where's Caroline?" he growled.

"You're her alpha. You tell me." I gave him a sleepy smile. "Guess you wish you'd been a little more forthcoming when I needed you to. Tit for tat."

He stared at me for a long moment. He wasn't handsome, not in the traditional way. He'd never be on a billboard or featured in a magazine. He was rough around the edges, like a really sexy mountain man—one capable of changing into a wolf and ripping your throat out at a moment's notice. He had a presence to him, a way of demanding attention anytime he was in a room. Right now, he was trying to use that same sense of charisma to get answers from me.

The pixies landed on either side of my shoulders, Inara haughty and amused, while Lowen had an implacable expression on his face. Brax eyed the two of them with a look of distaste before whirling and sending my coffee table sliding across the room with a well-placed kick.

"Rude animal," Inara said with a moue of disgust.

I patted next to her, mainly because she managed to evade the pat. "Shh, don't upset the alpha. You wouldn't like him when he's upset."

I realized what I just said and snickered.

"What's wrong with her?" Sondra asked, watching me with fascination.

"Nothing's wrong with her," Inara snapped. "She's just tired."

"This isn't a game, Aileen. You need to tell me where she is right now before someone gets hurt." Brax paced the small space, running a hand through his hair and making it stand upright for a moment.

"Did I hear you right? Were you just threatening one of my vampires?" a silky voice asked from my open door.

I cracked one eye open from where it had drifted shut and glared at the newcomer. "Does nobody respect a person's private space anymore?"

Both men ignored me. Liam stepped into the room, his enforcers at his back. A vampire several centuries my senior, Liam was a dragon given human form. He moved with the grace and confidence of a predator at the top of the food chain. Every movement he made held the potential for violence even as it looked like it belonged in a dance.

He had a maturity about him that said he'd been turned somewhere in his early thirties—something I envied him for. Who wanted to be stuck in their mid-twenties forever? He had dark hair and electric blue eyes that had a habit of seeing right down to the very core of a person, stripping away their paltry defenses. His cheekbones were sharp and his jaw stubborn, but his lips were utterly soft and kissable as I'd discovered during the one and only time I'd ended up kissing him. I claimed the distraction of my first blooding as the reason. He was the thorn in my side that just kept digging deeper.

"Hey there, baby ass-kicker, you're looking kind of rough," Nathan, his enforcer, said with a playful smile on his face. He was light where Liam was dark and acted like a flirtatious frat boy. I'd seen him kill, though, and knew he was every bit as deadly as everyone else in this room.

"I'm gonna kick all your asses as soon as I have my energy back." I gave up and let myself collapse on the couch, falling sideways.

"Aw, it's cute that you think that."

I made a grunt of argument. It was all I could manage with my current level of exhaustion.

"What are you doing here, Brax?" Liam asked. He moved with the grace of a tiger, beautiful and deadly, and oh so distracting.

"Your vampire is hiding one of our pups," Brax said.

Liam flicked a quelling glance my way. That would have normally made my night—I lived for pissing him off—but right now the effort was too much. I really just wanted him to go away and take all these other trespassers with him. He jerked his head and Eric, his other enforcer, strode for the hallway leading to the rest of the apartment.

"You won't find her," Sondra called after him, posting herself at the mouth of the hallway. "She's long gone."

Eric returned in moments and shook his head, confirming Sondra was right. She folded her arms and leaned back. All eyes turned to me.

"You're sure she was here?" Liam asked, fixing me with a stare.

"Her scent stops right outside the door," Brax responded.

I met their stares with as much energy as I could muster.

"I don't think you understand the severity of what is happening here," Brax began.

My eyes drifted closed as the conversation continued around me. I woke with a start, the taste of life and decadence on my lips. A weight pressed hard on my chest—Liam holding me down. One of my legs had curled around his. His eyes flared briefly as he finished licking the wound on his wrist.

"What the fuck?" I scrambled to seated as he stood and stepped away. "Did you just give me your blood again?"

He lifted one eyebrow, the superior expression on his face letting me know how stupid he thought that question.

I would have kicked the coffee table if Brax hadn't already knocked it out of the way earlier. Damn it. I just got used to bagged blood again. It had taken me weeks to be able to keep the stuff down after the last time I'd had a taste of Liam's blood.

"Don't do that again," I ordered.

"I will do what I must since you have already shown you can't take care of yourself. We needed you awake and alert for this conversation." He gave me a smirk. He knew exactly how difficult his blood would make my coming weeks. Yeah, I'd be supercharged for a few days. Stronger, faster, able to leap tall buildings with a single bound, but it came with a cost. That cost being the difficulty of keeping the bagged stuff down.

"When you two are done flirting, can we get back to business?" Brax asked. He'd taken a seat on the coffee table he'd knocked across the room and was leaning forward, his eerie blue eyes focused intently on me.

I glared at him, properly outraged at his presence in my territory now that I had the energy to stay awake and alert.

"From what I understand, Caroline needed a little away time from the farm you secluded her on. I understand the feeling." My smile was humorless. "All of this can be a little hard to take at times."

"No, you don't." Sondra stepped forward. "You can't. You're not a wolf. She's dangerous right now, both to herself and others. If we can't find her and she hurts someone, she could be put down."

I scoffed. "Like you were?"

Shame crossed Sondra's face before her expression firmed.

"Those were mitigating circumstances," Brax said, his voice a rumble in the quiet.

"It doesn't matter. Caroline won't let herself hurt anyone." Not physically at least.

"She's not the same person you knew," Sondra said.

"I was turned, and I managed not to hurt anyone," I said as a defense.

"You're not normal," Liam spoke.

"That's for sure," Nathan agreed.

Eric didn't give his opinion, just lurked in the background as he usually did, keeping an eye on things as he observed the situation around him.

Liam ignored the comment. "Most yearlings have to be heavily monitored for their first few decades. Before we had such strict laws governing their creation and rearing, they would rise and kill those closest to them when they tried to resume their normal lives. Their instincts often consume them, making it hard to establish control for a long time after their turning."

I shifted. This wasn't the first time I'd heard something similar. Evidently, I should have killed a whole army of people in my first year. The fact that I hadn't was a puzzle my sire and Liam were still trying to figure out.

"It's more than just her wolf she has to contend with. The demon taint has made her unstable," Brax said, sounding grim. "It's why I had to move her to the farm and extend her time there."

"What do you mean?" I asked. "I thought the demon taint was taken care of when Sondra bit her."

The look Brax leveled on me was both pitying and censorious. "Demon taint is not so easily remedied. She will have to deal with its effects for the rest of her life. The bite saved her life and preserved her sanity, but it still has a hold on her. She is stronger than other newborn pups. Her temper is shorter, which means it will be that much easier to snap and go feral."

"Feral? Like a wild dog?"

"Similar," Sondra said from my countertop, where she sat cross-legged. Glad to see she was making herself at home. "For us, it means a loss of self. The wolf takes over and becomes rabid. Its thirst for blood unquenchable. A feral wolf can never recover the person they were. They have to be put down one hundred percent of the time."

Some of my exhaustion faded away, and I looked from Brax to Sondra in worry. "Caroline's not feral."

"For now." Sondra's agreement didn't put my mind at ease.

"There are those in my pack who think I should have put her down as soon as we discovered the taint." Brax met my eyes with determination in his gaze. His mouth was pulled tight, and his eyebrows lowered in a frown.

My chest tightened, and a chill crept into my soul at his words. Why hadn't they told me any of this before? They could have revealed this information during any of the dozen phone calls I'd placed asking for news on her condition.

Liam appeared at my side and sat down, stretching his arms across the couch behind my back—his body coiled and poised for action. It was only then that I realized that I was making a growling, hissing sound, similar to the deep throated warning a cat gives when it's preparing to claw the face off its enemy. My fangs were down, and my hands were tensed and flexed as if they had claws on the ends of them.

Sondra leaned forward, one leg dropping down as she focused on me like a hunting dog sighting its prey. Nathan and Eric took a step closer, both watching me with caution. The room was poised for battle, the tension making it almost hard to breathe.

I took a deep breath, my shoulders lifting and dropping. My hands relaxed and my fangs returned to their hiding places in my gums. I'd discovered early on that vampires don't walk around with their fangs out all the time. Most of the time they were kept hidden. Strong emotions such as anger, fear, and lust could bring them out. Guess which one I was feeling at the moment?

"Why wasn't I told any of this?"

"You're not pack. Furthermore, Caroline made it clear she didn't want to see you."

Not pack. It always came down to an "us vs. them" mentality with these guys.

"I'll ask again. Where is she?" Brax's face was set and serious.

I kept my silence, meeting his gaze for a long moment. "She showed up last night and asked for a place to stay."

"And you didn't think to call us?" There was an edge to Brax's voice, and his frown grew more pronounced.

I lifted one shoulder. "It crossed my mind." I left out the part about how Caroline flipped out when I tried.

"Because you delayed, you've put her life needlessly in danger." Brax's tone was cold as his gaze shifted to Liam next to me. "This is what comes when you're too lenient with them."

My snort held all of the exhaustion and fear I felt. "This is what comes when you withhold important information just because someone isn't the same species as you. I begged you to let me know what was going on. I even threatened to blow-up your properties."

"And would knowing have made you act any different? You, the yearling who refuses to join a clan? Who hasn't even made the smallest effort to gain control of your instincts?"

Liam's hand landed on my shoulder, restraining me when I would have leapt for Brax.

"See what I mean?" Brax asked Liam. "She doesn't even know when she's fighting out of her weight class."

"Way I remember it, the reason you aren't some demon's plaything is because I saved you. Me, the baby vampire who doesn't know her weight class."

"She does have a point there," Nathan said with a grin.

Brax ignored his statement.

"Enough of this," Liam said. "The girl is gone. Aileen, do you know where?"

I hesitated. It galled to have to share any information with the jerk across from me, but if he was right, he held Caroline's life in the balance. At least for now, it would be smart to humor him.

"No, I gave her my bed last night and then went to sleep."

"You didn't see her leaving? Ask where she was going?" Sondra asked, a thread of judgment in her tone.

I shot her a derisive look. "You've seen me since arriving. I'm barely functional during the day. A herd of unicorns could have pranced through here, and I wouldn't have known the difference."

Brax didn't move and his expression didn't change, but I got the sense that my answer frustrated and disappointed him. He looked at Liam. "We'll need to take custody of Aileen in case Caroline tries to contact her again."

I stiffened and glared at him in outrage. No way was that happening. He wasn't the police. There'd be no taking custody of anyone.

"That won't be necessary," Liam said.

Brax's attention shifted to the vampire at my side. The wolf moved behind his gaze. To my new other sight, the shadow of a wolf cloaked him even as his power emanated in waves off him. It was like staring into the sun during a flare.

A cooler power, like that of the cold bite of an arctic night, flared as Liam tensed to meet him. You would think the absolute chill of his power would be uncomfortable. It wasn't. It called to some deep part of me that shifted in answer as if hearing the voice of a loved one after a long absence.

"It's my wolf and by her own admission she's been in contact with her. Your vampire has interfered with one of the most sacred aspects of our existence. If it was the other way around, your kind would have attacked en mass," Brax snarled.

"I don't disagree with the importance of locating your wayward wolf, and I'm well aware Aileen has trespassed on things she does not understand."

I shot him a glare at that last part. He ignored me, focusing on the wolf in front of him.

Brax watched Liam with a careful gaze. He seemed to be considering, weighing each of Liam's statements.

"Your vampire has already proven her inability to keep her nose out of things that don't involve her," Brax stated. Much of the antagonism had dropped from his voice, and the hint of a growl that had been there since he'd barged in had disappeared.

"This does involve me. She's my friend. She came to me for help." If he thought I was going to wash my hands of this, especially after what he'd just revealed about how close she was to a death order, he had another thing coming.

He shot Liam a glance as if to say 'see'.

Liam sighed and muttered, "You're not helping matters."

I folded my arms and sat back. By all means if he wanted to handle things, whatever they decided, I'd find a way to work around if necessary.

"Until your pup can be found, we'll take responsibility for Aileen," Liam said.

My head twisted so fast that I almost got whiplash. One of his hands dropped from the back of the couch to brush against my neck. I held my tongue, not because I trusted him or because that touch asked me to. I did it because I had no intention of letting him or his men keep me on a short leash. I figured it'd be easier giving them the slip than it would be Brax and his people. Not to mention I had a feeling my stay with Brax would be a lot less cordial this time, given the degree of hostility currently being aimed my way.

"She'll stay with us, and I, or one of my enforcers will be with her at all times. You have my word on it." Liam sounded firm, and I wasn't sure if that first part was directed at me or Brax.

"That doesn't fix the problem she's already created," Brax said, his gaze canny. "I wonder how the newly selected master of the Midwest would take it if he found out one of his own had misstepped so horribly. How would he handle it if the rest of our city knew the vampires have taken it upon themselves to interfere with our young? It might feed into some of the hard feelings that have been brewing over the last few months."

Liam was a frozen statue at my side, none of his feelings leaking through as he regarded the wolf with a lazy gaze. "You've made your point. To help smooth over this matter, I will attempt to locate the pup and bring her back to her pack."

Brax drummed his fingers on his thigh, studying me and the vampire at my side. He looked like he didn't like the proposal, but he couldn't find a reason to say no. Sondra, at his back, shook her head in disgust and hopped off my counter.

"Fine." Brax's acceptance was grudging. "You keep her close, and if by chance you find Caroline, you notify me immediately."

Liam gave him a sharp nod.

Brax's gaze swung to me. "And you?"

I let out a breath. "Whatever you say."

Liam turned his head, meeting my eyes with a catlike smile, as if he'd gotten everything he'd ever wanted. His hand behind me reached up to twirl a piece of hair around his finger. I narrowed my eyes at him and sat forward.

"Checkmate," he rumbled in a low voice, one intended only for my ears.

We remained seated as Brax and Sondra showed themselves out. The stairway rattled as they made their way down, even supernatural beings unable to navigate its length silently.

Nathan said, "That went well."

Eric, his hands clasped behind his back, made a small noise of disagreement. Liam pulled his arm from the couch behind me and leaned forward.

"What are you guys doing here anyways?" I asked. Not that I was complaining, for once. Without them, I got the sense things might have gone very differently for me with the werewolf alpha. I had a feeling I might have been kidnapped before the day was over, had Liam and company not shown up.

It was just strange, that was all, given the sun's height. It was just now beginning to set, and I could feel it as it began its descent. Twilight wouldn't be far away. While the myth that vampires couldn't go out in the sun was largely just that—myth—it was still true that it wasn't our natural element. I'm told that older vampires, ones that have matured enough to stay awake through the day, could go out in it without burning themselves to a crisp. They could enjoy the beach on a summer day, catch a wave and sun themselves. All the things I haven't been able to do for two years. The drawback being, they were significantly weaker and long-term exposure became uncomfortable. Or so I'm told.

Nathan and Eric looked at Liam. After a beat, Nathan said, "We heard the wolves were in the area and thought we'd stop by to see if you needed help."

I frowned at Nathan. Something about that story didn't add up. "You drove all the way from your headquarters downtown to my little abode on a rumor? During rush hour?"

Nathan once again looked at Liam before nodding. "Yup, that's what we did."

I turned to glance at Liam. He stared back at me, his gaze enigmatic. He looked relaxed and at ease as he rested against the couch, as if he'd just stopped by for pizza and a beer. If I didn't know better, I'd say he was pretty pleased about this turn of events.

"Did you have someone watching my apartment?"

His gaze sharpened, and the slightest bit of tension entered his muscles. That was a yes.

"I thought we had an agreement," I said, my eyes flashing with anger. "You leave me alone if I found one of Thomas's progeny, and I go my merry way."

Thomas was the vampire who had become the master of the city and the ruler for all the surrounding territory earlier this spring. He also happened to be my sire. I'd negotiated for my freedom before revealing that last bit. It should have been enough to buy me out of vampire interference, but as usual, things were stickier and more complicated than I'd anticipated.

"That agreement was with Thomas and Thomas alone." Liam relaxed back into the couch.

"He's your leader. How can you say that?" I said.

"As I recall, he only agreed to not force you into a clan or compel you to serve him; nothing in there about keeping an eye on you," he said with a lazy smile that exposed the points of his fangs.

Vampires. Always looking for a loophole.

"That also doesn't cover my own interest in you," he continued. He brushed one finger against the arm that displayed his and the sorcerer's mark.

I turned it slightly, looking at the mark emblazoned on my forearm. A normal—aka human—would assume it was a tattoo. In reality, it was an intricate piece of artwork that would never fade and told the world of my debts. When the sorcerer had first marked me, it had been a stylized lion wrapped in a vine with thorns. At first glance it appeared silver, but on closer inspection you'd see flecks of purple that looked almost metallic, as if someone had poured colored metal into the dye and then embedded it into my skin.

Since Liam had placed an unsolicited mark on me, it had changed. Now an oak tree grew behind the lion. At first, its branches had been bare of all but a few leaves, but now they were full, a green and earthy bronze joining the silver and purple. I had no idea what the addition of the leaves meant and doubted I would like the answer when I figured it out.

Liam gave the mark a pleased look. "It's taking root quite nicely."

I pulled my arm out of his grip, shooting him a displeased look of my own. "So, it would seem."

"That mark makes you my business. Whatever your agreement with your sire, it doesn't affect our relationship."

"We don't have a relationship," I said through gritted teeth.

"That mark says otherwise."

"Because you forced it on me."

He lifted one eyebrow. "We can spend the rest of your time here arguing semantics or you can pack. Your choice. You have ten minutes and then we're leaving."

CHAPTER THREE

I LOOKED AT him with a blank expression.

Humor touched his lips. "You didn't think you were staying here."

I kind of had.

His chuckle was warm and had more of an effect on me than I wanted to admit. "You heard me talking to Brax. Until your little friend is found, you and I are going to be living out of each other's pockets." He looked around with an amused expression. "And I don't sleep on couches."

Nathan smothered a smile.

My mouth dropped open. I wanted to argue, but didn't know where to go from there.

"You have nine minutes now. I suggest you grab your stuff, because one way or another we're leaving. Makes no difference to me whether you have clean clothes or not."

I held Liam's gaze for a long moment. What I found there convinced me he wasn't bluffing. He really would force me to leave with no clothes, even if he had to drag me out kicking and screaming. I huffed at him and stood, stepping around the other two enforcers and heading down the hall.

I entered my bedroom and headed straight to my closet to grab my gym bag. Bright orange and black, it was one of the few pieces of luggage I owned. I never traveled anymore so there wasn't a pressing need for real luggage.

"Have to say, this isn't how I pictured your room," Nathan said from where he slouched against my door jam.

I paused from where I'd been digging for a few shirts and took a moment to look around. My bedroom was my favorite room in the apartment. The floors were a warm golden brown, the kind of wood you couldn't get anymore. Though they were cracked and scratched in places, every one of those marks just added to their charm. I'd painted my walls a light bluish gray except for one. The wall behind my rustic wooden headboard was a deep gray blue that showed my bed off nicely. A quilted bedspread, also a grayish blue contrasted with the white with blue embroidery of the coverlet folded at the foot of the bed.

Caroline had taken the time to make the bed before she'd left. It was a comforting sight because it meant wherever she'd gone, she went willingly and not in a panic.

"What'd you expect?" I asked, busying myself with throwing three pairs of jeans in my bag.

"Nothing quite so feminine."

I paused and gave him a look complete with arched eyebrow. He shrugged, his expression sheepish. His view was one I'd heard before. I've found that once people learn you were a soldier, they assume certain things. A female soldier can't possibly be in touch with her softer side. No, we're hard core killers that prefer beef jerky and dressing in baggy clothes. It was complete bullshit, of course.

I resumed packing. "That's the great thing about being a woman in the modern era. I'm not defined by just one thing. I can be complicated. It's best you just assume I'm an onion."

Nathan wandered over to the canvas prints of photos I'd taken before being forced to assume a more nocturnal lifestyle. The one he examined was of a moss-covered staircase in castle ruins I'd taken when visiting Ireland. I missed photography. The night had its beauty, but nothing beat a sun-drenched landscape or a sunrise over the mountains.

"Where'd you get these?" Nathan asked.

I took advantage of his distraction to pull the Judge out of its lock box. A .45 caliber long Colt, the Judge was a revolver that I'd already used once to kill a vampire. If I was going into enemy territory, I'd do it armed. The gun was filled with a 410 round of my own making—silver nitrate that worked like a charm against vampires. They could heal a normal, lead round just fine, but the silver put them down and kept them down.

I stuffed the revolver under my clothes and looked at Nathan, who'd drifted over to another canvas, this one a photograph of a castle overlooking a meadow in bloom during early spring.

"I took them."

He looked over at me, impressed. "You've got a good eye."

I shrugged. I did. Before.

"I mean it," he said, his expression completely serious for once.

"Doesn't matter anymore. Photography is one of those hobbies where light is a crucial element."

He looked contemplative as he looked back at the canvas of the castle. "You could always try night photography."

Yeah, because I had so much spare time on my hands. I worked almost every night. On the few nights I didn't, I was too tired to pick up the camera.

I didn't feel like arguing with him, so I lifted a shoulder and said, "Perhaps."

"You ready?" Nathan asked, turning from my photographs. "Liam wasn't kidding about that deadline."

"I got that. I just need to grab a few things from the bathroom, and we can go."

I preceded Nathan out of my room. He shadowed me down the hall but didn't try to crowd into the bathroom with me. That might have been because it was the size of a postage stamp. It had enough room for me, and that was about it.

The linoleum floor was cracked and peeling in places, and the rest of the bathroom showed its age. The only thing it had going for it was the fact that it was clean.

Given Nathan had turned into my shadow, I figured Liam had ordered him to keep an eye on me. Such a lack of trust.

I opened the medicine cabinet and jerked back. Lowen sat on one of the shelves, his wings rubbing together, as he held one finger against his lips.

Seconds later, I heard a curse from Nathan and then the tinkle of bell-like laughter.

"We don't have long," Lowen said in his squeaky voice. "Your friend wanted us to give you this."

He held out a note that had been folded until it was roughly the size of a finger and nearly as tall as him. I took it and stuffed it in my pocket. Just in time too, as Nathan stuck his head in the bathroom, his expression annoyed.

"You about ready?" he asked.

I grabbed the toothpaste from next to Lowen. "Yup. Think this should do it."

Lowen grinned at me and gave me a thumbs-up. I gave him a small smile in return, shutting the medicine cabinet door, but leaving it ajar so he could escape. He probably had his own way in and out, but in case he didn't, I didn't want to leave him trapped in there until I returned.

"I don't know how you deal with having those pests around," Nathan said as I followed him back to my living room. His neck sported a welt the length of my forefinger—courtesy of the small sword Inara carried. I suspected her sword was covered in something poisonous, as a wound from it would smart and sting for days.

"They don't bother me," I said with an inner smirk.

We entered the living room to find Inara standing on my coffee table, engaged in a staring contest with Liam. He was still in the same position he'd been in when I left to pack, slouched back with one arm laying across the couch back and his legs slightly spread. He regarded the diminutive pixie with an expression of slight amusement.

I slung the strap of my bag over my head and adjusted it, so it was laying crosswise over my chest. Liam's gaze lifted to mine. His electric blue eyes held a fierce light of victory. I frowned at him. He might have me where he wanted for now, but as I'd proven in the past, I rarely stayed where I was put.

23

Inara made a sound of victory, in her mind, no doubt having won the contest. Liam stood and stepped toward the door.

"Don't forget, vampire. She's ours. Make sure she comes back to us in one piece," Inara warned, sounding fierce and deadly despite her small size.

"I understand, pixie. I will make sure she comes to no harm," Liam said, his voice and eyes oddly formal. He gave her a small bow, the movement graceful and straight from an older time.

Inara snorted, sounding just a smidge impressed despite herself. "See that you do."

Liam smiled, radiating charm and turning his already handsome face into a work of art. He held his hand out to me. "Shall we?"

I grunted and moved towards him, snagging my keys off the kitchen table. "Not like I have a choice right now."

"We always have choices. It's just a matter of whether they are good or not." His voice was a rumble against my ear as we walked outside.

*

Eric drove us to a hulking mansion close to downtown Columbus. You'd think these vampires would want to be somewhere secluded, somewhere they could let their fangs out without worrying a nosy neighbor would see them. Not these vampires—the gothic mansion they called home looked like it was straight out of the turn of the century, complete with pointed buttresses and a dramatic roof overlooking a topiary garden that was open to the public during the day. The place even had a wrought iron gate surrounding its manicured lawn that Eric had to use a remote to open.

The building itself fit my idea of a vampire stronghold, the location less so. If you walked a few streets over, you'd be on Broad Street—the main artery of downtown Columbus. Not just Broad Street, but on one of the busiest sections of the business district. At least during the day. At this time of night, this part of the city was deserted.

"Welcome to the Gargoyle," Nathan said in a cheery voice. "Your home away from home for the foreseeable future."

The neighborhood surrounding the mansion was not the nicest; there was a derelict home with boarded-up windows right across the street. Next to it was another, with an overgrown yard and paint that was peeling.

I looked back at the mansion, noting how many windows were lit up. Looked like they had a full house tonight.

"How many live here?" I asked. I'd been here once before, during the selection. The guys had told me the mansion acted as their home base, but I'd never gotten around to asking who all lived there.

I looked over to find Liam watching me with an enigmatic expression. I lifted an eyebrow. "What? Is that confidential?"

One corner of his lips lifted. "Not at all. Since you'll be living here, it would be pointless to keep such information a secret considering you'll find out for yourself soon enough."

I gave a nod of acknowledgment.

"All of the enforcers under my command, plus any human companions they have live here. Rarely are all of them in the house at once. Our territory covers a large area."

I didn't touch the idea of human companions. He already knew my thoughts on live blood. As long as he didn't assign me a companion, and the others showed no sign of abuse, we were good.

"They don't have their own homes?" I asked.

It's not like I wasn't used to the concept of keeping your people under one roof. The military kept its junior ranking soldiers in a barracks after all—but that was meant to be temporary. Vampires lived for centuries. Who wanted to live in a barracks environment for all that time? I shuddered just thinking of it. People all around you with little time to just relax. I couldn't think of a worse fate, and I had lived in barracks for a good long while. I'd been more than happy to get out of there when the time came.

He inclined his head. "Some keep a separate residence, but most elect to stay here when they can. Despite popular opinion, we're not meant to live isolated lives. We're as social as the wolves; we just show it differently."

The gaze he cast me held a hint of disapproval. For my own isolated living situation, no doubt. I shrugged it off. The solitude suited me.

Eric parked the car and we got out. Nathan grabbed my bag before I could.

"I'll show her to her room," he said.

Liam waved him on. "See that you do. Give her a tour as well then report back to me."

Nathan clapped me on the back and headed up the stairs to the tall wooden double doors. They looked like solid oak, stained a dark brown. It gave a certain majesty to the building, made you feel like it was out of a different era.

Nathan showed me to a corner room on the third floor. Bigger than possibly my entire apartment, it was more of a suite in a very swanky hotel than the bare bones barracks room I'd envisioned. The floor was made of a dark wood, with white and silver rugs dotting it. To the side was a sparse kitchen done with white cabinets, a dark blue tiled backsplash and stainless-steel appliances. A living room sat to the other side, the couch luxurious and inviting. On one wall was a large-screen TV complete with a surround sound stereo system.

I looked at Nathan in surprise. "This is my room?"

He nodded, looking happy about my reaction. "Yup, just for you."

I made a 'hm' sound as I stepped into the kitchen and ran my hand over the counter. Marble. Outfitting this place had cost a pretty penny.

"Are all the rooms like this?" I asked.

He shook his head. "No, each one is a little different. They've been designed with their occupants in mind."

"So, this is the guest suite," I stated, looking around impressed. If this was how they treated their guests, it'd be interesting to see how they treated their people.

A wide smile crossed Nathan's face before he moved to the coffee table and set my bag down. "Do you like it?"

I nodded as I opened the fridge. There were several bottles in there filled with thick, red liquid. "I thought you guys disapproved of the bottled stuff."

Nathan shrugged. "We do, but it's good to have on hand in case of emergency. Not as good as the live stuff, but it'll do in a pinch."

I shut the fridge door, not tempted by the blood. Liam's little perk-me-up would tide me over for a day or two, judging on my last experience with it. I didn't know if that would be the case with any blood taken from a live source, or if that was a special blend given his level of power and centuries of life. I suspected it was the latter.

I wandered into the bedroom and let out a low whistle. This room alone made my kidnapping worth it. The same dark wooden floor continued in here, light-colored rugs contrasting with it. The ceilings were vaulted with windows overlooking the gardens. On the opposite side of the room was a closet with one of those sliding barn doors that were suddenly so trendy. A full-length mirror gave the room the impression of airiness and light despite the fact it was night.

That's not what held my attention, though. No, the ginormous bed in the middle of the room did that all by itself. Elegant and simple, it looked like a cloud. My bed was nice, but this one was about three levels above it. If you fell asleep in that thing, you wouldn't want to get out of it come morning. One thing I enjoyed above all else was a good mattress. After spending several years sleeping on whatever cheap thing the military provided when I was lucky (I slept on the cold, hard ground when I wasn't) I'd embraced the decadence that came with having my own place and bought a nice mattress. This trumped mine.

"Like it?" Nathan asked, following me into the room.

I took a running start, leaping through the air to land belly down on the mattress, arms widespread.

"I'll take that as a yes," he said with an amused smile.

I took back what I was thinking earlier. Maybe living in a place like this wasn't the worst thing that could happen to a person. It was about as close to barracks living as a chicken was to a dinosaur. I could see why Liam's people didn't mind staying close to hand.

"You know, if you joined us, a room like this could be your very own."

I turned my head so my eyes met his and gave him a quelling look. "Nice try, but it'll take a little more than a nice room to tempt me to the dark side."

His lips quirked. "You haven't seen the bathroom yet."

I propped myself up on my elbows. That was true. A bathroom in this place would be worth checking out. Before I could move, a voice called out from the other room. "Hello?"

"In here," Nathan said back. He didn't raise his voice, so I assumed the newcomer was a vampire with the same exceptional hearing.

A man with red hair and pale skin stuck his head into the room. His plump cheeks and bright eyes didn't say vampire. They said normal guy with a desk job. He looked around. Spying Nathan, he bounced inside with all the energy of a puppy as he gave us a wide smile. On his heels came a tall, gangly man wearing glasses with thick black frames.

I sat up, wanting a look at these newcomers. The redhead had a disarming smile and didn't look like a cold-blooded drinker of the red stuff. His pale skin was the only thing that might have suggested vampire, but even that wasn't much paler than other redheads I had known. His companion didn't look nearly as friendly, but that was understandable given the fact the other man was probably friendlier than the rest of the people in this house put together.

"Ah, you're here," Red said, finished greeting Nathan. He bounced over to me and stuck out his hand. "I'm Richard. You can call me Rick, but never call me Dick."

I clasped his hand in mine. "Good to know. I'll make sure to remember that."

His eyes went slightly unfocused as his gaze turned inward for a moment. To my magic-seeing eye, it looked like light gathered around his head before dispersing almost as quickly as it came. His awareness returned, and his smile got wider. "I'm glad you're here, Aileen. I think we'll be good friends."

"Ah, ha. I guess my reputation precedes me." I looked over at Nathan in confusion, noting he looked fascinated by the interaction.

Did everyone in the mansion know about the stubborn yearling who refused to be absorbed into a clan? If so, how many resented the fact that I was going against the establishment? Humans liked to think they respected people who fought for their beliefs, but when someone tried to swim upstream, they collectively lost their minds and were incapable of appreciating the forward thinker until years, sometimes decades later.

"Not at all. I just have a bit of insight into the situation." Richard smiled as if he was amused by some inside joke of his. He didn't explain that ambiguous statement, turning and gesturing to the other man. "This is Theo. He's a companion."

"Companion?" My voice rose in question as I gave Theo a chin nod. The other man's nod was respectful, and he gave me a small, shy smile. He was cute with his curly mop of hair and the nerdy glasses.

Rick took a seat on my bed, leaning back on one hand and looking around the room in curiosity. "Yeah, companion. It's pretty much like it sounds. They provide company and blood to the vampires, usually it's an exclusive relationship but not always. There are a couple of free agents in the mansion for our brethren who have chosen to forgo keeping a companion for one reason or another. Theo's one, so if you get hungry just look him up."

The other man gave me an embarrassed smile before shooting a small glare in Rick's direction. It was a wasted effort, going unnoticed as Rick craned his head to look out the windows.

"And what do the companions get out of this relationship?" I asked, looking between the two men. I was careful to keep all trace of judgment out of my tone, not wanting to create waves this early in my stay. I know, a shocking thing for me to say, but one of the ways I'd survived in the military—heck even thrived—was by getting the lay of the land in any unit I entered. The people in this place were sure to be a tight-knit group. I had no intention of making things harder on myself than necessary.

Rick frowned thoughtfully. "Every person's reasons are different, but for the most part, I'd say they enjoy the longer lifespan and the fact that they're put on the short list for the kiss."

"The kiss?" I remember hearing about that before. I think it was how Kat referred to the act of changing a human into a vampire. "I thought it was difficult to turn people into vampires."

Rick lifted one shoulder. "That's true. You're the first on this continent to survive the change in a few years. Part of that is because we are extremely particular in who we turn. Our past is a cautionary tale about what happens when our species becomes overpopulated. The Black Death of the 1300s was evidence of that."

"What does that mean?" I asked.

"A plague wasn't the reason so many people died in that time," Nathan said from where he leaned against the wall, my bag sitting at his side. "We grew to be too many and couldn't control our population. What resulted, was one of the deadliest events in human history."

"That's why the application process is so rigorous. To prevent any megalomaniacs intent on establishing domination of the human race from being changed. Plus, we have to ensure compatibility and assess an applicant's chances of surviving the kiss. Even with all these measures, only about thirty percent rise that first night."

I listened, even as anger coiled deep inside. How had I gotten so lucky as to skip that process? By the sound of it, I would never have been on the list to begin with. That meant Thomas really had been acting outside their society's directives when he disrupted my life. And here I'd put him on the metaphorical throne for much of the Midwest. Go me.

"Companions are moved to the top of the line," Theo said, his voice quiet and surprisingly soothing.

I nodded but didn't comment. If he wanted to be a walking meal for a chance to join the undead ranks, bully for him. Not a trade I would have made, but to each their own.

Rick popped to his feet. "I'm glad I got to meet you. Everyone's been curious about who the new occupant would be since they started construction. Glad I was the first to welcome you to our humble ranks."

He swept out the room as quickly as he came, taking his whirlwind energy with him. Theo gave me a chin nod before slinking after Rick.

"What did he mean by 'since they started construction'?" I asked, staring after the two.

"You caught that, did you?"

I shot Nathan a quelling glance. He ran one hand through his hair looking abashed.

His answering grin was quick. "I guess there's no point keeping it from you. You're bound to find out sooner or later with this lot. They're all a bunch of gossips in this place." He stepped toward me, picking up my bag and setting it down next to me. He turned and sprawled out on my bed, making himself comfortable in the place Rick had just vacated. He folded his arms behind his head, his biceps bulging and his well-built chest on display. The oak tree that marked his allegiance to Liam was showcased nicely on his forearm. "This isn't a guest room per se."

I narrowed my eyes at him but didn't respond. Silence sometimes had a better effect on people than bombarding them with a ton of questions.

He sighed. "This room was always earmarked for you. After the selection, we had it renovated so it would be ready when you decided to come in from the cold."

"If," I corrected him.

He rolled his eyes but didn't fight me on that. "If you came in from the cold."

I looked around with new eyes. "Who commissioned the construction?"

"Does it really matter? It's yours now. Enjoy it. The companion you just met would have murdered his own mother for the opportunities you've been given."

I leaned close, careful to keep my body off his and set one hand on his chest. His body tightened under mine and a male awareness entered his gaze. I moved closer, as if to kiss him, before pausing. "And did he have a choice in being here?" My nails dug into his shirt, pricking the skin beneath as I met his gaze with dead seriousness.

He stiffened, any hint of desire vanishing.

My smile was grim. "Because I didn't. My entire life, the one I fought for, bled for—gone after a single night. Excuse me if I'm not as appreciative of the perks as you'd like."

His face softened, and he looked at me with an understanding I found uncomfortable. "You need to get over this. You're not the only one who has faced hardships and trials. Yours may be different than the rest of ours, but each of us have horrors in our past. Holding onto this anger will do nothing but poison you against any good that might come of your situation."

I sat up and looked away. His words had merit, and the concept was something I was working on. It was still hard. I didn't always deal with change as gracefully as I should. For the first two years after my turn, I'd buried my head in the sand hoping this vampire thing would just go away. That hadn't happened, and I'd spent the last few months trying to educate myself about this world, so I could be the commander of my own destiny.

Nathan popped off my bed, the seriousness of before forgotten. "I'll give you a moment to get unpacked while I familiarize myself with your TV. When you're done, I'll show you around."

"Don't you have anything better to do than play tour guide for me?" I shouted after him as he disappeared into the next room.

"Nope. Liam said I'm all yours for the night. So, resign yourself to my awesome company for the next few hours."

CHAPTER FOUR

GREAT. JUST WHAT I needed. A chaperone.

Impatience thrummed under my skin. I wanted to be out there searching for Caroline. Not sitting here twiddling my thumbs as Brax and his merry band of psychos closed in on my friend.

I took a deep breath and forced myself to relax. The good news was that Caroline wasn't quite the innocent college professor they probably assumed she was. She had almost as much street smarts as I did—a result of our misspent youth. She would know to stay away from her normal haunts and to keep from using her credit cards so they couldn't track her.

Most people wouldn't be able to track a person's credit cards, but despite all the mystical crap about this world, Liam and Brax have proven adept at manipulating technology.

That reminded me. I fished in my bag and pulled out my wallet before flipping it open. I thumbed through it. My search didn't take long. I had few credit cards; beyond my driver's license, a library card, and my business card for Hermes, there wasn't a lot in there to look through. My credit card was gone, as was the hundred bucks I'd had in there last night.

She'd taken them. Good. Liam or Brax would figure out they should track my credit card use before long, but in the meantime, what she'd taken should give her a head start.

It wasn't that I didn't understand the gravity of what Brax and Sondra had warned me about, but I also didn't trust them without reservation. I wanted to talk to Caroline first. If they just showed up and tried to force her back to the farm, I could see her snapping. Neither one of us dealt well with ultimatums—something the vampires and werewolves refused to acknowledge. If I found her first, I might be able to talk her around. And if things were as dire as Brax said, with her sanity in question, no way was I risking he would change his mind about putting her down. I'd figure something else out if I had to.

Until then, I just needed to figure out a way to slip my guard and then find her.

I threw my wallet on the end table and dug into the pocket of my jeans, pulling out the note Lowen had given me. It was tightly folded and looked a bit like origami.

I examined it with a frown. It would be easy to rip this thing and lose the message inside. I used a finger nail to pull loose one edge of the paper, and then with careful movements unfolded it bit by bit, working the paper as if it was a puzzle.

Finally, I had the message flat on the end table. It was definitely Caroline's handwriting.

Aileen,
They will be closing in on me soon, so I need to go. Don't worry about me, and don't look for me. I'll be fine. I never should have involved you in this. I'll never forget senior year, and please look after my cat.
Caroline

I folded the paper back up, my folds nowhere near as neat as they'd been before I unwrapped it. I tapped the paper against my thigh as I stared around in thought. I ignored the part about not looking for her. It'd been written with the purpose of allaying her pursuers' minds of my involvement should the note have been intercepted before reaching me. That I was sure of. The part about the cat and senior year was a message. I just wasn't sure of the meaning.

Caroline didn't own a cat; I didn't even think she liked them. She'd always been more of a dog person, which given her new circumstances, was probably a good thing.

Also, what did she mean by her reference to senior year? That was almost a decade ago, and a lot of things happened that year. I couldn't be sure which one she was referring to.

I stuffed the paper back into the pocket of my jeans to ponder later. For now, I had to keep up the charade and that meant unpacking. I grabbed the bag and headed over to one of the dressers. My things would probably need only a drawer or two. I opened the first drawer to find it filled with underthings. All with the tags still on them. I closed the drawer and stared at the dresser for a long moment. I bent to open another drawer, this one full of nice blouses and a few camisoles. I fingered one, sliding the tag out. My size.

Next, I walked over to the closet and slid the barn door to the side, revealing a space nearly as big as my apartment bedroom. It wasn't empty. Shoes sat like tidy little soldiers in their brackets and one side was full of clothes. I pushed a few aside, stopping to admire a nice leather jacket—again, in my size with the tags still on it. The price made my eyebrows climb, and I let out a low whistle. Expensive. Nice, but super pricey.

I wanted to shrug the new clothes off, ascribe it to them being in the wrong place. They were really for some other vampire who had just moved in, not me.

Even my inner ostrich couldn't bring herself to believe that—especially in light of the new information from Rick. No, whoever had commissioned this room had evidently found time to buy me a whole new wardrobe.

The question was why, and what strings were attached to all of these expensive little price tags.

I left the closet and its wealth of new clothes and headed back to the dresser. I chose one of the drawers and emptied it out, re-homing the clothes inside to make room for my own. Opening my gym bag, I grabbed the folded clothes and transferred them to their new home.

Finished unpacking, I frowned and pulled the bag closer to me, tilting it so I could see inside its depths. Empty. I unzipped both pockets, feeling around, even though I knew it was pointless. The Judge was gone. My hand knocked against something hard, my heart leaping in relief for a moment before falling again, as I pulled out a plain, leather-bound book.

"You again." My sigh was exasperated.

I tilted it for a glimpse at the spine, narrowing my eyes at the title *A Study of the Unexplained.* Under the title was a subtitle. *What Any Idiot Should Know About the Supernatural.* Looked like the book had given itself another title change. Last week it was calling itself, *The Adventures of the Criminally Stupid.*

The book had attached itself to me earlier this year during an ill-advised break-in to the shadow library hiding inside the Book Haven, a well-known independent book store in the area. I'd been hoping for a guide that would help me understand this shadow world. What I got instead was a sentient, smart-ass book that was only occasionally helpful. Previous attempts to read it had been met with frustration and circular logic. It only gave useful information when it suited it. The rest of the time it was little more than a paperweight.

"I'd rather have my gun," I told it before tossing it on the dresser.

I set my hands on my hips and glared at the bag as if that would make the Judge appear. Unfortunately for me, it didn't work.

Giving up on mentally willing it to make its presence known, I headed for the other room where I could hear Nathan had figured out the TV. He and I were going to have a long talk about boundaries.

"So, it seems there's a key item missing from my belongings," I said, stepping into the living room.

Nathan was sprawled across the couch, watching a baseball game. I paused at the incongruous sight of a lethal vampire watching something as normal as baseball, before shaking off the oddity.

He rotated his head to look at me, not moving from his spot. He shot me a lazy smile before going back to watching the game. "You didn't think we'd let you keep your little pea shooter, did you? We've got rules here—the first being, unaffiliated baby vamps aren't allowed to be armed on the premises."

"First, the Judge is not a pea shooter. It is a high-powered revolver that is easily handled and maintained."

"It's also ineffective against most spooks," he said, without taking his eyes off the TV.

"And yet I was able to kill Eleanor with it." I folded my arms across my chest.

"You got lucky; you probably won't be a second time."

I left that alone. There hadn't been any luck involved. I was prepared and had learned my lesson from my previous failures.

"How did you know I even had it?" I asked.

He tapped an ear. "Superior hearing, remember? I heard you take it out of your safe." He then tapped his nose. "Also, I could smell the gun oil you use to clean it."

I filed that last piece away. I'd known about the hearing—though mine was nowhere near as sensitive as his—but hadn't realized we also had a heightened sense of smell.

"Any chance I'm going to get it back?" I asked.

He shrugged. "Anything is possible; however, the chances of you getting that thing back while you're under this roof are improbable." He gave me a jaunty grin. "Liam decides who goes armed in the mansion."

And he wasn't my biggest fan at the best of times. Having just involved myself in an interspecies incident, I doubted he'd be cutting me any breaks anytime soon.

I rubbed my forehead and sighed. I did not like being unarmed in hostile territory. Worse, the ammo inside the Judge was my own special blend, complete with silver nitrate. None of my other weapons had ammo like that, so they would be useless against a spook until I could find time to create more.

Nathan switched off the TV and climbed to his feet. "Enough about your pea shooter. Time for the real fun of the evening to begin."

I gave him a frown at his nickname for the Judge and followed him on grudging feet as he steered me out of the room. If nothing else, the tour would at least give me an idea of the lay of the land in case I needed to find the best exit points.

*

The mansion, it turned out, was a bit of a maze. The areas I'd seen the last time I was here were only the beginning. In addition to the great ballroom, there were two other massive sitting rooms, a pool and sauna in the basement, as well as two wings set aside for the enforcers and their companions.

We made our way up from the basement as Nathan pointed out several other features of the mansion, including a section that he called the war room.

"Our weapons are stored in a locker in there." He gave me a sidelong glance. "I'd recommend not approaching unless you're accompanied by one of us. It's under twenty-four-hour observation, so we'll know if you trespass. The consequences of such an incident would be severe."

He gestured to the ceiling, pointing out the cameras so I would know he was serious. I suspected that the visible cameras were only the start of their security measures.

A man stepped out of one of the rooms, his silver-gray eyes meeting mine before his companion distracted him.

Seeing the other vampire, Nathan grabbed my arm and drew me away, trying to distract me with inane chatter. "Let me show you our entertainment room. It's pretty sweet."

I looked back over my shoulder even as Nathan kept marching me forward. Thomas watched me with an enigmatic gaze as his fellow vampire talked at him. Seeing where Thomas's attention had focused, the man paused and glanced my way, his eyes narrowing as he took in our retreating figures.

Nathan didn't release me until we were halfway across the house, and then only because I twisted my arm out of his grip. I had no doubt he let me escape, but I'd take what I could get.

"Does Thomas visit you guys often?" I asked in a calm voice.

Nathan looked uncomfortable, his shoulders tense as he avoided my gaze.

"Nathan?" I stepped in front of him, bringing him to a halt. "What is Thomas doing here and is he here often?"

"That's one way to put it."

I narrowed my eyes. It was not lost on me that he'd given a cryptic non-answer that failed to address the first part of my question.

"Does he live here?" I asked.

Nathan grimaced. That was answer enough.

I let out an animalistic growl, the sound wild and full of anger. My fangs dropped down and my hands curled into fists.

Nathan stepped in front of me and held up his hands, his face clear of any amusement for once. "You cannot confront him right now. He's the master of this territory. You make a scene in public, and he'll have no choice but to punish you. Believe me, you don't want that."

I took a deep breath and forced myself to calm. It wasn't like I planned to hunt Thomas down and attack him right this second. I wasn't an idiot. Thomas was powerful, perhaps more powerful than any vampire, with the possible exception of one of the vampire elders I'd met last year.

I wasn't sure of that last part, since I was still learning how to decipher things my magic-seeing eye showed me. What it had shown me of Thomas, was enough to impress on me the need to have a concrete plan and exit strategy, in the event I wanted to take him down. Even then, if I were ever to take revenge against him for what he'd done to me, I'd strike unseen from a distance, and make sure it could never be traced back to me.

My fangs folded back into my gums, and I glared at Nathan for a long moment before turning on my heel and striding away. His footsteps were nearly silent as he followed me down the hall.

Too bad his mouth couldn't be equally silent. "Where are you going?"

"To get my stuff. I'm not staying here."

It was his turn to dart in front and bring us to a stop. "Whoa, you know that's not going to work. You're in our charge until your little werewolf friend is found. That's the deal. No renegotiating now."

My glare should have set him on fire with the heat it was generating. "I didn't get a say in any of those negotiations."

He shrugged his massive shoulders, not looking the least remorseful. "Doesn't matter. That's how this cookie crumbles."

I breathed out through my nose. My temper simmered just below the surface. Not even in their stronghold an hour and I was already struggling not to burn the place down. There was more than one reason I'd chosen to isolate myself in my apartment and life. It was a lot harder to lose your temper when you were the only one present, and on the rare occasions when I did lose it, no one was there to see or judge.

I stepped around Nathan and continued down the hall.

"Where are you going now?" he called after me as he ambled after me. The sense of urgency he'd pursued me with earlier was gone.

"My room."

"Ugh, why? We're not done with the tour."

I didn't answer, continuing in the direction I thought my suite was located. Maybe. It was ridiculously easy to get lost in here. The mansion must have a charm that enabled it to be several times larger than it appeared from the outside. The mansion was big from the outside, but it wasn't big enough to house all that I'd seen so far.

"We still have the kitchen to see," Nathan said.

My pace slowed. No, no, don't get distracted. You're mad at him.

"We have a deep freezer. I believe some of the companions have a standing order with that ice cream place you like."

"Graeters?" I asked before I could stop myself.

He shrugged his broad shoulders. "No clue. I don't concern myself with human food brands, but from my understanding, the companions are very particular about their ice cream."

It'd be either Graeters or Jeni's. Columbus natives knew those two had the best ice cream flavors. Either one would hit the spot after the night I'd had.

I backtracked toward him. "Well, then. I guess I can spare a little time out of my busy night to check out this kitchen."

"And finish the tour," he added with a victorious smirk.

I frowned at him. That had not been part of the deal.

He guessed my thoughts before I could say anything. "You want ice cream; you've got to finish the tour."

I slid him a sideways glance. I bet I could find the kitchen by myself. Of course, given the size of this place, I could be wandering for quite a while. My shoulders slumped as I resigned myself to completing the tour.

"Now, on to the entertainment room."

I followed him with grudging steps as he led us through several more hallways, up a set of stairs located in what I thought was the back of the mansion and down another hallway. Unless he had a map somewhere for me, I didn't know how he expected me to find my way alone.

"Here we are," he said, stopping in front of an open entrance that had sound spilling out.

There was no door marking the room, just molding framing the archway. You had to step down onto a fluffy, beige rug that softened your footsteps, before transitioning into a mahogany wood floor. On one side of the room was a pool table, while a dark brown leather sectional sat on the other side in front of the biggest TV I'd ever seen. The room looked like the sort of place you'd find in a mountain retreat, but with all the amenities you could want, including a small kitchenette complete with wine fridge.

It was also occupied. There were two men in the middle of a pool game, while the sectional on the other side of the room was covered with several large bodies as they battled it out in a video game. The game paused as Nathan stepped down, reaching back and tugging me forward, when I would have stepped out of sight. We found ourselves at the center of several curious pairs of eyes.

It was like being the new kid in the middle of the school year. You didn't know what your reception would be—whether the others would welcome you, or treat you to the hairy eyeball and make snide comments to your face before pouring syrup into your locker.

"Nathan, who did you bring us?" one of the men at the pool table asked, pool cue clutched in his hand. His eyes were a pretty hazel, and he looked like a Viking of old—tall, fair, and sporting a beard that somehow made him seem handsome despite the fact I'd never been a fan of facial hair.

"This is Aileen. She'll be staying here for a little while," Nathan said, crossing the room to the wine bar and fishing out a bottle. He poured two glasses.

I stayed where I was, feeling like a gazelle facing down a pride of lions on the African plains. All of the strangers' eyes remained fastened on me. I couldn't read their intent, whether they were hostile, welcoming, or ambivalent.

"That's the stray yearling, right?" a man sitting in front of the TV said. He looked Asian and had shaved his head on either side, before dying his hair a bright blue and slicking it back from his face. He had a piercing in one ear and a tattoo crawling up his neck.

"That would be the one," Eric said, sitting up from where the couch had hidden his slouched form. He barely glanced in my direction before hitting a button and resuming the game.

Blue hair aimed a kick his way. "Hey fucker, I wasn't ready."

"Not my problem," Eric said with a negligent shrug.

The third man on the couch snorted. "He's just pissed because he's gotten his ass kicked for the last hour."

Eric didn't respond, mashing the buttons and staring intently at the screen.

"For that, I'm going to make sure all remember your name as a pathetic waste of characters," Blue said, standing and glaring at the screen as his thumb and forefinger moved over the game controller.

The third man shook his head and folded one arm behind his head. "As if you haven't had it out for him since we started." He aimed a lazy smile at the other two. He looked like a warrior from a long-ago era, one more used to swinging a broad sword, than a pen. His hair was dark, almost black, and his skin tan. He'd been turned later in life, if the crow's feet at the corner of his eyes were anything to judge by. His face looked like he'd lived and laughed and loved, the grooves just beginning to form.

"Shut up, Anton. You're just pissed you broke your controller when I pwned your ass on the last level," Blue said, not taking his eyes off the screen. His character switched between a bazooka and a sniper rifle to kill two enemies before he lobbed a grenade into a room.

The screen in front of Eric lit up, and his motions grew more frantic as he tried to lob his own grenade, only to have it rebound toward him.

Nathan stopped next to me and handed me a wine glass as a victorious cry rose from one end of the sectional and a muttered curse from the other side.

"What's this?" I asked, taking the glass. It was dark red, but lacked the consistency of blood.

"Blood wine. It's good. It's how we unwind after a long day. Thought you could use one."

I eyed it with curiosity. "I thought you said the only way we could get tipsy was to drink from an inebriated person." I frowned. At least that's what I thought he had said.

"Wow, she really is new," the Viking said, bending to line up his next shot.

I flicked a glance his way but didn't comment. He was not wrong.

Nathan frowned over at the pool shooter before turning to me. "This is an exception. It has wine and blood in it, but the wine is a fairy wine. The magic inside can make us tipsy if consumed in large enough quantities."

I now understood why my other-sight was seeing white lights fizzing and popping like bubbles in the deep red. That must be the source of the magic.

I hesitated, watching as Nathan took a generous sip of his own. Being tipsy in front of this lot didn't appeal. Any loss of control could mean bad things for me. Trust was not something I gave easily, and no one in this room had earned that.

Reading my hesitation, Nathan said, "Even then, it takes a few glasses before we feel the alcohol's effects."

I took a small sip and made a pleased expression. It tasted good. Better than wine and better than the bottled blood I'd been drinking. It popped and fizzed on my tongue. I didn't know if that was the magic or the wine, but the sensation was close to the bubbly nature of sparkling wine or champagne. So delicious.

"So, what's she doing here?" Blue asked, folding his arms over the back of the sectional and looking at me with dark, curious eyes. He didn't seem antagonistic, even if his question was borderline rude.

Eric set the controller down with a frown. "One of the new werewolves went on walkabout. Aileen has a close friendship with the person in question, and she's already been contacted once and let her slip away. Until the wolf is found, we're on babysitter detail."

I watched Eric in fascination; it was the most I'd heard him speak. Ever.

Blue raised both eyebrows and whistled. "I'm surprised the alpha didn't demand the yearling's head."

"He has a soft spot for her," Nathan volunteered. "She's saved his life a time or two."

I scoffed. "That man doesn't have any soft spots."

Not that I could find anyway. Brax was surrounded by a diamond-studded wall of unfeeling, by-the-book rules. My being an unclaimed vampire pissed him off because it violated his set of principles. Kind of like a certain vampire, who had forced me to come here, and then pawned me off on his second in charge. The two could have been brothers given how similar they were.

"She speaks," Blue said with a wicked gleam in his eye. There was a pop of air, and then he was standing next to me. "Is it true you shot our fearless leader?"

I blinked, trying not to show how impressed I was at his speed. Not even a split second had passed. I hadn't even seen him move, before he was beside me.

"Yes, three times," I answered after a moment. It took me a second to put his question together with the incident. It had been when Liam threatened to kill my family after he'd convinced them to do an "intervention" for my nonexistent drinking problem.

"Were you really stupid enough to give a marker to a sorcerer?" the Viking asked, leaning against the pool table.

Blue didn't wait for me to confirm, his face lighting up with excitement. "Let us see it. Let's see the mark."

My eyes went to Nathan, asking without words for him to save me from their interrogation. He kept his eyes focused on his glass as he swirled the wine around and took another sip.

No help from that quarter. Guess I should have expected it. These were his boys.

I sighed and held the glass carefully in one hand as I used the other to roll my right sleeve up, exposing the sorcerer's mark where it had melded with Liam's.

Blue took my arm, his fingers cool and gentle, as he tilted it so he could see it better. "Liam's marked her too."

The words brought everyone but Nathan and Eric's attention to us. The Viking set his pool cue down and advanced on us. "Where?"

Blue tugged my arm around, showing him the oak tree where it had bloomed with leaves behind the lion. "That's his mark."

Viking looked from it to me, his eyebrows lowered and a thoughtful expression in his eyes. His head swung towards Nathan. "Did you know about this?"

Nathan shrugged.

"What's the big deal about having his mark?" I asked.

Blue and Viking looked back at me, both sets of eyes more than a little impressed.

Viking's voice was a deep rumble as he said, "Liam doesn't mark yearlings. He thinks looking after them until they mature enough to be useful is a waste of his time. The only ones he ever keeps around are the ones he's made, and they were exceptional before he ever turned them."

"Has he marked you?" I asked. I knew both Eric and Nathan held his mark and was curious to see who else in this place had it as well.

Viking was wearing a t-shirt that hugged his chest and biceps lovingly. He turned his arm so I could see the forearm, where an oak tree spread its branches. Bigger than mine, his also had roots, making it similar to a Celtic tattoo I'd seen when I'd been human and thinking about getting one.

"All of his enforcers have one." Viking dropped his arm.

"I thought vampires wore the mark of their clan," I said.

The two shared a long look but refrained from commenting on my lack of knowledge. Since I didn't have the benefit of a vampire mentor willing to tutor me in all things of the fanged variety, I had to ask questions, even when it made me look like an uneducated hick. It forced me to don my reporter's mantle, thread-worn, and bug-eaten, as it was.

"Normally, that would be so. Enforcers are different. We're a clan unto ourselves. Instead of sharing the bond of blood or the same creator, we have *chosen* to be part of this fellowship and have passed rigorous testing for the honor," Viking said, watching me carefully. "Makoto is new to our ranks, so his is only partially formed."

Blue raised his arm and showed me the tattoo on his forearm. It was small and only sported a few scraggly branches. The green was faint and barely there in places.

I touched mine. Why was mine full of leaves and in full color when Makoto's was still in the beginning stages? It was a question I hesitated to ask in case there were ramifications that might make dealing with the enforcers difficult. Makoto had already demonstrated a speed far superior to my own. In a fight, I would lose. I wanted to keep things on as even a keel as possible. They might not be allowed to kill me, but vampires, even baby ones, could take a lot of damage before kicking the bucket. With the assistance of an older vampire to heal wounds, a lesson taught by these guys could get very painful indeed.

Neither one commented on the difference between mine and Makoto's mark for which I was grateful.

"What are you playing?" I asked to change the subject.

Makoto spared the screen a glance. "Halo. Ever play?"

I nodded. "A time or two."

That was a lie. Military guys loved this game, and to fit in, I'd learned. Not to mention, it felt good to beat their asses at something they assumed men were superior at.

Makoto's smile was slow and crafty. "Looks like we got a challenger, boys."

CHAPTER FIVE

"NO! HOW ARE you doing that?" Makoto howled as his screen exploded in red.

I smirked, my character on screen swerving, as I made for the spot he'd have to cross when he re-spawned. That was the third time in a row where I'd sniped him before he could do much more than pick up some extra grenades.

"Who cares how?" Anton said, his voice delighted. "She's kicking your ass. That's all that matters."

I was kicking his ass, and it felt awesome. Makoto was good. Better than I was, to be honest. I had to work my ass off to kill him as many times as I had. It helped that he underestimated me early on, giving me the opportunity to snap up the sniper rifle and a few other key items. All I had to do after that, was sit back in a few key spots, waiting for him to show. Then, it was a red parade for him.

I think even Eric was impressed. It was kind of hard to tell because the extent of his facial expression was a slight twitch of his lips as I, yet again, sniped Makoto's avatar from across the city.

Makoto cursed as the game kicked him back to a different part of the map. My avatar took off to get a bead on the grenade launcher I had a feeling he was going after next.

"Anton?" a feminine voice asked from the hallway. Pretty brown eyes in a heart-shaped face peered anxiously into the room.

"Catherine, my dearest. What is it you need?" Anton said, his voice lazy from where he sat watching me decimate Makoto.

Catherine stepped inside, her gaze flitting around. She was a pretty woman, human and delicate looking. That was all I had time to notice before being forced to return my attention back to the TV or risk losing my advantage.

"I thought you were coming to my room tonight," Catherine said, her voice holding the faintest edge to it.

Anton gave her a charming smile over his shoulder. "And I shall, my dear. As soon as I watch the yearling finish trouncing our resident game shark."

"Oh." Catherine didn't say anything else.

"Have you met our newest addition?" Anton asked her.

From the corner of my eye, I saw her shake her head. "Aileen, meet Catherine, my companion."

I hit a button, pausing the game. I gave her a friendly nod and a small smile.

"Nice to meet you," she said, her smile slightly hesitant before her attention went right back to the vampire sitting on the other side of the couch.

"Same to you," I said even though I had a feeling she was no longer paying attention to me.

She fixed Anton with an expectant look. "I'll just wait here, then, until you're ready."

Anton sighed, his lips curling up into a seductive look that he aimed at his companion. He patted the couch next to him. "You could always spend the time over here."

She giggled and ducked her head, an appealing blush staining her cheeks.

Makoto made a sound very similar to gagging. When I looked at him, he was staring at the TV as if he hadn't just made it obvious what he thought of the two's flirting. He hit the un-pause button as soon as he noticed my inattention.

I was forced to react, picking up several grenades as his avatar ran across the city. My fingers felt suddenly clumsy, fatigue causing me to miss the next shot. My eye-to-hand coordination devolved from there, and suddenly it was a struggle keeping my head upright.

Dawn. Somehow it had crept up on me while we played the game. I didn't remember the last time I'd lost track of the sun. Now, I was going to pay for it.

I hit the pause button, the controller sliding out of my hands as I struggled to stand.

"What are you doing? I was about to turn things around," Makoto said, his face outraged.

"I think it's time for me to find my bed," I said, the words tired sounding. I stumbled a few feet then lost my balance.

"Oh, my goodness, are you okay?" Catherine's surprised voice asked. "What's wrong with her?"

"Aileen?" Nathan's face appeared above me.

"Think I'll just stay here for a few minutes." I gave him a sleepy smile, my eyes drifting shut.

From far away, I heard another voice.

"What's going on?" It sounded like Liam

"The baby collapsed on her face." Makoto sounded insultingly pleased about that fact.

"Why is she so tied to the sun?" Viking asked, his voice a deep rumble. "She should have grown out of that after the first year."

There was a long sigh as Liam walked over to where I rested, eyes closed, on the floor.

"You got her?" Nathan asked.

"Yes," Liam said. A set of arms encircled and lifted me, cradling me against a strong chest. "I'll take her back to her room."

I snuggled deeper into the nice smelling shirt, rubbing my nose against it, and enjoying the rumble of his chest under my ear. It was soothing.

"Aileen, put your arms around my neck," Liam ordered. I resisted, my arms feeling like they had weights attached to them. "Aileen."

"Such a grumpy boots." My voice slurred with exhaustion. Grudgingly, knowing he wouldn't leave me alone until I did as he asked, I lifted one arm and draped it around his neck. I took the opportunity to nuzzle my nose against his neck, inhaling deeply his own unique smell—a blend of a spring storm and nighttime.

"You're a pain in the ass," he said. He didn't sound upset about that fact.

I let out a hmm, before sleep claimed me.

*

I jerked awake and sat up in bed, my head clear. I was alone. Even better, I wasn't in the entertainment room covered in marker graffiti or any other unsavory element. I swung my jeans covered legs out from under the covers. Good, Liam hadn't undressed me when he delivered me to my bedroom.

I couldn't believe I had been so careless as to get caught off guard by the dawn. Not only was it embarrassing to collapse in the middle of things, but it was a moment when I was at my most vulnerable. I would be hard pressed to defend myself in the event someone should try something.

I still couldn't figure out how it happened. I should have felt the sun before it ever cleared the horizon. This matter required some thought. It could be that Liam's blood had affected things. If this was going to become a thing, I needed to figure out a way to adapt. Maybe set an alarm on my phone that told me when it was time to retreat to the safety of my bedroom.

I set my feet on the floor. Perhaps a shower would clear my head and help me figure a way out of my current predicament. Out of the dresser, I grabbed a change of clothing before heading to the bathroom.

My feet stuttered to a stop and my mouth dropped. Now I knew what Nathan meant when he said the bathroom would tempt me to the dark side. About the size of my apartment bedroom, it was probably the most decadent bathroom I'd ever seen. It was straight out of one of those MTV 'Crash My Pad' shows. It had a sunken tub with room enough for three people and a shower that an entire football team could get clean in.

I let myself take it all in for a long minute. The place deserved that and more. I could spend days in this room, luxuriating in its spa-like atmosphere.

Sadly, the minute was all I could spare. Leaving the bathtub for next time, I headed to the shower, divesting myself of my clothes and playing with the sprayers for a few minutes. It took that long just to figure the system out. The shower was one of those that had multiple sprayers that could hit you from different sides and strengths. After that, it took another few minutes to get the temperature just right. I let the water pound down on the back of my neck with the perfect amount of heat and just relaxed.

It took some willpower to drag myself out of the shower and not just stand under the sprayer for the rest of my life. Dried off, my brown hair tied back in a bun to keep my clothes from getting wet, I cleared a spot in the fogged-up mirror and grabbed a toothbrush that had been sitting wrapped on the counter. My grayish blue eyes looked back at me from pale skin made even paler by the fact that I hadn't been outside in over two years. I was tall, five feet seven inches, and made lean from my work as a bike messenger for Hermes. It probably helped that although I could eat a small amount of food, it lacked the nutrients my body could process. As a result, I didn't gain weight no matter how many bowls of black raspberry ice cream I consumed.

I'd chosen a black t-shirt and a faded pair of jeans that fit me well but were loose enough that I could move if I had to. While the jeans would be a little warm for June, they would protect my legs if I ended up on my bike again.

Ready, I stepped out of the bathroom and froze at the sight of a pair of long legs attached to a lean body whose owner's head rested on my pillow. Liam turned from his perusal of the ceiling and gave me a lazy smile.

"You shouldn't have bothered with the shower. You're just going to get all sweaty again," he said.

I frowned at him. "What are you doing in my bedroom?"

His smile widened to hold a wicked edge. "Where do you think I stayed during the day?"

"Your own bedroom."

His expression turned amused. "And leave you with the opportunity to sneak out if you woke sooner than expected?"

Damn.

He let out a laugh, the warm sound brushing against me and sending tingles down my spine. He would be handsome if I didn't want to stab him in the eye half the time.

"I'm surprised you're here yourself given how busy you are," I said. "Where are your minions?"

He managed to turn his shrug into a thing of elegance. "They're all busy. I had a bit of time today and thought we could spend it together."

"You assume I want to spend time with you," I returned.

He didn't let my statement deter him. He sat up and swung his legs off the bed, standing in a graceful movement. "I suggest you put on clothes you can exercise in. I've decided to give you a little training this evening."

"I think I'm good. I have work anyways."

"Your first run isn't until one. You have a little time." He walked out of the room, leaving me to trail behind him like a lost little lamb.

"How do you know that?" I narrowed my eyes at him. "Did you call Jerry?"

Jerry was the owner of Hermes, and I had a hard time believing he would tell Liam anything. Jerry wasn't exactly the biggest fan of vampires. He only tolerated me because I was practically a newborn in vampire terms, and he owed my old captain a huge favor.

He tossed my phone over his shoulder. I caught it and looked down at it with a suspicious glance. It was unlocked, and my calendar was open. How did he unlock it? And what else had he stuck his nose into?

"Get changed, or you'll be training in what you're wearing," he called from the other room, his voice making it clear he was serious.

"I didn't bring any exercise gear," I shouted, trying one last time to get out of what was sure to be an embarrassing and painful experience.

"You've no doubt noticed by now that the room has been stocked with clothes in your size. Quit wasting time."

Yeah, and we'd be having a talk about how he'd got my sizes.

I stuck my tongue out at the door and headed for the dresser, grabbing the first pair of yoga pants I found. Pairing it with a sports bra and workout tank, I was ready in very little time. He was right; everything fit.

I appeared in the next room to find Liam standing in front of the fridge with a grimace of distaste as he held a bottle of blood up.

Seeing me, he closed the fridge and grabbed a glass from the cabinet. "Good, you listened."

"Like you gave me a choice."

"I've told you before. We always have a choice. It's just that some of those choices are acceptable and some not. You chose the one that allowed you to keep your dignity. This time." He slid the glass containing the blood towards me. "Since you listened, I won't force you to take blood from a live donor."

"Mighty big of you," I said in a dry voice.

He met my eyes with a serious gaze. "Make no mistake, Aileen, there will come a time when I force the issue. You need to learn how to drink blood from the source. Not only for your safety but for the safety of those around you."

I gave him my best stubborn look, the one that my mom used to get when she tried to make me eat my vegetables.

His gaze softened. "We both know it wouldn't take much for your will to break."

My look turned dirty. He was referencing the time when I'd been forced to take blood from him. One little cut on his neck and I'd latched on like a damn leech.

"I might surprise you," I said. Not the most original come back, but it was all I had.

He gave me a dark smile. "You just might." He walked around the counter. "Now, drink up. You're going to need the blood for what I have in store for you."

I grumbled but drained the glass as quickly as I could. My stomach tried to revolt against it as it oozed down my throat. My gag reflex nearly kicked in, and it was only through sheer will power that I managed to keep it down. Gone was the electric feeling of life that used to be there when I had a glass of the red stuff. Now, it was like ten-day old roadkill. It might technically have what you need, but it wasn't going to go down easy.

Liam's gaze was sympathetic. "It'll only get worse from here on out."

I set the glass down hard. "Let's go."

I didn't want to talk about my drinking habits. Not with him. Not when he was the reason I recognized the difference in the first place.

He held my gaze for a long moment but didn't fight me on it. Somehow that made me feel worse than if he had.

*

A hard blow to my stomach forced my breath out of my body. I fought the instinct to curl around the sore spot and kept my hands up, protecting my head from the follow-up fist.

"Move faster," Liam ordered, his voice so calm that just listening to it made me want to tear out all his hair—especially given the number of bruises already dotting my body. The man hit like a sledgehammer and had about as much mercy as one too. "Stop. Letting. Me. Hit. You." Each word was punctuated by a blow. One to my chest, one to my back, a kick to one thigh, a fist to the side of my head.

"I. Am. Trying." I tried dodging and received a cuff to the other side of my head for my troubles.

"Try harder," Liam barked.

It wasn't like I hadn't been trying for the last hour. He was faster. Stronger. And he wasn't afraid to use either against me. It was like trying to fight someone while standing in quicksand. My mind was willing; my body had to slog through a soupy, glop-like mess. Any benefit the blood might have afforded me had disappeared long ago. I was back to healing human-slow and feeling every one of the spots Liam targeted.

"Come on, soldier. Do something. Do anything."

I gritted my teeth and swung, knowing he wouldn't be there even as I started to move. He slid to the side, his lips turned up in that insufferable smirk he'd worn for this entire torture session. He kicked out with one leg, sending me crashing to the ground. My back protested as I hit with a hard thud. I lay there for a long moment, trying to get back my breath.

A movement out of the corner of my eye had me rolling out of range. Liam's foot landed where I'd just lain.

"Really? Kicking someone when they're down?"

He shrugged. "Your enemy won't give you time to catch your breath. Best you learn that here, where the worst you'll receive are some bruised ribs. Out there you could suffer a lot worse."

Nathan chuckled as he walked past us to the weight bench in the corner. "Don't let him kid you. He's just a perverse fuck."

We weren't the only ones using the gym in the basement. There were several moving from machine to machine. The human I met last night—I think I remember his name was Theo—was already lifting weights when Liam had forced this little training session on me. Nathan had joined us shortly after we arrived.

"You're a vampire. Use some of that speed I know you have," Liam ordered, ignoring his minion.

I was a yearling. The only speed I was capable of was the kind that allowed me to disappear after Thanksgiving with the family, so I didn't get stuck doing an entire kitchen's worth of dishes.

"Come on. Dig deep. Show me some of that stubbornness you're known for."

I'd really like to. If they ever gave me back my weapons, I'd be sure to.

We circled each other. Me, looking for a window. Him, probably trying to find a place he hadn't already abused.

Don't focus on the coming pain. Focus on what you can do. I wasn't going to beat him through strength or speed or even experience. It was clear I was outmatched in all three. That left trickery.

He threw a strike aimed at my face. Using one hand, I pushed it to the side and grabbed the back of his head with the other. I stepped forward, releasing the block and aimed for his head. He was gone before I could connect.

"Good, you're beginning to use your brain," he growled against my ear.

A heavy blow to the back of my knee and a hard push against my shoulder sent me crashing back to the ground.

"Again." He stepped towards me, and I popped to my feet. His smirk told me he'd planned to kick me again. Sadistic bastard.

He didn't wait for me to catch my breath, advancing on me faster than I could blink. The punch he threw was human slow. I slid to the side, already looking for the next one. There. I blocked, stepped forward, throwing several strikes and adding in a kick, trying to overwhelm his mind so that something might land.

It seemed to work. For a moment.

Out of nowhere, a force hit with the strength of a hurricane behind it. I crashed to the ground, the lights fading.

"Aileen?"

"You shouldn't have hit her so hard. She can't take our kind of damage," Nathan chided.

My eyes snapped open. Liam's concerned face above me and Nathan standing over him. I didn't think, just reacted.

I threw a punch, hitting him in the throat. He made a choking sound as I grabbed his arm and jerked, sending him off balance and rolling to a seated position on top of him. There was a shout behind me as my fists flew, raining down blows on his head, shoulders and chest as fast as I could move my arms.

Quick as a snake, he grabbed each wrist in an unbreakable grip, his eyes almost glowing as they peered up at me. His fangs peeked out of his mouth as he gave me a dark smile.

Before I could move, he rolled us over—me on my back, my hands held down next to my head, him wedged between my legs. "Knew you had it in you."

I snarled at him, beyond thought. Beyond reasoning. I lurched up, burying my fangs in his throat. He gave a guttural groan, his hands sliding from my wrists to cradle my head. Blood, that delicious giver of life, slid down my throat. It was nothing like that tepid stuff from my refrigerator. This was the real deal, sending energy zapping along my nerve endings.

"It's fine. Go." Liam's voice was hoarse and seemed to come from a distance, or maybe it was because I had better things on my mind. Like the arousal building at my core. An arousal Liam fed as he pressed his hard length against me. His voice muttered a few foreign sounding words; I was too far gone to even begin to guess what language he was speaking.

He buried his fingers in my hair, tugging lightly, and then a little harder until I unlatched. He pressed a hard kiss to my lips. I lifted, trying to rub all of me against him, need building deep inside, unlike any I'd felt before.

Everything felt more. More decadent. More wicked. Just more.

It was like being on a roller coaster with no seat belt, no guard rails, and no assurance that the next drop wouldn't be the last. Each kiss was intoxicating in its intensity.

He angled my head, nuzzling my neck before there was a sharp sting and then warm pleasure. Whatever I had felt biting him was nothing compared to this. A tidal wave of feeling swamped me, setting my entire body alight as need threatened to consume. A moan escaped me, and I writhed under him. His hold on me tightened, an animal-like growl escaping him.

"You're needed elsewhere," a crisp voice said, breaking through the haze.

Liam's lips slid from my neck, and his head came up with a snarl. His eyes were a blue bright enough to burn. They were the color of a raging, hot fire.

"Don't bare your fangs at me," the voice snapped. "There's been an issue, and your men are too afraid to interrupt you right now."

I came back to myself slowly, the passion fading enough so I could think again. I changed my grip so that I pushed Liam away. His eyes swung back to me, his fangs bared as he grumbled a warning.

"Stop moving. You've triggered his instincts. Give him a moment to calm," Thomas said, sounding irritated. "Liam, that's enough."

The blue in Liam's eyes faded to normal—still bluer than any other eyes I'd ever seen, but no longer so bright you'd be able to see them in the dark.

"Liam," Thomas barked.

The fangs in Liam's mouth snicked up and a look of annoyance crossed his face. He dropped one last kiss on my lips, his eyes soft, before rolling off me. "I heard you the first time, Thomas. There's no need to shout."

I wriggled to sitting, asking myself what had just happened. I'd attacked without thinking. Then I'd bitten him—again without thinking or any semblance of control. I'd lost track of my surroundings, which I was thankful to notice were clear of all but the two of us and Thomas.

Whoever'd had the foresight to vacate the room while Liam and I were rolling around exchanging saliva and other fluids would forever have my gratitude. Last thing I needed was to develop a reputation. Say what you want about equal rights, but there was a definite double standard between men and women when it came to sex. Liam would be the stud who got in the newbie's pants, while I would be the easy slut who let him.

I'd seen it time and time again. When my coworkers were mostly men, I'd learned to keep that part of my life separate. It was just good business not to date where you worked. It had meant for a lonely time in the military, but the drama-free workplace had been worth it.

Thomas arched an eyebrow. "Really? Because I've been standing here for several minutes trying to get your attention."

"What do you want?" Liam sounded like he was in a bad mood.

"As I said, there's been a situation that requires your attention, and Aileen is late for her appointment."

"What kind of situation?"

"What appointment?"

The questions were asked at the same time. For the first time since Thomas had interrupted us—a fact I'd be grateful for, just as soon as I got over the embarrassment—a trace of amusement showed on his face.

"One of the companions was attacked by what he is describing as a large dog-like creature. Probably a werewolf." Thomas's focus shifted to me as if he hadn't just dropped a potential bomb. "As for you, you have an appointment with one of our doctors to get checked out."

"This is why we have the newly turned under such strict security," Liam told me, his glare a fierce thing. "If your friend attacked a vampire's companion, it will not go well for her when she's found."

"You don't know it's her. There are a lot of things out there someone could mistake for a werewolf." I could name three off the top of my head. "For all you know, it's a rabid dog."

Liam jackknifed to standing. "I hope, for your sake, that you're correct."

I was on my feet in the next moment, blinking at the speed with which I moved. Come to think of it, the bruises and aches that had punctuated my movement before our horizontal wrestling match were gone. My body felt better than it had in forever. I felt like I could run a two-minute mile, jump a tall building and lift a car—all at the same time.

"I'm coming with you," I said.

Thomas stepped forward. "Appointment first."

"You keep saying that, but I never agreed to see a doctor. How do you guys have doctors anyway?" The spooks preferred to keep their presence hidden from humans. I had a hard time believing they would allow one to give them regular checkups. It'd be too easy for that human to expose them to other humans.

"Our vampires are capable of attending medical school," Thomas said, his eyes coolly amused. "We have a few who have an interest in the medical field and make it a point of keeping up with all new techniques and research."

"As for your appointment, we decided it would be best that you see one while you're here to make sure everything is as it should be," Liam told me.

"You decided? I take it, I don't have a choice in this."

Their silence was answer enough.

There it was. The thing that drove me crazy about vampires. They made decisions for me—without ever once consulting me. I wasn't a child and had no intention of handing my life over for anyone else to plan or guide. I'd done that once, and it had not ended well. Never again.

"We don't know how you were able to survive the curse that prevented Thomas from siring more vampires. We had your background checked and know you aren't one of his descendants. It's in everyone's best interests to figure out why," Liam said.

I studied him with narrowed eyes, trying to see if there was more to it than that. His explanation made sense, and it wasn't one I objected to. That didn't mean I appreciated them making these decisions for me.

"It can't wait until after we talk to the companion?" I knew before I asked the question what the answer would be but wanted to try anyway.

Thomas gave a small shake of his head. "This has waited long enough."

"I'll let you know what I find," Liam said, his eyes intent as if to impress on me his sincerity.

My hopes fell. They weren't going to budge.

Seeing my capitulation, Liam took a step toward me and touched me on the arm before departing, leaving Thomas and me the only ones standing in the empty gym.

CHAPTER SIX

"HOW HAVE YOU been?" Thomas's words were stilted and formal.

"Besides the fact that my friend is missing, and I'm being forced to stay in this house of horrors, I'm just hunky-dory."

Thomas's lips quirked to the side. "I don't know. You and Liam seemed like you were having a good time."

I gave him a deadpan look. We were not going to discuss that. Not now. Not ever. "Let's get this over with. I have work in a few hours."

Actually, probably sooner. I didn't know how long Liam had spent training me.

Thomas inclined his head and turned, leading the way. I followed, assuming this doctor wouldn't care that I was in yoga pants, a workout shirt, and covered in sweat.

"You haven't used the car I gave you," he said.

I kept my face expressionless as I kept pace with him. "No."

"Is there a reason? I can get you a different car if there's one you like better."

"I don't need a car. My bike is enough."

"I beg to differ. I've met Jerry's other couriers. All of them have some form of vehicular or magical transportation. A car would only increase your profits by saving you time."

"I'm fine." My answer was short and to the point.

"There are no strings attached if that's what you're worried about," he said, his voice calm and reasonable.

There were always strings attached. Nothing in this life was ever free.

My silence was answer enough. Thomas didn't accept that. "You're being ridiculous. It's a gift. Denying it only hurts yourself."

My snort was full of scorn. "I think I've had enough of your gifts."

"You're talking about your turn."

I didn't answer. I hoped we got to where we needed to go soon, because this conversation was one I'd planned to never have.

"You must know it was never my intention to abandon you," he said, his voice coaxing.

I rounded on him with a snarl and fangs bared. He drew up short, his eyes flashing a warning I refused to heed. "You killed me. You destroyed the person I was, made me into a monster afraid of being around my own family for fear I might hurt them. Your abandonment was the only good thing you ever did for me."

"I can understand why you're angry," Thomas said, his voice infuriatingly calm. "But, you need to look at this as a gift. You'll live for a very long time. If you would just accept your circumstance, you'll find this life can be a good one."

"It was not one I chose," I shouted at him. Of all the things wrong with what was done with me, that was the one that continued to haunt me. He'd stripped my options from me when he made me what I was. He'd taken any dreams I had and turned them to dust. Even if I could get past everything else and embrace my vampyness, I couldn't get past that. Not yet. Perhaps not ever.

There was a long silence between us—one full of anger and bitter feelings on my side, and regret and something I couldn't define on his.

We came to a stop in front of a door. We were on the first floor in a section Nathan had showed me yesterday.

Thomas met my eyes, his expression calm and totally at odds with the writhing mass of feeling currently residing in my stomach. "What's done is done. I can't change it and don't even know if I would if I could. Your existence has been a gift to me."

My lip curled. I bet it had. The vampires had a weird rule. Only those capable of siring other vampires could be selected as the master of the region. My timely appearance was what enabled him to take the city and make it his when it would have otherwise gone to a much less charming vampire. For all that I railed at Thomas and wanted to take a hammer to his head, I knew he was the lesser evil of the two. Didn't mean it didn't burn.

He blinked in acknowledgment of the irony. "As much as you may dislike me, you'll see that you need me. This is a cold, hard world you've found yourself in. You're going to need allies, and it's my duty to ensure you're prepared whether you like that or not. Keep that in mind."

"Don't forget. We have a deal," I told him. "I allowed you to claim me as yours, but you agreed to stay out of my life."

"That agreement only holds so far. I cannot make requirements as your sire." He stepped closer, the deadly predator that had enabled him to claim the city present in his eyes. "But be warned, this city is mine as is everything in it. As its master, I still hold power over you."

Finished with his speech, he opened the door and gestured me inside, his expression back to the bland politeness of before. I held his eyes for a stubborn moment before preceding him into the room.

It wasn't like most doctor's offices. That was for sure. One—it was in a mansion full of vampires. Two—it lacked the sterile brightness of most medical offices I've been in. It looked like a regular home office, granted nicer than I was accustomed to with its antique wood furniture, expensive artwork, and heirloom decorations. The only nod to the fact it belonged to a doctor were the medical instruments laid out on one of the tables and an examination table tucked into the corner of the room.

The office was warm and cozy and invited its occupants to sit down with a cup of tea or maybe a glass of scotch. The man standing next to the desk didn't fit this scene. He was a caged tiger that looked like it had already eaten the zookeeper. Wild, and convinced nothing could ever challenge its spot in the food chain. Arrogance showed in every line of his posture. Arrogance and superiority.

"You're late," he barked before we were even all the way in the room.

"Yes, there was an unexpected complication," Thomas said in a smooth voice.

The other man sneered, but refrained from saying anything else. "Is this her then?"

He studied me from eyes that would have been beautiful, if they hadn't been glaring at me. He was tall, with skin the color of coffee, eyes a light hazel, and a face that invited sin.

"It is," Thomas said.

The other man tilted his head toward the table. "Get on."

"With a bedside manner like that, I'm surprised you don't have more patients," I said in a dry voice as I made my way to the exam table and took a seat, feeling like a teenager about to have a checkup.

"What would I do with more idiots running around?" the tiger asked. He stepped closer, picking up a stethoscope and putting one end to his ear.

"How does this work anyway? I thought the thing that made us was magic. How can science help figure this out?"

"Be silent." I kept my response to myself and complied. He listened for a moment then moved the stethoscope again. "Breathe deeply."

I took a deep breath.

Thomas stood across the room, his arms folded over his chest, and a watchful expression on his face.

The doctor stepped back, setting the stethoscope down on the desk behind him and picking up a needle. I couldn't help my grimace. I'd never been a fan of needles.

The doctor gave me a dry look. "You're a vampire with fangs more dangerous than any needle, yet you're afraid of this tiny little thing?"

I shrugged. "It's not a rational fear."

One side of his mouth quirked up. "Phobias so rarely are."

He prepared my arm as expertly as any human doctor I'd ever met. Better even, because as a vampire, he had an instinctual feel for where the vein was.

"To answer your question, the critical component of our transformation is magic, but it acts more like a virus. It's spread through blood and saliva much like a human STD," he explained in a grudging voice.

"And looking at my blood under a microscope will show you this magical virus?" I asked.

"Not exactly. We've found that certain markers are produced when the virus is present. Those will also tell us a little about the human you were."

As he talked, I caught movement out of the corner of my magic-seeing eye. Little black dots, the size of ants oozed out of his skin and marched down his arm to where he was holding me. The little ants disappeared into my skin, making it quiver and dance under the sting of phantom bites.

I jerked my arm away, or at least I tried. The other man held tight, not letting me budge an inch.

"Is there a problem?" Thomas asked.

"She's fighting me."

"Of course, I'm fighting you. You're hurting me," I said through gritted teeth. I put more strength into trying to pull away until we were in the oddest arm wrestling match I'd ever been in.

"Joseph."

"I don't know," the man holding me snapped.

"Let go of me." My mouth felt crowded as my fangs came out to play. It was now more than merely small ant bites and the little suckers had made it all the way up to my shoulder.

"Almost done."

The pain crested, and I screamed as it coursed throughout my body. Fuck this. This exam was done. I balled up my fist and hit Joseph with everything I had, which was a lot since I had Liam's super-charged blood coursing through me.

Joseph's head turned with the force of my blow. His grip didn't budge. He turned back to me and licked the blood off his lip. "That all you got?"

I drew back for another blow. Thomas appeared, grabbing my arm and forcing me down so I was lying flat on the table.

The black ants poured out of Joseph, biting and stinging as they burrowed their way into my body. I writhed and kicked as the pain invaded.

"Damn, she's a fighter."

"Will you hurry up?" Thomas growled. He glared at the other man, holding me down quite easily.

"Yeah, yeah." Joseph's forehead furrowed in concentration. "That should do it."

He withdrew, the ants disappearing as if they had never been—only the memory of the pain they caused remaining.

Joseph released me and stepped back. Thomas did the same, though a tad slower.

"What just happened?" Thomas asked, his voice thunderous. "You said it wasn't supposed to hurt her."

I struggled to sit up—one thought on my mind. Kill.

Joseph looked thoughtful. "Yes, she had an interesting reaction."

That lamp would do. It was the closest object.

I was up off the table, the lamp in my hand. Thomas looked around, my name on his lips, just as I brought it down on his head. He fell to a knee, blood flowing from an inch-long gash. Joseph's mouth fell open as he wavered between looking scandalized and entertained.

I brought the lamp down again, missing his head this time and getting his shoulder. The world retreated in a red haze as I became consumed with the thought of removing Thomas's head from his shoulders. My memory got foggy after that.

*

I came back to myself to the sound of shouting. "What the hell is going on? I leave you with her for a couple of hours, and this is what happens?"

Hmm, that sounded like Liam.

I shifted only to find my movements impeded.

"Easy there, enforcer. He had no choice. The woman went apeshit on his ass. It was actually pretty funny."

"She already didn't trust you before this. How is she going to trust you now?" Liam's voice was hard.

Answer—she wasn't. If Thomas thought I was antagonistic before, just wait. I was going to blow his mind with the hostility I treated him to now.

"I know." Thomas didn't sound happy. "It wasn't supposed to happen like that. I was assured that it was painless, and she wouldn't even feel it."

"I'd like to know how she performed that little trick," Joseph said. "I've never had a patient feel my aura when I scanned them. The way she was acting, it was like she could see it."

"How is that possible? There's nothing to see. It's magic," Thomas said.

"I've no idea," Joseph said.

While they talked, I investigated my surroundings. The reason I couldn't move was because I was tied to the bed with a series of straps, each as thick as my arm. They glinted in the light.

I squinted. Was that? Yes, it was. The straps had silver in them. I'd be willing to bet all that I owned on that fact. They were perfect for keeping a vampire from attacking during one of their exams. If they'd used them before, it might have prevented me from walloping Thomas upside the head.

I let my head fall back. I wasn't going anywhere until someone came and undid these.

"You learn anything?" Liam asked.

"Her development is delayed, which is no surprise really, given the fact she hasn't had regular access to a master vampire's blood since her change. On the plus side, I think I figured out how she survived the change when the hex that Thomas suffers from should have killed her," Joseph said. "It might also explain why Thomas has no memory of her turning when he can remember his other attempts."

"How?"

"I don't think she was fully human before the change."

"How sure are you of that?" Thomas asked.

"Not one hundred percent. It's hard to get an accurate read since the transition would have rewritten much of her former makeup. Her vampire side is very strong and resisted the scan."

"Even her cells have her stubbornness." Thomas sounded half-admiring, half-aggravated.

"We've checked her family history and found no evidence of any other spook in their bloodline," Liam said. "Both her sister and niece show as fully human as do her parents."

I gritted my teeth. So much for my efforts to protect them. What would have happened to them if they'd come back as anything other than human? Would Jenna have been changed? Would they have changed her seven-year-old daughter, or would they have waited until the child was an adult?

"That's not all. Best I can tell, she had a nasty piece of protective magic lying dormant at her core. Once the change started, it would have triggered its defense. Even a routine magic scan set it off. Had I been any less experienced, I'd be lying unconscious on the ground. It's possible that when Thomas attacked her, it retaliated by wiping her from his memory."

"Could that magic have kept her from succumbing to the hex?" Liam asked.

"It's not only possible; it's probable."

There was a long pause.

"I do wish her sister showed some of the same traits. I would've liked to have studied her more in depth," Joseph said in a wistful voice. "I've never seen anything like the magic crouching inside her. Something capable of circumventing Thomas's curse would be worth studying and trying to replicate."

Thank God for small miracles. Looked like Jenna and her daughter were safe for now.

I didn't let myself dwell too deeply on what they'd revealed. Not when they were liable to discover me awake at any moment. That would come later, when I had time to process it.

At the moment, there was nothing I could do with that information anyway. Furthermore, it sounded like Joseph wasn't even sure that I *hadn't* been fully human. For all he knew, the magic he sensed was something I'd picked up after my turn. A lot of weird shit had happened to me this year, any of which could explain his observations.

I was human before. I know I was, and no vampire doctor with black ants inside of him was going to tell me different.

"Is there anything else?" Liam asked.

There was a short pause. "There is something, but I need to confirm it first. It would help if I could perform other magic on Aileen."

"No." Two voices voiced the answer.

"Not until we know why she reacted the way she did to your magic," Thomas said. "I would prefer it if my yearling didn't try to kill me every time she saw me."

"Perhaps it would have helped if you had thought of that before." Liam's voice was cool.

"Is this going to be a problem, deartháir?"

"That would depend on you and how you respond to this situation you've created."

"I've told you it wasn't my intention to cause her pain," Thomas retorted.

"You've said that before, but you have a history of badly misjudging situations when it comes to those you sire. Be very careful this does not turn into another situation like with Connor."

There was a crash and then Thomas said in a voice throbbing with power, "You forget who you're talking to. I am the master of this region and this city, and I will not be challenged."

"And I am the council's enforcer—their head enforcer. We have too few new vampires to sacrifice even one to your pride. If I judge her mental or physical state to be negatively impacted by interactions with you, I will pull her from this territory. You're not the only vampire who has had challenges with siring another. We cannot risk losing even one of our yearlings to negligence and stupidity," Liam said, his voice colder and more authoritative than I'd ever heard before. "Don't fuck this up."

There was another crash. I flinched as a door slammed hard enough to shake the building.

"You live dangerously, old friend," Joseph said.

"Thomas is many things, but he's not stupid. He won't strike me down for speaking hard truths. He recognizes the wisdom of my words even if it sticks in his craw."

"You weren't entirely fair to him. Connor wasn't his fault. Neither was this. We couldn't have predicted her reaction."

There was a heavy sigh. "We're past fairness. He claimed the selection by the smallest of margins. Had she made a different choice, we would have all suffered the consequences."

"Perhaps," Joseph said, sounding unconvinced. "Either way, your yearling is awake. It's best you free her. The last time I got close to her she tried to stick a broken lamp in my heart."

There was silence, and then Liam appeared in my view. We looked at each other for a long moment. His thoughts were hidden behind an impenetrable wall. Joseph didn't appear behind him, which was probably a good thing, considering I might have tried to attack him again.

"You gonna let me up, or are you going to just stand there?" I asked.

"I'm considering leaving you there," he said, arching one eyebrow in an arrogant look. "What could have possessed you to try to beat Thomas with a lamp of all things?"

My shrug was ruined by the fact that the straps prevented me from moving more than a centimeter. "I thought it time to redecorate. Everything in this office is an antique. Vampires included."

I didn't want to admit my attempt at homicide by lamp hadn't been entirely voluntary. I'd snapped, and the poor lamp paid the price.

He bent a censorious look on me. "Had Thomas been a different vampire you would be dead right now. We don't typically suffer such insults from our yearlings. You're lucky that your circumstances are rather unique, and that Thomas has need of you."

I sighed. He was right. Attacking a master vampire—the master of this region— was a quick way to commit suicide. My existence might shore up his power base and legitimize his claim to the region, but we all knew he was powerful enough without me that it would be easy to decide he was better off with me dead.

He reached out and undid the straps, remaining close as I massaged feeling back into my legs before sitting up.

"What did you find out from the companion who was attacked?" I asked.

There was a long pause as Liam examined me. I avoided his eyes. I didn't want to talk anymore about what happened or why. I didn't want to talk about the fact that I might not be human, that I might never have been human. I wanted to focus on a problem I could solve.

He let me have that. "The companions were largely uninjured. There was no sign of a bite or claw marks on them. They were mainly shaken up by the experience."

"What did they say happened?"

"A large, wolf-like animal rushed them when they were out doing the grocery shopping for the household. They said they were able to lock themselves in their car before the animal rammed it a few times and then jumped on the roof."

Hmm.

"Did you find evidence of a werewolf?"

Liam shook his head. "Not conclusive evidence. There were dents in the side where I assume it attacked the car and the roof had huge indents too, but that was it."

And I bet he hadn't called in any of the werewolves to see if they could pick up anything the vampires missed. Sometimes, the arrogance and superiority complex on both sides of the divide was enough to choke on.

"How fast is a werewolf? Is it normal for a human to be able to outrun one?" I asked.

The werewolves I'd seen were all insanely fast. I'd be hard-pressed to outrun one, and I was a vampire.

"Companions are faster and stronger than a regular human, courtesy of the bite and the blood their benefactor shares with them, but a werewolf would still be faster."

That's what I thought.

"You have nothing to suggest it was Caroline." I felt a little relief at that. It meant I still had time to figure something out.

"Caroline would be the reasonable choice. Brax's wolves know better than to attack us. None of them want to start a war," Liam pointed out.

"This wouldn't be the first time one of his wolves acted against him. That's not even considering that there is no evidence to even suggest this was a werewolf. Your companions may have just over-reacted to an aggressive dog."

That would be the simple answer, but even I didn't believe it.

"You can tell yourself whatever lies you need to believe, but we both know your friend is running on borrowed time. The best thing you could do is help me find her."

I kept my mouth sealed shut, not wanting to argue about this. I didn't know what I was going to do about Caroline. On one hand, I didn't want to hand her back to Brax when she'd made her wishes known. Doing so would make me the biggest of hypocrites, considering I fought so hard against joining a clan and refused to acknowledge the sire/yearling relationship. On the other hand, I saw what they were saying and knew the dangers of trying to figure this out by yourself. I'd be lying if I didn't say going it alone was hard—

perhaps one of the most difficult things I've ever done.

I just needed time to talk this out with Caroline. Whatever was decided, she needed to have a say in it. I knew first-hand what it was like to have your choices taken away from you after your very species had been changed without your permission. No way was I going to subject her to that.

A thought occurred to me. "How long was I out?"

Liam frowned. "I don't know. Long enough for me to question the witnesses and get back." He pulled his phone out of the back of his pocket. "It's three a.m. now."

"I'm late." My shift for Hermes was supposed to start at one. "Jerry's going to kill me."

He was still a bit sore about losing Tom.

"I need my phone." I swung my legs off the table and hopped down. I also needed a ride back to my apartment to retrieve my bike.

"Use this." Liam dangled his phone in front of me.

I grabbed it and sent a grateful look in his direction. Pressing the buttons in quick succession, I waited as it rang.

"Hermes Courier Service, we'll come to you. What are we delivering for you today?" Beatrix crisp voice rang out over the line. Unlike when she addressed me, she sounded almost chipper and professional.

"Beatrix, it's me. I need to talk to Jerry."

The cheeriness dropped from her voice. "You're late."

"I know. Just let me talk to Jerry."

"It won't make a difference. I've already had Ruth fill in for you."

I closed my eyes and pressed my lips together. "I understand, and I apologize for my tardiness."

There was a beat of silence over the phone, and I imagined Beatrix looking at it and wondering if I'd been taken over by some outside force. It was probably the first time she'd heard me apologize.

"I'll ask Jerry if he wants to speak to you." Beatrix's words were grudging.

"Thank you."

The line started playing music, one of the generic songs you hear in an elevator.

"Aileen." Jerry's deep voice rumbled over the telephone.

"Jerry, I know I'm late, and I'm sorry about that. There were unforeseen circumstances. It won't happen again."

"You know, I took a chance on you because the Captain said you wouldn't give me problems, and that you were one of the best soldiers under his command. Events of late are making me question my decision."

There was nothing worse than being so totally in the wrong and knowing there was nothing I could do about it. I prided myself on my professionalism. It might not have been my dream job, but I tried to be the best I could at it. That meant showing up on time and carrying out my commitments. Showing up late—worse not showing up at all, was not the persona I wanted to project.

This little debacle would cost me—not only in money and possible future routes but in respect. Once that's lost, it's doubly as hard to regain.

"This won't happen again," I promised.

His sigh was heavy. "You can't promise that, not with the vampires in your life. It's just going to get worse. I hope you recognize that."

"It won't. I won't let it."

Liam's eyes flared, but he didn't interrupt. With his superior hearing, he could probably hear both sides of the conversation.

"I hope, for your sake, you can figure this out. You're at a crossroads, and I won't let you drag us down with you."

There was a long pause where I was afraid to say anything for fear it would end with me out of a job. My cash reserves weren't great and jobs that would allow me to work only nights weren't exactly thick on the ground.

"I'll give you one last chance," Jerry said. I felt my heart clench with relief. "You miss one more drop off. Have one more problem with a client. If a client stubs his or her toe while you're there, you're done. Do you understand?"

"I'll make this work," I promised.

"See that you do." Jerry's voice didn't hold a lot of optimism in it. I couldn't blame him for that. I still had my job, and for now it would have to do. It would take time, but eventually I would prove I was an asset.

CHAPTER SEVEN

IT WAS TOO late to do anything about my job today. Even if I'd wanted to, it would have been an exercise in futility. In a little less than three hours, the sun would be up, and it would be lights out for me. I considered a moment. Maybe not, now that I'd gotten a pretty big dose of Liam's supercharged blood.

I shook my head. No, I needed to proceed under the assumption that I had my normal restrictions. I didn't want something like last night happening again.

"You don't need that job," Liam said, his voice bland.

I looked at him and raised an eyebrow. "Unlike you, I haven't spent several lifetimes accumulating wealth. That job pays for my rent and all those other pesky little details that come with living."

Once, in addition to providing for my lifestyle, the job also sheltered me from vampire society while giving me exposure to the spook world. That wasn't the case anymore. The bell has been rung on my status as a vampire. There was no going back. However, Hermes still provided an income and allowed me to learn about other spooks.

For all that vampires were at the top of the food chain, they weren't the only dangerous things out there. It paid to know as much about this shadow world as possible—especially since I didn't enjoy the same protections as most vampires. Being a runner for Hermes offered me that. It also meant I had contacts throughout the community that I suspected even Liam didn't have. I could be wrong. He'd surprised me before.

"You could work for us." He met my gaze with a challenging stare of his own, not letting the astonished skepticism faze him.

"That'll never happen."

His lips quirked in a half smile. "You never know. I'm sure you once said you'd never stay in a clan home and yet here you are."

He did have a point there.

"Some things are non-negotiable. Giving you lot that much power over my life is one of them."

He chuckled, the sound warm. "We'll see."

"No, we won't."

I made my way out of the doctor's office, not seeing any sign of Joseph or Thomas. I counted that as a blessing. Even though Liam's blood had helped me heal any wounds they may have inflicted trying to get me strapped to that table, I was still tired—like I'd been up for three days with zero sleep. I didn't want any more run-ins before I recouped some of my energy.

It wasn't long until I found myself totally turned around. With no one to guide me, I'd made a few guesses as to which way would lead back to my room. I could have sworn this was the way Nathan and I had come last night.

I wandered down another long corridor, cursing space-warping magic.

Hearing voices coming from a hallway I had just passed, I about-faced and headed in that direction. If nothing else, they should be able to point me in the right direction. I found myself in a familiar, bright space full of gleaming stainless-steel appliances. It was the kitchen Nathan had shown me last night. Unlike before, several people occupied seats around an island, while a few others busied themselves cooking on the huge stove or chopping ingredients.

All eyes turned to me, curiosity on their faces. Judging by the fact they were in the kitchen, and all the vampires I'd met had expressed distaste for solid food, I assumed they were human.

Theo turned from where he was preparing something on the stove. "Aileen, what are you doing down here?"

A few of the humans shared looks before turning their focus back to me. The curiosity remained, but there was something else on some of their faces. Something a little less friendly.

I didn't want to admit I was lost, but I also needed to think of a good excuse to be down here. "Nathan gave me a tour yesterday and might have mentioned there was ice cream in the freezer." I gave him a sheepish smile.

Theo looked around before grabbing a hand-towel and drying his hands. "Ah, yup, I think there's still some left. Let me get you a bowl."

"I can get it myself if you point me in the right direction," I said, stepping forward.

"No, no. I'll get it for you. Just have a seat, and I'll pull it out." He waved at the island where three people sat.

I hesitated before I headed in their direction, finding a seat on the end and perching on it with a stiff smile. The humans watched but didn't say anything. It was awkward, like I was some kind of zoo animal they were examining for possible signs of aggression.

I didn't know if it was because this was typically their domain and they had rarely seen a vampire breach it, or if my reputation preceded me. It couldn't be because they hated vampires. They were all companions, or at least I assumed they were companions because they were in a mansion stuffed to the brim with vampires.

Theo busied himself in the industrial size freezer, shifting things around as the man and woman by the stove turned back to their work.

The rest of us stared at each other in silence until Theo set a bowl filled to the top with purple ice cream stuffed with giant chocolate blocks in front of me.

"Black Raspberry." I couldn't help the excitement in my voice. It was my favorite flavor.

Theo stepped back and leaned against the counter behind him. "Nathan mentioned you asked about it, so I figured it was a safe bet."

I dipped the spoon in the freezing awesomeness and stuck it in my mouth, rejoicing at the tart sweetness that rested on my tongue. It wasn't quite as good as Liam's blood, but it was damned close.

"Never seen a vampire eat ice cream before," a blond-haired man said from two seats down. He was tall, thin, and sported a scraggly beard. Young, but then they were all young. Most of the companions looked no more than their mid-twenties.

I paused in savoring the unexpected treat and looked sideways at him. There were several ways I could take that statement—especially given the smallest tinge of hostility I could hear in his voice. Maybe I was reading into it, letting some of my insecurities frame how I received their responses.

"Then they're missing out, because never tasting Graeter's Black Raspberry ice cream would be a tragedy." I stuck another spoonful in my mouth to illustrate my point.

"That's true," the woman by the stove said with a smirk. Her dark brown hair fell halfway down her back and had a reddish tint to it. "Ice cream is what makes the world go 'round."

I pointed my spoon at her and nodded. Finally, someone who recognized the absolute need to have it in your life.

The man snorted. "It's weird. My patroness said eating human food could impact her strength. I wouldn't risk it. It's just not worth it."

"Not even for steak?" Theo asked, his expression teasing.

The blond shook his head. "Not for anything. Those who receive the kiss have a responsibility to do all they can to support the clan. Risking their health and development for some fleeting pleasure spits on that duty."

I dragged the spoon over my tongue. Well, I guess that answered that. Definitely hostile. Or at the very least, jealous.

"I don't know. It would be hard to face an eternity without all my favorite foods," a woman with dainty features and a sweet smile said. "Just imagine, never tasting sushi or lasagna again."

"My patroness said the taste of blood more than makes up for the loss of food," the blond said, a trace of haughtiness in his tone.

The woman by the stove rolled her eyes. "Don't mind Pierce. He's a pompous, know-it-all at the best of times."

"Since he heard about you jumping the line, he's been like a bear with a thorn in his paw," the man at the stove said. He had skin the color of dark mahogany and a beautiful smile.

Pierce looked like he'd bitten into something sour. "You all weren't happy to see another take your spot. Don't even try to pretend otherwise." His angry glare moved from one to the other. His eyes settled on the woman at the stove. "Deborah, you were just saying earlier how you didn't think it fair that some random stranger off the street got turned when you've been waiting eight years."

Deborah flushed and turned her eyes back to the pot of simmering red she was stirring. Marinara unless I missed my guess.

Theo stepped in, his brown eyes earnest. He gave me an embarrassed smile. "Pardon my friends, Aileen. They're a little out of sorts after the attack."

Pierce folded his arms and leaned back, looking oddly satisfied.

I looked around, noticing who avoided my eyes. Pierce met my gaze with a stubborn tilt of his head and jutted out his jaw as if he was waiting for me to chastise him. I didn't know how the vampires in this place typically interacted with them, whether such talk would be considered an insult or not.

I decided to focus on more important things then what they thought of my presence. "Attack? You mean the one Liam was investigating earlier?"

He nodded, looking somber. "Yeah, that's the one."

"Is the person attacked okay?" I looked around the room, careful to keep my expression sympathetic. "Who was attacked?"

"It was Theo and Catherine," Deborah said, turning to face me, while keeping one eye on her pot. "Thanks to Theo's quick thinking, neither one was hurt."

I made an appropriate sound of appreciation, my gaze flicking back to Theo.

He blushed and ducked his head. "I did what anybody would do."

Pierce rolled his eyes, looking disgusted at the entire exchange.

"That's impressive," I said, ignoring Pierce.

"It was," Deborah agreed. "He saw the wolf in time and got him and Catherine into the car before it could hurt them."

I glanced at the woman with the sweet smile. Catherine, I think that was the woman from last night.

Seeing my look, the woman said, "Catherine found the experience a little traumatic. She's in her room resting right now."

"And you are?" I asked.

"Sheila." She gave me another sweet smile. "My patron is Kato, one of the new master's lieutenants."

I had no idea what that meant, but by the way she said it, I imagined it was supposed to be impressive.

"My patroness is a lieutenant as well," Pierce said with a superior smirk. He slid a look Theo's way. "Unlike those of us who are unclaimed, I hear all of the latest news."

Deborah rolled her eyes. "Yes, yes. It's very impressive that your patron is so high up. We're all companions here; you're no better than the rest of us."

Pierce curled his lip. "At least mine isn't an enforcer."

Deborah slammed down the spoon she'd been using to stir the pot. "Don't you dare talk about Noah like that. He's worth more than some upstart clan member hoping to get selected to the new master of the region's inner ranks."

I took another bite without taking my eyes off the two of them. This place was like a real-life soap opera, complete with drama and hidden agendas.

Theo held up his hands in a placating gesture as he stepped between the two as they glared at each other. "That's enough. This isn't a conversation we should have in front of company."

All eyes came back to me. I gave them a small smile and set my spoon back in my now empty bowl.

Sheila watched me with an amused glint in her eyes. "Is it true that your sire had no idea of your existence until you declared it at the selection ceremony?"

I cocked my head as I considered. It had been less of a ceremony and more of an outright brawl, but perhaps blood sport was what passed as ceremony with these people.

"That about sums it up."

"What was it like waking up a vampire with no prior knowledge of this world?" Deborah asked, forgetting for a moment her disagreement with Pierce.

I looked down at my bowl and wished more ice cream would magically appear in it.

Seeing the discomfort on my face, Deborah said, "I'm sorry. That's probably an insensitive question. You don't have to answer if you don't want."

I studied her. She looked sincere. It was the only thing that convinced me to speak. "It was difficult. I thought I was going crazy at first."

"How did you survive the bloodlust that takes all the newly turned?" Theo asked, his gaze intent. I looked around to find all of them looked interested in my answer, even Pierce.

Their fascination made sense. If they were companions hoping to make the change, they would want to know what was in store for them. I doubted they'd learn anything from my experience. It had been far from the norm, based on what I'd heard.

"I had a little help from someone in my old command. They were familiar with this world and got me through the first few weeks. Once I stabilized, that person helped me get out of the military and set up a life here." It was a heavily sanitized version of events, and I made sure not to mention any details that might be used to identify the Captain. They probably weren't bad people, but their loyalty would be to their patrons first. I didn't want something I said being used to hurt the Captain later on.

I owed a lot to that man. I didn't like to think about what might have happened had he not been on duty that night.

"Impossible," Pierce scoffed. I fixed him with a stare, arching one eyebrow. He didn't let my look phase him, secure in his own convictions. "You're lying, or at least concealing the truth. There's no way it only took a few weeks for you to rejoin the world. A vampire's bloodlust is near uncontrollable in the beginning. Some human, or even another spook, would have no chance in controlling you."

I gave him a grim smile that held little humor in it. "You've been turned into a vampire, have you? You have first-hand experience in what it's like?"

Deborah allowed herself a small smirk as Pierce's mouth snapped shut, even Theo looked slightly aggravated at the other man. It seemed I wasn't the only one who disliked him. He mistook the power and position of his patron as his own. I hated people like that, and I especially hated when they called me a liar.

Pierce didn't have a ready retort.

"I didn't think so." To the rest, I said, "Once in Columbus, I got a job with Hermes and have been working there ever since."

"How did you know what to do to survive?" Sheila asked.

I shrugged. "I figured it out and picked up tips here and there."

I left out the fact that my knowledge of spooks was seriously lacking. Every one of them probably knew more about vampires than I did. As companions, they had an all-access pass to the vampires' habits and traits, something I hadn't had much exposure to. I'd learned more about my own brand of spook in the past twenty-four hours than I had in the last year.

"It must have been tough," Theo said with a sympathetic glance.

I inclined my head.

Pierce scoffed. "She got an easy pass to the top of the food chain. Some of us have been waiting years for an opportunity like that, and she had it dropped in her lap."

"Pierce," Sheila said with gentle reproach in her voice. "You know Thomas, because of his power, has an exemption from those rules."

He grimaced but didn't challenge the small, gentle-looking woman.

I pushed back from the island, being sure to hold Pierce's gaze with my own. "Some opportunity. I would gladly give it to you if I could."

I gave the rest of them a small nod before leaving the kitchen without another word. Their voices trailed behind me.

"Pierce, that was rude," Sheila said.

"What? We were all thinking it. Sarah said she won't even claim a clan. Spoiled bitch. Any one of us would have killed to be in her shoes, and she's just throwing it all away."

"Pierce, you can't say things like that." Theo's voice was a quiet rumble.

"Aren't you mad?" he asked. "You can't even get a proper patron. They pass you around like you're a whore."

There was a long pause. "It's not her fault. She didn't choose this. We did."

Their voices faded as I continued out of hearing distance. They'd given me a lot of food for thought. From the sound of it, the patron/companion relationship wasn't quite the symbiotic give and take that Nathan and Rick had portrayed it as last night. At least from the companions' perspective, the vampires seemed to hold all the power, controlling who claimed a companion as their own, and who was turned, and when.

I could understand their resentment. I'd be resentful too, if I'd toed the company line for years only to find someone had not only skipped to the front of the line, but also turned around and given the finger to all of the traditions and rules that came with the lifestyle.

The glimpse into their thought processes was useful, and I made a note to talk to Theo about his attack at a later date. Maybe when he wasn't surrounded by the rest of the companions. I also needed to track down Catherine and get her perspective on what happened. I still stood by my assertion that it wasn't Caroline, but in case I was wrong, I needed all the facts. Finding out who, or what, was responsible for their attack would get some of the heat off Caroline until I could locate her.

I walked through several more hallways before coming to a stop. I was in the same predicament as I'd been in before I stumbled on the kitchen, lost and with no idea how to get back to my room.

My stomach cramped painfully, and I set a hand on it. That was new. My stomach hadn't given me problems since my change. That it was happening now, concerned me. Was it the ice cream? I'd been careful in the amount I ate, keeping it to just one bowl. While I did get sick if I overconsumed human food, it usually took quite a bit more than what I just ate. I shouldn't be having trouble right now.

It cramped again, my insides twisting and curling in on themselves. Sweat dotted my forehead. Pain. A lot of pain.

Seeing a staircase that looked familiar, I made my way up it and thanked every god I knew when I recognized the corridor. I wasn't far from my room.

Moments later I was lying on my bed and praying that my stomach would just stop hurting. Dawn couldn't be too far off. For perhaps the first time, I wished with all my being for its presence and the blissful unconsciousness that came with it.

My cell phone rang, the sound muffled from where I'd stashed it under my mattress. I hadn't wanted to take the chance that Liam or Nathan would see it and decide to take it—for monitoring purposes.

I answered before looking at the caller ID, my voice tight with pain. "Yeah?"

"Aileen?" Caroline's tinny voice came over the line.

I sat up, wincing as my stomach cramped before forcing the pain away. "Caroline, where are you?"

"I'm somewhere safe."

That was vague.

"Where?" I didn't know how I would get to her by dawn, but I'd figure out a way even if I had to steal one of Liam's goon's cars to do it.

"It's better that you don't know. Just know I'm safe. I'm sorry I got you involved in this. I didn't realize how much trouble it would bring to your door."

"Don't worry about it." The last thing I cared about was the trouble this had brought. I'd find a way to deal with any repercussions one way or another. "It doesn't matter. What matters is keeping you safe." And making sure she didn't attack any humans or start a war between the vampires and the werewolves.

There was a pause as I listened to her breathing.

"Caroline, I think it would be best if you came in. Let me talk to Brax for you. Maybe I could negotiate some type of compromise."

Her breathing became harsher, a hint of a growl creeping in. "Now, you sound like them. You're on their side, aren't you?"

"No, that's not what this is about. Right now, everyone is hunting you. I'm just trying to look out for you."

"Turning me over to them isn't how you help me, Aileen." That was a definite growl.

"I'm not saying I want to turn you over, but they can help you if you let them."

"I don't need help," she snapped. "And that's pretty hypocritical coming from you."

"What's that supposed to mean?"

"They told me about you. How you refuse to align yourself with the vampires or accept any help from them?"

"That's—"

"So, excuse me if I don't put a lot of stock in your suggestions right now." Her voice was bitter.

I took a deep breath around the hurt blooming in my chest. She was right, but so was I.

"Can you honestly tell me you're not a present danger to yourself or anyone who might bump into you on the street?" I asked, my voice low.

Her harsh breathing was my only answer. That's what I thought.

"Because I only spent a few minutes with you, and you nearly ripped my head off when I challenged you," I said, not showing any mercy. "I'm a vampire, Caroline, and even I was worried about what you would do if I pushed too hard. Can you truthfully tell me that if a human got up in your face or started arguing with you that you wouldn't lose it on them?"

There was a small snarl.

"Listen to yourself right now, Caroline. I've barely started pushing, and you're already losing control. How will you feel if you hurt someone?"

There was another snarl and then a small whine. My heart tugged painfully. It did not bring me joy confronting her on this, but I couldn't let her make a mistake and possibly hurt someone.

I waited as her breathing slowed, and she got a hold of herself. A thought occurred to me. "Caroline, were you anywhere near German Village this afternoon?"

"What are you talking about?" Her questions sounded frustrated and confused.

"Just answer me. Were you near Third Street today?" Did you happen to attack a pair of humans getting into their car? That question went unvoiced for fear I'd lose her. The other fear, the one I refused to admit to myself, was that she'd been responsible for the attack, and even knowing that, she was refusing to come in.

"I don't know what you're talking about."

"Caroline—"

"No. I know you mean well, but it's not going to work." Her voice held a steely resolve that I knew from experience meant she wasn't going to budge. "There are things about this that you don't understand. I'm sorry I got you involved, and I'll figure this out on my own. Thanks for your help before; I appreciate it."

"Caroline!" A dial tone buzzed in my hand. "Shit."

She was gone.

Moving slowly, every movement precise, I set my phone down on the nightstand. I couldn't afford to break it as it was my only phone and the way Hermes contacted me for jobs. Breaking it would cut me off from the rest of the world, something I couldn't afford right now.

Oh, but I wanted to.

The urge to break, rend, and tear ate at me. Before I could give into it, I threw myself back on the bed and forced myself to take deep breaths. In through the nose, out through the mouth. Again and again.

When I could think past the rage, I opened my eyes. The pain in my stomach helped bring me back to myself. My sigh was heavy.

That could have gone better. The conversation had revealed Caroline wasn't going to listen to reason, and I didn't know if it was because of the transition to werewolf, or the demon taint Brax maintained still infected her. I was going to need to track her down and force her to be reasonable. Before that however, I needed to figure out what I was going to do with her when I did find her. That problem could very well be more difficult than the other.

Until then, I needed to survive the pain in my stomach now that the adrenaline of Caroline contacting me was fading.

CHAPTER EIGHT

SOMETHING PATTED MY cheek. I waved my hand and rolled over, hiding my face against the covers. A hand shook my shoulder, and I groaned, trying to worm under the pillow. So tired.

"Nope, time to get up, baby vampire," Nathan's cheerful voice said from above. The covers were whisked off me, then a pair of hands gripped my ankles and pulled. I gave up after a brief struggle, and let my eyes close as he pulled me across the floor. Fighting him was too much work.

I was almost back to sleep as he dragged me across cool tile, then picked me up and set me down, so I was sitting up, my back supported against the wall. There was a small sound before freezing water rained down on me. I sputtered awake, gasping as the cold stole my breath. There was the sound of a camera clicking as I lurched for the faucet.

Nathan pocketed his phone as I shut off the water and turned to face him, dripping wet and wide awake.

"What the hell?" I snapped.

He shrugged his mammoth shoulders, not looking the least perturbed in the face of my anger. "You wouldn't get up. This seemed like the best way."

My eyes widened. "You put me in the shower and used freezing water on me."

He grinned, unrepentant. "It worked, didn't it?"

He took his phone out of his pocket and flashed it at me. The home screen said 5:24 on it, a full three hours before sunset. I stared at the time and felt a sense of wonder. Except for when Brax had woken me, I hadn't been up this early in years. Unlike yesterday, I didn't have the same exhaustion and mental fog pulling at me. I actually felt functional. It was something I had lost hope of being possible.

"Thought that might shut you up," Nathan said, his smirk satisfied.

I looked back at the water faucet. "All I needed to stay awake was freezing cold water?"

He snorted. "Hardly. Half of this is the blood Liam shared with you yesterday. The cold water helps. Shocks the system."

I blinked at him, and he rolled his eyes.

"Come on, get showered and then dress. If you hurry, you can see daylight before the sun sets." He sauntered out of the room as my heart leapt at the promise. Day. It had been so long.

I was showered, dressed and in the front hall in less than ten minutes. Granted, my hair was still wet and slicked back in a messy bun, my face bare of makeup, I wore a pair of capri yoga pants and a t-shirt with a skull and crossbones on it, but I was ready for the day.

Nathan smothered a smirk at the sight of my eagerness and looked to his right. I followed his gaze and blinked as Liam stepped into the hall, hands behind his back, his eyes warm as they surveyed me.

"What are you doing here?" I asked in surprise. I hadn't realized I'd have an audience for this little excursion.

"I wanted to be here for this."

I tilted my head and narrowed my eyes, considering his statement. Before I could finish questioning it, Nathan opened the doors, sunlight spilling across the foyer floor. I edged back when the light would have brushed me and stared at the golden rays as they danced across the wood. It was so pretty. It reminded me of summer days and cook-outs and chilling with friends by the pool.

I crouched and placed my hand right in the shadows next to where the sun's light faded. So close. All I had to do was move my hand an inch, and I'd be touching the sun for the first time in two years.

For all that I craved the light, wanting it with every fiber of my being—a great yearning that had been gnawing at me for years—I couldn't bring myself to move that last little bit. It was like I was stuck on a precipice, and one wrong move would send me tumbling into the abyss.

My desire for its warmth was only matched by my fear of its pain. The light had almost killed me once when I was too weak and starved for blood. How did I know it wouldn't hurt me this time? They'd told me repeatedly that I wasn't a typical vampire, my development somewhat delayed. How did I know this wasn't another area where I was seriously lacking?

Liam knelt beside me and set his hand next to mine. He held it there for several moments and then moved it, so it rested on top of mine. With slow movements, each one pausing to give me time to resist, he edged my hand toward the light.

I made an incomprehensible sound of protest and fear as we crossed that threshold between light and dark. Liam gave a wordless sound of comfort, turning his head and pressing his lips to my hair. Then it was over, my hand fully in the light. He released me and sat back.

I stayed there, turning my hand, feeling the sun on my skin. It tingled—the sensation not quite painful but not comfortable either. I could feel the strength I'd begun to take for granted fading and a familiar tiredness beneath it all. It wasn't so all-consuming that I felt like I needed to lie down, but it was enough that I understood why vampires preferred the cover of night for their business.

Liam brushed a tear from my cheek, and I realized they were wet. I brushed the tears away with the hand not in the light.

"Would you like to try standing in the sun?" Liam asked, his voice a quiet rumble.

"Is it safe?" I didn't know what the normal rules for this were. How much protection did I have from the sun? Enough to stand in it unsheltered? Or would that be the piece that sent me into flambé territory?

"My blood has strengthened you. At this time of day, when the sun is weak, you should be safe."

"So, if the sun was stronger?" I asked, turning to him.

His gaze was sympathetic as his eyes roamed my features. "It would mean considerably more pain and possibly death at your stage of development."

I nodded. Still, seeing a sunset again was something I'd never thought possible; reading between the lines, I took that to mean that the sun at midday wasn't necessarily going to always be out of reach. The stronger I got, the more of it I could take.

I made it to my feet and took a deep breath. Before I could think too deeply about the risk I was taking, I stepped forward. The knot at the center of my being uncurled, and I looked up, squinting against the bright light. Birds chirped, and I could hear cars and the noise of people going about their busy lives. All sounds I associated with summer.

Everything was so green and bright and shiny. The sun was hot against my cool skin. I forgot how frickin' hot it could be when under its direct light. My skin prickled uncomfortably like it sometimes did at the beginning of a sunburn, the sensation a familiar one from my childhood.

I stepped further outdoors, Liam and Nathan at my back. My feet pointed me at the topiary garden before I could think. It had been so long since I'd seen flowers during the day, and I don't think I'd ever seen a topiary garden in sunlight.

The two let me wander for a long time, until the sun was setting, and the street lights had come on. It was only when the sun had fully sunk behind the horizon that I headed back to the mansion where Nathan waited. Liam must have slipped off at some point. Maybe while I'd been laying on a bench staring up as white, fluffy clouds made their way across a blue, blue sky.

"Liam had other duties to attend to this evening," Nathan said in answer to my questioning look.

And did those other duties have anything to do with a certain runaway werewolf? I slid Nathan a sidelong look, noticing the tight line along his jaw, as if he was waiting for an argument. I took that to mean he had no intention of telling me where

Liam had run off to. I couldn't really blame him; I wasn't one of them. Also, I was planning on a little solo work myself.

"I had a few plans for the evening myself." I headed to the mansion. "I don't suppose you could give me a ride back to my place, so I can pick up my bike?"

He shot me a look that asked what game I was playing. "Why would you need your bike?"

I shrugged. "I have a few runs for Hermes tonight and need it for transportation."

"You're not working tonight," Nathan said. "You're slated for another fun-filled night in the mansion."

"I have to work, or I'm going to lose my job. Liam said it was fine. Check with him."

He frowned at me, not trusting my words for a minute. Smart vampire. In this case, I was telling the truth. I did have to work.

He pulled out his phone, hitting a button and then holding it to his ear as it rang. "Nathan, what is it?"

I could hear Liam just fine, despite the phone not being on speaker. I guess in addition to being able to tolerate the sun now, I also got a bump in my hearing.

"Liam, the yearling is telling me you gave her permission to work tonight." Nathan raised an eyebrow in my direction and smirked, fully anticipating his win. I gave him a tight smile back.

Liam sighed. "Not in so many words, but I did tell her we wouldn't get in the way of her making a living."

That wiped the smirk off Nathan's lips. My smile widened.

"She can't be unsupervised," Nathan said, turning away as if that would keep me from hearing the conversation. "The wolf is still missing, and you know Brax will take any reason to snatch Aileen off the street to take her out of the equation."

"I'm aware of all that. You're just going to have to accompany her on her courier runs."

Nathan's head jerked, and he glared at me over his shoulder. Heh. Looked like it was Aileen 1, vampire babysitter 0.

He hung up without saying another word, not taking his eyes off me.

I sauntered past him. "You might want to wear comfortable shoes for this."

"We're taking the car, Aileen. I'm not chasing you down while you ride along on your bike," he yelled at my back.

I waved. That worked for me. It meant an easy night of being chauffeured from client to client. Compared to a normal night on the bike, that was practically a vacation.

*

"What is this place?" Nathan asked, observing the teeming mass of humanity before us with a scowl. He'd come by his grumpiness honestly. The night had not been an easy one for him as he traipsed behind me on each of my deliveries, some of them in the not-so-good parts of the city. One of them had been to a downtown sewer. That had reeked, and he'd complained over the last few hours that he could still smell its stench on his clothes.

At each delivery, he had to sit through comments and derision directed his way by my clients—most of whom had grown used to and tolerated my presence. The addition of another, new vampire, had been enough to bring some of the old prejudices to the forefront, most of which had been directed at him.

Vampires were not popular with many other spooks. Because they were so powerful, vampires sat at the top of the food chain and didn't concern themselves about the little guys. As a result, much of the spook world feared them, but also didn't like them. Since Nathan was with me, they'd assumed he was as powerless as I was. Hence the insults. Something I'm sure the enforcer had not encountered in many, many decades.

It had been an education for him. One I had enjoyed immensely, since he couldn't retaliate against any of my clients. Not without jeopardizing my job, which I'd made sure he knew was not allowed.

The latest delivery on my schedule was set to be dropped off at the annual summer food truck festival, which was located on the green in front of the Commons. Whoever planned this event always misjudged the amount of people attending. There were over a hundred food trucks crammed on a little bitty green square packed with scores of people sampling the different cuisines.

We stood on the outskirts, watching as a band played on the stage to our right and people elbowed their way to the front of the lines. Say what you'd like about Columbus, but we took our food very seriously. I'd never lived anywhere else that had the variety and number of amazing restaurants. Whatever type of cuisine you wanted, you could find it here. We were a test market for many restaurant chains and a surprising number of franchises had sprung from our little city.

Another reason my turn hadn't been welcome. It was impossible to enjoy living in a city with such a diverse culinary scene when I couldn't fully avail myself of the delights.

"It's a food truck festival," I told Nathan.

"A what?"

I sighed. He was so knowledgeable about modern American life, it was hard to believe that this was what made him show his considerable age.

I pointed at the trucks. "They cook and serve food out of their trucks. Most of these are from Columbus, but some come from different parts of the state to participate."

"Why would they want to cook out of a truck? Wouldn't it be cramped? And unsanitary?"

I shrugged. "Cramped, probably. Unsanitary, unlikely. These trucks are basically mobile kitchens with the same health requirements. The overhead is lower than a brick and mortar restaurant, and they can go to their customer base rather than waiting for it to come to them."

Plus, they charged an arm and a leg for the experience.

"Why are we here?"

I pointed at my bag. "The recipient is in one of these trucks. I need to find him and deliver the package."

"It can't wait until this," he waved at the roiling crowd, "has dispersed?"

I shook my head. "The deadline will have passed by then, and the punishment clause will kick in. I'd prefer not to be a dishwasher for the next week."

As a punishment, it wasn't so bad. Definitely not the worst one I'd faced. Still, I had better things to do than wash dishes, and I refused to have a black mark on my record for a tardy delivery.

"Just follow me and don't bite anyone." I didn't wait for a response, setting off into the crowd. The brief had said the truck would be bright yellow and have big letters spelling out The Hungry Satyr. I glanced down at the map that had the truck's location highlighted on it. Nathan staggered out of the crowd, his brow furrowed, as he looked around him with extreme dislike.

"I think someone grabbed my butt," he said with a disgruntled frown. I stifled my smirk and kept my smart-ass comment to myself. "Let's get this over with before I have to start removing hands. Do you know where we're going?"

I folded the map and stuffed it in my pocket without looking down, as I gave him a jaunty grin. "No clue. We may have to split up to find it."

He leveled a censoring look on me. "Nice try, but where you go, I go."

I shrugged and turned on my heel, setting off to make a circuit of the main area with Nathan trailing behind me. It was slow going as the crowd pressed in on us. Most trucks had a line twenty to fifty people deep. That didn't include the gawkers trying to get a look at the menus.

The fan favorite trucks, the ones that had already built a following, had lines so long that they had to double back on themselves. One of the trucks was from a fried chicken place located in the Short North, a trendy part of the city known for its art and food. The restaurant used its truck to extend its brand, reaching those hungry people who weren't up to trekking down to the busier part of the city or contending with its horrible parking.

"These are some oddly named restaurants," Nathan said. "Who's going to want to eat at a place called the Sticky Bun or the Cat's Meow?"

I looked at the trucks he indicated, a bright blue one with cats all over it and a pink and yellow one with what looked like donuts.

"I would, for starters. The Sticky Bun has some of the best cinnamon rolls in the city."

Hmm, cinnamon rolls. I took a step in the truck's direction only to be brought up short by Nathan's hand on my elbow.

"Nice try. You've got a job to do, remember?" Nathan said with a flat look.

I sighed. "It'd only take a minute. The line is short in front of that one."

It was true. The line was only a few people deep, not because it wasn't good but because people came here for a meal, and the Sticky Bun was known for its dessert. Later in the evening, they'd probably do good business, but for now, it was pretty slow.

"You shouldn't be eating more food—especially after your ice cream last night."

I gave him a sidelong look but didn't say anything. Guess I was right to be cautious of the companions. It hadn't taken them long to reveal what they knew to the vampires, small though that information might be.

"You haven't had any stomach pains, have you?" Nathan said, his manner nonchalant.

My shoulders tightened, and my gait hitched before smoothing out. I took us toward an offshoot section of the festival. As it had grown larger over the years, the festival's organizers had taken over adjacent areas, including a smaller green next to the main one and a parking lot across the street.

"Because if you have, it would be the first sign that your body is starting to suffer effects from your diet."

"And what other effects might arise?" I asked.

Nathan's dark eyes came to me, and his face tightened as if I'd just confirmed a suspicion of his. "Your stomach will become more intolerant of solids. You'll develop headaches as food puts more toxins in your body. You'll have slower healing, less strength. Eventually, you won't be able to tolerate the sun, and it'll cause you extreme pain. You'll be as weak and defenseless as if you haven't consumed blood in a week."

The longest I'd ever gone without blood was thirty hours, and by the end of it, I could barely function. It was the closest I'd ever come to a rampage, and I'm not entirely convinced I wouldn't have gone on one except for the fact that I was so stinking weak I could barely lift my arms. What would a week with no blood look like for me?

I didn't respond to his explanation, turning over his words and considering each point. The stomach pains had already arrived, and they'd nearly flattened me.

Yesterday's dawn had been a welcome reprieve from them. I'd have to see about the rest of his claims. Part of me wanted to discount everything he'd said. I'd been eating solids for years. Granted, never a lot and not every day, but enough that I remained suspicious of his assertions. Wouldn't these symptoms have arrived sooner if they were going to come? Why start now?

"There's the food truck," I said, leaving the topic behind for now. I'd worry about this later, when I actually suffered from the effects. For now, I had a delivery to make.

The truck had a good-sized crowd in front of it, though not quite as large as the trucks in the main court.

"The Hungry Satyr?" Nathan squinted at the sign and then made a pained grunt. "Don't tell me its manned by a satyr."

I shrugged. "Okay, I won't."

"That's not even a good name," Nathan muttered. "Why doesn't he announce what he is to everyone he meets?"

"You sound like an old man right now," I told Nathan, bypassing the line and moving to the back of the truck and knocking.

"Hey! No cutting," a middle-aged man with glasses said. He had a bit of a belly and was wearing open toed sandals. "We've been waiting thirty minutes to place our order."

"Keep your sandals on. I'm not here for food," I snapped back, banging on the back door again.

"You better not be," the woman beside the man muttered.

Nathan chuckled, pleased that I was the one they were targeting with their verbal bad will. Neither one of those two would try anything physical even if I was here for food. They'd mutter and huff, but in the end let me have my way, content to shout their anger in my wake. At another time, I might have fucked with them just for the hell of it, but I had a schedule to keep and a babysitter to shake.

"Argus, come on. Open up. I have a delivery." I waited a beat. When the door didn't budge, I sent a kick its way. Stupid satyr and their stupid games.

"Need some help, baby." Nathan's arms were folded over his chest, and he had an amused grin on his face. He got a kick out of watching me struggle it seemed. "You'll owe me though."

I let out a huff of air. Not a chance. Owing another vampire anything did not factor into my life plans. Especially not one who worked for the bane of my existence.

"Thanks, but I've got my own way of doing things." I thumped the door one last time. "Last chance, Argus, or I give it to the nymphs."

The door opened, almost hitting me in the face. Nathan pulled me out of the way in time, his quick reflexes saving me from a black eye or busted nose.

"You wouldn't dare," Argus said. He was a hot mess, his face red and drenched in sweat. His dark hair plastered to his head and kept out of his eyes by a bandanna. He wore a simple white shirt and long pants that covered his goat legs and hooves. He wore no shoes, and I briefly wondered how he passed health inspections.

Except for the hooves and legs, he looked nothing like what I'd pictured. He wasn't particularly attractive, his nose too big for his face and his eyes too small. His middle and arms were also just a little too soft when compared to Greek art featuring his kind.

He was a hell of a cook though. The crowd in front of his truck could attest to that.

I lifted an eyebrow, ignoring the fact that I'd almost suffered an unfortunate accident and projected the calm, confident courier I hoped to someday be. "Wouldn't I?"

"You'd have to deal with the punishment clause."

"I tried to deliver in good faith. The clause doesn't kick in when the recipient acts like a dick and refuses delivery." I gave him a grin.

He gestured at the front of his truck. "Come on, A. You see the crowd I'm dealing with. It's been like this all night. D called off, and I'm barely keeping up with orders as is."

I sympathized. In the few minutes he'd been out here talking to me, his customers had started getting restless, more than one glaring at us as if they could mentally force us to stop distracting the god of food they'd like to worship with their ten-dollar bills.

"The harpies are making my life hell too," he continued before I could say anything, the pent-up frustration of the evening spilling free. "They keep sabotaging the generator and poaching my customers when I come out to fix it. I think one of the little jerks was in here messing with my food earlier."

"That all sounds like it would be frustrating," I said, not caring in the least. "I've got your package so you should be able to at least serve your specialty for the rest of the night."

His eyes lit up, and his gaze went to my bag. "Is it the good stuff?"

"They're from the Strix on Fourth. You know they don't truck in anything but the best." I dug out my phone, clicking through the Hermes app to the screen where he could verify delivery. "Your secret ingredient straight from Greece. Should make your gyros taste out of this world."

Just saying it made my mouth water. As I said, Argus was an amazing cook. He did Greek with a twist, and that twist was what kept people coming back for more, and had them standing in line for long periods in the heat. It would have been nice to grab some food from him before I went on my way, but in light of my conversation with Nathan, that might not be the best of ideas.

Argus put his thumb on the screen and drew back when it gave a low hum. It turned green, signaling he was the correct recipient. The app was a weird melding of technology and magic that I didn't profess to understand. I just knew it worked, and if someone tried to cheat the system, consequences that were better left unimagined befell them.

"Ah, before you go, I've got a job for you," Argus said as I turned over his package.

I'd thought he might.

Nathan stiffened at my side. "I thought you said his delivery was your last job for the night."

"Who's this?" Argus asked, pointing at Nathan. He looked him up and down with a derisive glance.

"No one important," I told Argus as he folded his arms over his chest and looked down his nose at us. To Nathan, I said, "We give our clients the courtesy of extending a job if there's need."

Nathan looked disgusted at the thought of prolonging this experience. I fought to hide my snort. This was a short night for me. If he thought this was bad, he needed to tag along on some of the nights that went until the sun was threatening the sky.

"Is this going to be a problem?" I asked. "We can call Liam again if you have another issue with this."

Nathan fixed me with a flat glare, and I took that as a sign to get on with it. Covering my victorious smile by turning back to Argus, I asked, "What do you need from me?"

Argus' arms relaxed, and for the first time since we interrupted his night, his expression lightened. "I need you to get the harpies to lay off me. My secret ingredient will help, but if I keep having to deal with their pranks, I'm not going to be able to keep up with demand."

I nodded. It wasn't an atypical request since Hermes couriers often served as an intermediary between the different species. We walked in that weird no man's land where we had no firm allegiances to any of the sects. It enabled us to be impartial when acting as a mediator—or as impartial as any of the spooks ever got. All the species had prejudices against the others, so it wasn't something we did all that often.

"Point me in the right direction, and I'll see what I can do," I said. "You know I can't promise."

Argus nodded, his expression saying he didn't really care. "I'll send the fee to the usual place."

"See that you do."

"They've been hanging out around the stage. No doubt to steal food from the unwary." Argus clicked his teeth.

Sounded like them. I'd never known a harpy who didn't get a kick out of stealing from a human, especially when it involved food.

I tucked my hands in my pockets and strolled off, Nathan an unhappy shadow at my back.

Argus shouted after me, "Tell them I don't want them within ten feet of my truck."

I waved a hand in the air to acknowledge his statement before the crowd swallowed me as I pushed through it, making my way back to the stage. It seemed to have doubled in the time I spent talking to Argus, and it was an effort to make any forward progress.

For all that I'd given Nathan a hard time about his dislike of the festival, I wasn't much better off. Crowds set my back to itching and triggered a mild case of claustrophobia. I could feel any good humor draining away bit by bit as I forced my way through, leaving me cranky and out of sorts by the time we found our way back to the stage.

"Where are these harpies?" Nathan asked close to my ear. "I'd like to get this over with, so we can get out of here. All these people are getting on my nerves."

I watched the crowd for a minute, trying to spot my quarry. "We may need to spread out. Argus was right. They tend to congregate around large crowds so they can snatch food from humans. They turn it into a game to see who can be the most daring."

Nathan eyed me for a long moment.

"What? You're the one who wants out of here faster. Otherwise, we could be here for an hour or more while we search." He didn't look convinced. "You don't have to go far and can keep me in sight. It's not like you can't run me down with your superior speed anyway."

He looked around the crowd, noting how tightly crammed they were into the space. Not a speck of green existed between one folding chair and the next. It would indeed take hours to search this place.

"Fine, but you don't leave my sight, and you stay in this area." He pointed his finger at me for emphasis.

I held up my hands up in agreement.

"I mean it. You won't like the consequences if you test me, and I know Liam would agree with me."

"You got it. Don't leave the area; stay within eyesight."

He gave me a long look, making it clear he didn't entirely trust me, before turning and moving through the crowd as he scanned for the harpies.

I waited a beat, watching him as he observed the crowd with a heavy frown before I circled in the opposite direction. I hadn't lied. It really would have taken us hours to piece through this crowd, so it was a good thing I already had an idea of where they were hiding.

Harpies were women, who for all intents and purposes, were half birds. That meant they favored high spots. I'd done several jobs for the flock in the past and had acted as an intermediary between them and Argus during the last food festival. I made my way to the left side of the stage, careful to stay where Nathan could see me.

When I was on the edge of the crowd, I looked up into the dark shadows by the stage and jerked my head, nodding toward a spot to the side of the crowd that was relatively private. There was a rustle of feathers and the shadows swirled, letting me know my request had been received.

I turned and walked, scanning the crowd to make it seem like I was still searching. When I reached the spot, I waited. It wasn't long before a lean woman with sharp features clad in a thin t-shirt and jeans with holes in them strode up. She had motorcycle boots on her feet and looked like the type who would be perfectly happy to stomp someone to death with those boots. At the moment, she looked human as long as one didn't peer too closely, her wings and more birdlike features hidden so the normals around us didn't freak out at the spook in their midst.

Her eyes were fierce as they met mine, and her thin mouth stretched into a smile showing her pointed teeth. Her head cocked in a very birdlike manner as she said with a thick accent, "Little vampire, I see the satyr went whining to you again."

I leveled an amused look on her. "Did you expect any different, Natalia? I heard you were sabotaging his generator again."

She waved a hand and scoffed. "He has no proof. The old goat is paranoid and likes to blame others for his own neglect."

It was possible she was telling the truth—Argus did have a tendency to be cheap when it came to anything but food—but the sly look in her eyes told me she or one of her sisters had a hand in his generator's unreliability over the past few hours.

"How 'bout you leave him alone and focus on a more challenging quarry?" I said.

Her eyes sharpened, and she tilted her head in interest. "What did you have in mind?"

I nodded toward where Nathan was moving through the crowd. "I know you and your sisters love a good hunt. The vampire should prove challenging enough for you."

Her eyes slid to Nathan, who chose that moment to look up, spotting us talking on the edge of the crowd. His brow furrowed, but he didn't look overly suspicious. Not yet.

"Ah, I had heard the bloodsuckers were trying to lock you down, little vampire."

"They're having a bit of trouble closing the deal. I'd like to take payment for their meddling by making their lives as difficult as possible."

Her red lips tilted up in a smirk. "Sneaky, I like it. You would have made a fine harpy."

I inclined my head, taking the statement as the complement she meant it as.

She watched Nathan with an avaricious look. "We have never toyed with a vampire before. They are not our normal prey."

"Your flock would have bragging rights."

She slid me a sidelong glance. "If he did not tear us apart first."

There was that. "I doubt he'd take such actions with all of the humans around. Bloodshed would only draw attention, and he wouldn't welcome that."

"This is true." Her face took on a set cast, a bit of the bird peeking through. Her hands shifted toward claws and the brief outline of wings could be seen before she twitched her back and the mirage disappeared. "Very well, little vampire. We will leave Argus to cater to his humans, so we can play with your friend."

Suspicion dawned on Nathan's face, and he opened his mouth as he started for us. "Aileen!"

Natalia whistled, a sharp sound that pierced the air. Several women descended on Nathan at once. To humans, it would appear as if the women came from all directions to mob an unsuspecting male, but to those of us used to seeing the unexpected, the harpies came from the sky, swirling around him and obscuring me from his view.

He cursed even as their hands darted all over him, tugging on his clothes while not letting him catch a hold of them. The high-pitched screeches and giggles could be heard even from this distance, making it clear the harpies were having fun with their new prey.

"You should leave before he gets loose," Natalia said, her eyes focused on where her flock harried Nathan. "You have my appreciation for the entertainment."

I shot her a grin and took off with a small wave, letting the crowd swallow me. A few steps and it would be impossible for him to know which way I went. Now, I could get back to the business of tracking down Caroline without Liam or his flunkies getting in the way.

CHAPTER NINE

AN ONLOOKER IN the crowd caught my attention as I passed. He failed to notice me, as his focus was on the spectacle the harpies were creating with Nathan. A wolf. Was he here for the festival? I doubted it, given the way he now scanned the crowd as if looking for someone. I ducked behind a tall man and his gaggle of kids.

Nope, I was willing to bet the wolf was here for me. Brax had probably set him to tailing me in the event Caroline made contact, or I slipped my leash and went after her. For someone who had only met me a handful of times, he had a pretty accurate assessment of me.

I used an app on my phone to flag down one of those personal lift services that people looking to make extra money joined. They could use their personal cars to give people a ride to their next destination. Basically, a taxi but less formal. It was less expensive than a traditional taxi but still more money than I should be spending. Desperate times called for desperate measures. Without a ride, it would take me half the night to walk to my destination from here.

My luck seemed to have turned, because there was one circling the block. I clicked on the app and watched as it headed toward me. I kept walking in its direction, not wanting to stop and give either Nathan or the wolf an opportunity to catch me.

A minivan pulled up in the distance, and I checked the app. Looked like that was my ride. I exchanged pleasantries with the human and took a seat in the back, my stomach a bundle of nerves until we pulled away.

"Did you enjoy the festival?" the driver, a middle-aged man wearing glasses, asked while looking in the rear-view mirror.

I gave him a tight smile. "It was a little crowded for my tastes."

He nodded. "I hear that. As I get older, I find myself enjoying busy places less and less. Was the food good at least?"

"Very tasty." It had smelled tasty at least, and the number of people massed in front of those trucks would seem to suggest the same.

"You there alone?" he asked.

Evidently, this ride was going to be full of conversation.

"No, I was with friends but decided to come home early." I looked out the window, trying to show my desire for quiet.

He took the hint and went back to driving, the city passing by in a blur of lights.

My phone rang, the face lighting up with Liam's name. I sighed and clicked the button to silence it. That hadn't taken them long. It rang again almost immediately. I switched the ringer off, knowing from experience he was liable to blow up my phone until I gave in and answered.

The driver's eyes met mine in the mirror. "Your boyfriend seems determined to get in touch with you."

"What makes you think it's my boyfriend?"

His smile flashed. "Only a boyfriend would be that persistent."

I made a noncommittal sound, grateful when he fell silent, keeping his own counsel for the rest of the drive.

We pulled up in front of my apartment, and I hopped out of the back. "Thanks for the ride."

I didn't wait for an answer, ducking my head and making my way to my apartment. The stairs rattled under me as I took them two at a time. I figured I didn't have a lot of time before Liam or one of his guys got the idea to swing by here and check.

Normally, I would have avoided it for that reason, but there were a few supplies I needed before I started my hunt.

The door stuck as I unlocked it and tried to swing it open. I growled, setting my shoulder against it and shoving it open, stumbling inside and slamming it shut after me.

"Inara, Lowen. Out here, now." I headed for the bedroom, grabbing a backpack, a change of clothes, and my back-up weapon. It didn't have the silver ammo, but it was better than just relying on my fists.

"I see you managed to give your keepers the slip," Inara said, fluttering to take a seat on top of the lamp on my nightstand.

"Did you really think I couldn't?"

She shrugged her delicate shoulders. "I had my doubts about your abilities. You have not proven yourself especially adept up to now."

I shot her a glare, grabbing a disposable cell phone from the back of my dresser. I took the one I'd been carrying and removed the battery before slipping it into the bag. It might be a sign of paranoia to think Liam had the capability to track me through it, but the resources he had at his disposal had surprised me before. I didn't want to chance him interrupting at an unfortunate time. Best to be cautious rather than regretful.

"Ah, you're back," Lowen said as he flew into the room.

"Did neither of you think I'd be able to give them the slip?" I asked, straightening and glaring at the two pint-sized pests. Two blank stares met mine, neither expressing a confidence in my abilities. "Unbelievable." Again, I questioned what had inspired me to allow them to stay here.

"What did you want?" Inara asked, tossing her hair over her shoulder. "I have better things to do than watch you pull things out of your dresser."

"I need to know anything you know about Caroline and where she might have gone." I put the last item in the bag. That should be enough to tide me over for the next few days. I didn't really intend to evade Liam and Brax long-term—to do that, I'd have to leave the city—but I wanted to be prepared in case I was gone longer than I planned.

"What makes you think we know anything?" she asked.

I leveled a knowing gaze on her. I wasn't going to be sidetracked with her questions. "She left a note. I know you were awake when she left, and you're a nosy little pest who likes to keep an eye on things."

Inara gazed at me with narrowed eyes, the jeweled colors in her wings flickering slightly.

"Don't be mean, Inara," Lowen said reproachfully before she could say anything.

Inara met his eyes with a mutinous gaze. He wore a stubborn look of his own. Whatever she saw there must have convinced her because she sighed. "Fine, I won't play any games. Amusing though they might be."

My shoulders relaxed. Good. I didn't think I had time to go round and round with Inara, not before Liam or Brax showed up to tow me back.

"Did she say anything before she left?" I asked.

Inara shrugged. "She left her note and said something about calling in a favor."

I frowned. Who did she know that might owe her a favor that would get the wolves off her back?

"She also said to tell you things aren't as simple as you thought; that something you were involved in before made staying with the wolves impossible. Something about research you'd asked her to do for you," Lowen said, his big eyes concerned.

Of the two pixies, he was a little less hostile and more willing to live in harmony. Inara's mood changed as quickly as the phases of the moon. Sometimes she was cordial and others she rejoiced in making my life as difficult as possible. Her information might not be entirely trustworthy, if not for Lowen's endorsement.

A favor and research. It wasn't much, but it was more than I had a few minutes ago.

"Okay, thanks for the help. You might want to make yourself scarce over the next few hours. Both the vampires and the wolves will come back here, and I don't want either of you caught in the crossfire."

They shared a look and Lowen took off. Inara rose in the air, her wings a blur behind her. "We'll be fine. We have a place we can disappear to for a little bit."

I nodded, throwing my bag over my shoulder and heading for the front door and the bike that waited next to it. Several black Escalades pulled into the parking lot just as I opened the door.

"Shit." I slammed the door and backed away from it. Their reaction time was a lot faster than I'd given them credit for. Who knew that one little yearling could inspire this sort of response?

Inara hovered at my shoulder. "You won't be able to go out that way."

"I see that." My voice sarcastic.

This was bad. If they caught me, they would put me on lockdown, and the chances of escaping a second time were damn near zero.

There was no back way out of my place either. The window in my bedroom was easily seen from the parking lot, and the window in the bathroom was too small for me to fit through, let alone my bike.

"I can get you out of here," Inara offered.

I looked at her with suspicion and more than a little disbelief.

She gave me a dry smile. "Your witches aren't the only ones capable of magic."

Fair enough. I'd seen crazier things in the course of the last two years.

"It'll cost you," she said with a cheeky grin.

"What sort of cost?" I asked. The last time I negotiated with her, I ended up with two unwanted roommates, and this seemed like a much bigger deal.

"A favor."

"What kind of favor?" I asked. That was a pretty broad term and could mean anything.

A heavy hand pounded on my door. "Aileen! I know you're in there."

"Do you have a choice?" Inara asked.

I stared at the door. Not really. Not if I wanted to find Caroline.

"Break it down," I heard Liam order.

"It cannot hurt any around me, and cannot involve my death or someone else's, or any body part being severed from my body." It said something about the kind of life I was leading that those were my conditions.

"Done."

"Can I bring the bike?" I asked.

She rolled her eyes and fluttered away, her wings a blur of color.

"Does that mean yes?" I whispered. There was movement beyond the door, the kind that said they were preparing to breach it.

I wheeled the bike after Inara, following her down the hall.

"In here," she said from my bathroom.

It took some doing, but in moments, the two pixies, my bike, and I were all crowded in my postage stamp bathroom with its peeling paint and cracked linoleum.

There was an explosion at the front door, then heavy boots, as the intruders moved into my apartment.

Inara said a long word—one that was lyrical and resounded through the air with a thunderclap. There was a moment where nothing happened, and then it was like the world spun and kept spinning. It halted with a sickening jolt, my stomach lurching painfully.

I blinked up at a white ceiling, my bike half on top of me, and the two pixies hovering above me with slightly disgusted looks on their faces. Better them, than the irate vampire who had been moments from breaching my bathroom.

The heavy thud of footsteps sounded from above us as I found myself in a bathroom much like the one we'd just left.

"Where are we?" I asked.

Both pixies shushed me. Lowen pointed upward and then curled his fingers and pointed to his ears.

"I don't know what you're trying to say," I told him. His movements made no sense and had nothing in common with the nonverbal communication I'd dealt with in the past.

"Be quiet, you idiot, or they'll hear you," Inara hissed, zooming close to bat me on the nose. I jerked back in reflex even though her tap hadn't really hurt. It was surprising, more than anything else.

I looked up, as indistinct voices drifted down from above us. I couldn't make out the words, but I thought one voice sounded very similar to Liam's. Pushing the bike off myself, I stood and stared around in disbelief before tilting my head to look up again.

She wouldn't have. The guilty look on Lowen's face and the crafty one on Inara's said she very much would. I dropped my head into my hands and groaned. How was I going to explain this to the current tenant? I wasn't an expert on such things, but I was pretty sure he was going to flip when he came in here to use the bathroom and found a woman with a bike standing here.

A flick to the top part of my ear sent pain shooting down it. I cradled the offended appendage and glared at the over-sized insect hovering next to me as she held one finger to her lip in the universal sign of hush. She, at least, understood nonverbal cues.

I nodded and bent a nasty glare her way before flipping down the lid to the toilet and taking a seat. If we were going to be stuck here for a while, I might as well make myself comfortable, or as comfortable as I was likely to get, sitting in a stranger's bathroom with two pixies.

I turned my eyes to the ceiling, listening as the boards above creaked and groaned as Liam and his men moved around. It took over an hour before they gave up; much longer than I thought necessary, given how tiny my place was. Did they think I was hiding in a dresser drawer or something?

Even after the apartment above fell silent, we remained motionless. Liam was a tricky vampire, and I wouldn't put it past him to have stationed someone in my apartment in case I turned up.

The bathroom door creaked open, startling me into standing. A tall man with shoulder-length copper hair and a face full of hard plains slouched against the door frame, observing us. He held a coffee mug in one hand and raised it to take a long slip, not taking his eyes off me.

I watched him with mouth slightly agape, speechless for once. It crossed my mind to say this wasn't what it looked like, but the shock of his presence had frozen me in place, stealing my words and making even a pretty lie impossible.

His lips quirked at some hidden amusement, and he straightened before turning and disappearing into the apartment. I stared at the door he'd left ajar for a long moment, fighting the urge to hyperventilate. I was pretty sure Liam or one of his guys were still hanging around somewhere, and a cop car showing up to arrest me would probably call their attention in a big way.

"Inara," I said in warning.

She fluttered out of the room without answering. Lowen rose from the sink, hovering before me. "It'll be fine. You'll see."

He followed the other pixie.

How could it be fine when they'd involved a normal in spook business?

Alone in the bathroom, I dropped my head into my hands and groaned, running the events of the night back in my head and trying to figure out a way I might have made this end differently. If only time machines were real, along with magic.

Well, it did nothing to postpone the inevitable. Might as well get this over.

I stood, grabbing the bike and maneuvering it carefully out of the bathroom, careful not to scratch the walls. Bad enough I was trespassing where I didn't belong, no need to damage their home as well.

The apartment had the same set up as mine, so it only took a few steps until I was in the kitchen and living room area. The man who'd found us in the bathroom stood in the middle of the space, coffee mug in his hand. Another man with eyes of the brightest green, the type you find in spring after weeks of rain, sat in an armchair near him. His hair was ash-blond, and his features delicate where the other man's were hard.

Inara and Lowen perched on a set of floating shelves that had been screwed into the wall, various types of potted plants dotting the space.

All eyes were on me. Again, I wished for a time machine or a way to gracefully exit without ever having to speak. Even now, my mind was blank.

"Your guests have mostly left," the blond said, his lips curving in a charming smile. "Although they have left sentries across the street who are on the lookout for your return."

I blinked at the statement and looked between the two again, noticing for the first time that Lowen and Inara had made no attempt to disguise their presence and that the two strangers did not look particularly surprised to see pixies flying about.

Obviously, they weren't human, but I didn't have enough information to guess what they might be. When the two men had moved in at the beginning of the summer, I remember suspecting they might be spooks but had somehow managed to forget in the months since. That wasn't like me, and I had to wonder if maybe I'd had a little help in forgetting.

I turned a troubled gaze on Inara and Lowen where they swung their tiny feet as they watched the room with curious eyes. Could pixies affect memory? It would make sense, given how they liked to play pranks on anything bigger than them. If they had messed with my memory, their time as my roommates was about to come to a very violent end. I had enough troubles without bringing a spotty memory into it.

"That's good to know," I finally said. It was the only thing I could think of, given the circumstances. Whether they were human or not, I was still an unexpected visitor, one who hadn't received permission before I'd appeared in their bathroom. If it'd been my apartment and one of them had appeared unannounced, I would have attacked before they even cleared the bathroom door and asked questions later.

There was another awkward silence.

"This is Cadell," the blond said, gesturing at his copper haired friend. "I am Niall."

"Aileen." I fidgeted with the bike handlebars, my eyes going between the two.

Niall and Cadell shared a look that was hard to interpret. Niall's gaze held meaning as Cadell shook his head slightly before he looked away, his lips tightening.

Niall gave me a small smile. "You're welcome to stay here until it's safe to leave."

I stared at him for a moment, considering. The people watching my apartment were unlikely to leave anytime soon. I had a feeling they were there until I was located. It's how I would have done it, had I the resources and desire to find someone so I could lock them up.

"I doubt they're going anywhere. Is there a back way out of this place?" I asked.

Cadell moved, seeming to uncoil from where he stood. "Yes, the downstairs apartments all have a front and back door."

That's what I figured. The apartments on the bottom had a few more amenities than the ones on the top, which was why my little place was significantly cheaper.

I hesitated to follow him to the back door, curious about them and how they seemed to know Inara and Lowen—because they did know the two pixies. I was willing to say quite well, given the familiarity Inara and Lowen treated the space with.

As I turned, I noticed an item on their kitchen counter, a piece of paper bent in complicated folds until it formed a crane.

"Caroline was here," I said. She was the only person I knew who folded paper into weird shapes when she was stressed. She'd picked up the habit after reading an origami book when we were kids.

I turned back to Cadell and Niall, fire in my eyes and ready to do some damage. "Where is she?"

"For someone we did a favor for, you're awfully demanding," Cadell said, his chin tilted down and his body posed to intercept me should I offer violence.

I regarded them with narrow eyes. That was not the answer I was looking for.

"Inara?" My voice cracked through the air like a whip. She or Lowen were the ones responsible for this. There was no doubt in my mind.

"She got here the same way you did," Inara said after a pregnant pause and a look from Niall. He was clearly the one in charge.

"Why?"

Inara shrugged. "The wolves were at the door, and she was frantic to get out without them catching her. I just facilitated the escape."

I closed my eyes and dropped my head. I'd missed her by minutes when Brax pounded on my door. "When did she leave?"

"That night. A few hours after you did," Niall said.

I sighed. So close. If only I'd remained at home, I might know where she was right now, and this whole situation could be resolved.

"Did she tell you where she was going?" I asked, hoping, but knowing it was probably a futile question.

He shook his head. "Nothing beyond what your pixies have already told you."

"They're not mine," I said, shooting the two in question a dark look.

"It is considered an honor to have a pixie queen and her consort deem you an acceptable companion," Cadell said in a stiff voice.

I arched an eyebrow and shot Inara a considering look. "A pixie queen?"

Yeah, I could see that. She had the air of royalty and certainly treated others with the attitude I'd expect of a queen. And now I owed that queen a favor. When would I learn?

94

"How did Caroline seem when she left?" I asked, turning the conversation back to what was important at the moment. I'd worry about unnamed favors later. Perhaps when that favor was being called in.

"Upset. Anxious," Niall said. "Her control over her second form is still shaky. We gave her a glamor to help, but it will not last long and won't keep her from the change in the event of strong emotions."

"Glamor? You're fey?" I didn't know much about the fey, but I seemed to remember that you weren't supposed to say thank you unless you wanted to owe a huge debt they could call in, however they wanted. I tried to remember if those words had crossed my lips tonight.

"Sidth," Cadell snapped, his eyes flashing dangerously.

I held up my hand. "Okay, sidth."

I didn't know the difference between fey and sidth or why he seemed to dislike the first term. I'd always thought fey covered all the categories in their brand of spook. Guess not. That was good to know, if only so I didn't step on any land mines with my customers in the future.

"Your information has been helpful," I said stiffly, trying to express my gratitude while not getting too close to the sentiment.

Niall's eyes flashed with amusement as he hid a small smile. Yeah, yeah, I bet it was funny watching the vampire turn into an awkward idiot because she didn't know the rules of etiquette for the sidth.

"Cadell will see you out so you can continue your search for the mac tire dorcha."

I nodded, letting Cadell pass before beginning the awkward maneuver of turning my bike around in the small place. Inara zipped over to land on my handlebars, perching on them as I wheeled the bike after Cadell. It took only moments to reach the back door.

Cadell went out first, stopping and peering around with eyes that saw much more than any human's. I suspected given the way he looked at the shadows that his night vision was as good as mine.

Inara lifted off the bike as I wheeled it outside. "Be careful with your friend, Aileen. She's different than you remember. Treat her with extreme caution."

For once, Inara seemed serious and without the chip on her shoulder that normally characterized our interactions. I gave her warning the respect it deserved and nodded. Lowen had similar reservations before; it was disturbing to hear her echo the sentiment.

Cadell contented himself with watching the shadows as I wheeled past.

"See you soon, vampire." The words were soft and had an edge of finality to them as the night engulfed me. Had I not been a vampire, I doubted I would have heard the send-off.

CHAPTER TEN

MY FIRST STOP after leaving my neighbors' apartment was not far, and had me heading to the strip of city lying between Columbus and the edge of Grandview. Columbus was a weird city that had townships woven throughout its border. On a map, it looked like several Pac-Men had eaten away at its edges to carve out individual townships that made up the surrounding area. It's why, although the area I was in was technically Columbus—paying Columbus taxes—to locals, it was considered the less-nice section of Grandview and came with the perk of Grandview schools.

Caroline's mother lived in a townhome there and had since before Caroline and I graduated high school. One of the few good things Mrs. Bradley had done for her daughter was remain in Grandview so Caroline could finish her schooling without having to transfer.

Caroline was closer to her dad, but he had business in Germany and spent a good part of his time there. Her mom was her only family in the area. While I knew Caroline was unlikely to go to her mother's condo, I was hoping Mrs. Bradley would at least have an idea of where Caroline might have gone. My information on Caroline's habits was a few years out of date.

Mrs. Bradley's townhome was in a small building that contained three other townhomes. The complex was sandwiched between Fifth and King, two streets that saw a lot of traffic. Close to the university, she was surrounded by college kids on either side. Her place wasn't quite as rundown as mine and had a spacious backyard to make up for the lack of curb appeal from the front.

I wheeled the bike to a stop against the side of the building, out of sight in case Brax or Liam sent any of their people to do a drive by of the area. I'd spent the last thirty minutes making sure there were no hidden watchers, so I felt reasonably safe walking up to her front door and knocking.

No answer. I waited several seconds and knocked again. "Mrs. Bradley, it's Aileen. I need to ask you about Caroline."

I heard movement inside and stepped back from the door, waiting until it opened. Mrs. Bradley peered through the crack, her eyes red-rimmed and her nose bright red from crying.

"Mrs. Bradley, are you okay?" I asked, concern in my voice.

"Aileen, do you know where my baby is?" she asked, her voice thick. "I know something is wrong."

The smell of booze wafted out, making sense of her state. Mrs. Bradley, for as long as I'd known her, had a bit of a drinking problem. She'd hidden it rather well when we were kids, and the only way we'd known she wasn't like the other moms was because we discovered her stash of empty bottles. After the divorce, she didn't bother hiding it anymore.

"Why do you think something is wrong?" I asked. I knew what was wrong, but it surprised me that she did. She existed in a fog and rarely noticed the world around her, or if she did, she forgot any hard truths shortly after learning them.

"Caro hasn't been by to see me in a long time." Her eyes were watery, and she was the picture of a broken woman, her hair lank and unwashed around her face, wearing sweats with food stains on them. She was a far cry from the fashion plate of our childhood. I'd known she had problems, but the extent managed to shock me. "She usually stops in every other week to help me clean and make sure I have everything I need."

Mrs. Bradley left the door open as she shuffled back to her seat in front of the TV. I hovered on the edge of the doorway, conscious of the fact that I couldn't enter unless she gave me express permission.

"Mrs. Bradley, how about you invite me in and I ask you a few questions about Caroline?" I asked, giving her a hopeful smile.

The fog cleared from her face for a moment, and she looked at me with something like fear. "I can't do that. Only the monsters need an invitation into your home."

My smile faded, my expression turning thoughtful. Two years ago, I would have thought such a statement necessitated a visit to a mental health facility. Now, I had to wonder if there might be something more to Mrs. Bradley that I had never seen before.

Suspicion joined the fear on Mrs. Bradley's face, and she clutched at something. My gaze dropped to the fire poker that now rested across her lap. It looked like cast iron, heavy enough that a blow from it would hurt if it landed.

"Are you a monster, Aileen?" she asked.

"Of course not, Mrs. Bradley." I kept my voice calm, not wanting to send her into a rage that could cause her to harm herself or me. "You've known me for many years. I used to spend the night at your house near that park. Do you remember? You had a cherry blossom tree in your front yard. We took pictures in front of it on the first day of school every year."

Her grip on the poker relaxed and her focus turned inward. "Yes, I do remember that."

My shoulders loosened, and I felt relief.

"Caro said you haven't been yourself since coming back," Mrs. Bradley said, her gaze suddenly direct as if it could see straight through me. I fought a sense of unease. "You might not be Aileen anymore."

There was a depth of knowledge on her face that gave me chills. Yes, I think there was more to Mrs. Bradley and the housewife I'd always assumed her to be. I don't think either Caroline or I had ever given her enough credit.

Her hands tightened on the poker, and I took a step back.

"Aileen?" a familiar voice asked from the sidewalk behind me.

"Mom?" I blinked at my mother, standing there watching me with surprised eyes and clutching several bags of groceries. "What are you doing here?"

"Caroline asked me to look after her mom while she was away on a research trip." My mom joined me at the door. She was shorter than me, with warm brown eyes and blond hair that had reddish highlights when the sun hit it just right. She was a bundle of energy wrapped in a small package that belied the backbone of steel she possessed. She aimed a kind smile at Caroline's mother. "Hello, Grace, I have the groceries you asked for."

"Who's that?" Mrs. Bradley asked, squinting at my mom.

My mom's sigh was quiet and sad. "It's Elise Travers, Aileen's mother. I was here last week."

"Last week?" It was clear by Mrs. Bradley's tone that she didn't know what my mom was talking about. She eyed my mom suspiciously.

I grabbed my mom's arm to prevent her from stepping inside.

"What are you doing, Aileen?" My mom had the tone of voice that I remembered from my childhood—the one that said I needed to think very hard about my answer, because she was about to rain down a mother's wrath. Only difference was, I was no longer a child, and her wrath didn't contain quite the level of threat it once had.

"She has a poker in her hand, Mom, and she seems very confused."

"Oh, Aileen." Her voice was sad, but this time it was me making her that way. "She's not a threat. I've been coming here for the last few weeks with no problem."

I didn't let go of her. She might not have had a problem before, but the way Mrs. Bradley was looking at me said she might now.

My mother sighed. "I thought the facility was supposed to help you with this paranoia."

I blinked back at her, shocked, and remembered that she thought I'd been in a mental hospital dealing with my nonexistent PTSD and alcohol problem. It was something Liam put in her head to explain my absence and something I'd let her believe to protect her and my family.

In the darkest part of night, I sometimes wondered if the other reason I'd let the belief stand, was because it was just too hard to be around them and their constant well-meaning judgement. They thought they knew the world, and they didn't. Trying to explain that to them, was like standing on top of a mountain and shouting a warning to the town below that an avalanche was coming. Frustrating and heartbreaking.

"Mom, this has nothing to do with that. She threatened me with a poker before you showed up. I don't want you going in there alone."

She huffed at me and shook her head, making it clear she didn't believe me. "I'm going in there to help her. If you're so worried, you're welcome to join me."

With her invitation, the invisible force keeping me out disappeared, leaving me free to follow her inside. Despite that, I almost blocked her entrance. Mrs. Bradley watched us with suspicious eyes, not at all convinced we weren't monsters.

"You've given the monster entrance," she said, flicking an angry glance my mother's way.

My mother's laugh was humorless as she headed for Mrs. Bradley's kitchen to put away the groceries that she'd bought. "I can vouch for the fact that my daughter isn't a monster."

Mrs. Bradley didn't take her eyes off me, her hands moving over the poker in her lap. Her preoccupation with that thing had a sinister edge to it, and I made sure to stay close to where my mom made herself busy in the kitchen washing dishes.

"I don't remember her being this odd when I was a child," I said, not taking my eyes off Caroline's mother.

My mom looked up from the cleaning she'd undertaken. The house had an odd, musty smell, and it was easy to tell that the trash hadn't been taken out in a while.

"That's what happens when you're gone for years," my mom said, a hint of disapproval in her tone. "People change, circumstances change."

I ignored the disapproval—it had gotten easier over the years, though it always stung, like a splinter you just couldn't dig out of your hand. She hadn't approved of my decision to join the military, and my lack of focus—her words—since I got out hadn't helped matters.

"Why wouldn't Caroline tell me she was so bad off?"

Mom busied herself scrubbing the counters free of an odd sticky substance. "My guess is she was ashamed and didn't want anyone to know. Her mom's mental state has been deteriorating for a while now. This is a bad day for her. Normally, she's a little better."

"Still."

"You have no one to blame but yourself." Her voice was crisp. "You made it clear when you came back that you wanted to keep a distance between yourself and everyone else. She respected that distance."

I flinched at her words, unable to argue. I had made an effort to keep myself away from everyone, even as I couldn't bring myself to cut off contact entirely. It didn't make it any easier to hear.

"Why are you here, Aileen?" my mom asked after a long moment. Finished putting the groceries away, she rested her hands on the counter and gave me a hard stare.

"Caroline hasn't been answering her phone and wasn't home. I was hoping her mom could help me figure out where she'd gone."

My mom's smile was hard. "Her mom isn't likely to be of help to anyone. Not even herself."

I saw that. This trip was going to result in a dead end.

"I assumed you would be at the facility for longer," she said, not taking her eyes off my face.

I went very still, fighting to keep any expression off my face that might give away my guilt. "They said I was all better and free to go."

I met her eyes and tried to project sincerity. Unfortunately, this woman had changed my diapers and seen me through my troubled teen years, as well as a short phase in middle school where everything out of my mouth had been a lie. She could smell my fabrications from a mile away with her fine-tuned mom sense.

She arched one eyebrow. "I was under the impression that it was a year-long program."

A year long? What had Liam been trying to pull? And who would have the money to send anyone to a facility the likes of which Liam had pretended to work at? It was the type of place only the filthy rich would have been able to afford. Something I was decidedly not, and neither were my parents.

"I guess I wasn't as bad off as everyone assumed." This was true, since I had neither PTSD nor an alcohol problem. My issues were of a more permanent nature, but tell that to my mom.

"You didn't go, did you?" she asked, her voice flat.

Damn. She was like a lie-sniffing dog.

"I can't believe this, Aileen." She slammed the rag in her hand down in the sink. "How could you do this?"

"Me? I'm not the one who ambushed their daughter and accused her of being mentally unstable and an alcoholic. Neither of which have any merit."

"Don't you lie to me," she snapped back, her voice ugly as her eyes flashed. "You know you're not right."

My chest heaved at the unfairness of that statement. "I'm different than I was before, yes. That doesn't mean there's something inherently wrong with me. Just because I don't do what you want doesn't mean I'm flawed. It means I'm an adult capable of making my own decisions."

"Bullshit. I'm your mother. I know when something is wrong." She pointed a finger at me.

I turned away and took a deep breath. Mustn't lose my temper and chance showing her what that something wrong was. I had a feeling she'd prefer an alcoholic over a vampire.

When I spoke again, my voice was level. "I have a stable job and an apartment. I even have friends." Granted, they were odd friends, and not the sort you let around your family. "It's not like I'm homeless, living on a street and unable to function in society."

"Aileen." Her voice turned pleading. Next, she'd turn on the waterworks. I loved my mother, but she was as manipulative as the day was long.

I hardened my heart. If I let her continue, she would find a way to turn this around until even I thought I might have a problem. I couldn't let her do that, especially in light of all the issues I was already dealing with.

"No." I kept my voice firm and even. "We're not talking about this anymore. This is my life, and I'll live it how I choose. You can either accept that and respect my boundaries, or you can get out of it. Your choice, Mother."

I met her gaze and tried to put all my resolve behind it. Much as I loved my family, I couldn't let them keep doing this to me. It was hard to listen as they listed all the things they thought wrong with me, and dangerous for them if they kept crossing the limits I set.

The tears that had been threatening her eyes dried up, and she met my gaze, her jaw clenching. The stubborn woman that I'd butted heads with on many occasions as I'd grown up was there in her eyes.

"You're just like him," my mom said, the comparison sounding ugly.

I stilled. "Like who?"

Before tonight, I probably wouldn't have questioned the comparison, assuming it was of my dad. Except my dad and I had never had much in common, and she had never sounded like that when talking about the dad I'd grown up with. After listening to the conversation about my possible spook heritage, I had questions. Lots of them.

My mom looked away, her jaw hardening.

"Mom, who am I like?" I asked in a measured voice.

"I'm not talking about this anymore," she snapped, her voice cold and hard.

"What are we talking about, Mom?" I asked, my voice high and tight. Suspicion was crowding close the more she evaded. I didn't want to think what I was thinking—that my dad might not be my dad. That was too horrible to contemplate, even as her actions drove that thorn ever deeper.

"I'm done with this conversation." She made a sharp gesture, cutting me off. "Since you don't want to take the first step toward getting better, I'll leave you to live your life the way you want—without me in it."

Her words were like a punch in the stomach—almost worse than the questions about my dad. I hadn't really thought she'd take that choice. I'd thought the ultimatum would force her to see that what she was doing wasn't helping, that it was making things worse between us. Seemed I'd done that anyways.

She threw the rag into the sink and stepped around the counter, grabbing her keys and tossing a goodbye in Mrs. Bradley's direction.

"Mom, don't do this." My voice was small as I tucked a shaking hand into the back pocket of my jeans. I hated fighting with her. I always had, but I couldn't let her continue as she had been. I just didn't have it in me.

She stopped in the doorway. A sniffle reached me and then she rubbed her eyes. "You know where to find me if you decide you'd like help."

She hesitated, and for a moment, I thought about calling out to her, promising anything to take the hurt out of her voice. She walked away, and I said nothing to stop her.

Mrs. Bradley cackled, her laugh breaking me from the emotional morass I was venturing into. "Perhaps you're not such a monster after all."

I sniffed, sucking back any emotion that might be trying to leak out of my eyes. "What do you know of monsters, Mrs. Bradley?"

She moved back and forth in her chair, and I realized it was one of those rocking chairs that looked like a normal armchair. She contented herself with rocking for a few moments, staring off into the distance.

For a moment, I thought she might have gotten lost in her own world, and I considered leaving. She spoke before I could take a step toward the door. "They're all around us, though you'll never see them."

She rocked for several more moments, muttering to herself. I stayed where I was since she still had the poker clutched in her hands. I didn't want to chance that she would go after me with that thing.

"It's best that they keep to their own kind, Lena," she said, using the nickname from when I was young and innocent. "Humans and monsters just aren't meant to be together. Bad things happen when the two intersect."

"What happened to you, Mrs. Bradley?"

Her gaze turned faraway, and her face grew haunted. "The monsters got a hold of me and made me a monster too."

My eyes were thoughtful as they rested on her. She was human, or at least she felt human to my senses. It was possible that I wasn't picking up on her spook factor, and that someone like Liam or Brax would be able to sense more. Not that I could ask either one of them for their help, even if we were on speaking terms. I imagine it was why Caroline asked my mom to take care of hers rather than having one of the wolves do it.

There was a chance they'd see her mom and know what was wrong, but there was also a chance that they'd consider her a threat to their secrecy. Caroline and I wouldn't risk her mom's life without being dead sure that what we were doing would help her in the end.

"Is that what happened to you, Aileen?" she asked.

My mouth quirked. At least she was back to referring to me by my name and not as a body replacing monster.

"Yeah, Mrs. Bradley. That's what happened to me too."

She nodded, her eyes sad. "I'm sorry I couldn't save you."

I shrugged. "It is what it is."

"I saw my daughter last night," Mrs. Bradley said, her voice distant. My heart leapt at the unexpected piece of news. "The monsters had got to her too, and she wasn't my baby anymore."

I ventured closer, taking a seat on her coffee table to make myself seem smaller and less threatening. The spot was still far enough out of reach of her poker that I could stage a hasty retreat if need be. "Where was this, Mrs. Bradley? Where did you see Caroline?"

"She wasn't my Caroline anymore." Emotion thickened her voice and a mad light entered her eyes.

Okay, I wasn't going to be able to reason with the current Mrs. Bradley. She was a little too close to the edge for that, and I didn't want to upset her more for fear she would shut down, and any information I needed would disappear into the twisty corridors of her mind.

"Where did this monster who used to be Caroline appear to you?" I asked, my voice hesitating over the word monster.

"She was in my dreams." Mrs. Bradley's smile was wistful and serene. "She was running from something, darkness all around."

I sat back, disappointed in the answer. I'd hoped for something more, something a little more helpful.

"She's not going to be able to escape it, Lena. It'll chase until it catches her. It's going to consume her, and I'll never see my baby again." Mrs. Bradley turned towards me, her eyes made scarier by the utter calmness in them. An emotion that had been missing from her until now. "Just like it got you."

Her words sent a chill down my back, despite the fact I knew she was a few cards short of a full deck.

"It's time for you to go now, my dear," she said, lifting the poker. "And don't come back."

"Wait, Mrs. Bradley. I need to ask if you know where Caroline is, where she might go. There are people looking for her, monsters looking for her. It's important I find her first."

"Oh, my dear," Mrs. Bradley's expression was pitying. "The monsters have already found her."

"What?" I asked. It was the only question I had time for before Mrs. Bradley raised the poker and swung at me. I dodged, the iron coming down hard, scraping the coffee table where I'd been sitting moments before. "Mrs. Bradley, wait. What are you doing?"

I evaded another swing. This one taking out a few objects on the end table. The woman was surprisingly spry given her mental state and age.

"Sorry, my dear. No monsters allowed here."

She wound up for another swing. The backs of my legs bumped against the couch, and I clambered up and over its cushions, knocking over a lamp as I vaulted over the end. The poker buried itself in the cushions, and Mrs. Bradley pulled it free with a rip, the cushion's insides coming out in a flurry of white.

"Mrs. Bradley, it's me. It's Aileen. You've known me since I was two," I said, holding out a hand, palm facing up to show I wasn't armed.

She hesitated in the middle of her next swing, the poker over her shoulder, and blinked at me. Confusion in her face as she looked around the wreckage of her living room. "Aileen."

I breathed a sigh of relief. She recognized me again. Thank God. I didn't want to be the one responsible for anything happening to Caroline's mom, even if it was an injury that was self-induced. "Yes, Aileen. How about we put the poker down, and I'll get this straightened up?"

She looked around, the confusion draining from her eyes and that familiar set expression taking hold again.

"Uh oh," I said. This wasn't going to be as easy as I thought.

"I know what you are," she said, her voice deeper and more confident. She pointed the poker at me, her expression vindictive. "And you won't take me like you took my daughter."

"I don't plan to do anything to you, and I would never hurt Caroline," I said, desperate to get her to see reason. I'd run out of places to go, and I was hemmed in on both sides by a fallen end table and her TV. The door to outside was behind her. The only way to it was through her, something I couldn't bring myself to do.

"You're a liar, Lena. You always have been." She didn't sound upset, her voice calm.

That was kind of true. Though, I hadn't realized Mrs. Bradley knew about all those times Caroline and I had lied to get out of trouble or to get into it.

"Aileen Travers, I rescind your invitation to this home. Never darken its doorstep again." She stepped aside, her bearing that of a warrior goddess and her eyes watchful.

A force exploded in my chest, and a thunderclap deafened me. I was propelled out of the house, flying through the air, my shoulder clipping the door as I burst out of it. I landed hard on my back on the walkway out front, the breath exploding from my chest as I blinked up at the lamp post over me.

"Goodbye, Aileen. I'm sorry I couldn't save you from the monsters," Mrs. Bradley said. She was back to seeming like a frail old lady, nothing like the Valkyrie that had managed to toss me out of the house with just a few simple words.

I rolled to my side, my body not quite willing to find its way upright quite then. "Wait."

She didn't pause, her door closing with a sense of finality.

CHAPTER ELEVEN

I COLLAPSED AND groaned. That had hurt. A lot. My body still ached from her rescinding the invitation.

I hadn't even known that was possible. Sure, I knew I needed one to enter a domicile inhabited by a human since I'd had a few unfortunate encounters with the strange barrier in the past, but I hadn't known that rescinding it resulted in a physical expulsion. Learn something new every day.

I forced myself to sit and looked around. What now? Mrs. Bradley had been less than helpful. All she'd given me was a bunch of muttering about darkness swallowing Caroline. Given her apparent knowledge about monsters and evicting vampires, I was willing to give more credence to Mrs. Bradley's dream than I would have otherwise. It still didn't give me much; definitely not enough to find her.

All I'd gotten for my troubles was a bruised ass and ripped jeans. I fingered the rip and curled one lip. Another pair destroyed. Apparently, I was way harder on my casual wear as one of the fanged than I'd ever been as a human. This was the third pair I'd damaged this month. At this rate, I'd need to make another trip to the thrift store.

Before that, I needed to go on a little excursion to the north side of the city and see a sorcerer about a tracking spell. Destination decided, I retrieved my bike and climbed on, setting my feet on the pedals.

I really didn't want to go and see the sorcerer. Last time, he'd managed to force me to pull out my own eye. Not an experience I wanted to repeat, but for Caroline, I just might have to.

I set off on the bike, making my way to one of the numerous bike paths. Over the past few years, Columbus has made a serious effort to turn itself into the Seattle of the Midwest. In addition to an influx of hipster restaurants, it's torn up many of the city's streets, remodeling them to make them friendlier to cyclists by installing bike lanes. It was safer for those of us who choose to travel by two wheels rather than four, and it also made it easier to bike from one end of the city to the other without having to worry about getting hit by a car on a busy road.

After a short ride that snaked through campus and then a longer jaunt along the bike lane on East Seventeenth Avenue, I turned onto the Alum Creek bike path, which would take me over to the eastern side of the city and let me out right next to Easton. It was only a short ride from there to the office building that I suspected the sorcerer owned.

In all the times I'd visited his office, I'd never seen any sign of other tenants. Just him, and on rare occasions, the receptionist I suspected was a mirage created by his magic. Granted, I usually arrived at night when most sane humans were home with their families, but there still should have been some sign of a normal's presence. Like a security guard standing sentinel in case anybody needed to check in, or the rare person working late—at least that's how the movies always portrayed it. I'd never worked an office job before, so I wouldn't know.

The sorcerer's office was on the top floor of the building, which meant I bypassed the elevators, not wanting to bother with them when the stairs were nearly as fast.

I was only breathing lightly once I reached the fifth floor, thankful for the increased stamina being a vampire gave me.

This time there was no receptionist waiting, no click-clacking of computer keys, or answering of phones. I paused on the threshold, glancing around the small welcome area before continuing through the double doors across the room. Unlike the first time, they didn't lead into a humongous room filled with a night sky as its ceiling. For a moment, I saw a mirage of the typical boardroom found in offices like this, a long table lined with chairs, a white board in the corner, and one of those starfish speakers for important meetings.

Beneath that image was an alchemist's dream—one that would have been at home in some medieval castle of old, complete with beakers of odd colored liquid on tables, and old leather-bound books on the tables and shelves. It was a room I'd been in twice before.

I blinked, and the boardroom disappeared, my magic-seeing eye breaking the illusion. Funny, I thought the alchemist room would be the one to disappear since it bent the laws of physics. Not the case.

The sorcerer wandered in from another door, giving a glimpse of stone steps spiraling down behind it. He was absorbed in the book he held and didn't immediately notice my presence. It gave me a rare chance to study him.

Peter Barrett, as I'd come to know him, looked like a teenager, although he asserted to anyone who'd listen that he was actually decades older. His exact age was a mystery, but I knew he was older than fifty. How much older was still the question. Tall and gangly, he had limbs that he'd yet to grow into. Given half the chance to mature, he'd be considered cute once he'd grown into the angles of his face. His green eyes were among the most vivid and beautiful that I'd ever seen. All this was ruined by the fact that he was a complete and utter asshole.

I'd never been one to condone violence against the young and innocent, but Peter had pushed me right over that line. It was a good thing he wasn't actually a teenager, or I'd feel like a monster in truth.

He shuffled over to one of the tables, his lips moving as he mouthed whatever he was reading. It would have been endearing if he wasn't a little ass prone to shitty behavior.

He reached up, pushing a lock of dark hair back from his face, copper flashing at his wrist.

That bastard.

"I see you found a use for the cuff, after all," I said, my eyes narrowed on him and my jaw tight. That was funny—and not in a ha-ha way—given the amount of grief he'd put me through after I'd stuck him with the copper genie cuff that cut him off from his powers. Given the torture he'd subjected me to because of it, I found it interesting he would be wearing it again.

He jerked back, the book falling from his hands with a thump, his eyes wide and startled. "Aileen, how did you get past my wards?"

My steps hesitated. What wards? I hadn't noticed anything on my way in here. I didn't want him to notice my confusion—information was a weapon best wielded carefully—so I shrugged. "Maybe they're not as good as you think they are."

He bent a displeased look on me, attitude oozing from him. "Not likely. You did something. I know it. What was it this time? A null bomb? A charm from the witches? Or maybe you got something from the same place you got this?" He raised the hand that was wearing the cuff.

"It's funny you mention that. Why are you wearing it?" I asked, tilting my head. "Given it cuts you off from your magic, wouldn't you want that as far from your person as you could?"

He lifted his chin in a bullish manner and covered the cuff with one hand. "I'm running an experiment."

I arched an eyebrow. Right, and I had a unicorn stuffed in my pocket. I'd play along for now. "Oh? What kind?"

"I'm trying to create a spell to unlock something of this nature, so that the next time a presumptuous vampire tries sealing me away from my powers, I can open a can of whoop-ass on her fanged head that she will not soon forget." He gave me a meaningful look.

I returned it with a humorless smile and tapped the skin under my left eye. "Oh, I won't forget. Don't you worry about that."

He jerked slightly, covering the movement by raising his chin. If that thing got any higher, he'd be staring at the ceiling.

I stepped closer, trailing my hand along the wood of the table closest to me. I drew it back and rubbed my fingers together, grimacing at the dust clinging to them. This place would definitely never pass a white glove inspection. That was for sure.

"You need a maid. This place is disgusting," I told him, looking around in distaste. Now that I'd noticed the dust, I noticed other things, like empty McDonald's wrappers all over the place and a pile of dirty clothes in the corner.

"You volunteering?" he asked, the words not quite disguising the unease in his voice.

It was enough to pull my attention back to him. Behind his bravado, I thought I detected a trace of fear, which was laughable because I should be the last thing in the world he feared. Unless he lived in anticipation of my wicked zingers.

I stepped closer, noting how he edged back and looked away.

"You're afraid of me?" I asked, disbelief clear in my tone.

His bright green eyes came back to me and he scoffed, the sound making it clear what he thought of that sentiment. I straightened and looked him over. That's what I thought.

I drew closer, my eyes narrowed.

"If you didn't come here to clean up for me, I suggest you go," he said, bending to pick up the book that had fallen and placing it on the table.

I cocked my head. Something was different about him—I just couldn't put my finger on what. Something beyond the trepidation sticking to him like a coating of sweat. He had a thin five o'clock shadow along his jaw, much fuller than the last time I'd caught him trying to grow a beard, and he was taller than I remembered.

A grin stretched across my face as I figured out what it was. "You're trying to get older. That's why you put the genie cuff back on."

His eyes widened, even as his mouth dropped open in outrage. "I did no such thing! This is for experimental purposes only."

"Uh-huh," I said, not bothering to keep the smile from my face as my tone made it clear I didn't believe a word he was saying.

"Get to the reason you're here so you can leave me in peace," he snapped, power flickering around his fingertips in green arcs. My skin twitched in response, remembering how it felt to have that magic popping and crackling along my nerve endings—worse than electricity ever felt.

"I need a tracking spell," I said, losing interest in teasing him.

His laugh had little in common with humor and a lot of disbelief in it. His eyes hardened. "You couldn't afford it."

"Look, it's a spell you've done for me before."

His brow furrowed in confusion. I sighed before leaning forward and tapping the skin under my eye again and gave him a meaningful look. The penny dropped and understanding dawned.

He shook his head. "She's with the wolves on their territory. I'm not risking a war with them just so you can check on her."

"You afraid of a few people with a serious moon allergy?" I asked, folding my arms over my chest.

He snorted. "Hardly, I could snap them in half with barely a thought. However, they outnumber me a hundred to one and fighting them off would take time and energy from other pursuits—ones that pay quite a bit better."

I wiggled my jaw as I considered how much to tell him.

He'd shown an attachment to Caroline in the past—enough that he put aside his hatred for me for the most part—to help me when the demon had her. It was an attachment that concerned me when she'd been human. As a wolf, she would have more protection should he try to practice any of his shenanigans on her, but did I really want to risk it?

Without his help, it would take me three times as long to track her on my own. Each night she spent on the run was another night for Brax to grow fed up with her stubbornness and give the kill order. So yes, it was worth it. I hoped.

"Caroline escaped from their little compound in Kentucky," I said, making my decision as I leaned against the table. "She's back in Columbus and on the run. From what Brax tells me, things might not go well for her if we don't find her first."

Peter paused in rearranging his beakers and frowned. "That's not good. They don't like it when a pup bucks the system. They'll feel the need to hunt her down and make her a lesson, to prevent others from doing the same."

That did not fill me with confidence about turning Caroline back over to Brax. It put even more doubts in my head than had been there before.

"Brax said there were those in his pack who'd urged him to put her down because of the demon taint." I wouldn't let them treat her like a rabid dog. I'd fight a second war, one with more at stake than the first one, to prevent any further harm from falling on Caroline.

His frown turned troubled, his gaze turning inward as he looked around the room with unseeing eyes.

I pressed my advantage. "You see why I'm eager to find her before Brax and his pack does."

"Yes, that would be in her best interests."

"So, you'll help me by putting together a tracking spell?" I asked.

His gaze focused on his hands, and he seemed lost in thought.

"Peter? You'll help me, right?"

He looked up at me, regret in his eyes. "I can't."

"Why not? Do you need more ingredients? Fine, I can give you my other eye." I wasn't happy about that, but it would grow back. Probably. It might be able to see the same shadow world that my left eye did, but at least I wouldn't be seeing two versions of the same thing all the time.

He flinched and shook his head—the movement frantic. "No, no. That won't be necessary."

I stared at him with narrowed eyes. Something was up. That was not the reaction of the sorcerer I remembered. "It's not a big deal. You know I'd do anything to help Caroline, and it'll grow back."

Faster if I sucked down some of Liam's super-charged blood.

"No, that won't work," he said, turning and busying himself with rearranging items on another desk.

"Why not? It worked the first time." Frustration crept into my tone. This was supposed to be an easy transaction. I told Peter what I needed. He'd hem and haw for a few minutes, maybe blather on about payment, before eventually giving in and helping me.

He slammed down a book. "First—it didn't work the first time. The spell didn't react the way it should have, and I refuse to chance a rebound with a spell I already know doesn't work properly."

I blinked at that, my mouth opening to ask what a 'rebound' was. He continued before I got the chance.

"Second—that spell only works once. Using it to track Caroline again would be pointless."

"What about another spell?" I asked, not wanting to give up. "There must be something in your bag of tricks."

"I'm not a magician," he snapped, power swirling around his hands. Seeing it, he flicked his hand and it disappeared. "I cannot just whip up a spell whenever it suits you."

I cocked my head. If he had the cuff on, he shouldn't be able to draw power or use it. The fact that he could meant he'd either been successful in his experiments, or that there was something more going on than he had chosen to share.

"Not even for Caroline?" I asked, watching him carefully.

He shook his head, avoiding my eyes. "Much as I'd like to help you, I can't."

I tapped my fingers on the table, giving him the stare I used to give Privates. The one that said I meant business.

"She said she was going to call in a favor," I said slowly, mulling over the information I'd spent the night uncovering. My neighbors had given me a couple of vague pieces, but that didn't mean they weren't relevant. "She didn't come to me for that favor, and you're the only other spook she knows."

Peter paused in rearranging his table, a guarded look on his face.

"Does the reason you won't help me have anything to do with that favor?" I asked.

"Don't be absurd. She wouldn't even know where to find me."

Hm. That was true. Although, he did spend several days with her after she was first turned, before Brax kicked him out. It was possible he'd told her how to contact him or given her one of those summoning charms he'd given me when we were hunting the draugr.

"Somehow, I just don't believe you," I told him.

"I don't care what you believe. I can't help you, and I'm asking you to leave."

The door I'd come through burst open with a crack and an invisible blast that felt like someone had punched me in the chest. I was guessing that blast was Peter's ward breaking. Liam, accompanied by Nathan and Eric, strode into the room.

"It seems you were wrong, Nathan. Our previous talk with the sorcerer did get through to him," Liam said, barely glancing at Peter before his eyes landed on me.

Peter flinched, and he drew his arms in to cross them over his chest, looking like he was almost hugging himself.

I looked between the two. So, it wasn't me he'd been afraid of. Rather, he feared what Liam would do when he found out about my little visit.

"Are they the reason you won't help me?" I asked, giving him a warning look. I hoped Liam had missed the question about the favor Caroline may have been after. It could be I was wrong, and she hadn't come to Peter, but if she had I didn't want to tip off my hand.

"Not the only reason," Peter mumbled, avoiding looking at the three vampires.

Nathan wandered through the room, shuffling through Peter's papers, moving his things. Peter made a sound of protest when Nathan picked up a beaker of oily liquid, but he didn't challenge him. Not like he would have before. It was out of character for the arrogant sorcerer to let me see just how much Liam and company scared him. Nathan's lips quirked at the sound, and he held the beaker a moment longer before setting it down and moving away from the table full of interesting liquids.

"What did you do to him?" I asked, tilting my head toward Peter.

Liam arched one eyebrow in a superior expression that had my fingers tingling with the need to smack it right off his face. "Nothing he didn't deserve."

That answered nothing. I let my frustration show on my face.

"We simply had a little chat about what would happen the next time he decided to take his frustration out on you," Liam said, his voice soft and calm.

I bet that conversation had been one-sided and contained a physical expression of Liam's feelings. Whatever happened had left a big enough impression on the sorcerer for him to treat me with a level of caution approaching fear.

My lips tightened.

"You're angry. Why?" Liam asked.

Oh, I don't know. Perhaps because I suspected Liam and his minions had done something to the sorcerer—that something involving a closed fist. Something that instilled enough fear in the man that he was still affected. It had been two months since the eye incident. Human memories were short. Nothing less than a traumatic experience would have had such an effect.

"It's nothing he hasn't done to others," Eric said from his post by the door. It was a surprising admission from a man who didn't speak much.

Peter made a sound of disbelief. He hunched in on himself when Eric turned cool eyes his way. Peter reminded me of a rabbit in the presence of a much larger, fearsome predator. It was not a visual I thought I'd ever associate with the man who had so casually tortured me on our second meeting.

Liam stepped closer, distracting me. His blue eyes pinned me in place. He was beside me before I could think to avoid him, his hand coming up to cup the back of my neck.

"I thought we had an understanding," he said, his breath whispering across my ear.

I pulled back slightly, putting pressure on his grip. It tightened, not hurting me, just letting me know I wasn't going anywhere just yet.

"You would stay in our care, and we would allow you to continue with the job you feel is so important."

I set one hand on his chest but didn't respond. There was an undertone of anger in his voice—one that sent shudders down my back, not all of them stemming from fear. A part of me found the danger radiating from him exciting. It was the same part that reveled in the taste of blood and screeched for the destruction of my enemies. It was the crazy, suicidal part that I'd gotten good at ignoring. Mainly because listening to it led me into dark waters that would pull me under given half a chance.

"Nothing to say?" he asked, his voice a sultry rumble.

What did he want me to say? That I'd do it again given half a chance. That my loyalty to Caroline meant any word out of my mouth would be a lie if it in any way threatened her well-being. I'd failed her once. I wouldn't make the same mistake again, even if that put me in hot water with Liam and the vampires.

My only regret was getting caught.

"How did you know I'd be here?" I asked. I was interested in learning how he'd tracked me, so next time I wouldn't get caught.

He chuckled, the sound a dark rumble as his eyes watched me like I was a fascinating specimen. "Where else would you go to track down your friend?"

"Could have gone to the witches," I said.

He shook his head. "Their price would have been too steep, and the sorcerer has already demonstrated an attachment to her."

I did not like that he knew me so well.

My frustration seemed to amuse him, draining some of the intensity from his eyes and leaving the normal Liam behind. He released me and stepped back.

"Besides, the sorcerer has already agreed to work for me on locating Caroline."

Wait, what? My eyes went from Liam to Peter and then back to Liam before returning to Peter as I processed that statement, unable to believe what I'd just heard. "You're working for them?"

I took back any regret I had that he'd probably been tortured. My only hope was that they'd made him suffer.

"It's not like they're giving me much of a choice," Peter snapped. "Believe me, I want as little to do with vampires as possible. That goes for you too."

"You're a sorcerer. Aren't you supposed to be all powerful?"

Nathan snorted, the sound anything but amused. "Maybe if he was fully trained or had reached maturation. For now, he's on the low end of the spectrum and will be for a few decades more, I'd wager."

Shock silenced any question I might have, as I turned incredulous eyes on Peter.

"Oh, shut up," he snapped before I could say anything. "This is all your fault. I never would have been on their radar if you hadn't messed everything up."

"Me?"

"Yes, you. I had a good thing going before you decided to make that mark permanent. Everybody thought I was my master, so they left me alone." He gave me a fierce frown—one with enough heat to it to have incinerated me where I stood.

"It would have made little difference had you been past your maturation," Liam said, his voice amused. "Thomas was most put out to learn his yearling had a sorcerer's mark and her master had gone so far as to use it to hurt her." He looked at me with a somber expression. "Furthermore, he had a very strong reaction to learning what the sorcerer did to your eye."

There was a hesitation before the word 'reaction' as if Liam had to think of a less violent word than the one he'd originally come up with.

Peter flinched at Thomas's name, his face going ghost-pale and his shoulders rounding.

So, it wasn't only Liam and his men who'd been involved in this. Thomas too. For someone who wasn't supposed to be in my life unless I invited him, he was sure finding lots of ways to interfere.

"You know she won't forgive you for helping them catch her," I said, ignoring that for the moment. "You help them and any chance of a friendship between you two is over."

Not that there was much chance either way. At this point, I'd say anything that might keep him from handing her over to them.

"That's enough." Liam's voice cracked through the air. "You've put me in a difficult position. The wolves know about your little adventure and are calling to have you turned over to them. Their accommodations would be much less nice than the ones we've provided."

"Not to mention, I'm seriously pissed you sic'd a pack of harpies on me," Nathan said with a scowl. "They stole my wallet, phone, and even my lucky penny."

"I've been lenient with you because of your unique set of circumstances. That ends now." Liam gestured, and Nathan sighed before ambling over to me. "See her to the car and don't let her out of your sight again."

I started to protest but was cut short by Nathan as he guided me to the door. "Come on, Aileen. Don't make it worse than it already is."

"It's not my job to make yours easy," I snapped, feeling like a two-year-old put in time-out.

"Yeah, yeah. Tell it to someone who cares," Nathan said, his tone bored and disinterested. One hand settled on my arm, the grip confining but not bruising, as he led me out of the room.

CHAPTER TWELVE

I TRIED TO shrug out of his hold, but Nathan jerked my arm, his grip tightening. "That's enough. We're going to sit in the car until Liam concludes his business. I'll drag you out of here if I have to." Nathan's tone left no room for argument, the fun-loving, laid-back guy of before, gone.

He escorted me the rest of the way in silence, his anger a live thing around us. Guess he really wasn't happy about the manner in which I'd ditched him.

He put me in the car and climbed in after me, forcing me to scoot to the other side or be sat on. Nathan pressed a button in the key fob he held and all the locks in the car clicked on.

"That's a little much, don't you think?" I said, fixing him with a narrow-eyed stare.

He shrugged his massive shoulders. "Is it? Given your tendency to run, I think it's best to be cautious."

"You're mad at me," I stated.

He fixed me with a flat stare. "That would imply I care about you one way or another."

Yup, definitely mad.

I sighed, trying to decide if I wanted to attempt to fix this or not. While Nathan's loyalty lay with Liam, he had proven a valuable ally in the past and keeping on good terms could help me in the long run.

We sat in silence for several minutes, each consumed by our own thoughts.

"For what it's worth, I'm sorry I set the harpies on you." And I was. Sort of. Not because I wouldn't have done it again, but because it had been necessary.

The leather seat creaked as Nathan shifted, facing me more fully. "Do you have any idea the hot water you've put us both in? Liam's not happy. Don't let his little routine in there fool you. There will be repercussions—not just for you but for me too. I haven't failed a mission. Ever."

"Is that what you're upset about? The fact that I showed you up in front of your boss?" I could sympathize with that as I hated when the same happened to me. No one wanted to look like a fool in front of someone they respected.

"Never mind. You'll understand soon." Nathan sat back and faced forward. His hard expression made it clear he was done talking.

The quiet between us was not an easy one. It was uncomfortable and full of the weight of unsaid things. It was the sort of quiet that came when there was a regard for one another—the sort I usually only had to worry about with the people I cared for. Not the sort of thing I associated with Nathan. We weren't friends, nor were we likely to become friends given he drank gladly from the vampire Kool-Aid, while I tried to get as far from it as possible.

The driver and front passenger doors opened, saving me from any further awkwardness.

"Get what you needed?" Nathan asked.

I pressed my lips tight together to keep from asking if Peter had given Liam a way to track Caroline, knowing they were unlikely to share, and not sure I wanted the answer.

"We got a piece. Evidently, it'll take time to create the rest." Liam didn't sound happy about that.

Eric started the car and pulled away from the office building, one that blended in with the rest of this side of town. Nothing marked it as anything unusual. Nothing that shouted 'sorcerer's stronghold here'. As with so much of the spook world, it was as nondescript and ordinary as everything else in the area. It was no wonder humans never suspected the presence of the supernatural. How could they when we blended almost seamlessly into the everyday world?

"You're quiet, Aileen," Liam said. "I expected a lot of questions about what we got from the sorcerer."

Precisely why I hadn't bombarded him with those questions, since I knew he'd withhold the answers just to aggravate me.

"Just thinking about my next move," I said.

"There will be no next move. After your little escapade with the harpies, you're on lockdown. You're not going anywhere but the mansion, where you will stay until your friend has been located." His words had a note of finality to them.

That he thought things would work out that way was downright hysterical. He should know by now that the more he tried to put me under his thumb, the harder I'd try to escape.

"You know I'm not a prisoner, right?" I asked. "Certain law enforcement types would frown on this attempted kidnapping."

His chuckle was warm and brushed against me with the feel of a fur-lined glove. "There's no attempt about it. You're caught, my dear. Resign yourself to your fate."

I was quiet for a long moment as I faced forward.

"What did you think to accomplish by this?" Liam asked. "You must have known we'd track you down eventually."

I shrugged. Yes, but I thought I'd have longer before that happened.

"What did you plan to do with Caroline when you found her?" Liam looked over at me, his eyes somber. "With your current lack of power, it's likely she would kill you the first time you upset her."

"Whatever you say, however you try to convince me, I'm not going to believe she's lost hold of herself," I said, meeting his eyes. "She's still Caroline."

"As you are still Aileen?" he asked, no judgment in his voice. My face darkened as I got his reference.

I looked away without answering, folding my arms and watching the city pass outside the window. His sigh was heavy before the leather creaked as he turned to face forward again.

Now what? I was caught, and by the sounds of it, they didn't plan to give me the chance to repeat my little excursion. Whoever they put on me would be twice as guarded against any attempt to escape. How was I to help my friend if I couldn't even look for her without bringing the vampires, and by extension, the wolves down on her?

A phone rang, the sound splitting the quiet.

Liam fished it out of his pocket, hitting the button and holding it to his ear. "Go."

I could hear Makoto as he gave his report. "Boss, there's been another incident. This time it's bad. There are bodies."

"Where?"

"Off Third Street in German Village. I've already sent two enforcers over there to secure the scene, but you said you wanted to be apprised of anything to do with our little problem."

"Are they ours?" Liam asked.

There was a hesitation before a softly voiced, "Yes."

"Okay, I'm on my way." He hung up and set the phone down before letting out a soft curse. "Looks like you're going to get a crash course in exactly what your friend is capable of."

My skin turned cold at the implication. I bit back my protest, knowing it wouldn't make a difference. They were already convinced Caroline was responsible for these deaths. It would take proof to convince them otherwise.

Eric turned the SUV, pointing it towards German Village where the site awaited. It wasn't too far from our original destination, just a few blocks south of downtown Columbus. This area was one of the oldest neighborhoods in the city. It was partially settled in the 1800s by German immigrants, giving rise to the name German Village. It was also probably why Columbus had such a strong German influence, stemming back to the city's founding. It was now a coveted area of town for couples. The historical houses, wrought iron fences and carefully cultivated lots were a hipster's dream property. The area was also walkable and home to many of the unique features that made Columbus an interesting place to live.

Eric turned down a street not far from the Book Haven and its secret bookstore that catered to spooks. He navigated slowly down the brick streets, careful not to scrape the sides of the SUV on the surrounding buildings. This area was not built with modern conveniences in mind. The streets were narrow and from a time when your own two feet were your primary mode of transportation. They were a real bitch to clear during winter.

Eric parked several streets over, and we disembarked, Nathan taking his place at my elbow in case I got it into my head to bolt again.

We turned down the street, following Eric as he led the way to the site. It announced itself through smell first, the stench of human bowels and dead meat greeting me before I'd rounded the corner. Under it were the delicate notes of blood that even now, sated from the blood I'd drunk this morning and feeling slightly sick at the sight of the bodies before me, called to me with a siren's temptation.

The scene was enough to turn even the strongest of stomachs. It looked like a slaughterhouse but without the organization or purpose. The closest I'd come to anything like it was in Afghanistan when a soldier walked over an IED and set it off. The force of the blast had ripped him to pieces before he'd even known what was happening. That had haunted me for months. If I was being truthful, it haunted me still. This new scene would join it in my nightmares.

Whatever did this had ripped its victim to pieces just as effectively as that IED. Judging by the fact there were too many arms and legs in the small alley, I was guessing there'd been more than one victim. One was a little more intact than the other, but that wasn't saying much. The torso and head were still attached as they leaned against the brick wall, but the person's arms had been ripped off and strewn across the ground in several pieces.

I moved closer, careful not to step in the blood pooling around the torso. I thought I recognized the person. It was difficult to tell with the face frozen in a rictus of terror, but she was familiar. Her long blond hair had turned almost pink from all the blood, and her heart-shaped features were missing the sweetness from our first meeting.

Catherine. I wasn't sure, but I thought it might be.

My stomach turned as I noticed a bone that had been largely stripped of flesh.

"Are those teeth marks?" I asked, my voice weak.

"Yes." Liam crouched near one of the pieces, lifting a ribbon of flesh away to get a better look at it.

It looked like some animal had chewed on the bone, cracking it and then sucking out the marrow. Behavior typical of a dog or wolf, but abhorrent when you thought of the person that bone used to belong to.

The other person would need DNA testing to be definitively identified. Their body was unrecognizable. Like the other, it had been ripped apart, but whatever had done this had demolished it. The torso was in two pieces, the spine visible, and what was left of the intestines on the other side of the alley. There weren't enough pieces, which meant the attacker had probably eaten part of them.

"The head's missing," I said in a low voice, looking around. It could be hidden under some of the other pieces or further down the alley. I stayed where I was, not willing to disturb the scene any more than we already had. The brick alleyway was slick with blood, as if someone had poured a vat of it all over the place.

"The head's not missing," Liam said, his voice grim as he stared down at the ground in front of him. An odd shaped blob rested on the cobblestone, bone peeking out with what might be blood-matted hair mixed into the mess. It had been crushed so that it was virtually unrecognizable.

"What's she doing here?" Anton snarled, advancing on me.

I took a step back, the sight of an angry vampire distracting me from the scene. Nathan pushed me behind him, stepping to meet Anton.

"She shouldn't be here," Anton spat, his eyes finding me over Nathan's shoulder. The black in them seeming to bleed over into the white as his fangs dropped down.

"Anton, that's enough," Liam's voice cracked through the air. He straightened from where he crouched, his eyes doing that eerie glowing thing as he stared at the other vampire.

"Her meddling caused this," Anton responded, his voice heated.

"That's enough, my friend." The Viking from game night stepped forward, taking Anton by the shoulder and steering him away. "Why don't you take a breather?"

Anton sent another snarl my way before stalking off into the night.

Viking turned back to us, his eyes flicking over me in derision before he turned his attention to Liam. "Forgive him. His companion is among the dead."

Liam nodded, his face grim.

"What was Makoto thinking sending him here to stand guard?" Nathan muttered.

Viking flipped him a dark glance. "Perhaps he had no choice seeing as three of our own were forced to track down the yearling. Again. We're understaffed since we also have to provide security for the master."

"Enough. This situation is bad enough without fighting amongst ourselves," Liam said, his voice brooking no argument. "Daniel, tell me what you know so far."

Daniel and Nathan stared each other down for a moment longer before Nathan's body relaxed, and he stepped beside me instead of in front. Daniel's gaze moved over me, something in his eyes making it clear that he held no more love for me than Anton.

It was a significant change from last night when there had almost been a camaraderie building. I didn't want to admit it, to them or myself, but the loss of that hurt. More than I thought it would. I missed being part of a team. I missed the jokes and the teasing and the sense that there was someone who'd guard your back no matter what came.

I had no one but myself to blame. I'd even gone so far as to make sure there would be no chance that I could build it into something better, but it stung just the same.

"From what Anton shared, Catherine said she was tired of being cooped up and wanted some fresh air. She likes the cream puff pastries from Schmidt's and had planned a short excursion for one."

Damn. I was right.

My heart clenched in sympathy. No wonder Anton wanted my head. I hadn't known her well but from what I'd seen of her with him, the two had seemed like they'd had real feelings for another.

"Theo volunteered to go with her. We think he's the other victim."

Theo? I looked at the other body with sad eyes. The man had struck me as shy but nice and the thought of him lying dead and unrecognizable was more depressing than I wanted to think about while standing among those who now viewed me as an enemy.

"Have Makoto run his DNA through the system and compare it to the body. I want a firm confirmation."

Daniel nodded and walked away without glancing in my direction.

Liam crossed the alley over to my side. "This is why we're so hard on our newly turned."

"You still don't have anything proving it was Caroline," I said in a soft voice. "Why would she come after the same companions from last night? She hasn't been a wolf long, and I doubt she knows who any of the other spooks are."

I certainly hadn't when I'd first been turned.

"Vampires have a distinctive smell to a wolf's nose," Liam said, his eyes thoughtful as he stared at the bodies. "Perhaps her wolf became confused and thought they presented a threat."

Maybe. Or perhaps her wolf thought it was me, then lost control when the companions had no doubt panicked.

"I still don't believe it," I said.

"You can lie to yourself all you want, but you and I both know she's the only one who would do this."

I didn't know what I believed anymore. This scene looked like the site of an animal attack. While there were many spooks that could have caused a similar scene, the chances were very small. It would have to be a pretty big coincidence for some unknown spook to attack these two in the same way a werewolf would.

I didn't want to doubt my friend, but the two victims had punctured a gaping hole in my defenses.

"Brax will be here soon. He'll be able to tell if Caroline was present." Liam's face was grim. "If she's responsible, it could have grave repercussions."

"What do you mean?"

Liam looked down the alley, his gaze distant as if he wasn't seeing the bodies, but something else. Something worse.

"Brax will not want to give up one of his own. He is many things, but he'll protect his wolves to his last breath," Liam finally said. "Thomas is new to his position, and the murder of a companion cannot go unanswered. Not if he wants a stable power base. He'll want to make an example. Your friend makes the perfect sacrifice."

I took a deep breath and released it.

His touch whispered across my shoulder as he gave me an enigmatic glance before moving away to give me privacy and time with my thoughts.

"Caroline, what have you gotten yourself into?" I whispered, staring at the macabre scene before me.

I didn't know if I was going to be able to protect her from what was coming. Worse, I didn't know if I should. The friend I remembered wouldn't have been capable of this. Not in a million years.

If she did somehow do this, it meant that Anton was right. My actions caused this, and I played a part in innocent deaths. Something I had sworn I would not let happen. Emotion tightened my throat and a burning started behind my eyes. I couldn't deal with this now. Maybe later in the dark of night when I was alone. But not now.

I owed it to Catherine and Theo to find their killer and deal with them. Friend or not.

Liam and Nathan gave me the time to come to terms with this new development, discussing the scene in quiet voices as we waited for the wolves' arrival. While we lingered, I forced myself out of the dark morass of emotion that threatened to overtake me and studied the scene. I wasn't a crime scene investigator and most of what I knew came from watching detective shows or reading books. That didn't mean I couldn't notice something the others had overlooked. I might not know what it meant now, but knowledge was power, and observation was something I was good at.

What were they doing in this alley? If they'd been going to Schmidt's, they'd parked a fair way past it. Granted, parking in this area around dinner time was a bit tricky, but there would have been many better places to park closer to the restaurant. Also, I didn't see their car.

Could they have been chased down this alley? If so, why would they have turned away from the more populated parts of the city? If it was me, and I was being chased by a monster, I would have made a beeline for the biggest number of humans in the area. At least, when I'd been human I would have.

That sounds callous, but most people have a strong will to survive. The recriminations and self-hatred would come later, after the threat had passed. During the threat—it's every man or woman for themselves.

"Woo, she's a messy eater," Clay said from my side. I controlled my jump, knowing that's what Brax's beta wanted. A tall, lean man, with short blond hair and pretty blue eyes, Clay looked over the scene with an amused grimace. As beta to Brax, Clay was number two in the pack. I hadn't had many dealings with him, but he'd struck me as easygoing but competent in his job. He took care of the things Brax didn't want to, or didn't have time for.

Brax stood by Liam's side, Sondra at his back. The alpha and Liam acknowledged each other with a nod before Brax moved into the alley, his eyes scanning the scene.

"It's possible this wasn't Caroline," I said.

"Nose doesn't lie, babe." Clay tapped his nose as he stepped forward, uncaring of the blood as it squelched under his shoes. He crouched next to Catherine, placing one hand on the brick to steady himself and then leaned close, inhaling deeply, his eyes shifting to the ice blue of his wolf. He straightened, his eyes changing back to their normal blue. "Yup, our girl was here."

I stared, unseeing at the scene. The news freezing my insides. I'd hoped. I'd prayed that we'd been wrong, that by some miraculous turn of events, Caroline hadn't been part of this.

"Could the smell have been faked?" Liam asked, his face emotionless.

"Anything can be faked," Clay said, standing. "I doubt it, though. I spent some time with the girl after her turn. This is definitely her."

"Then you're sure Caroline Bradley is the one responsible for these deaths?" Liam asked.

Clay glanced at his alpha, turning the responsibility over to him.

Brax picked up one of the limbs with his gloved hands and examined it closely. "These bite marks are inconsistent with her bite."

"What does that mean?" I asked, afraid to hope.

He handed the bone off to Clay before moving onto the next piece.

"It's possible her bite has changed. The demon taint has affected her and made her transformation unstable. Her wolf is not as static as ours. It can be larger following some changes and smaller others," Clay said.

"But this is different than her bite in the past," I said.

Clay frowned and hesitated, as if he didn't want to confirm that. "Yes, it's different."

"It's still likely that she's the one responsible," Sondra said from the mouth of the alley. Her eyes were sad as they took in the scene.

"But not definite." I could work with that. This changed nothing. I still needed to find her, talk to her and get her side of the story before deciding what needed to be done.

"Even it isn't her, it's only a matter of time before she loses her grip," Brax said. "The full moon is in two days. The chances of her surviving a change with her sanity intact with no support from the pack are very small."

"Why is the pack's support so important?" I asked.

"In the first years after welcoming our wolf, it can be difficult to maintain a sense of "self" through the change and after. We're pack animals. We need that social bond to be healthy. We're stronger with the others around us. With a pack, you can rely on the older members to guide the change and safeguard your identity when you might be too weak to do so for yourself," Sondra said. "Without a pack, most wolves, especially in the beginning, go mad. Some never come out of their first change. It's why we're so diligent in hunting down those who might have been bitten in an attack or by accident, so we can bring them into the pack before it's too late."

"Aileen, we need to know where she is," Brax said.

"I can't help you because I don't know." It was the truth. I really didn't know. "She called me a few days ago and apologized for getting me involved. When I tried to get her to meet with me or at least consider some kind of compromise that would involve contact with the pack, she flipped out and hung up."

"How did you get that call?" Nathan asked. "We've been monitoring your phones."

That confirmed one suspicion and made all my precautions worth it. I didn't answer him, not wanting to give up my secrets so easily. They'd guess eventually but maybe not until after the next call.

"What did you do to her that scared her so badly she's willing to risk her sanity?" I asked. Because that was the real question. Caroline wasn't stupid. If they'd explained to her what they'd just told me, she never would have run. Her mom's grasp on mental health was shaky at best. I doubt Caroline would have done anything to risk hers.

Brax's attention focused on me, the great power that followed him around like a pet ratcheted up to nuclear intensity. "What makes you think we did something?"

"She wouldn't have just run like this. Not without a reason. Something happened to make her pull a disappearing act. I want to know what it is before I help you."

He cocked his head, the predator in him coming out. "So, you do have an idea?"

I shrugged. "A few."

Liam advanced on me. "The time for games is over. There are dead on the ground—people I swore to protect. Tell us what you know."

"Doesn't work like that," I said. "I won't hand her over—destroy our friendship—without knowing why she ran in the first place. If I do, this will just happen again, and next time she won't reach out to me first." They needed my help, whether they wanted to admit it or not. The only question was if they could get past their alpha-ness and superiority complexes to see that.

I might be a novice at the spook stuff, but I knew my friend and I knew how humans thought.

"There was an incident about a week before she ran," Sondra said, the shadows playing across her face sharpening and softening her edges as she walked into the alley. Her high-heeled sandals clicked against the brick, the shoes at odds with the otherworldly grace in her movements.

"What kind of incident?" Liam asked.

"The kind that shook her confidence and caused her to shut down," Sondra answered, holding Brax's eyes with a small, sad smile. "Until then, she seemed accepting of the wolf. She wasn't happy about having her life disrupted, but she was willing to learn and gain control."

"Her demon taint was stronger than expected," Clay explained. "One of our other new pups had difficulty controlling their wolf and attacked her. Caroline's wolf took over and defended her, but savaged the other wolf."

"We tried to make her understand that her response was self-defense, but her wolf's reaction to a minor infraction was extreme. She didn't just subdue her attacker, she nearly ripped her head off."

"It is an understandable reaction for one of us," Brax said. "Our world is brutal and requires a certain amount of violence to survive. We didn't blame her or hold her at fault."

"I think she was afraid of the wolf within after that," Sondra explained in a soft voice.

"It didn't help that the demon taint has made her wolf a little different than the rest of the pups," Clay inserted. The violence around him didn't seem to bother him as he maintained his good ol' boy charm. It made me revise my assumptions. Anyone who could keep a smile on his face while surrounded by this much carnage was a lot more twisted than I'd thought.

"How so?" Nathan asked.

"She's bigger than the normal werewolf. Faster. Stronger. And I suspect her wolf's needs are slightly different than the norm as well," Clay said.

I wonder if they had told her all this. If it made her feel even more out of sync than she had before. She would have felt isolated, like a freak who didn't belong. It's hard to trust, when you're afraid the people who should be helping you are one bad mood from pronouncing you too much trouble.

"She left me a note," I said, choosing to trust that they'd told me the truth. Trust had to start somewhere and even if I found Caroline, I wasn't sure I could help her. This would take knowledge and finesse much greater than I possessed. I pulled the folded-up note from my pocket and handed it to Brax.

His brow furrowed as he read over it before handing it to Liam. "What does this mean?"

I shrugged. "I don't know, but she doesn't have a cat."

"No, she doesn't," Sondra said, peering over Clay's shoulder to read the note once Liam had passed it over. "It was one of the questions I asked when she first woke up. We usually foster any animals until the pup is ready to resume their life."

"Senior year, that's high school, right?" Nathan arched his eyebrows in question.

I forgot that as centuries old vampires they might not be up on current school lingo. "Yeah, it's high school."

"Would she go back to the school?" Brax asked.

I shook my head. "I doubt it. We both hated that place. Neither one of us could wait until it was time to get out of there."

"School's not in session. Might be a good place to hide, especially if you're familiar with the layout," Sondra said.

"Were there any places there that you guys liked to hang out?" Brax asked.

"Not really. Neither one of us were the type to skip class and any extracurriculars took place in the classrooms."

"I don't care. It's a lead. We need to send someone over there to check it out," Brax told Clay.

"On it, boss." Clay pulled out a cell phone, his voice hushed as he walked out of the alley for some privacy.

CHAPTER THIRTEEN

"ANYTHING ELSE YOU can think of?" Brax asked, arching an eyebrow.

I rubbed my hands together as I stared at the bodies, feeling like the worst sort of traitor. "Yeah, my downstairs neighbors talked to her before she left. She told them she was calling in a favor and to let me know that not all is as it seems."

I left out the part about how those same neighbors weren't exactly human and how they'd shielded her from detection when Brax and Sondra had paid me their little visit. Those were not my secrets to tell.

"It's odd she would tell such a thing to a stranger," he said, his eyes never leaving my face.

I shrugged. "He's a charming guy."

In every sense of the word, I suspected.

Clay stepped back into the alley. "I sent a couple of wolves to check out the high school. We should know something soon."

"I don't suppose you'd let me speak to the wolf Caroline savaged," I said, lifting an eyebrow.

Brax studied me before sliding a sidelong glance Liam's way, asking without words for his thoughts. Liam's arms were crossed over his chest, his face inscrutable. He looked dark and dangerous, the kind of man whose very presence threatened your piece of mind—the bogeyman with the face of a fallen angel.

"She may see something you missed," Liam said after a long pause. "She's shown a certain talent for this sort of work."

"More like she's a trouble magnet," Nathan said, his lazy humor peeking through for a moment.

"Either way, I don't see how you have much choice at this point," Liam said. "The city's master isn't going to be happy about this latest turn of events, and he'll hold you responsible since Caroline's one of yours."

Brax's face darkened, but he didn't argue. He looked resigned, determined.

Sondra paled, her eyes going to the bodies before coming back to me. There was something in her gaze, something I almost thought might be pleading. That couldn't be right, though. Sondra was a fierce warrior. Self-assured and confident in her abilities. There was nothing I could do that she couldn't do one hundred times better.

There was subtext here that I just wasn't getting. Frustration at my lack of knowledge ate at me.

"I can bring the pup around tonight," Brax said.

"Not tonight," Liam responded, looking up at the sky. "We'll be here a few hours longer, which will put us too close to dawn. Bring them tomorrow, first thing after sunset."

I started to protest. If catching Caroline before she did any more damage or went insane was so important, then we should do anything that might find her a priority.

Liam silenced my protest with a cutting look. "Unless you'd like to take blood straight from the vein."

I closed my mouth and hesitated. My gaze falling on the bodies.

"I thought so."

It was the last line I hadn't crossed. The few times I'd drunk from Liam didn't count. He was a vampire, and it was unlikely that I could kill him should I lose myself in the taste of blood.

"I'll do it," I said, not looking up. "I'll drink from the vein."

I crossed my arms over my stomach to hide the tremble in my hands as I stared at the bodies. There were times you had to bite the bullet and do the things that were hard. When you screwed-up as badly as I had, it meant sucking it up and doing what needed to be done, sacrificing if necessary. It was the only way to make amends.

"From Thomas. You'll take blood from your sire's vein," Liam said, making his demands clear, his gaze drilling into the top of my head.

My head lifted in surprise, and my mouth parted in denial before I bit it back. "What would be the repercussions of such an act?"

His expression softened. "Does it really matter?"

Did it?

My lips firmed. "No, but I still want to know."

Caroline was worth the sacrifice, and if it meant I didn't have to stand at another scene like this one, I'd take the chance.

"It will strengthen you and give you the ability to stay awake longer while the sun is up." He hesitated before continuing. "It will deepen your connection with your sire—bring it more into line with what it should be."

"Will he be able to control me?" I asked through numb lips. "I've heard that a sire can compel their yearlings."

Liam's gaze went to Brax and his wolves.

"I'll bring Lisa by before sunrise," Brax said before stalking off into the night, his two wolves shadowing him.

Liam waited until the three were well out of hearing range before answering me. "It might, though you have shown a surprising resilience to any form of influence."

The way he said that made me think he'd tried at some point only to fail.

"Most sires form some sort of connection with their yearlings; the form of that connection depends on both the sire's needs and the yearling's strengths."

"How much control did your sire have over you?" I asked, my voice calmer than my mental state, which had turned into a gibbering fool begging me not to consider this.

"I was not a typical case," Liam said after a long pause.

My gaze went to Nathan. "How about you?"

Nathan looked from me to Liam. "He could compel me to act against my will if necessary."

"Still? He could do that still?" I asked, not looking at either of them.

"It would be much harder than it would have been a few centuries ago," Nathan said. "But that is not how the relationship is typically handled between sire and yearling. Most only use the compulsion to help the yearling gain control in the first few years."

"But not all?"

There was another hesitation. "No, there are cases where such a relationship is abused."

That was the way of the world. The strong taking advantage of those who couldn't protect themselves. I never thought I'd be the one who couldn't protect myself.

I looked at Liam, fear in my eyes. "You're asking me to trust someone who has never shown me he deserves it. If I drink from him and he gains control, there is nothing preventing him from taking over all aspects of my life."

He could force me into a clan, get me to quit my job. Hell, he could force me to kill my family, and there would be little I could do to stop it.

"I know you don't believe me right now, but Thomas isn't like that. I can't guarantee he'll never compel you, but he'll do it only when it's in your best interests."

That was little comfort. I hate when people say "it's for your own good". That's like saying you're too stupid to know what's best for you. Maybe what I've chosen, while not the smartest way, is the way that works for me. My entire life I've been a square peg trying to fit into a round hole, and I'm tired of it. Going my own way, while difficult and often dangerous, was still better than giving up who I am for a false sense of safety.

A small part of me wanted to refuse. It was only a day's difference; it couldn't matter that much in the grand scheme of things. Only, I knew battles were won in moments. Show up just a few minutes too late and you might arrive just in time to pick your dead off the ground. Every second counted, and I wouldn't do anything to knowingly prolong this. Not when Caroline's mental and physical wellbeing were at stake.

I looked away, not willing to argue his words. It would accomplish nothing.

"Do you need me here for this next part, or can I wait in the car?"

Liam looked like he wanted to say more as he examined the set of my face. He sighed and then nodded, gesturing at Nathan to accompany me.

We didn't speak as we headed to the car. Eric had managed to accomplish a minor miracle in this neighborhood and snagged a parking spot just down the street. I opened the back door and slid over until I was sitting on the opposite side of the car from where the murders had taken place while Nathan climbed into the front passenger seat.

"Aileen."

"I don't want to talk about it," I said, staring out the window. "Talking about it won't help."

There was a sigh. "Alright. I can understand that."

Good. The rest of the time passed in silence as I stared out at the buildings in front of me, wishing my life was different.

*

Eric parked in front of the mansion, he and Nathan exiting the vehicle without a word, leaving Liam and me sitting in the darkness. Liam was motionless, his eyes on me. I didn't bother looking at him, not in the mood to argue, or banter, or whatever it was we did.

"I'm not doing this to punish you," he said, speaking for the first time since he'd gotten into the car.

I didn't respond, letting my silence speak for me. I felt like a rebellious teen brought to heel and about to face the music. It was not a good look on me, but I couldn't force myself to act in a more mature fashion. Not when I felt my choices and freedom slowly slipping away.

"After your little escapade, the wolves no longer trust that I can control you. We need them as allies. This will bring you more fully into our ranks and give you a little breathing room when it comes to them. With Thomas as your sire in truth, they will trust he has a handle on you." Liam's gaze turned towards me, his gaze burning into the side of my head.

Sensing he wanted something from me, I pulled myself out of the deep morass of self-pity I'd been indulging in. "You don't have to explain, Liam. Baby vampire, here. I won't know any better anyway."

With those final cutting words, I shouldered my way out of the car, walking towards the house. There was a pop of air, and then Liam was stalking along beside me.

"You're being stubborn and childish."

"Whatever you say, enforcer."

I took my time mounting the steps, feeling like a death row inmate going to my executioner. Liam's frustration kept pace with me as we entered the mansion.

"Where are we going to do this?" I asked, stuffing my hands in my pocket and looking around the luxurious entry way with feigned boredom. "I assume you already called ahead to let him know."

Liam's gaze rested on me, thoughts hidden just beneath the surface of vivid azure eyes. "Follow me."

He turned and led the way through the mansion until we were at the section Nathan had warned me about that first night. The area he said was monitored by both cameras and magic. Guess it served as Thomas's place of business, or maybe they did all their weird drinking rituals here.

We stopped in front of a dark wooden door that felt as imposing as any principal's door I'd ever had to knock on. Guess this was it. My skin felt clammy with sweat, and my heart raced as my stomach tried to twist itself into knots.

Liam's hand on mine stopped me from twisting the knob. His eyebrows were furrowed as he stared unseeing at the door. He seemed to be wrestling with an internal demon.

"Shore up your mental defenses and maintain a sense of self," he said in a soft voice that barely reached my ears.

He let go of my hand and stepped back. I gave him a questioning look over my shoulder as I opened the door and stepped through. His expression was impenetrable, giving me no notion at what was going through his head or what that warning was meant to do. Help me? If he'd wanted to help, he could have made it so this wasn't a requirement.

Left with those cryptic words, I turned to the room, a home office, by the looks of it. One that fit in an opulent mansion filled with vampires. Despite the fact it had a raised ceiling and was done in dark shades of brown, the place managed to seem inviting. On one side were floor to ceiling bookcases filled with an impressive number of books, as well as items that Thomas must have picked up on his travels.

The desk was on the other side of the room in front of oversized windows looking out on the topiary gardens. It was made of simple lines and clear of any clutter. Thomas stood with his back to me, hands clasped behind him, as he stared out at the garden. His dark hair curled against his neck, and he was wearing a charcoal gray suit that lovingly flowed over his body.

He'd been wearing a similar suit the first time I met him, and I could see how the younger me had fallen for his suave charm. He'd managed to seem sophisticated and charismatic in that bar full of twentysomethings wearing tight jeans and polo shirts. He'd seemed different from the people I'd hung out with for the past year, and I'd been reckless and desperate to forget the war.

"Why did you give Nathan the slip?" he asked without turning.

The window cast a reflection against the dark, and I could see a wisp of a woman, pale faced and exhausted looking. His reflection's eyes moved slightly so he could study me, watching me without seeming to.

I shrugged, not caring if the gesture translated or not. "I had things I needed to do that I couldn't with him shadowing me."

"Things like visit Caroline Bradley's mother?" he asked.

The question threw me. They couldn't have known about that, or else they would have pulled me off the street rather than allow me to wander further.

My surprise must have shown. "We had surveillance set up in case her daughter decided to visit. Unfortunately, our people didn't realize you were to be apprehended until it was too late."

Huh. Lucky me.

I glanced at the chair, considering sitting for just a minute before discarding the idea. I had too much energy to try to confine myself to the chair, and I didn't like the thought of him towering above me.

"How did your visit with your mother go?" he asked, his voice idle. His apparent lack of interest didn't fool me. He either knew exactly what had happened, or he found the answer to be important. I didn't know him well enough to tell which it was.

"Why does that matter?"

His shrug was negligent. "You're the only vampire currently maintaining a relationship with your human family. I'm curious what such a relationship looks like."

"You didn't see your family once you became a vampire?" I asked.

His gaze turned back to what was outside the window, the expression on his face turning distant. "It was a different time. Magic was the same thing as evil. My family wouldn't have welcomed me back home. They would have tried to stake me and drag me out to meet the sunlight—for the good of my soul."

Put that way, my problems with my mother didn't seem so dire.

"My mother senses something different about me, but I can't tell her what that is. It's led to tension."

"Yes, certain humans are able to discern on some level when the supernatural world encroaches. She must be a sensitive."

I huffed, my laugh not quite humorous. "She seemed to like Liam well enough."

"Liam is centuries old and has had much practice in hiding his true self. You're barely a candle against the vastness of his existence."

Well, that put me in my place quite nicely.

Thomas turned from the window, his face grave as he studied me. He stepped closer to his desk, reaching to pick up a goblet of what I suspected was bloodwine.

He took a sip, his eyes never leaving me. I stayed very still, not knowing what he was looking for, but feeling like I was on the precipice of something dangerous—something that could snap me up and make me bleed before I could even think to defend myself.

"What is it you want, Aileen?"

I started. "I thought Liam would have told you."

His arched eyebrow and as his lips twitched with amusement. "Yes, he's informed me of the situation."

"Then you already know."

One finger tapped against the glass as he stared at me, some of that otherworldly stillness invading and making me very aware that this was the master of the city—a being that had left his humanity behind long ago.

"That is not what you want," he said after a long moment where my instincts begged me to find the nearest exit and flee. "I'm interested in knowing what it is you want."

I tilted my head, confusion stealing through me. "I don't understand."

"It's simple. What do you want? You've made it clear that I stole your life, made you into the monster you are." He gestured to me with his glass. "What is it you want? What would you have been without my interference?"

I had never considered that question. "I suppose I would have continued on with my life. I would still be in the military."

Maybe I would have met someone by now, be on my way to a promotion. I didn't exactly know. I didn't often think about what might have been. It was a pointless exercise. All that mattered was my current existence. Everything else was just useless wishes.

"Somehow, I doubt that," he said, his lips curling.

Some of the exhaustion peeled away, and I gave him a glare. "What would you know?"

He gave a half chuckle. "Quite a bit. Let me remind you. You were lost, searching for something more. Your entire life you've been lonely, so alone that sometimes you couldn't stand it."

"What would you know about any of that? You don't even remember that night."

"I know, because that was who I was searching for. Someone whose life was so meaningless that they would embrace the gift I had to give them. That they would risk everything to have it." He pointed at me with the glass he was holding. "I don't remember the exact manner of your making, but I do know I wouldn't have taken someone happy with their place in the world."

"You don't know anything," I hissed, my inner vampire taking control for a minute.

"I know you're lying to yourself," he said, his voice perfectly calm. "And you still haven't told me what you want."

"I just did."

"No, you told me what you thought your life would be, what you would do. You shared nothing about what YOU want."

"Why does it matter?" I asked, suddenly tired of these questions. "I'm doing what you guys want. Nothing else matters, right?"

The look he gave me was pitying, the kind you'd give someone you thought was too stupid to live. "You really have no idea who we are."

My mouth snapped closed, and I met his sympathetic gaze as I fortified my defenses, surrounding my heart with ice, determined to remain unfeeling.

"Can't we just get this over with?"

He slammed the glass down and was in front of me before I registered the movement, fangs exposed and a dark light in his eyes. He grabbed my shoulder, preventing my instinctive retreat. "No, Aileen, we can't." His voice was full of a forced patience. "This is not some feeding where you gulp a few drops down and send the donor on their way. You are asking much of me. This is a sacred bond, and I would know the person I am establishing it with before doing so."

Fear was a thick coating on my tongue. Memories flashed of the last time he was this close to me, his teeth buried in my throat and my life flowing out of me no matter how my mind fought. Paralyzed, with no way to defend myself.

My heart pounded in my chest until I could feel my pulse fluttering at my neck like a bird trapped in a cage. My hands went ice-cold, and I fought to keep from whimpering. Vampires didn't show fear. Even baby ones with more anger than sense.

His gaze focused on me as he registered the terror I fought to hide. His hand loosened and for a moment he looked sad before his mask slid down. He moved away, his form full of sinuous grace.

"Now, what is it you want from life?" he asked, his back turned toward me.

There was a lump in my throat that kept the words trapped inside. I took several deep breaths through my nose, clenching my hands into fists to hide their trembling.

My voice, when I forced it past that lump was subdued. "Caroline and my family safe. That's all I want."

His head bent, something I couldn't read in his posture. "That's good enough for now, I suppose," he said, in a voice so soft I wasn't sure if I was meant to have heard.

He was before me in an instant, moving with that supernatural speed both he and Liam possessed. My eyes fought without success to keep up with him.

A bloody wrist was held to my lips. I flinched but was held motionless by his hand at the back of my head.

"Drink and be mine," he crooned, his voice a deadly lullaby.

The blood was cool against my lips, and an icy tingle spread from where it touched, as my mouth filled with saliva. It's draw pulled at me despite my mental reservations. My will fought its lure in a losing battle.

His thumb massaged the back of my neck in a subconscious caress meant to be soothing.

"Come now, my dear. This is the path you chose." His eyes were all I could see, the glow of them filling every space of me, even as untasted blood dripped down my chin. The words were an echo of that long-ago night when the younger me died.

I gasped, the blood filling my mouth, flooding my taste buds with bliss and power. It felt like I'd stuck my tongue into a light socket and was trying to gulp down liquid electricity. Painful. Tingling. And, oh so, fulfilling. It felt like someone poured energy into me, filling me to bursting, until my skin struggled to contain itself.

Liam's words from before came back to me. I could see now, what he meant. Already the pieces that made me Aileen, threatened to submerge under the tidal wave that was Thomas. His power ate away at me, huge chunks at a time. It was a struggle to retain myself in the closest to an out-of-body experience I'd ever had.

Someone could have walked up to me and put a knife in my back and I doubt I would have noticed, as long as I kept sucking down this blood.

Even as the blood coated my throat and sent power washing through my veins, I pulled the shreds of my mental defenses around me, building them up one painful tree at a time. When I could no longer summon the will for trees, I built shrubs, and bushes, and formations of rock around the core of me.

My mental defenses weren't like others. They weren't formed of hard walls or castle fortresses. They were organic and pulled from nature. As flexible and tenacious as I was, from the stubborn spruces, the hard oak, and the wild roses protecting the secret bits of me.

He might have the rest of me, but he could not have that. It was mine and mine alone. Even when every scrap of me begged to hand itself over, no questions asked.

"That's enough. Any more and you would be in danger," Thomas hummed, his thumb brushed against my jaw before gradually exerting pressure and pulling his wrist free with a pop.

I slowly came back to myself laying on the floor, staring up at the wooden beams of his ceiling. His office was very manly, was the odd thought that struck me. Thomas crouched next to me, showing no signs of the lethargy that was quickly invading my limbs.

"What was that?" I asked through lips that had gone mostly numb, like all of that energy had deadened their nerves. The blood still pumped through my veins, a fire making its way down each of my limbs and then back to my core.

"That, my dearest, was a proper feeding." Thomas peered down at me with an amused expression. "You'll be fine in about an hour. Your body just needs to process it and burn some of the excess power off."

I started to sit but didn't make it much further than the thought. My body refused to move. It was almost as if I'd had a really good workout, one that had left every muscle in my body pleasantly lax and unwilling to go through the effort of moving.

A faint feeling of worry threatened to steal the cloud of bliss I was riding on. I pulled my attention from it, not willing to give up this contentment. I'd been worried for so long. Scared and alone. Thomas would fix that now.

He bent and picked me up, cradling me to his chest as he walked toward a leather daybed I hadn't noticed before. Probably for all his donors, the snarky side of me said.

I blinked, a little more of the contentment I'd been feeling fading away as he laid me down. His hand brushing against my cheek as he took a seat beside me.

"Now, let's test this connection of ours, shall we?" he asked, his fangs denting his lower lips.

I gave him a sleepy smile, my thoughts fogged and seeing no problem with that. Why would I? A connection to my sire would only strengthen me and him. It was a sacred thing. I didn't know why I had fought against it for so long.

"Who helped conceal you from me?" he asked, his voice all I could hear, drowning out the rest of the world.

"Hmm. I'm right here." What an odd question.

Amusement glinted in his eyes. "I could grow to like this version of you."

My smile widened. "Because I don't challenge you?"

"No, because you look happy. It's a look that agrees with you." His expression was soft.

"Happiness is an illusion. Short and fleeting. Here one moment and gone the next."

He brushed back my hair. "Who is it that instilled in you such a dark outlook in life?"

"Someone who no longer matters," I said, the dark memories threatening to steal more of the cloud I floated on, making my perch in this drowsy dream world even more precarious.

"He must have meant something at one time, macushla, for you to hold tight to such a sentiment."

I shifted, my eyes falling from his as the contentment faded until it was no more than a wisp across my senses.

"Who was it that helped you hide what you were after your making? Who instilled such fear in our kind?" he asked, his voice pulling at me, tugging at me until I wanted to reveal my deepest secrets.

"Why do you need to know that?" I asked, trying to think past the cloying cloud in my mind, actively fighting it now.

"Because, _macushla,_ that person did you a grave disservice. I would have his name," Thomas said, the gentleness falling from his voice as a hint of steel threaded through it.

I winced and shook my head, the movement becoming violent as the words surfaced in my head. "No, no. He helped me."

"Did he?" That silken voice twined around me. "He left you knowing nothing about your new state. Not how to protect yourself or how to navigate the world. My enforcer tells me you had not seen sunlight since your making. What kind of monster deprives another of the sun?"

"It's not like that." The mental forest trembled around me, disturbed by my inner turbulence much as a storm would have rustled the trees and thunder shaken the ground.

"I can make you tell me," Thomas said.

The world around me froze, time standing still at that one statement. My mental forest settled and a calm similar to the contentment of earlier took hold, but this time deeper and stronger.

"Do your worst. Sire."

He drew back, his eyes narrowed, his fangs turning his handsome face into something out of this world. I sat up on the couch taking advantage of the space as he stood, pacing from one end of the room to another.

The fact that he hadn't already compelled me, told me he couldn't. It made hope leap in my chest. Hope that Liam's advice had given me some semblance of freedom, that my free will hadn't been subsumed under his.

He grabbed the bloodwine off his desk then set it down without drinking it. While he was distracted, I threw my legs over the side of the day bed until I was sitting upright. My first instinct was to put distance between me and the item that had been privy to my weakness. I forced myself to wait, knowing that his blood had affected me in ways I did not fully understand. The only thing worse than staying seated, confined here, was standing and chancing falling flat on my face.

I did not want to show weakness. Baby vamp I might be, but I was a badass infant capable of keeping my feet under me at all times.

"Aileen, one day you're going to see I'm right—that this world you are now a part of is not the worst fate you could bear, and that I saved you from a life of mediocrity," Thomas said, his back to me as I pushed myself to standing. I wobbled but somehow managed to remain upright.

"Hell will freeze over before that day comes." Confidence rang in my voice.

He turned to me, whatever emotions, whatever frustration he'd felt, masked by the confidence in his expression. "I am sure all children tell that to their parents."

I raised an eyebrow at him. "I've already got parents. You're not among them."

I didn't wait to be dismissed, making my way toward the door knowing my time upright was limited. Already my muscles wanted to collapse like wilted leaves of lettuce.

"I'll expect you to report for weekly feedings from now on. You're weaker than you should be," Thomas said.

I stopped with one hand on the door, turning back to him with a scathing glance. "The deal was one feeding for one interview with one of Brax's wolves. This experience will not be repeated."

His words pelted my back as I stepped out. "I believe you have said that you would never take my blood before tonight. Keep telling yourself those lies if it makes you feel better."

CHAPTER FOURTEEN

I MADE IT as far as one of the sitting rooms before I collapsed into a chair, my legs unable to carry me any further. Without Thomas watching me, I gave up on trying to present a strong front, content to just rest for now. His blood was still playing havoc with my system.

If it didn't settle down, this would have been for nothing. There was no way I'd be able to talk to the wolf in this condition. I refused to let that happen, not after what I risked.

My eyes closed, and I slowed my breathing, in and out. In and out. Forcing my heartbeat to slow with it.

Silver lining in all this—I got the sense that the connection with Thomas didn't allow him to compel me, or at least not to the extent that I feared. I'm sure if he exerted enough raw power into the compulsion I wouldn't stand a chance, but that had been the case before as well. I'd learn eventually how far this connection extended, whether he'd have access to my thoughts and innermost self. I'd have to deal with that when the time came. Not now. I had more important things to worry about.

Liam walked around the corner, his focus on where I was sprawled in an armchair. His lips quirked with a trace of amusement, and I fixed him with a hard stare. Nothing about this matter was funny.

"I'm surprised you made it this far," he said.

I grunted. "Me too. I feel like half my bones went on sabbatical."

"Only half?" he asked, arching one eyebrow.

"The other half is too stoned to move."

"Ah." His chuckle wrapped around me in a warm embrace. He moved to the armchair across from me and sat down, his body as lithe and sinuous as a cat's. His sprawl was nothing like mine—which was more of a boneless flop. His was a thing of beauty. One that seduced and spoke of dark pleasures.

"Thanks for the advice," I said in a stilted voice.

He inclined his head.

"Why'd you help me?" I asked, unable to resist. His warning about staying separate made a difference. I just couldn't tell how much of one yet. "I doubt Thomas would appreciate your interference."

The look on Liam's face was thoughtful. "Perhaps not immediately, but I have faith he'll see the wisdom in my actions eventually."

He was either naive or just stupid. I couldn't tell which. Thomas, in my eyes, was a power-hungry asshole who wanted things his way now. I doubted he would ever appreciate the fact that Liam had helped me maintain some distance in the connection.

"I don't know what you see in him," I said.

Liam rubbed his finger against the arm of the chair as he tilted his head. "You see him through the lens of a few interactions. Perception is rarely reality. I have the benefit of centuries of exchanges to pull from."

I made a sound of disgruntlement. If he said so. I didn't plan to take his word on it, though. What I'd told Thomas was the truth, this had been a one-time thing. I didn't plan on giving him any further opportunities to sink his hooks into me. Not unless it was absolutely necessary.

"Do you know when Brax's wolf will get here?" I asked. Sunrise was less than two hours away, and my experience last night had made me wary of cutting it too close.

"She's already here. That's why I tracked you down."

I struggled to sit up. "Why didn't you say so?"

"You looked so content sitting there, I didn't have the heart to disturb you," he teased. His expression turned serious. "You need to remain still for a while longer to let your body acclimate to the blood. Thomas has a lot of power and his blood packs quite a punch."

"I don't have time for this," I said, finally fully upright.

Liam was next to me in the next moment, pressing me back into the soft cushions, his face close to mine. His eyes flicked to my lips before he gave me a wicked smile. "You have more time than you think. Consuming Thomas's blood has the nice benefit of enabling you to resist the sun once it rises."

I paused and gave him an intrigued look. "You mean I won't be tied to its coming and going?"

What would it be like to have so much more time in my life? I could finally take on more runs, which would mean I could stop living hand to mouth and finally make some decent money. It wasn't too bad with the long nights of winter, but during summer my hours were seriously curtailed. Shortened hours meant less runs, which meant less money.

"For a short time." He gave me a meaningful look. "Unless you make it a regular habit."

I grimaced at that statement. Tempting though it was to be free from the prison of the sun, I didn't think it was enough to make me come over to the dark side.

"What's with your sudden insistence that I tap his vein regularly?" I asked. My bones felt like they had a bit more substance. Liam was right, much as I hated to admit it. The few minutes we'd been talking had gone a long way to restoring my strength.

He studied me with a thoughtful expression as if he was trying to decide how much to tell me. "I've said before that you're not a typical vampire, even for a yearling. One of the ways your making is different than others is the fact you were not given regular access to your sire's blood, or any other master's blood, for the first year of your making."

"And you're trying to make up for that now," I said.

He inclined his head.

"Why?"

There was a pause. "There are certain benefits that come with drinking from your master for the first few years after the turn."

I nodded, pretending to understand even though his answer left as many questions as it answered.

I rested my head against the back of the armchair and watched him from under veiled eyes. His was the sort of face I could watch for hours. That is, until he opened his mouth. Then, I just wanted to punch him, more often than not.

"You two were made by the same sire," I said, tired of my own drama. They'd called each other brother once, which I'd learned didn't mean they were actually related but had shared the same sire.

"Yes, our sire was very old at the time of our making." His expression turned distant.

"Were you made at the same time?" I asked, curious in spite of myself.

"Near enough by vampire standards. In reality, we were turned thirty years apart." His eyes came back to me with an odd light in them.

"Which of you is the oldest?" I asked, my lips stretching in a playful smile.

His eyes glinted in the light, his expression turning seductive. "Which one do you think?"

A non-answer. I should have expected that. Still, it was a challenge I couldn't resist.

I tapped my lips thoughtfully as I studied him. It would make sense if Thomas had been the elder, but something stopped me from making that assumption. There was just something between the two of them that made me think differently. Liam was almost protective of Thomas, much like an older brother would be of a younger one.

"You're the eldest," I said, taking a chance.

His lips curved, but he didn't confirm or deny. "You should be feeling better now."

I frowned at him, knowing a subject change when I heard one. I couldn't argue with his statement since I was feeling a lot better. Actually, even better than I would feel normally, now that I thought about it. My body felt like there was a current running through it, like I could do an Iron Man and then go for a nice hike up a mountain afterward.

"Fine, have it your way," I told him, letting him know I was on to him. "Where is Brax's werewolf?"

Liam slid to standing in an otherworldly movement that had me blinking. Sometimes I forgot that he wasn't quite human until he did something to remind me.

"I had Nathan show them to one of our interrogation rooms," he said.

He kept pace with me as we made our way through the mansion. I kept an eye on the halls we turned down, wanting to better understand the layout so I wouldn't keep getting lost.

"Wow, not my first choice for questioning someone," I said. "Would have preferred to keep them comfortable so they were more likely to share."

People tend to clam up the warier they were.

"I've found fear is a powerful motivator in convincing people to talk," Liam said, humor in his voice.

I gave him a sidelong look. Hm, I could see how that might work for him. He'd scare the piss out of them, and they'd fall over themselves trying to say whatever it took to get him to go away. It was something I was unlikely to ever pull off, though. I lacked the necessary scariness that would make such a maneuver effective. Perhaps it had something to do with being a baby vamp.

"This is us," he said, stopping in front of a heavy wooden door, one just like every other door on this corridor. Nothing marked it as an interrogation room.

"You coming in with me?" I asked.

"Yes, I'm as curious you are to see what drove your friend to such desperate actions."

I thought as much, but the confirmation was nice. Perhaps I could use his presence.

"Let me take the lead," I said. I'd paid a steep price for this and wasn't willing to have him take over.

He nodded. "For now. If I feel the need, I will take control of the interview."

"Guess I'll just have to make sure you don't feel the need," I muttered.

There was a light touch on the small of my back, and then he reached past me to open the door, pushing it open. I took a deep breath before stepping through.

The woman waiting was not what I was expecting, nor was the room. Instead of an austere, grungy interrogation room straight out of a TV or movie set, it was a warm and welcoming sitting room. There was a dark gray couch and other comfortable looking chairs around the room. The coffee table had an array of bright magazines, and the room was painted a pale, sunny yellow. Everything was designed to put you at ease, to say come in and have a seat while we have a conversation.

I gave Liam a dark look over my shoulder, and he grinned un-repentantly at me, knowing exactly what I had envisioned when he said interrogation room. A dungeon this was not. Tricky, tricky vampire.

The wolf was a petite woman with wavy, blond hair and a pixie face. She wore a bright green sundress and greeted us with a happy smile, standing when we entered. This was the woman Caroline attacked? That didn't seem right.

"Are you Aileen?" she asked in a light, high voice, giving me a nervous smile. "They told me to wait because you had questions for me." She fidgeted, twisting her hands in front of her as she waited for my answer.

I smiled, hoping it didn't show how off balance her presence put me, and held out a hand for her to shake. She took it with a grateful smile, and I felt a smidgen of relief that my people skills hadn't completely deserted me.

"I'm Aileen. Sorry to keep you waiting so long."

She smiled again, the expression lighting her face. Her makeup was flawless, understated and elegant. This was a woman who had probably never been unpopular. She was all sweetness and butterflies, and I could easily imagine her in a sorority before making a graceful transition to adulthood. It wasn't a combination that should have set Caroline off. Granted, the two would probably have never have become besties—the woman in front of me was too normal for that and would have bored Caroline and inspired reluctant distaste, but not antagonism. Caroline would have just consigned her to being unworthy of her notice.

"I'm Lisa. It's nice to meet you."

"How long have you been a werewolf?" I asked.

She blinked and sputtered out a laugh. "That's a personal question."

I forced myself to give her an answering smile, even as I felt impatient. She must know Brax sent her here to answer my questions, most of which would be personal on some level. "Sorry, I'm new to the whole vampire life myself, and Brax led me to believe you were in a similar situation. I apologize if I overstepped."

"No, no. That's perfectly understandable. I remember when I first transitioned I was always looking for others in a similar stage as I was." She clasped her hands in her lap and shared a conspiratorial smile. "It helps to have someone who understands what you're going through."

"Exactly," I said. Not really. At least for me. I was too much of a loner for that.

"I've only been two natured for about a year and a half," she confided.

"Really?" I asked. A year and a half and she was still at the farm? I'd been under the impression from Caroline that they usually only secluded wolves for a year, so they could gain control over their other self. That this woman had to stay longer meant either there was something about this process I didn't understand or her control was very shaky.

"How'd you become a werewolf?" I asked, curious how the wolves went about choosing the people they planned to change.

She got a sheepish look on her face. "It was a bit of an accident."

How does one 'accidentally' become a werewolf? I thought Brax had more control over his wolves than that.

"My boyfriend is a werewolf," she said as if that explained everything.

The look I gave her was blank. I didn't understand.

Seeing my confusion, she blushed before leaning forward and confiding, "We were intimate a little too close to the full moon, if you know what I mean."

No, I had no clue what she meant. I raised my eyes to Liam, asking without words if he did.

He took pity on me. "Their control over their wolves gets shakier around the full moon. Passion has been known to snap that control. If any part of him changed during sex, his bodily fluids would have the potential to carry the lycanthrope virus. In rare cases, it has been known to spark the change in a partner."

Lisa looked slightly uncomfortable at the revelation.

Liam continued with a cool look in her direction. "I thought Brax had counseled his wolves on being careful around such times so as to avoid such a circumstance."

She bit her lip, looking slightly abashed. "He had, but we figured since I was on the list for the bite anyway, there would be little harm in it." Her eyes were avid as she leaned forward. "Plus, sex with a werewolf around the full moon is really intense. The inner animal comes out, if you know what I mean."

My eyes widened slightly, and I nodded. I did understand this time.

Liam retained his hard expression. "You realize your boyfriend would have been punished severely for disobeying his alpha. Brax has killed others for less."

She looked shamed, her chin wobbling and her eyes filling with tears. One escaped to roll down her cheek. She looked no less perfect for the show of emotion. When I cried, I tended to turn a blotchy red, my eyes looking like a puffer fish and my nose looking like it had a severe sunburn.

"I know. Since finishing Brax's punishment, he refuses to talk to me. I haven't spoken with him since that night." She sniffed. "I hope he knows I never meant for any of this to happen."

Liam looked unconvinced. Both of us studied her with a laser focus.

"What happened between you and Caroline?" I asked in a soft voice, trying to appear sympathetic.

She looked up at me, her eyes still watery. "It was my fault."

"I'm sure it was an accident," I said, giving her an excuse.

"I know better than to corner a new wolf." Her hands twisted in her lap, the picture of a remorseful woman. "I've just been so lonely being the only girl on the farm. I thought it might be nice to have a friend. All of the other wolves don't like me much because they think it's my fault Jonathan got in trouble."

"Of course, that's understandable," I said with a warm smile.

"It is?" Her look was hopeful.

"Yeah, I was in the military for several years, and it was always nice when I found a female friend. Guys are great, but they sometimes don't get everything we're going through."

I ignored the look Liam shot me, one that said he suspected someone had invaded my body.

She gave me a relieved smile. "Exactly. I just thought we could help each other out."

"Give each other tips?" I said, helping her along.

She nodded. "Yeah. Maybe even cover for each other when one of us needed a few minutes away to get ourselves back under control. I mean Brax and his people are so nice, but I think they forget sometimes what it's like."

"You know, I'm going through some of the same things. These older vampires, they just don't understand. They're all about rules and nit-picking everything I do. It's enough to drive a person mad," I said, flicking a glance Liam's way.

Her eyes went to him to as if she had just realized he was in the room with us. Panic flitted over her features, and she leaned forward, her hands gripping my arm, "Please don't tell Brax I said anything against him. He's a good alpha, but he wouldn't understand that sometimes us girls just need a moment. He might punish me for such thoughts."

My eyes narrowed. I kept my sly smile inside.

"Sounds like a pretty awful person to punish you for such a natural way of thinking," I said in an idle voice.

"Oh no, he's great. I mean, he's set in his ways and he can be a little harsh sometimes."

I nodded as if I agreed with every word she said. "Right. Sounds like you don't like him at all."

"No, that's not what I said," she denied, her gaze going from me to Liam and back again.

My voice was puzzled. "First you say he's great, then you say he's harsh. That you'd face punishment for saying anything against him. Does that sound like the alpha we know, Liam?"

Liam's eyes rested on me, warm with a slight quirk to his lips. It was a long moment before he looked back at Lisa, his eyes turning wintry. I shivered at the thought of such a gaze being turned on me. I'd faced his stony expression before, so I knew exactly how unsettling it was when the stone-cold enforcer came out to play.

"Nope, sure doesn't," he said.

"You're twisting my words," Lisa said, frustration beginning to show on her face.

I studied her for a moment, my mouth pursing just the slightest bit. Maybe. "Back to Caroline, what was it about being friends that she took issue with?"

Lisa stared at me for a long moment before jerking up one shoulder. "She invited me into her room, and then flipped out when I touched her things."

"So, it wasn't friendship that pissed her off. It was you invading her space."

"No, she invited me."

I made a face as if I understood. "But, I thought you said you pressured her."

"Yes, to be friends. That's all."

"So, it's her fault?" I asked.

"Yes." Her face blanched. "I mean no. It's just being a new werewolf can be hard. I think she lost control for a moment. That's all. Everything since then has gotten blown way out of proportion."

"Now, you're saying she over-reacted to what happened," I said in a flat voice, not bothering to hide my dislike for her anymore.

She scowled at me. "I don't think I like your tone. I'm not here for you to cast accusations and blame me for things that aren't my fault."

Bitch was good, playing the whole 'we women have to stick together' card before transitioning to righteous indignation. Too bad I'd dealt with that sort of thing more than once in my life. It stopped having an effect on me a long time ago.

"No, you're here because your alpha ordered your presence. I doubt he did it, so you could lie and misdirect us," Liam said from his corner, his voice a cold wind. He fixed Lisa with a gaze that said he was wondering what she would look like with her throat torn out and her blood gushing down the front of her pretty dress.

She blanched, reading the intent in his gaze, her gaze going to me for help.

I shrugged, allowing my amusement to show through. "Don't look at me. I've heard very few truths out of you since I sat down."

"That's, that's—"

"Unfortunate," I finished for her. "How about you try a little harder to tell us what happened? Otherwise, I'll leave you in a room alone with Liam. He's kind of upset with me because I took a bit of a breather from all this earlier tonight. He might enjoy working his frustration out on you."

Liam's lips curved in a dangerous smile, his fangs denting his lower lip and giving no illusion about just how he would get the information.

"You can't do that. Brax won't let you." Fear showed in her eyes. I think we were finally getting to meet the real Lisa.

"I think he would if it meant learning what actually happened that night." I leaned forward, my face set in a cruel expression. "I'm told some vampires can see memories from blood. He's pretty old. What do you want to bet he has that ability?"

"Please, help me. I didn't do anything. I'm not lying." Her eyes pleaded with me. A nicer person, a less determined person might have felt bad. Not tonight. She'd picked the wrong person to play her games on.

I rubbed my chin and leaned forward, resting my elbows on my knees. I gave her an easy smile. She blanched. Hmm. Guess that smile needed work. "If the next words out of your mouth aren't the truth, I'm walking out that door. It's best that way, believe me. Right now, I'd like to dismember you piece by piece then watch as you heal, so I can do it again."

My smile held all of the dark yearning and terrible wrath that I concealed on a daily basis. I let some of my darkness peak through. This time she flinched, her mouth shutting so she could watch me with the intensity of a rabbit faced with a wolf. Pretty funny since she really was a wolf.

"Caroline is my best friend. One of my only friends. You did something so horrible to her that she fled a place that was supposed to make her feel safe, at a time she needed it most." My voice was a low thrum in the quiet. The yearning for violence might have scared me a few years ago, but now I embraced it. She had to believe I would hurt her if she lied to me. Had to believe I'd make her wish she was dead.

She'd brought this on herself when she did whatever it was that sent Caroline fleeing into danger. I wouldn't forgive her for that, and if scaring her was the most I could do, I'd take it.

"She found out I was still seeing my boyfriend. The alpha decreed that we weren't to have contact until he approved." The sneer in her voice made it clear what she thought of that order. "I don't think she planned to tell anyone, but I had to be sure. Jonathan can't go through another punishment."

"What did you do?" I asked, my voice doing that weird growl thing that happened when my emotions were too close to the surface.

Lisa gave a negligent shrug. "I just planned to threaten her a bit."

A yowl escaped me, the dangerous sound similar to what a cat makes when they mean business. The sound was deep, and promised pain for anyone stupid enough to keep pressing me. It was a warning.

Lisa jerked, her lips curling to expose teeth that were a lot sharper than they had been a moment ago. I tensed, ready to act if she thought to attack me. She settled down when Liam shifted forward, violence in every line of his body.

"Nothing too bad. I cornered her in her room. Said some things."

"You're lying again," I threatened, my voice full of power that had an odd reverberation to it.

"I let my wolf out. It was just supposed to scare her, but she flipped out. Next thing I knew, I was on my back, and she'd almost ripped off my arm. Clay and Sondra came in then." Lisa crossed her arms over her stomach, looking defiant even as her eyes moved between Liam and me. "Happy now?"

I held my body very still, the urge to go for her throat very strong. She'd just admitted to terrorizing Caroline, and she didn't even acknowledge that she'd done anything wrong. Yes, her blood would look very nice decorating her front.

"Aileen," Liam warned.

I took a deep breath and sat back. She wasn't worth it. Such an action would put the final nail on the coffin of Liam's conviction I needed someone watching me at all times. I was better than that, even if it would be satisfying to make her pay for her actions.

"What happened after that?" I asked.

"Nothing." Her eyes shifted away from me.

I snarled and darted forward, my fangs brushing her throat. "What did I say about lying?"

"I left a few presents in her room. Made her think I'd be coming for her again, but with more wolves this time."

I sat back, my fangs retreating into my gums as I looked over my shoulder at Liam. He was just behind my chair, his body poised for action. I kept my smile to myself, seeing he'd bought my act. "You have anything else to ask?"

His chin tilted down as he met my gaze for a long moment. His face was thoughtful. "No, nothing else for the moment."

The door opened to reveal Brax in the doorway, his face a dark cloud as his eyes went straight to Lisa. He didn't say anything, his power rolling into the room like a pack of angry wolves. The glow of it to my magic sight seethed with rage. It was a burning, living thing.

Lisa flinched, hunching into the couch and looking terrified of her alpha. I couldn't bring myself to feel an ounce of sympathy for her. She'd brought this on herself.

"I'll be taking my wolf now," he said, his voice a dangerous thrum in the quiet.

Liam didn't protest. I remained in my seat, watching through veiled eyes as Lisa jumped up looking like a shade of the confident, sunny woman I'd met when I first came in. She scuttled to the doorway, careful not to brush against Brax as he stepped aside to let her out.

He lingered once she disappeared, the power that had saturated the room pulling back until he wore it like a cloak. He pinched the bridge of his nose, looking suddenly tired.

"Why was nothing done to protect Caroline after the first attack?" Liam asked.

It was a question I should have asked, but fury and rage were too close to the surface to make speaking right now a good idea. Worse, I could feel the familiar burn behind my eyes that said I wasn't far from a crying fit sparked by all this surplus emotion. It wasn't that I was sad. It's just when I was thrown into a rage, my body sometimes got confused, which caused that awful thing called tears. It had been the bane of my professional life, and I'd learned the best thing to forestall it was to go silent until I got my emotions back under an iron grip.

Brax's sigh was heavy and tired sounding. "We didn't know what caused the altercation. Neither of them would tell us, and we assumed it was because Lisa threatened Caroline's personal space. It's happened before with other pups."

The chair arm cracked under my grip. Neither Brax nor Liam commented, though they both glanced in my direction.

"I knew there was something more between them, but I had to tread lightly. You managed to get more out of her than my people did. Good work." That last piece was aimed at me.

"Does this change anything?" My voice was tight and raw from the stranglehold created by my turbulent emotions.

Brax hesitated, the expression on his face answer enough. I went back to staring at the wall. "I'm sorry, but the former problems still remain. We need to find her before she hurts anyone else."

CHAPTER FIFTEEN

I CLOSED MY eyes and let my head fall back against the chair, listening as his quiet footsteps moved down the hall. There was a rustle of movement as Liam came to sit on the couch Lisa had occupied moments before.

"Where did you learn to do that?" he asked.

"Do what?" I asked, without opening my eyes.

"Question someone. Get them to make mistakes and then capitalize on those mistakes to get at the truth."

I made a small sound of amusement.

"You were quite skilled. For a moment, I thought you were falling for her act. I even thought I might need to save you. Force her hand."

"Did you now?"

"Hm. Yes, I had a whole plan worked up. One where you would instantly recognize my genius and worship at my feet from here to eternity."

My snort of laughter startled me, and I opened my eyes to find Liam regarding me with amusement, a warmth in his face that sparked a flicker of heat in me.

"Too bad you ruined my plan."

"I'm known for that. I've got quite the reputation," I said with a small smirk.

His chuckle rumbled through the room. "What made you suspect she was playing you?"

I shrugged. "Hard to say. I just had a feeling that something wasn't right." I thought a moment. "It helped that I know Caroline. She wouldn't have snapped without reason. It was easy to see through her with that background."

He made a thoughtful sound. "I know many who would have fallen for her routine even with intimate knowledge of the other party. Hell, even Brax admitted they missed it, and he doesn't miss much."

Good to know I'd impressed them.

"Did you receive interrogation training in the military?" he asked, the question jolting me to alertness.

A laugh escaped me. "That's a fanciful spin on things."

His gaze told me he didn't share my amusement.

"Does my record show that training?" I asked, my face still crinkled in a slight smile.

"No, but I know that the military doesn't always put everything in the record, especially when you're on special assignment."

I was quiet a moment, lost in thought. "I'm afraid it's nothing as clandestine as that. I was combat camera, so I got good at observing people. Things happen fast downrange. The only way to get a shot is to know it's happening before it actually happens. Also, since public affairs was usually spread thin, they had me interview the soldiers I went outside the wire with for news stories they could write up." I gave a negligent shrug. "Turns out I was good at it."

Liam tapped his fingers against his knee, his face thoughtful. "I think there's more to it than that, but we'll leave it for now."

I gave him a sardonic look. "Mighty kind of you."

Before he could respond with the teasing comment I could see brewing, Nathan stepped into the room. "That was entertaining. Who knew the baby was a natural?"

I looked at him, puzzlement on my face. It took me a moment to understand. "There are cameras in here."

And microphones if Nathan had heard the questioning. I should have picked up on it earlier when Brax mentioned something. I had just assumed his super hearing had been responsible.

"That's why we call it the interrogation room," Nathan said in a bright voice as he took a seat on the chair next to me.

Rick bounded in after him, his energy bouncing after him like an eager pet. He crashed into the couch next to Liam and took a seat. "What do we think? How long before Brax is forced to put her down or exile her? Two months? Three?"

"Why would you say that?" I asked.

Rick's lips curled up in a feline smile. "That woman is trouble with a capital T. Given half the chance, she'll upset the balance of the pack."

"He can't just kill her for that," I protested.

"He can if she crosses the line and her actions challenge his rule," Liam said in a soft voice.

"She's a brat, but that seems a little harsh," I said.

"Not really," Rick said. "I very much suspect the bitch manipulated her boyfriend into changing her. It's probably why Brax separated them and forbade contact. He was probably hoping to give the guy a chance to shake her influence off."

Rick seemed very sure of that assessment, and I couldn't argue after talking with the woman for a few minutes.

"So, why doesn't he just exile her?" I asked.

"He can't until her control is better," Liam said. "To do otherwise would risk the same problems he faces with Caroline."

"Corrective punishment isn't likely to work on a person like that," Nathan said, sounding disinterested. "They're too busy blaming everyone else rather than taking a good look at the reason for their suffering."

I yawned, my jaw cracking with the force of it. Sleep tugged at me. I resisted, knowing I'd lose the battle soon.

"You lasted almost an hour past dawn. Congratulations." Liam stood.

"Better head to bed before you fall flat on your face again," Nathan said with a wicked grin. "Next time you might wake up with a few things drawn on your skin in permanent marker."

I pulled a face at him before I frowned and stood. He had a point. I had no idea how long I had before sleep became less of a choice and more of a reality.

"I'll escort you," Rick said, jumping to his feet with an energy I was jealous of.

Despite the power boost Thomas's blood had given me, I was starting to drag, every movement taking a little bit more effort than the last.

Rick was quiet as we walked up the stairs, humming under his breath. I plodded next to him, grateful for the silence. Much of the night had been depressing. I still had no clue what to do and was too tired to think of something at this stage.

I was grateful when the door to my room came into sight. Rick touched my elbow, drawing me to a halt. His gaze was unfocused when I turned to him, and I hesitated, not sure if I should ask questions or leave him to his thoughts.

"Remember that the shadows can be your friend in times of desperation," he said, his vague words not making any sense.

"What does that mean?" I asked as he moved down the hall.

He turned around and gave me a drowsy smile. His eyes still had that same unfocused look. "You'll figure it out, or maybe you won't, and you'll die."

What the—was he high? Could vampires even get high?

Left in front of my door with more questions than answers, I shouldered it open and headed for the bathroom. The night called for a hot shower before I crawled between the sheets, and I had just enough energy left for one before I entered slumber land.

Hair still wet and wearing a pair of sleep shorts and tank top I'd found in the dresser, I crawled into a bed that was more comfortable than any I'd ever had before. I closed my eyes and drifted off in moments, for once grateful for sleep's cool, dark protection.

*

A soft tap came from the door as I entered the kitchenette in my suite, my stomach growling and my fangs aching. I eyed the door with disgruntlement before calling, "Come in."

I didn't wait for whoever had disturbed me to respond, heading for the fridge and the cold meal that awaited me there.

I grabbed a glass from the cabinet and a bag of blood from the refrigerator, already dreading forcing the stuff down.

"Hello," a soft voice called from the doorway.

"Over here," I said, frowning at the blood. I'd never had this problem before being exposed to the stuff in Liam and Thomas's veins. I threw the bag on the counter and looked up, surprised to see Sheila dithering in the doorway. "Sheila, what're you doing here?"

"Since Theo is gone, the companions have been asked to provide blood meals for you until a replacement can be found." Her voice stumbled over the word "gone", and her eyes moved around the room as if searching for a place to alight. One that would shield her from the implication of that word.

"Ah." I didn't know what else to say as I stared at her, nonplussed. After a long moment where I tried to frame my refusal in polite terms—ones meant to cause little offense even though the offer repulsed me—I settled on saying, "I thought you already had a long-term companion. I was under the impression you only provide blood to that vampire."

Her smile was troubled and didn't reach her eyes. "That's correct, but we have no other uncommitted companions. We were asked to draw lots to see who would provide for your needs."

A laugh escaped me. "Draw lots? Am I so repulsive?"

She didn't answer, her eyes dropping to her feet.

"Ah, guess that answers that." I popped the top of the blood bag, pouring it into the glass. Good to know the companions were so scared of me they needed a lottery to determine who got the duty of feeding me.

"It's just that all of us were close with Theo. He was well liked here," she said, looking uncomfortable.

The blood pouring into the glass paused as I hesitated. "And you blame me for his death."

She flinched and jolted back a step. "No."

"I suspect as a companion you know vampires have heightened senses and can tell when the human body reacts with indicators of a lie," I said in a conversational tone. We could hear when a heartbeat sped up, the slight rasp of an inhale and see the beads of sweat that were all signs someone was uncomfortable. It could sometimes be used to discover lies. Not every time. I suspected a sociopath would be able to fool the enhanced senses, but Sheila didn't fall into that category.

Her stricken expression told me she did know that. She fell quiet, her big eyes watching me as if I was a snake about to strike. I sighed. Way to go, Aileen. You've terrified the poor girl into a stupor. I became more and more the vampire every day.

"It's fine, Sheila. I understand. You can go."

She jolted, betraying her wishes by glancing at the door. "But, I'm supposed to provide blood."

I gave her a humorless smile. "Sorry, I don't plan to drink from someone who is visibly afraid of me. You might stab me with a stake by accident."

"Um, that doesn't actually work." Her words were hesitant.

I sighed and closed my eyes, praying for patience. "I know. It's just an expression. Go."

She looked chastened as she turned to leave. "You should stay away from Deborah. She had a crush on Theo."

"Did she now?" I asked, not really caring.

Sheila nodded. "Not that she had a chance. He and Catherine were never far apart, even after Catherine gained a patron."

That was interesting. I spoke before she could leave. "I thought vampires and their companions had an intimate relationship."

She hesitated by the door, the call of freedom visibly pulling at her. She swallowed the urge in a display of bravery I hadn't thought her capable of. "It can be, but not always. Sometimes it's just a friendship or akin to a parent-child relationship."

Hm.

She waited, fidgeting in place as I stared at her blankly for a long moment before realizing what she wanted. I flicked my hand in dismissal.

I took another long gulp of the blood after she was gone, choking down the stuff and wishing for the days where this actually tasted good. Now, it tasted rancid—like milk three weeks past its expiration date. At least it would keep me fed for another night.

The visit with Sheila had unnerved me more than I wanted to admit. It wasn't only the enforcers who saw me as being partially responsible for the deaths last night. Seemed the companions felt the same way. It added to the guilt and sense of wrongness that I was already dealing with.

I sighed, setting the glass on the counter. It was only half drunk, but I couldn't force any more of it down. Perhaps in a little bit. Even telling myself that lie didn't work. I put the glass in the fridge to keep it from going bad, just in case.

My elbow bumped into something on the counter as I turned, the book that followed me around like a pet dog lying innocuously face up. I leaned next to it, staring at it with repulsed fascination. I liked books as much as the next person, but it was disturbing when one could just move around under its own power. A witch had told me it was an item of power that did not mean me harm. That could change, and I suspected I would never see it coming.

"Don't suppose you have an answer to my problem?" I asked it, only half joking.

It had provided semi-decent information about the demon taint before. Feeling slightly stupid, I waited a moment but nothing happened. Didn't think so. I turned away, somehow bumping the book and knocking it to the floor, though I could have sworn I was nowhere near it. I squatted next to the open book, frowning at it in consternation. That wasn't creepy or anything.

It'd fallen so it was lying open, face down, practically asking for me to pick it up and see what it had to say. I shook my head, knowing I should just walk away. It had tried this trick before, and until now I'd made a point of ignoring it. Not this time.

"This had better be good," I warned it. "Or I'm going to find a lighter. I'm sure a place like this has a fireplace—or a dozen."

Before I could talk myself out of it, I picked it up and glanced at the text on the page. What I found was unexpected. Instead of something that might help me calm a werewolf, or a weapon that might force an angry one to sleep, the book had a hand-drawn picture of a room. I bent closer. Books. Lots of them.

I recognized that room. I'd been in it during my ill-advised excursion to the supernatural bookstore, and I was pretty sure I'd been lucky to escape with my life and this book.

There was no other text on the page, just the drawing and another page with a picture of the bookstore keeper and an empty spot next to him.

"That's not helpful," I told the book before shutting it and tossing it back on the counter.

I didn't understand. It had always been semi-helpful in the past. Yes, the information was often vague, but it had at least gotten me pointed in the right direction. That picture must mean something, but I had no idea what.

Not ready to leave the room and chance encountering some of the now unfriendly inhabitants of the mansion, I settled on the couch in the living room section of my suite. Nathan, Liam, or whoever they appointed as my babysitter for the night would be around soon. I was actually slightly surprised they weren't already here.

Maybe they figured little Sheila would keep me occupied for a bit, or perhaps they were enjoying a blood-filled companion of their own. Either way, it left me some breathing room. Fat lot of good that did me.

I still had no idea where Caroline was or what I was going to do when I found her. My little chat with Lisa last night had shed some light on why Caroline had pulled her disappearing act, but it didn't change the fact that she was waist deep in shit and sinking fast. The dead bodies complicated things even more. I wasn't even sure what the right thing to do was anymore.

It had all gotten so fucked up, and in such a short time. I'd been here before. Only thing left to do was put one foot in front of the other and hope you were moving in the right direction. Standing still. Questioning yourself. Dwelling on your failure would not solve any problems. Action solved problems, and I'd get to it as soon as I figured out what I should be doing.

My cell phone rang from the bedroom, distracting me from my thoughts. Not that they were good thoughts anyway.

I thought about leaving the phone unanswered but hoisted myself off the couch with reluctance. It could be important. Only way to find out was to see who it was.

I'd put the battery back in last night. The vampires had caught me, so it was pointless to try to keep them from tracking it. The phone was no help, showing a number but no name to go with it. I clicked answer and waited.

"Aileen, are you there?" Caroline's scared voice came down the line.

"Caroline. Where are you?"

Soft sobs filled my ear, making my heart sink even further. "I screwed up. I need your help."

"Okay, Caroline, just stay calm," I said, fighting for that state myself. "I can help you but I need you to stay calm."

"Yeah, you're right. I need to stay calm."

I pressed my palms to my eyelids trying to ignore the prickling behind them.

Caroline started speaking before I could say anything. "It's just, there was so much blood. I've never seen that much blood before, and the bodies—they were both dead. I don't know what happened. There were so many pieces." Her voice was ragged, and she sounded like she was on the verge of a panic attack.

"Let's not think about that right now. We're staying calm. We can deal with that later." I waited a beat as her breathing slowed, still fast, but she didn't sound like she might pass out or turn into the wolf at any moment. "Where are you? I'll come get you, and we can figure this out together."

Her breath rasped in and out. "Yeah, you're right. I don't think I can do this alone. I need help."

"Yes, you can trust me."

"Do you remember our senior trip in high school?" she asked.

My eyebrows furrowed. "We didn't go on our trip."

"Right, where did we go instead?" she asked. "Be there in one hour, and Aileen?"

"What?"

"Come alone."

The phone went dead in my hand as it fell to my side. I sat down hard on my bed and stared at my hands, feeling cold.

"You get all that?" I asked in a soft voice.

Liam uncoiled from where he rested his shoulder against the door frame and crossed the room. "Yeah."

I nodded, feeling like the worst kind of traitor. "You won't hurt her."

His eyes held mine. They were sympathetic even as they were unyielding. "I can't make that promise as I'm sure you're aware."

A tear slipped free, and I looked away. Yeah. I was aware.

"Where is she?" he asked in a soft voice.

"You'll need me for this," I told him, meeting his eyes with grim purpose. "She'll have more than one exit planned, and she'll stay under cover unless she sees me."

His fangs came out, his eyes fierce. "That will not happen."

I raised my eyebrow, unimpressed. I didn't feel much of anything at the moment. Just numb. As if a different Aileen had taken over my body—one forced to do what was necessary, even while it felt like the worst kind of wrong. I felt defiled to the very core of my being. What was one angry vampire?

"I need to talk to her," I said, holding his gaze and not letting the anger in his eyes phase me. "You'll give me that, or I'll call her back and warn her you're coming."

He was across the room, his hand around my throat as he picked me up and held me effortlessly against the wall next to my bed. "It's unwise to threaten me. I've given you more leniency and understanding than any other vampire in my command. Do I need to remind you of where you stand?"

My soft chuckle held little humor. "Go ahead. Do your worst. You still won't catch her without my help."

His fingers tightened around my throat, just a small movement, not hurting, just threatening. I let my conviction fill my gaze. I wasn't budging on this one. If he didn't like it, he could pack sand.

He drew closer, his smell wrapping around me as his eyes mesmerized. "Why? This action will only hurt you."

I flinched at the truth. "Those are my terms. Take them or leave them."

His hand loosened. I didn't move, remaining still as he drew closer and rested his forehead against mine. He sighed, his breath tickling my lips.

"You want to bargain? Very well." He drew back, a dark smile playing across his face. "You will owe me ten nights."

I blanched. "For what?"

He tilted his head. "That is for me to decide."

"Fine, but I want her safety guaranteed." I lifted my chin.

He shook his head. "You could not afford the price tag that came with such a guarantee."

"Still." I was willing to risk it.

"No. All I will promise is to try to keep her alive. Brax, and her own actions are the only thing that can guarantee the outcome." His face was serious as his eyes drilled into mine.

I took a deep breath and released it. Fair enough. I didn't like it, and there were too many things that could go wrong, but I could see how his hands were tied.

I looked away from him and stared unseeing at the wall. Moment of truth.

"I got kicked off the senior trip when I accidentally set fire to the chemistry lab during an unsupervised experiment." It was too late to change my mind. All I could do was hope. "Of course, I was covering for Caroline at the time. She stayed behind to keep me company. We spent the entire week on top of the abandoned railroad tracks over near the Scioto river. We told stories to each other as we drank the liquor we stole from our parents' secret stash."

Liam squeezed my shoulder, his face neutral as he turned to where Nathan leaned against the door frame.

"I'll call Brax and explain what's happening," Nathan said in response to the unvoiced order from Liam. His eyes came to me for a moment before he turned and disappeared into the other room. His footsteps faded as Liam waited with me.

I didn't look away from the night outside, too drained and tired. What I wouldn't give to be able to roll back into this bed and just go to sleep, let the night pass me by. Sometimes being a vampire sucked.

CHAPTER SIXTEEN

I'D TAKEN A long, scalding shower, wishing the heat would wipe away some of the emotional grime I felt. Tears cascaded down my face for several moments before I got a hold of myself. Crying wouldn't help things. My decision had been made, my course set. Sometimes being a friend meant doing what was necessary even if it hurt the other person in the short term. I saw no other way that didn't lead to death for someone. I doubted Caroline would see it in that light, but that was something I would have to live with.

There were a lot of things I had to find a way to live with in this life. Someday I feared those things would become more than I could bear, and I would crumple under their weight.

Dressed, my hair tied back in a ponytail and my face free of makeup, I padded into my bedroom collecting things along the way. My phone ringing brought me to a stop. I stared at it for a long moment, not wanting to answer. Nothing good ever came of answering that phone. Evidence—last time I answered I'd ended up betraying one of my oldest friends.

Hermes calling.

Shit, I had a run tonight that I was late for. I grabbed the phone and clicked answer.

"Where are you?" Jerry rumbled, the sound having only the barest resemblance to his normal voice. This version was deeper, like a volcano on the precipice of eruption. You knew when it went it was going to take out everything in its path.

"Not where I'm supposed to be," I said.

"And, are you planning to get to your pickup anytime soon?" he asked, that volcano bubbling ominously.

I stopped putting on my shoes and sat on the bed. My silence was answer enough.

"One day," he said. "You kept your promise for one day."

I closed my eyes and rubbed my forehead. "Yeah. I did."

There was a crash on the line. When Jerry came back, his voice was calm. It was scarier than the volcano had ever been. "You leave me no choice." I really hadn't. "Aileen, you are no longer employed with Hermes Courier. Henceforth, you are banished from our offices and no longer operate under our banner or protection. Hermes will never work with you or deliver to you."

My exhale was tremulous. That hurt more than I thought it would. My job was important to me. I might bitch and groan about it, but a large part of me had found purpose in it, and I'd made connections that would have been otherwise impossible.

"I understand, Jerry. And, I'm sorry."

His sigh was heavy. "I didn't want to do this, but you left me no choice."

My throat was tight and my voice wobbly as I said, "I know."

"They're going to come after you now. Every spook with a vendetta against the vampires will consider you fair game."

I nodded, forgetting he couldn't see me.

"Consider joining a clan," he said, his voice barely audible. "It will provide protection."

My laugh sounded soggy. "I doubt that's a possibility anymore. Thanks, though."

"What are you going to do?"

"I'll figure something else out. It's no longer your problem." I cleared my throat. "I appreciate everything you did for me. I know it hasn't always been easy and wasn't something you ever wanted, but I thank you anyway."

There was a heavy silence. "Ah, lass. You know better to say thank you to a fey."

I snorted lightly. "You never confirmed your species, so those rules don't count."

"They always count," he returned, his voice normal. There was a pause. "Good luck, Aileen."

"Thanks."

The line went dead before I could say anything else.

The phone dropped into my lap. I was unemployed now. I'm sure once it sunk in and I processed what had just happened, I'd feel panicked, but for now I just felt resigned. The question of what I was going to do, how I was going to live without an income, was too big for my mental state now. Like so many things tonight, it was a problem I would have to solve later. Perhaps when my rent came due and I was unable to pay it.

*

The hour flew by and the moment of reckoning loomed over me like a freight train barreling down the tracks. A part of me had thought I would come up with some brilliant but insane plan by now—one that would magically fix things and save both Caroline and myself from our mistakes. Nothing came to mind, which left me standing alone at the base of the tracks ten minutes before the meet time.

The tracks were exactly how I remembered, an old wooden bridge crossing the river. On this side, the tracks extended to within ten feet of Riverside Road before disappearing. Trees framed it on either side, since the riverfront had been turned into a metro park. There were old brick buildings just up the bank, remnants of a time in Columbus's history where all goods flowed under the power of the river.

Liam and his men, as well as Brax and his pack, waited in the shadows, leaving me to draw Caroline out alone. It kind of felt like I was in a high stakes thriller blockbuster. They'd fitted me with a wire so they could hear what was said and so they could ensure I held up my end of the bargain.

I looked at the train tracks above me and sighed. It was time.

Climbing the short hill to the tracks didn't take long. Standing on top of them, I looked around. No sign of Caroline. No sign of anyone, really. Liam and Brax had done a good job of keeping their people hidden so it looked like I was alone. Not surprising, considering both were apex predators, and this wouldn't be the first prey they hunted.

I walked out onto the tracks, careful to watch my step. Some of the boards on this thing weren't stable. They were old and twisted, a few missing, forcing me to widen my stride to jump over them. Twenty feet away from the bank I stopped before turning and looking out over the river. An inky black blot against the sky, it was lined by the shadowy shape of trees around the edges. The moon was out, almost full. Another day and it would be. It was clear tonight, the moon's light made it easy to see by—even if I had not been a vampire.

I stuffed my hands in my pocket and watched the river flow by, the moon reflected in its dark depths—its lights dancing across the surface. Wind blew my hair away from my face as I let myself be, let myself just feel the night around me, the insects singing and the railroad bridge creaking under me. It was so peaceful. Quiet, with a solitude that called to my deepest self.

"You always did like this place at night," Caroline said from several feet away.

I didn't jump, nor did I look away from the river and starry sky before me. "So did you."

Caroline looked out at the river, a small smile on her face. "Guess that's why we're friends."

"I thought you were my friend so you could cheat off me in math class."

She snorted. "Hardly. It was always you looking over my shoulder, if you remember."

A smile broke across my face. "Oh, yeah."

Her lips twisted in an answering smile, and she looked down and away. "Thanks for meeting me, Aileen."

I grunted.

"No, really. I mean it. I know I haven't been easy these last few months, what with locking you out and then showing up out of nowhere." Her shoulders hunched, that same edginess she'd had in my apartment making another appearance. I took my hands out of my pocket, not wanting to get caught unaware if she flipped.

Not that it would do me much good. Both Brax and Liam had seemed certain that if she changed and attacked me, I would stand little chance. Her wolf was evidently much stronger than my vampire, and since neither would chance giving me a gun after last time, I would have to face her with nothing but my fists. Cheery prospect that.

"What happened?" I asked.

"I thought I could handle this by myself, and I can't." Her voice was raw and her eyes glassy as she admitted that. "It's just too big for me, and I don't have enough experience with the wolf. I need someone at my back."

"Let me bring in Brax, then. He can help with your wolf much better than I could," I pleaded.

"No, you can't do that," she snapped. "I don't know if he can be trusted. There are things going on here that you don't understand. His pack is part of it, and I'm not sure which of his wolves are compromised."

"Caroline."

"I said no." Her voice took on a deep timber, her eyes shifting and her wolf peering out at me. To my othersight, that wolf bared its fangs, power flicking around it uneasily.

"Okay, let's just stay calm." I held up my hands.

She took a deep breath, closing her eyes and visibly calming. The wolf beside her faded slightly until it was just a shadow clinging to her shoulders. Present, but not moments from ripping out my throat.

"I am trying to stay in control. It's like there're two Caroline's fighting for my body, and one of them is so very angry," she admitted, her voice desperate as she looked at me. "You bringing him up over and over, when you know I don't want to go back to that place, isn't helping matters," she said, her voice strained.

"You know I'm just trying to help. What did you mean about his wolves being compromised?" I asked, changing the subject and getting her mind off Brax.

She took a deep breath and shook herself, like a dog shaking off rain. It was a mannerism unlike Caroline, bringing home the point that this was my friend, but it wasn't, too.

"You know that project you had me work on earlier this year. The one that resulted in this?" She gestured to herself.

"Where you traced the Bennet lineage?" I asked. How could I forget? It was responsible for our current predicament.

"That wasn't just the descendants of just any random person, was it?" She stalked along the steel girder of the railroad tracks, her balance perfect as she moved back and forth, unable to stay still.

"No, it wasn't," I admitted.

"Who was it?"

"A vampire. A powerful one."

"And you got me got involved in that." The words were an accusation.

"Yes."

"It didn't occur to you the danger you were placing me in," Caroline's voice deepened, her wolf moving closer to the surface. Before, I'd only caught glimpses, flashes of it. Mostly its head, an impression of its body. Now, it was closer to fully formed, and it was big. Bigger than it should have been.

"I didn't think they'd go after you," I confessed.

"Well, they did," she snapped, her voice breaking. "Do you know what it's like to be trapped in your own body, unable to think or do anything but feel horror at what is happening to you?"

Yes. My words didn't leave my mouth as I stared at her with sorrow. Admitting such a thing wouldn't help and wasn't even important right now.

"I don't know how they learned about you," I said. "The only place we were together was that gala you dragged me to."

She stilled. "What do you mean?"

"The vampires were there. They were all over the place. It's why I put distance between us and then dragged you out. I hoped it would keep you off their radar. Guess I was wrong." I took a step closer. "I still don't know why they targeted you. It's not like I'm worth anything, and they couldn't have known about the research."

"They did," she admitted, her voice cold. "I don't know how, but they kept asking me about it. I should have left it alone after, but I didn't. I wanted to know why my life had been ripped apart, so I kept digging. That's when I found it."

"Found what?"

"His descendants are still alive, and they're right here in Columbus." Her face shone with victory.

"I don't understand how that's pertinent to what's happening," I said, wishing we'd been able to keep that little tidbit secret. With Liam and a half-dozen other vampires listening, this information was bound to get back to Thomas. How long before he tried to ruin other lives by turning them into little, baby vampires whether they wanted the change or not?

"It's the reason for everything," she said, her voice close to a growl. "I thought I could track down the why, maybe get some closure, but they're too smart. They keep covering the evidence."

"Caroline, I need you to stay calm," I said. She was close to losing it, her eyes taking on a wild gleam, her gestures frenetic.

"They almost caught me in the alley, but I got away," she said.

I stilled. "What alley? Where?"

"The one in German Village," she said.

I took a deep breath, the sensation almost painful. "What did you do when they almost caught you?"

I didn't want the answer, not really, but I couldn't stop myself from asking.

"What?" She seemed disinterested in the question, waving it away. "That's not important right now."

"Did you kill those people?" I asked, my voice brittle.

Her movements stopped, and she gave me a sidelong look, suspicion dawning. "Why are you asking that?"

"It's important," I said, my throat tight. "Did you kill those people?"

She stared at me for a long moment before twitching and shaking her head. "What? No?"

"You may not remember," I said, unable to let this go. "I'm told that your memories can get spotty near the full moon for the first few months."

"What are you talking about?" Her eyebrows furrowed in confusion.

"The people in the alley way. Did you kill them?"

"What? No. How could you think that?" She looked horrified at my accusation.

"Your scent was there, and when you called me you kept talking about blood," I said.

She threw up her hands. "Yes, I was there, but I didn't kill them. I arrived after they were already dead. The blood may have made my wolf a little excited, but I didn't murder them."

I fell quiet, thinking. Could she be telling the truth?

"How could you think that?" She appeared genuinely hurt that I thought she had killed them. "You know me. You know I'm not capable of that. For God's sake, I was a vegetarian until this whole werewolf thing happened."

"You were?" That was a new development.

"Yes!"

"Since when?" I just couldn't picture it. Caroline loved burgers.

"Since a year after you left," she said, her voice still outraged.

"That doesn't mean you didn't kill them," I said in a soft voice. I wanted to believe her, but she made it hard. She barely seemed in control. I could see her losing her temper and doing something she would regret later. Hell, I'd been in her shoes once upon a time, was still in her shoes on my worst days, if I wanted to be honest. Sometimes the only way I held on was through a wish and a prayer. Perhaps she hadn't had my luck.

"Come on, Aileen. You know me."

"I thought I did," I admitted. "I'm not so sure anymore."

She laughed. It was a bitter sound. "Then why are you here if you think I'm some homicidal wolf on a rampage?"

My throat locked down, and I was unable to think of a lie. The shame showed on my face, and I found it hard to meet her eyes.

"You didn't," she said, denial in her voice. Her eyes went over my shoulder. "Please tell me you didn't."

My voice was steady and seemed to come from far away as I straightened. "You need more help than I can provide. Look at you. Since we've been talking, you've almost lost your grip on the wolf twice. You're a danger to yourself and others."

She screamed, a long sound that turned into a howl. "I can't believe you. You're a hypocrite."

"Yeah," I admitted in a soft, defeated voice. "Feels like it right now, too."

Dark shapes swarmed across the ground, their movements a blur. Some were in their wolf form as they stalked along the bridge. Liam appeared at the other end, behind Caroline, cutting off her escape as Brax padded along the rail behind me.

Caroline snarled, falling into a defensive crouch as she looked between the two. Her eyes had taken on an amber sheen, and her fingers were tensed into claws.

"You're going to let them kill me," she accused, her eyes swung to mine.

"No one is going to kill you. They just want to help," I said.

"You don't know them. Brax will put me down if he thinks I've tasted human blood." Her voice was guttural.

My gaze turned towards him, a question in them. The grim look on his face did not allay my concerns.

"Stupid, Aileen. That was always your problem—acting first and then thinking of the consequences later." Caroline's voice filled with pain as her body twisted.

Within moments, a wolf stood in her place, the change faster than it should have been given her age. I took a step back, finally seeing why Brax and Sondra had been so convinced that Caroline was a danger. She was double the size of other wolves I'd seen, her head even with my shoulder and her fur shining white in the pale moonlight.

The wolf snarled, the sound dangerous, calling to the primal part of me. The one that recognized long ago that humans were not the top of the food chain. It was the part that originated from a time when our ancestors lived in caves. It sparked an immediate flight response.

"Caroline, calm down. They're not going to kill you. I made them promise," I said, backing away from the wolf whose head towered above mine.

"Aileen," Liam yelled, flying forward almost faster than my eyes could track. "Run."

I couldn't do that, struck with the sense that the moment I turned my back on her she'd rip my head from my shoulders. Not to say anything was stopping her from doing that now.

"Caroline." My voice rose in warning and fear.

Her paws inched forward, her head lowered in a hunting pose, her eyes tracking my every movement. Her nostrils flared, scenting the fear I couldn't stuff far enough inside. Another growl came, this one so low it was almost silent. Only the vibration of it felt, the sound of danger.

Caroline wasn't in those eyes. This was a predator. One that decided I had to go—whether that was because it was hungry, or saw me as a threat, I didn't know.

My eyes went to Liam, closing fast as he moved with a spook's speed to cover more ground than a human ever could. It still wasn't going to be enough. She was too close, and I was too slow.

"Caroline, no!" Brax roared from behind me, the alpha in his voice. Power flowed from him. The wolf's paws paused before she shook off its effects, advancing on me with that same stealthy creep.

Her muscles bunched. I threw myself to the side—her teeth closing on my arm instead of my neck. I screamed, a long, thin sound of pain as those teeth savaged my arm. They unlatched to close on my leg, her head shook hard once. There were twin roars, one a wolf's and the other the pissed off sound of a big cat crossed with a very angry bear.

Caroline released me, dropping me to the tracks and sprang backwards. Liam landed between us, fully vamped out. His fangs lowered as he hissed, his eyes glowing with that electric blue. Claws tipped each finger as he crouched in front of me. Brax's wolf barreled into hers, forcing her further back.

Pain savaged me, fire flaring up in my arm even as my leg went numb, the cold of a glacier's ice sheet inching up the limb. The two extremes competed with each other as I struggled up.

"Stay down, Aileen. You're bleeding out," Liam ordered, his voice otherworldly. He didn't turn to see if I obeyed. I did, but only because I was too weak to fight off the compulsion. I could see the veins of his power reaching out to me from him, soothing my worries and convincing me that he was right.

My eyes slid shut, and I slumped to the ground, my head bouncing off the steel track like a rag doll's. It was too much effort to get up anyway.

"Caroline," I whispered.

The wolf's ears swiveled forward as she looked my way. She made a hurt sound, almost a whimper and then she bounded over the side of the tracks. There was a splash below, followed by several more, as Brax's wolves followed her.

I pulled myself along the tracks until I could look over the edge, the effort stealing the last of my strength. Blood coated the wood and metal under me, drops of it falling to the water below. Down the river, I could just make out the ripple of water as a wolf paddled along, letting the current do most of the work. Several wolves trailed behind, falling farther behind as the bigger wolf widened the distance.

She was going to get away, and I didn't know if I was glad for that or upset by it.

Nathan was beside me before I could decide, rolling me over and distracting me from the sight of Caroline's retreat. "Aileen, stay with me." His hands busied themselves. Pain crashed through the numbing cold as he tightened his belt around my leg, creating a tourniquet. I screamed and tried to move away. He held me down, making sure the makeshift tourniquet was tied off before taking off his shirt and pressing it hard to my shoulder. The new pain was too much, and I blacked out for a moment.

"Liam, she needs you," Nathan shouted, his voice tight.

I opened my eyes as Nathan stared down at me, his face tight with worry. Impossible. The bite must be making me hallucinate. I thought I read that in the book. Werewolf bites could be toxic to vampires, especially baby ones who didn't have the sense to get out of the way in time. Nathan would never be that worried for me, not the pain in the ass yearling they got saddled with.

Liam's face appeared next to Nathan's, his eyes wild. "Aileen, stay with me."

I smiled. My face was numb, my body cold, so at least I hoped it was a smile. I didn't feel much of anything anymore.

"Get Brax," Liam ordered.

I might have imagined it, but his fingers felt gentle as they touched my face. "You, stupid girl. Why didn't you run?"

"Then the big, bad wolf would have bitten off my head," I said in a slurred voice. "I'm rather attached to it."

"You believe us now about how dangerous she is?" he asked, his mouth tight as he felt along my neck for my pulse. It struck me as odd. We had one; it was just significantly slower than a human's. Hm. I raised my head and looked at my thigh. Perhaps I'd already be dead if my pulse was stronger. Didn't the pulse have something to do with how fast you bled out?

Maybe. It was hard to think right now.

"She said she didn't do it." Why was it so hard to think? My eyes fluttered shut. Liam shook me. Hard. I couldn't bring myself to care.

Fire across my cheek. "Ow. What was that for?" I asked in a plaintive voice.

"You need to stay awake." His voice was urgent.

Something occurred to my foggy brain. "Why aren't I healing?" I raised my head. "Why aren't you healing me?"

"I've already tried. It's why you're not dead. Caroline's wolf's bite is more toxic than anything I've encountered. Brax may be able to help," Liam said. He looked up, his expression darkening. "Where is he?"

"He went in after the pup," Nathan said, sounding as angry as Liam looked.

"If she dies, I will take it out of his arrogant hide," Liam snarled.

"Not his fault," I said, my teeth chattering. My breath rasped out. Why was it so bloody cold? "Caroline should be the priority."

"Bullshit," Liam snapped. Ah, there was the autocratic dick I was used to. It was a comfort to know he was there in all this, like a horsehair blanket designed to abrade and keep you on your toes. "He should have seen to you while he sent his pack after her."

My laugh was a disjointed, broken thing. "Su-such a know-it-all."

The tracks vibrated under me as footsteps approached. Sondra ran up, her eyes full of the wild and her hair an untamed mess around her face.

"Where is your alpha?" Liam demanded, power in his voice.

The colors floated in front of me twining around me like loving cats before darting after Sondra. "Such pretty colors," I said in a quiet voice.

"He's gone after her," Sondra said, strain showing in her voice. I turned my face toward her, surprised that the loving cats had turned feral as they twined and nipped at her.

Her wolf flexed and fought under her skin, power rising in green waves as they tried to force Liam's strands away.

"That won't work," I said to myself. "They'll just slip in the cracks."

Liam's gaze turned to me, and I smiled sleepily up at him.

"We need him here. She'll die if the toxin is left unchecked," Nathan shouted. The argument between them faded into the background as the color in Liam's eyes grew until it was all I could see. He was my sole focus, the rest of the world unimportant.

"What pretty colors, Aileen?" he asked in a soft voice.

I blinked slowly, knowing there was a reason not to tell him but unable to remember why. I turned my head to look back at where Sondra was fighting unsuccessfully against Liam's power as it tightened its grip around her. "Them," I said with a soft smile.

So pretty.

I turned my eyes back to Liam, smiling up at the shapes that surrounded him. They smiled back at me. "They're all so pretty."

"Brax can't help her anyways. Caroline's bite is beyond his control." Sondra's voice came from a distance.

"Thomas has more raw power. He's like the sun, look at his power too long and you'll go blind," I confided. "Yours is a finely hewn blade, beautiful and deadly. Wielded with a surgeon's precision."

The magic that stemmed from his core reached out and touched mine gently, brushing against my skin much like a cat would the object of its affection. My magic arched up, twining around it before his pushed it back inside me with a gentle nudge.

"You can see magic." His voice was hushed and full of awe.

I made a lazy sound of agreement. I no longer felt the cold or my body, just a spreading contentment.

"Aileen, stay with me." He sounded desperate. I wondered why. "Aileen, you can save yourself. You can see where the wolf's bite has spread."

I struggled to lift my head, glancing down at myself for the first time. Liam's hands were gentle as he helped me raise up until I was half-sitting, his weight at my back supporting me. Oh yeah, he was right.

"I'm covered in oil," I said, surprise in my voice. With my othersight, I could see black splotches spreading over my body, smothering the slight flicker of magic that resided in me. The taint had already traveled to cover my entire arm and leg and was now spreading through my core.

I lifted a hand to touch a spot and pulled it away, turning it this way and that in fascination. The black didn't transfer, which I found even more interesting. I touched another spot and another, until I was rubbing at them with a single-minded fascination.

"They won't come out." My head fell back to look Liam in the eyes. "None of the black will come out. I think it's killing me."

Pieces of the black flickered with a burnt umber, making it look like someone had painted me with the colors of Halloween.

"If you can force it out, I should be able to heal you," Liam said, one hand coming up, his thumb brushing against my cheek. It felt good, and I closed my eyes to savor the feeling, one of the only things I could feel at the moment.

"Don't know how," I confessed.

"I'll teach you." His lips touched my forehead as he smoothed back my hair. "Do you remember the first time we met?"

My laugh was raw. "Yeah, you threw me into a kitchen island. Broke several of my ribs."

"And then I showed you how to heal yourself, right?"

That's right. It was the first time I'd realized that the healing could be focused.

"Have you been practicing?" he asked.

"Every now and then." More like every chance I could get. Mostly just small stuff like a cut on my hand, but I was a little better than I'd been when I first started.

"Do that now. Only this time instead of directing it inward, corral the taint and push it out."

I tried. I tried so hard, but the tendrils that rested at the core of my being refused to obey. "I can't. It's not working."

He rocked me back and forth. "No, no. You can. You can see what needs to be done. Just do it. I know you, you're more stubborn than this. Where's the woman who survived impossible odds to become a vampire? Where's the woman determined to make it on her own? Be that person. Beat this. Do it now."

169

Tears leaked out of my eyes as I turned my focus inward, my thoughts sluggish. My mental forest rose up around me, the one I'd first created to protect my thoughts from telepaths. It had begun sticking around even when I wasn't actively trying to guide against mental attacks. I was beginning to think it was the manifestation of my soul. A whimsical thought, I know, but it was comforting to think my soul was the shape of a forest. A place of peace and tranquility where nature could flourish.

That's how it was normally. Right now, there was the smell of rot in the air, and the trees around me looked sick. This was the reason I couldn't force the black ichor out. It hadn't just infected my body, but the heart of me as well.

My bare feet whispered across the land as I walked my forest, noting where the trees' roots were beginning to decay. I hadn't the first clue as to what was needed to fix this. This task seemed too big for me, too far along. Maybe if I'd had the thought sooner.

I came to the large oak in a clearing that I suspected resided in the center of all this. The oak had two visible wounds on it and was leaking the black oily substance that pervaded the rest of this place.

As if in a dream, I walked up to it and touched it, my fingers coming away covered in black sludge. I stood back and looked at the tree. Already leaves were falling as whatever this was drained the life from it.

I stepped close and put my hand on the tree again, closing my eyes and envisioning a bubble around the taint. My thoughts fought for purchase, wanting to run in all kinds of directions. Gradually though, I felt that bubble flicker into place, containing it. For the moment.

I had no idea what to do now. I couldn't stay here forever working to contain this thing. Eventually, I'd run out of energy. Already I could feel myself flagging. Not to mention staying here would be the equivalent of being in a waking coma.

Last time I was here, I used the power from Liam and Peter's marks to drive away the demon. Perhaps they could help me this time too. I reached for those strands only for them to slip out of my grasp time and time again, the effort exhausting me.

"Shit," I said, looking up at my tree.

The shadow of a wolf appeared at my side. It bared its fangs at me, and then attacked the dead spots on the tree, ripping pieces of it away. Pain flared, like someone was ripping pieces of me away.

I screamed and flung out my hands. The wolf flew back, hitting the ground with a yelp and disappearing.

I panted in the aftermath, my strength spent. Going back to the tree, I touched the damaged parts. They were smooth with no hint of the black ichor.

I glanced back at where the wolf had disappeared. So that's why. Made sense. Sometimes the only thing to do with rot is to cut it out at the source.

I turned back to the tree and attacked the weak spots, my hands forming claws as I yanked and pulled, scooping out the bad. This was a dream, with dream rules. It meant I was able to yank and carve out the wood of the tree, when in the real world, I would have needed a chainsaw or an ax. Perhaps Liam could have done it with his bare hands, but he'd had centuries to strengthen.

Pain bit and nipped at me as I worked. It was like someone was taking a dull spoon to my psyche and carving it up one small bite at a time. I screamed and worked faster. This would not defeat me. I would not go out like this.

I worked until I couldn't see anymore, until the tree's sap flowed free of the black. Then I collapsed face down on the dirt, the world around me turning dark.

CHAPTER SEVENTEEN

WATER SURROUNDED ME when I opened my eyes. It was dark, the gloom unrelenting. I opened my mouth and choked as the liquid ran into it. I thrashed, fear of drowning swamping me, my hands beating at the sides of the metal coffin I found myself in. For a long moment, I thought they'd buried me, thinking I was already dead.

I screamed, and did my best to pound on the lid, trying to force it up. It resisted before sliding away. I exploded from the water, dragging in a deep breath as soon as I was out.

Panting, I clawed at the gunk covering my eyes, wiping them clear as best I could. My hands were red, and I looked down at the water I sat in. It was black with a ruby tinge. Blood. They'd put me in a coffin and submerged me in blood.

My gorge rose.

"Don't you dare throw up any of it," Nathan ordered from the corner of the room.

I swallowed back the vomit, my chest heaving as I tried very hard not to think about what coated my body. I might have been a vampire, but I still had a human's squeamishness. Not many people I knew would welcome the idea of bathing in someone's blood. At least no one out of the Romanian dark ages. There was a countess around then who liked bathing in young virgins' blood, thinking it would keep her young; I had no such illusions.

"Why am I sitting in blood?" I managed to get out through the panic threatening to steal my voice. There was no way all of this had come from just one person. The average human body only holds about 1.2-1.5 gallons of blood. There had to be several gallons in this thing.

"The bite was pretty brutal. You almost died. Thomas and Liam thought this was the best way to make sure you didn't," he said.

"And how many people did they kill to ensure that?" I asked.

His lips twisted. "None. It's all vampire blood. Your conscience can rest easy."

"Vampire blood?"

"Best thing for healing. Full of power and restorative properties. You should feel honored. I don't remember the last time they opened a vein for someone."

I looked down at the blood cradling my lower half. "This is too much to have come from just the two of them."

Nathan held out his hand. I grasped it and let him help me out of the metal coffin. My legs wobbled under me, and I would have fallen if Nathan hadn't caught me, uncaring as the blood stained his clothes.

"You underestimate a master vampire's healing ability. They both had to top up on human blood a few times, but they were able to fill the tub with just the two of them," he said as he helped me over to a chair.

"What happened?" I asked.

He tilted his head as he looked at me. "How much do you remember?"

I glanced away, one hand going to my leg. It was healed, the skin smooth through the torn jeans. "Caroline biting me." And then escaping. "Did they catch her?" I was afraid of the answer.

"No, she got away."

I nodded. I remembered her swimming away, her larger size giving her an advantage over the smaller wolves trying to catch her.

"She seems to be one of a kind," Nathan said, sounding unhappy about that.

"What do you mean?" I asked.

"The alpha forgot to mention that her bite can be highly toxic to anyone. Something about the demon taint affecting things again. It's why Brax was unsuccessful when he tried to pull out the toxin, and why Liam couldn't heal you when you were injured."

I blinked. "Wait, didn't she attack that woman, Lisa, I think her name was?"

"Yeah, her bite hadn't fully developed yet." He leaned against the wall.

He watched me with enigmatic eyes as I tried not to touch anything on me. I'd never been a fan of dirt, and blood was even worse. It covered every inch of me, and I knew if I licked my lips I'd taste it. Tempting as it was to experience the high their blood would no doubt give me, I needed to be clearheaded.

"Where are Liam and Thomas now?" I asked.

"Giving the alpha the third degree. They're not exactly happy about how things turned out," he said in a sardonic voice.

"It's not his fault," I said in a quiet voice.

Nathan snorted. "He withheld valuable intelligence about the danger she posed. If you hadn't been hurt, it could have been one of us. Not to mention she killed the companions."

"She said she didn't," I said. "She got there after they were already dead."

"And you believed her? After this? She almost killed you. She damn near ripped off that leg. Do you have any idea how long it would take you to regenerate that? Decades."

I was silent a long moment. All that was true.

"She's dangerous, Aileen. She can't be allowed to roam the city unchecked. I'm not even sure at this point if Thomas will allow her to live. Demon taint is very serious, and a wolf that can kill with its bite alone is a weapon he won't allow his enemies to have." Nathan straightened. "You should prepare yourself for the worst."

I stared up at him, unable to respond.

His shoulders bunched before he relaxed. "Come on. You should get a shower and clean up. You look like a murder victim right now."

"More like Carrie at the prom," I said.

He chuckled. "You're right. Only you don't have the cool powers."

True. Baby vampires were notoriously weak when it came to raw power. It'd be a century or more before I became any kind of player.

I let him lead me to a shower that was thankfully part of the same suite I'd found myself I in, since it meant I didn't have to walk around the mansion letting everyone stare at me. Even for a vampire stronghold, I would present quite the sight. He left me alone in the large space, with a shower as nice as the one in my room. What did they do—design every shower in this place with a hedonist in mind?

I discarded my ruined clothes on the bathroom floor and stepped under the warm water, letting it rinse the blood off me. I didn't let myself linger, even though I felt fragile after my brush with death—the closest I'd come in a very long time—since my turn in fact. There wasn't enough hot water in the world to wash that experience off.

I didn't have the luxury of indulging my weaknesses either. Caroline's life depended on me finding a solution to the problems facing us.

Despite her attack on me, I believed her when she said she didn't kill those people. Call me crazy or naive, but I know she would either have told me the truth or not remembered it at all. Even if it was a lie, I owed it to our friendship to verify it.

Her talk of Thomas's descendants had gotten me thinking.

I stepped out of the shower, having scrubbed myself clean three times over, and wrapped myself in a big, fluffy towel—the kind you find in really high-end hotels. Clothes had been folded and left for me on the toilet. I wasted no time in getting dressed.

Nathan waited for me on a sofa in the next room. One wouldn't guess he was a century-old vampire from the way he watched his cell phone. He would fit right in with people my age who never seemed to lift their faces from their smart phones anymore.

Hearing me, he clicked a button and stuffed the phone in his pocket. "Liam wants you to stay here for now. He'll be down once he's done."

"I have a better idea. Why don't you take me to see the rooms of the companions who died?" I suggested.

He hesitated, the request unexpected.

"Look, you're all convinced she's the murderer. It won't hurt to let me take a look at their things." I shrugged. "If I find nothing, I find nothing. Maybe it'll even help me process this shit."

He frowned in consideration and studied me, looking for an angle. I kept my expression expectant without trying to seem impatient. There wasn't an angle. I really did just want to look around.

"Fine, but you don't go anywhere but those rooms, and you don't try anything like escaping to go find the mad wolf." He pointed his finger at me.

"Deal."

He sighed and looked up at me. "I have a feeling I'm going to regret this."

"Only if I'm right."

He shook his head.

*

Catherine's room looked like a unicorn had thrown up in it. It was a frilly, pink, purple, and blue mess. Not exactly a room I pictured a companion occupying.

"This was her room?" I asked in a skeptical voice. It looked more like a preteen's.

The bed was wood carved with four posts that she'd hung gauzy sheets from. The coverlet was white, and there were pink and blue pillows at the head of the bed. It was a princess bed—the kind that featured in many a young girls' fantasies growing up.

She had a makeup table, one covered in various shades of eyeshadow, lipstick and nail polish. There were also stuffed animals all over the place.

Nathan looked around and nodded. "Yeah, this is hers. Anton always complained about feeling out of place every time he visited her here."

"What was their relationship like?" I asked, curious. He had seemed to have a great deal of feeling for her, but that could also have been the shock of her death.

"Fraught with tension." Nathan circled the room in the other direction.

"Really?"

"Yeah, they were a bad match. We all knew it, but nobody interferes with companions."

"The vamp code?" I asked with a sly smile.

He snorted. "Something like that. Anton's never been one to be tied down to one person. She was his companion, but he also had others. She was the jealous sort. It created a lot of tension."

"I thought it was an exclusive relationship," I said.

"It's exclusive one way. The vampire partner doesn't have the same restrictions. Some vampires see humans as little more than pets. You can feel affection for your pet, but they often won't let themselves feel more." He eyed a picture of a young Catherine with her friends in a pink, glittery frame with a hint of distaste.

"Sounds charming," I said, my voice sarcastic.

"Hm. Yeah. When you live as long as we do, it grows wearying to watch people die. After a while, it just doesn't seem worth the effort to get close only to have their light blink out in a flicker of a moment," he said. There was a hint of sadness in his voice, lingering behind his eyes that made me think the observation was a personal one. "Most of our families have long since died. A few of us track our descendants, check in on them from time to time. Even that becomes difficult after a while."

"Sounds like a lonely existence." One I would share in a few decades. It was something I tried not to think about. What would this world be like without my parents in it? My sister? My niece? How would I bear it when every person I'd known had gone into death's embrace? It was enough to keep me up at night, which was why I tried to live in the moment. If I was lucky, I wouldn't share that fate for several decades.

"It is. Why do you think Liam has been so insistent you cut ties?" he asked, spearing me with a hard glance. "The longer you hold on, the harder it will be when they go. We've all experienced it."

"You gave up possibly decades of knowing your family to spare yourself a little pain?" I asked.

"I know we seem cold to you," Nathan said, the humor that was normally in his voice absent. "It's not true. We experience things more deeply, more vividly. The deeper the connection, the greater the possibility of insanity when that connection is cut."

I looked away from his piercing eyes. I was willing to take the chance. You didn't walk away just because you knew it was going to hurt someday. As a human, I knew my days could be cut short at any moment. That's why you had to live to the fullest, because one day there wouldn't be any more sunrises and you'd be left staring into the dark wondering if you did everything you could to enjoy the short time you had. I think these vampires had forgotten that. Maybe I would too, eventually. Maybe they were right, and I was courting insanity by clinging to my human family. Some risks were worth taking.

I stepped close to her makeup table and started riffling through the drawers.

"What are you doing?"

"Person like this, I'm betting she had a diary of some kind." It would fit with the woman who had put her stamp on this room.

I opened the last drawer and felt around it, coming up with nothing. Reaching further into the space, I patted along the back and felt along the top. My fingers brushed against a hard ridge. There was something there—something taped against the wood. I pulled it free and stood up.

A journal, a little bigger than my hand, rested in my hands. It had yellow stars on the front and one of those key latches.

I opened it, flipping to the last couple of entries. If there was anything useful in here, it would be towards the end.

He visited me again last night. I worry sometimes that we're letting our feelings get in the way of what's important. Once we have the kiss, there will be no reason to sneak around. He keeps saying it won't be long now, that he has a plan. I hope so. This charade is becoming tiring.

Two days later, there was another entry.

He's asked me to lie for him. I couldn't deny him, even as my doubts are creeping in. What if my patron finds out? What if the rest of the enforcers are onto us? I don't like how the head enforcer, Liam, questioned me—like he knew I was lying.

This started as a game, but now it's so much more. I don't know what I would do if I lost him, even as I realize my patron would turn me out if he figures out I've been sneaking around behind his back. I must have faith in my love and his promises of eternal life, but sometimes I fear he's lost sight of that in the desire to punish the bitch who continually rejects the gift she's been given.

I was guessing I was the bitch in that entry.
A few pages later.

We've found a way to hurt her. It's the perfect plan, and after we'll take her place in eternity. We're going out again tonight, and this time I won't lose courage at the last minute.

The last entry was dated the night she died. Guess we all knew how that ended. I sat down on the bed and looked around. The journal had been helpful in confirming my suspicion there was more to her and Theo's death than was immediately evident. But, I still didn't have the full picture.

For starters, who was this 'he' she wrote of? Theo? He was dead too, so if he was a part of this, it was only as a bit player. Someone else was pulling her strings. I needed to find out who.

"Let's head to Theo's room," I said, closing the journal and standing with it.

His room was one floor down in the section Nathan told me belonged to the male companions. The two genders were separated by floor. Those who served high-ranking vampires had bigger rooms on one end of the hallway versus those whose vampires had a lower rank.

Hierarchy even here. Why was I not surprised?

"This should be Theo's room," Nathan said.

I didn't question him as I followed him into the dark room. Nathan flicked on the light to quarters that were as different from the one upstairs as a butterfly was to a hawk. Both flew but the manner in which they traveled was night and day.

Theo's room was done in neutral colors, his furniture strong blocky pieces. It was a nice room and utterly devoid of personality—nothing on the walls and no items around the room pointing to who he was as a person, nothing that said what kind of life he led. It was as impersonal as a guest room or something found in a hotel—a pretty picture but almost sterile in its beauty.

I walked around the space, looking everything over carefully. When I completed the circuit, I could have told you no more about the occupant's personality than before exploring, besides the fact that he liked brown. Maybe. Or perhaps he'd picked that color because of how neutral it was. The room wasn't overly masculine.

I opened an old, wooden armoire, the only thing in the room that seemed out of place. It was empty. Of course, it was. I closed the doors and frowned.

"Does this place seem weird to you?" I asked, not sure if it was just my imagination.

"What do you mean?" Nathan set down a coffee coaster he'd picked up.

"There aren't any personal items."

Nathan shrugged. "There're books."

"Every one of them old or a dictionary. No thrillers or mysteries or sci-fi. Just leather-bound books. Nobody reads that kind of stuff. They're the books you pick up in antique shops so you can stage your public bookshelves so people think you're worldly and smart." I knew this because my mother did it. She staged the shelves with old-looking books and items she'd collected through years of life. My father and sister had always teased her about it.

"Perhaps he just likes old books." Nathan drifted over to the bookshelf in question.

Maybe. It still seemed weird.

This place felt like a dead end. I settled on the bed, staring around the room.

"Are you done now?" Nathan asked.

I didn't answer. Perhaps it had been arrogant to think I could find a clue when I was sure the vampires had examined these rooms as well.

My eyes fell on the floor before the armoire. There were scuff marks on the wood, as if the heavy piece of furniture had been dragged into place. I got off the bed and bent in front of the piece, touching the floor gently. It looked like only one of the legs had left a mark, probably because the felt under it had worn down. The rest of the legs were protected against scratching the floor.

"I think I found something," I said.

"What?" Nathan asked from the door.

I didn't answer, too busy moving the armoire. With my increased strength, it was easy to shift the piece of furniture out of the way to reveal the wall behind it, covered in paper and notes and photos.

"What's that?" Nathan asked from the other side of the room.

I shook my head. "I don't know."

I stepped closer to the wall and the papers the armoire had hidden. Smart of Theo to use the furniture to cover whatever this was. Smarter than most. It's easy to find things stuffed in books or furniture—but behind it? Few people think to check there. I certainly wouldn't have. Not without the markings on the floor as a hint.

Nathan examined the papers next to me, a frown on his face. "Why would he want to hide this?"

"That is the question," I said.

"It's a list of names and places." He pointed to one of the photocopies. "This looks like the type of thing found in old family bibles. I remember my father recording births and deaths in ours. This looks like the same thing."

I pulled that piece of paper off the wall, looking closely at the names. "I recognize some of these."

"From where?"

"From when I was researching Thomas's descendants. These names are the same."

"Are you sure?" he asked.

"Yeah. I mean, a few are new, but Thomas, Martha and Elijah Bennet—all of these names popped up in my research." I looked up from the paper and gazed at the rest of the documents. "Why would Theo have all this?"

"Maybe he planned on helping Thomas find his descendants." Nathan sounded just as troubled at this revelation as I was.

"How would he have known about Thomas's curse and its fix?" I asked.

"It's no big secret. Most of us realized something was wrong. You don't become a vampire of Thomas's power and standing and not have yearlings to shore up your power base. Maybe he talked to a witch and came up with a solution in the hopes that Thomas would offer him the kiss," Nathan proposed, not sounding entirely convinced of his reasoning.

"He wanted to be a vampire?" I asked.

Nathan rolled his eyes. "They all want to be vampires. They enjoy the pleasure of the bite and the perks of our lifestyle, but make no mistake, they're here for their chance at the kiss."

"I thought one of the perks of being your companion was an extended life."

"Extended, not eternal—or as close to one as a human is going to get. Not to mention a companion is always a second-class citizen, even under the most attentive of masters." He looked over at me with a quirked eyebrow. "How many of your generation are satisfied with such a classification?"

Fair enough.

"Wait, hold on. Baby vampires have as little power or status as companions." And do for a long time from what I can gather. "Why would they sign up for that?"

"I doubt they realize that. All they see are the big players and think they can be that after the change."

"Even if it means their death?" I asked, because that was the most likely outcome given how much difficulty the vamps had in turning one of their yearlings.

"They all think they're the ones to beat the odds," Nathan said. "They're actually kind of vicious competing for the slots. Anything goes."

"Their masters don't stop it?" I asked.

Nathan lifted one shoulder. "No reason to and many believe you need a certain level of grit to survive the change."

I pulled a face before turning back to the wall. The companion relationship sounded kind of depressing—for both parties. Not exactly what they'd tried to sell me when I first turned up in the mansion.

A pair of names near the bottom caught my eye. They were half-hidden behind another page. I bent and pulled both pieces off the wall.

"Are you sure you should be doing that?" Nathan asked.

"What makes you say that?"

"I don't know. Maybe there was a rhyme and reason to the way he had this arranged." Nathan moved one hand in a circle encompassing all the chaos.

I looked back at the wall. He had a point, but I didn't understand the method to Theo's madness. That made all this organization pointless. Might as well look at it in a way that made sense to me.

I turned my attention back to the two pieces of paper I held, one a drawing of some type of sigil. The other two names with photos under them.

"That's Theo," Nathan said, pointing at the photo on the left. He was right. Theo was younger, his eyes almost feral and his hair a different color, but it was definitely him.

"And this is Lisa," I said in a soft voice, looking at the photo on the right. Again, it was a younger version with different hair and a fierce expression at odds with the cheery bubble-head I'd interviewed earlier, but it was her. "Her name's different here."

Alissa Benedict. Theo's last name on this was the same. Looking closer, the two seemed to share a resemblance. It was there around the eyes and mouth. Sister and brother, maybe? Cousins?

"I think they're related," I said. The wall held Thomas's descendants. The upper half paralleled my own research as far as I'd been able to track them. That must mean the lower half contained the missing link—the one Caroline said she'd found shortly before her abduction. It made sense that they would change their last name Bennet to Benedict if they thought someone was hunting them.

I looked back down at the papers in my hand. "That would mean these are Thomas's descendants. Caroline said they were in Columbus."

What sort of coincidence would have led Theo here right under Thomas's nose when he most needed him? Too big of one. There was more to this.

There was a thump next to me as Nathan slumped to the floor, blood flowing out from a wound on his back. Theo stood over his body, his head tilted and a sinister smile on his face. "Good job. You put it all together. I'd say congratulations were in order."

I took a step back. How? What? Dead man walking. Why did these things always happen to me?

I started to shout for help. He raised his hand, an unrecognizable object in it. Black flooded out then I dropped to the ground too.

CHAPTER EIGHTEEN

MY SHOULDERS SENT lancing pain through my body, my hands suspended overhead, and my feet barely brushing a dirt floor. I jerked, coming awake with a start. I was in a barn or maybe a shed. Dim light filtered in from the outside. It was quiet—the kind of quiet that said I was far from civilization.

Caught and strung up like a deer carcass. My head pounded from whatever he'd used to make me unconscious. "This is really becoming an unwelcome habit," I muttered.

"You often wake up in the secret lairs of your enemies?" Caroline asked in a tired voice from a few feet away.

I craned my neck, twisting so I could look over my shoulder at her, surprised to find someone else sharing the murder shack with me. A thin, ragged-looking Caroline glared back, a worn and weary expression on her face. Locked in a cage just big enough that she could sit upright, but not stand, she looked like she'd gone a few days without sleep or a bath. She was curled in a ball, her naked limbs wrapped around herself, protecting her modesty.

"What're you doing here?" I asked.

She made a small noise of disbelief. "Same as you I'd imagine. Our lovely hosts captured me, stuffed me in this cage, then showed up with you half an hour ago."

My shoulder throbbed where she'd bitten me as if the wound knew its maker was near. "How did they get you? Theo's human, and last I saw, you were more than a match for any human."

Caroline's laugh was raw and tired sounding. "You'd think so. Werewolves tend to fall unconscious after a shift—even demon-tainted ones. He knew where to look. I never had a chance. Next thing I knew, I woke up naked in this cage."

I nodded. I supposed it made sense. Expending that much energy on shifting every muscle, bone and fiber in your body would put anyone in need of a little nap.

"Did he hurt you?"

My body tensed for the answer. There wasn't much I could do right now if he had. It would have been better to leave such things until after we'd escaped, but I had to know.

She shook her head. "No, he's mostly stayed away except when he brought you in."

My muscles relaxed as I counted one piece of good news in this. It occurred to me she might be lying, but if she was, it was something we would have to deal with once we were safe.

Caroline slid me a sidelong look through the bars of her cage. "Sorry about the shoulder and leg, by the way."

I nodded again. There really wasn't much to say to that. She'd almost killed me — but she hadn't. I don't think harming me had been her intent either. Unfortunately, apologies weren't a one-size-fit-all band aid. Even if I could accept it, I doubted Brax or the vampires would.

"I did try to turn you into the wolves," I said.

She laughed, the sound closer to the real thing. "Yeah, you did. Did you really think I killed those people?"

I grimaced. It was all I could manage hanging from the ceiling, my hands numb and my shoulders protesting their abuse. "They had very convincing evidence. Your scent. The demon taint on the bodies. Then there was the fact you almost killed me."

"Still."

"Yeah," I said in a soft voice. "Still."

We were silent for a long moment, giving me time to look around. I revised my earlier opinion of the space. This was definitely a shack or maybe a shed. Not that I knew the difference between the two. It had been stripped of anything that could be used as a weapon or tool to escape. Smart. Doubly smart when you considered the likelihood of either of us getting free of our bonds.

The shack smelled musty and damp, and the faint sound of furtive movements convinced me we had company of the rodent variety. A cat would take care of that. I craned my head back, looking up at the wooden beams above me, noticing the holes in the ceiling that let in the first rays of the morning sun.

Great. I was strung up in what looked like a serial killer's hideout, and the sun was coming up. Just what I needed.

I twisted my hands, trying to pull them loose or at least ease the strain in my arms. No such luck. Worse, I was pretty sure the stinging in my wrists was from silver, making my predicament that much more painful.

"Can you break your cage?" I asked, trying to distract myself from the discomfort.

"I tried already," Caroline said from where she huddled in the corner of it, careful not to let any more of her skin than necessary brush against the wires. "This thing is silver; even attacking it in my werewolf form didn't do anything."

I looked over at her, noticing the way she was crouched and the barely veiled pain in her eyes. "All of it?"

183

Caroline's grim look was all the answer I needed. If the bottom was silver as well, it meant her naked skin was lying unprotected against what was essentially poison to both of our kinds.

"Shit." I yanked hard on my arms, growling when my shoulders screamed in protest before giving up for the moment.

"Such a way with words," Caroline said in a dry voice. She made a soft sound of pain as she shifted, and a new patch of skin came into contact with the silver.

"We're going to get out of this," I said, trying to project conviction in my voice.

"Are you trying to convince me or yourself?" she asked.

"This isn't the first time I've been locked up awaiting death," I said.

"Oh? And how did you get out last time?"

I grimaced. "I didn't really. That came later."

She aimed a dour look my way. "Not helpful, Aileen."

I gave her a jaunty smile, or as jaunty as I could manage in these circumstances. I didn't want to be a downer, but our situation was not good. Even for me.

To my othersight, my chains as well as Caroline's cage had a slight aura to them—one that made me think it was more than silver keeping us here. Talk about overkill. Silver by itself would have been more than enough to keep both of us put. Some type of spell on top of that? Our odds just kept getting worse and worse.

Still, I couldn't let her give up hope. I'd been in bad situations before, and I knew that you had to stay in the right frame of mind. You never knew when the slimmest of chances to escape might come along. You had to be ready to take advantage, and that meant keeping your wits about you and staying determined.

"I thought the military trained you guys for situations like this," she said with a baleful look.

"They mostly teach how to evade capture, or techniques to hold up under interrogation. Either way, I never went to the SERE course so I'm fresh out of ideas." SERE stood for Survival, Evasion, Resistance and Escape. It was the course the military sent its badasses to and involved a no-holds-barred training regimen designed to prepare soldiers for the possibility of capture. The program was pretty brutal from what I'd heard, so I'd never volunteered to attend. There were just some things in life I never wanted to survive. That was one of them. "Somehow, I don't think name, rank and social security number is going to help us right now."

That got me a sound of grim amusement from Caroline. It felt like a win, even as worry grew inside at her state. She was pale and sweat gleamed on her forehead as the ball she'd huddled into tightened.

"Do you know why they're doing this?" I asked.

She opened her eyes and looked at me. "No, but I know they've been planning this for a long time. They're the descendants you asked me to track down."

"I figured that part out," I said. "I mean, they should be on our side. Not working to kill us."

She shrugged. "You know as much as I do."

There was a creak as the door in front of me opened and the dim rays of the morning sun filtered through. I blinked against the bright light, feeling that familiar lassitude invade my limbs. Thanks to the blood bath Liam had forced on me, I wasn't in any danger of falling asleep. Yet.

A familiar face peered in disgust at me from the door. Lisa looked pissed to see me awake and hanging from the ceiling. "You've got to be fucking kidding me," she spat.

She stalked into the shack, her gaze going from me to Caroline. A growl came from Caroline's cage and my friend was suddenly crouched, her body poised to spring at Lisa.

"Shut it, kujo," Lisa snarled.

"My, my, I had no idea you were so involved in this," I said, turning her attention to me. That was a lie. An inkling had begun forming when I'd seen her photo on Theo's wall. There were also the bodies in the alley. Theo was human. There was no way he could have done that to Catherine and the other. That left Lisa. I suppose it was possible there was another werewolf involved in this, but I doubted it. Often the simplest explanation fit.

Her glare turned my way, and she paced closer to me. "You have no idea what you're talking about."

"What is Brax going to do when he realizes your role in all this?" I asked.

"He'll rip her spine out," Caroline said before Lisa could, her voice close to a growl. "He dislikes traitors."

"And you working to frame Caroline could be constituted as betrayal," I said as if just realizing the truth.

"That's not what happened," Lisa said.

"I don't think Brax is going to believe that. Do you, Caroline?" I said.

The amused noise Caroline made sounded odd coming from a throat half transformed to that of a wolf. It was a thing out of nightmares, your darkest fears given voice. "Not a chance in hell."

"Ah, well, it's been nice knowing you," I told Lisa with fake sympathy.

"There's no way he's going to find out," Lisa said, her voice defensive. I kept my inner smile to myself, seeing the chink in her walls.

"Isn't he, though?" I asked. "He's a very bright man. I'm sure your photo on Theo's descendant wall is going to be a very big clue, and when Nathan wakes up to identify Theo as his attacker, that'll be another glaring arrow pointing right at you."

"Your enforcer friend is dead," she snarled.

I kept my worry to myself, not letting her see how her words affected me. I prayed he survived. As many personal issues as I had with the vampires, I wouldn't wish most of them harm. Nathan, especially. He'd grown on me over the past few days—kind of like fungus.

"Are you sure?" I asked, sowing the seeds of doubt. "Do you really think your human could kill a vampire? We're pretty hardy, you know. Hell, I've survived a hole in the stomach and kept going, and he's way older than me. It'd take a lot to put him down."

Her mouth tightened, letting me know I'd scored. Good. Let her think on that. I wasn't bluffing either. I had no idea how much a vampire of Nathan's age could take, but I was banking that Theo's little magic charm didn't have enough juice to kill him.

Before she could respond, Theo appeared behind her. "What are you doing here?" She whirled. "You! What is this?"

She waved at Caroline and me. Theo's face tightened as his eyes went to the two of us. He strode in, grabbing his sister's arm and yanking her out.

"We talked about this. You're supposed to keep your distance and let me know if the wolves make any suspicious moves."

"That was before you kidnapped the vampire's bitch. They're involved now and Brax is beginning to ask questions." She lowered her voice. "Dangerous questions."

"I don't care," Theo snapped, sounding nothing like the well-mannered man I'd met in the mansion. "He's your problem. Your presence here could jeopardize everything. Go home."

She yanked out of his grip and spun on him, the skin on her face rippling as if the beast inside was fighting to get free. "We're not done talking about this."

He made a frustrated sound. "Fine, but not here."

She jerked her shoulder and preceded him out of the shack. Theo paused before following her, his face turning slightly towards me. "I'll deal with you later."

I bared my fangs at him. "I look forward to it."

He made a derisive sound of amusement, walking over to the wall where there was a switch. He gave me a smile before flipping it. I jerked and screamed as pain darted down my arms, my feet dancing across the bare dirt in a painful arc.

Caroline shouted at him to stop, throwing herself against her cage again and again.

He watched us with a nasty little smile before he flipped the switch again. My unwilling jerking came to a stop, and I stilled, an agonized moan escaping me.

"Next time you back-talk, I'll leave this on while I attend to my business," he told me.

I didn't have time to answer, my breathing painful as I struggled to gain my strength back. He sauntered to the door, pulling it shut behind him. My ears picked up the faint rattling of the chain as he locked the padlock.

"Aileen, are you okay? Aileen?" Caroline's voice rose in panic as I failed to answer.

I managed to say, "I'm fine." My head sagged forward. What was that? Electricity? Whatever it was had made itself felt. My nerves still fired with remembered pain.

"You're not fine," she snapped.

"I'm close enough," I told her, forcing my head back up. She needed me to be strong. I could at least pretend at it to keep her calm.

She sat back and let out a breath of relief, my response having convinced her I wasn't about to kick the bucket right then and there. "We need to get out of here."

"I know. I'm working on it," I assured her.

"No, you don't." She looked at me directly, desperation on her face. The wolf so close to the surface that it felt like there were two beings present in one body. To my other sight, I saw the burnt umber and black that I associated with the wolf flickering around her body like a halo. "Tonight's the full moon. If we're not out of here by then, I won't be able to control myself during the change."

I stilled, memories of the last time her wolf had attacked me rising in my mind. Fear coated my tongue and it took effort to control my breathing. If it was that close to a full moon, she didn't need my panic contributing to her lack of control.

"We're going to get out of here," I promised. Hopefully, before her wolf ate me.

"I hope you're right," she said, leaning her head against her drawn up knees. "Otherwise, I very much fear you're going to have to kill me."

I felt an instant denial form—one that originated from the very core of who I was. In no realm or timeline, not even a parallel one with an evil version of myself, would I ever consider such an act. "That's not happening."

"It will if you have even an ounce of caring left for me," she said. "If I turn, I won't be me. I'll be a monster intent on your flesh. If that's the case, the kindest thing you can do for me is put me out of my misery."

"It's not going to come to that," I said. "We're going to get out of here."

She didn't respond, her silence letting me know just how hopeless she felt.

We were each quiet, consumed by our thoughts as the day deepened and the morning wore on. I fought sleep with every ounce of my being, drawing on the strength of Liam and Thomas's blood to stay awake. Knowing what tonight might bring, I didn't want to chance falling unconscious, knowing the next time I woke might be to the jaws of Caroline's wolf ripping out my throat. So good to know my fate once again would be decided based on my susceptibility to the sun.

Before long, the shack door opened to reveal Theo. He strolled inside, his face fixed in that affable geniality that had fooled me before. He didn't look like a murderer or a back-stabbing bastard. He appeared to be a regular guy—perhaps a little bland-looking and definitely too nice for his own good. Too bad this nice guy happened to have kidnapped two women and was planning their grisly deaths.

"Have to tell you, I expected you to be out for the day already," Theo said, coming to a stop in front of me. "I'll talk to that charm-maker. She promised that it would keep a vampire of your strength out for an extended period."

A charm. That must be how he got into the Gargoyle with all its protections. I was betting he had more than one—each tailored for a specific purpose. It must have been how he got so close without either Nathan or me knowing.

"Perhaps they'll give you a refund," I said.

He stared at me for a moment, his lips twisted in wry humor. An emotion not reflected in his eyes, which were cold and unfeeling. "What did I tell you about back-talk?"

He moved to the switch, looking at me as if he expected me to protest or beg. I stared back, blank faced. He made a sound of humor and then flicked the switch. I screamed as my back bowed, my muscles seizing so hard I thought I might be in danger of breaking something. The pain stopped, leaving me panting.

When I got myself under control it was to the sight of Theo, only steps from me as he watched in fascination. "It's my own design," he said. "Tailored for spooks. A blend of magic and human ingenuity. You see, electricity, by itself, hurts but is fleeting. Pair it with a little magic, and it creates something beautiful."

I didn't answer, meeting his gaze with determined eyes as I forced down the pain. Runners will tell you it's mind over matter—that you can do anything, endure anything. That's bullshit. Everyone has a breaking point. Everyone. The trick to dealing with pain isn't ignoring it. It's embracing it, letting yourself feel it in its entirety, while knowing all things are fleeting. It allowed me to focus on something else—something greater. Currently, that something was what I planned to do to Theo when I got loose. Hint—it wasn't going to be pretty.

"Thought you were dead," I said. "Whose body did we find with Catherine?"

He straightened, giving me a sardonic look as if it amused him that I wasn't a whimpering, gibbering mess. "Pierce. It wasn't hard to convince Catherine to bring him along. He always had a thing for her and thought he could play protector and perhaps earn some points with his patron."

"Did she know what you had planned for her?" I asked, struggling to stay present.

I hadn't liked Pierce the one time I met him. He struck me as arrogant and full of himself, but he hadn't deserved what Theo had done to him. I could only hope his death was quick, and he hadn't been conscious for long, given how much damage had been done to him.

He lifted one shoulder. "She should have—I made it clear on more than one occasion how pathetic I found her—but I doubt it. She was too easy to seduce. It was almost a joy to watch the shock and betrayal in her eyes when she realized what was happening."

"Why are you doing this?" I asked. "You must know you won't get away with it. Liam is having the DNA from Pierce's body run against yours. They're going to figure out you weren't the victim. What are you going to do then?"

DNA testing, unlike on TV, took weeks. They might eventually figure out it wasn't Theo in that alley, but it would take time. Time, I didn't have.

"Yes, but by then you'll be dead, killed by your friend. Such a tragedy that," Theo said with a fake sad face. "And Theo will pop back up telling a story of how he ran and hid after being wounded." He walked back over to the switch. "Best part about this is that it will come out that I'm his descendant, his one ticket to a yearling now that you're dead."

"That's what this is about? Becoming a vampire?" Caroline asked, her voice disgusted.

I echoed the sentiment. He had to be kidding.

He paused, looking over at her and cocking his head as if he'd forgotten she was there. His hand moved to a different switch. Caroline screamed, the sound of an animal in pain. I jerked at my restraints as I watched her writhe, biting my tongue against any protests. If he knew watching her being tortured hurt more than anything he did to me, he would make sure to use her the next time he felt the need to make a point.

So, I watched and said nothing as he made her suffer—self-loathing a ball of snakes in the pit of my stomach.

He let up on the switch and watched with a half-smile as Caroline's sobs of pain filtered through the air. "At first it was about being a vampire. That was before."

I didn't say anything and neither did Caroline, both of us watching as he waited expectantly. A long moment passed before he gave a smile of victory, as if we were dogs that had just learned a trick. He continued as if nothing had happened. "My master opened my eyes to all the wrongs Thomas has done our family through the years. How he is the reason for so much suffering and chaos." He paced toward me, his face taking on the look of a zealot, someone so convinced they had the right of it that even incontrovertible proof held right under their nose wouldn't convince them otherwise. I hated zealots.

"Thomas lost track of his descendants more than a century ago," I said, knowing it was useless.

A blow landed against my ribs, the pain negligible compared to what came when he flipped the switch. "Exactly. He should have turned us then instead of allowing our line to be hunted through the decades."

"You know it was Steven who was responsible for all that."

Fire landed on my cheek.

"Of course, I know that. Who do you think raised me and my sister after he killed our parents?" After that revelation, he paced away from me heading towards Caroline.

"Why do you care anymore if Steven is dead?" I asked, needing to distract him from her. I couldn't imagine what horrors that vampire had visited on two young children, the descendants of his enemy. Their childhoods would have been difficult. Maybe horrible enough that Theo had a driving need to please his former captor? Enough to carry out his agenda even in death?

He looked over his shoulder. "Another thing that can be laid at your feet."

I watched Theo with wariness, not bothering to deny the accusation. I didn't kill Steven, Thomas had, but I might as well have given it was my blood that proved Thomas had a yearling. That was enough to make him master of this territory, giving him permission to challenge Steven. Everything after that could be blamed on me. I didn't feel guilty about it. Steven had been a monster, responsible for so many deaths and the one I blamed for Caroline's change. Sondra might have been the weapon, but he's the one who put everything in motion.

"This is revenge," I said in understanding. It finally made sense—not why he wanted revenge. I didn't understand that given Steven had killed his parents and probably subjected Theo to a horrible childhood, but if revenge was his motive, it explained why he had struck at Caroline. All for the purpose of making me suffer.

Theo clapped. "Very good. Tomorrow night when she changes—she won't be able to fight it—she'll rip out your throat. Added benefit, this way will no doubt cause both of you maximum pain and suffering. When the vampires find out she killed another one of theirs, they'll be forced to retaliate."

"I doubt it," I said. "They barely blinked when they thought she'd killed you and Catherine. It won't be any different for me."

He lifted an eyebrow, the corners of his lips half twitching into a small, barely-there smile. "Do you think so? Really?" he stepped closer. "Those were companions. Humans. Expendable. Your sire is among the most powerful in their ranks. They won't let an insult like that stand."

I kept my chin lifted, not letting him see how his words affected me, sending a chill down my spine.

"Enough talk. Time for part two of today's plan." Before I could respond, he flipped the switch. Pain coursed through my body, growing and growing as he watched. This time he didn't end it, just waited as my screams got louder.

The blood's power kept me awake and conscious long after I prayed to pass out. It felt like an eternity, all of it spent in purgatory, before my body shut down, allowing blessed darkness to claim me.

As I drifted off my last thought was that I really hoped that the next time I woke, I wasn't staring into the jaws of a demon wolf.

CHAPTER NINETEEN

"I DON'T CARE what you want. This was a bad plan," a woman shouted. There was a rumble where I couldn't quite make out the words as I raised my head, feeling woozy. Leaves stuck to my cheek, and my skin felt like little ants were biting every piece exposed to the sun beating down on my unprotected skin. "Why couldn't you have just left well enough alone? We were free. Why did you have to go and screw it up?"

Another low-voiced rumble. The woman sounded like she was moving closer, soft footsteps crunching over the thin layer of dead leaves. "I don't care what you want. I'm done. I didn't agree any of this shit."

"You're part of this too," Theo said, his voice low and dangerous.

"I'm not," Lisa snarled. I could barely see them out of the corner of my eye as she rounded on him. "You and he made sure of that when you decided to throw me away. This is on you, and only you, brother dearest."

"And what about the companions you killed?" he asked, a sly look on his face. "The ones you ate?"

Lisa looked horrified and slightly sick to her stomach. "That was an accident. I thought we were just going to scare them, get Caroline banished. Nothing would have happened if you hadn't cut the woman."

"Yes, but something did happen," he said with a gloating smile. "And you lost control and killed two people belonging to the vampires. What do you think they'll do to you when that comes out?"

Lisa was quiet for a long moment. I kept still, feeling that my continued unconsciousness was more useful than trying to plant more doubt in her mind.

"Better that come out, rather than for Brax and the vampires to learn we played a part in the death of these two," she said. "Besides, I'll just blame you. Tell them you stabbed the woman and man and my wolf took over. Brax will understand."

She sounded like she was trying to convince herself of that.

"You don't know that," Theo argued.

"I don't care. This is your problem," she spat.

"So, go. I don't know why you're here if that's what you think," he snarled.

She snarled back, the sound animalistic. "They already know the role I played in driving Caroline out of the pack. Brax isn't an idiot. How long do you think it'll take him to put the two events together once he finds the family tree you so stupidly left where she could find it?"

The derogatory way she said 'she' left me in no doubt who she meant. I tensed my arms, feeling rope tying them down so I lay flat, face down on the ground. Not enough that they planned to kill me through wolf attack, but they'd staked me out in the sun like this was some fucking B-movie horror flick.

My exposed cheek felt hot and tight, as if I had the mother of all sun burns, and the back of my neck felt like one giant blister. How long had I been out here? I closed my eyes, turning my face so the burned cheek was lying against the cool ground. At least I hadn't burst into flame yet.

There was a slapping sound and then a cry of pain. I cracked open my eyes, squinting against the bright sun. Theo cradled his cheek as he glared at his sister.

"You don't get to do that to me anymore," Lisa growled. "I'm stronger than you now. Courtesy of the life you forced me into. Think about that the next time you want to hit me."

She turned her back on him, advancing on me. I watched, unable to move as she crouched next to me, fumbling at the rope wrapped around my wrists. Seeing I was awake, she said, "You'll tell Brax I helped you. That when I found out what my brother was doing I tried to fix it."

"Yeah, whatever you say," I mumbled, knowing if I disagreed she might decide her chances of surviving were better if I weren't alive.

Movement shifted behind her.

"Watch out!" I cried as Theo appeared, a tire iron in his hand. She started to turn when he brought it down hard on her head, the crack of her skull loud in the sudden silence, his face a murderous mask.

Lisa dropped to the ground unconscious, blood pouring from the wound on her head. Theo panted above her, the tire iron clutched in his hand.

"Bitch," he spat, throwing the tire iron to the ground. "You want to get soft; you can join them in their fate."

He grabbed his sister by the feet, dragging her across the clearing to a tree. There, he sat her up before stalking back out of view.

I hissed at her. "Lisa, wake up. You need to shake this off. Get up now."

The crunch of snapping branches alerted me of his return, and I fell silent again, dropping my head back to the dirt as I played unconsciousness. I watched through cracked eyes as he took a bungie cord and wrapped it around her feet before doing the same with her hands. Next, he took a chain and finished tying her to the tree. The same aura that had been on Caroline's cage and my chains in the shack covered the silver he used on Lisa.

Finished securing his sister, he made his way back over to me, checking the chains that still tied me to the ground. I feigned sleep, not wanting him to know I was awake lest he decide to fix that. My bonds must have passed his inspection because he aimed a kick into my side, one that had me fighting not to grunt or groan—the bastard had a pretty sharp kick—before he wandered out of view again.

I waited several moments, listening before I lifted my head and looked around as I took better stock of the place where I'd been staked out. I was in a small clearing on mostly flat land, trees all around. They were young trees as evidenced by the thick underbrush that surrounded me. To be honest, my new accommodations didn't tell me much. I could have been anywhere in Ohio.

Lisa was still unconscious against her tree. I scanned the clearing as far as I could with my limited mobility, my gaze coming to a stop as a pair of bare feet came into view.

I released the unconscious breath I'd been holding at the sight of Caroline slumped, boneless against the ground. Unlike me she wasn't tied face-down, her arms held immobile by stakes in the ground. She lay on her side, her face slack in sleep, the pinched, tight look from earlier gone as she rested, blissfully unaware of our current predicament. Looking closer, I could just glimpse something barely visible around her neck—a collar with a silver chain attached to it running from a loop in the front to wrap around the base of a tree. It was thinner than the chain he'd used on Lisa, probably so it could snap when the demon wolf made her appearance.

I dropped my face back into the dirt, trying to ignore the discomfort in my body. This wasn't good. Nobody knew where we were, and given where I estimated the sun to be, I figured it was already late afternoon. There were four to five hours until the sun set.

I tugged on my arms again, testing the strength of my bindings. My right arm didn't budge, but the left had some give in it that hadn't been there before. I turned my head, trying to get a better look at that arm, rotating the wrist so I could see it better. It looked like Lisa had undone one of the loops.

Perhaps if I could loosen it just a little more, I could slip free. My wrist twisted and jerked as I tried to fight loose, my heart leaping every time there was the slightest give. It wasn't much. Soon the skin around my wrist turned bright red as the rope and chain bit into my skin, abrading it until blood oozed from the marks.

The afternoon slid by as I struggled to free myself, each moment ticking by with an inevitable finality. When I couldn't summon the strength to continue, I rested for a moment, my eyes sliding shut as the sun sapped more and more of my strength.

Forget the fact that I was tied down. Given my current state, I wasn't sure I could make it more than a few steps once I did manage to free myself. The sun felt more taxing than it had just a few days ago. Could be because it was at its strongest and most intense, or maybe it was the fact that I'd been lying out here exposed for an indeterminate length of time. Maybe I was just weaker despite the top me up from Liam and Thomas. Torture tended to do that to a person. If I survived, I'd have to ask Liam.

I gritted my teeth, tugging and pulling on my arm as my hand slipped an inch, and then two out of the loop. The skin at my wrists tore further, the blood making the task a bit easier. With one last final wrench, I pulled my hand free before collapsing face first back into the dirt, the last of my energy sapped.

My eyes drifted shut as I promised myself a break. Just a minute, and then I'd go back to working myself free. My body relaxed into the earth's cool embrace as I drifted, half aware of the sun blazing down on me and half dreaming.

I was on a rocky beach, the shoreline a mass of rugged cliffs behind me, and the water a dark, stormy gray before me. This weird half-existence tugged at my focus, and for a moment I felt myself slipping back into my body, the sun an insidious thing above me.

"Aileen." Liam's deep voice pulled me back into the dream. I looked over to find his gaze steady on me, his hair a mess as if he'd been running his hands through it, and his clothes in a state of disarray. Normally, he was well dressed, his outward appearance another facet of the cool confidence and seductive vampire that was Liam. At the moment, his shirt and pants looked like he'd been wearing them for days, wrinkled and mussed. His skin was sallow, the skin under his eyes bruised and delicate-looking.

"Liam," I said in surprise, not sure if I was dreaming or if the link had finally started working.

"Where are you?" he asked, his voice urgent.

I blinked, looking around the rocky beach I found myself on while hoping it was all real.

"I don't know." The skin over his skull drew tight. "There are trees around us."

Liam's head turned as if he was listening to something I couldn't hear. For a moment, I thought I heard voices and then the murmur faded.

"I need more information," he said. "Can you tell us anything?"

"Can't you track me? I thought that was what the mark is for." I fought despair. There wasn't a lot more to tell.

"I've been trying, but someone has been hiding you from us." Frustration was a live thing in his voice. "I don't know what's changed, but this is the first time I've gotten close to you. Even now the connection is tenuous."

Maybe because I got my hand free?

"I don't know where I am, but I can tell you who is responsible for my current circumstances," I said. If I didn't make it out of here, perhaps I could still make sure Theo paid for this. I'd prefer to live, but in the absence of that I would settle for vengeance from the grave.

"Good. Nathan said he never saw his attacker."

"He's alive?" I asked. I hadn't dare hope that Theo had been wrong about killing the enforcer.

"Barely. Whatever was used on him would have killed him if I hadn't felt him fading and been close."

I felt relief. Last thing I wanted was to have the enforcer's death on my head. "It's Theo. He's the one who did this to us."

Liam looked shocked and vaguely disbelieving. "That's not possible. He's dead."

I shook my head already anticipating his denial. "No, Pierce is the one who is dead. I'm sure once the DNA results come back they'll confirm that."

His brow furrowed. He looked like he was considering the ramifications of what I'd revealed.

"Liam, Caroline is here." The carefulness of my tone must have warned him because he focused on me with a guarded expression on his face. "The full moon is tonight."

Understanding dawned as well as fury.

"He's planning to use her wolf to kill me," I said, struggling to keep my voice even. Freaking out wouldn't help matters. I needed to remain calm if I had any hope of getting out of here alive.

"Something is blocking Brax's connection to her," Liam said. "He hasn't been able to get an idea of her location either."

"Lisa's here too," I said, not sure if that would help or not. At this point, I figured the more information they had the better. You never know when a single piece might come in handy.

"The woman Caroline attacked?" Liam sounded surprised.

"Apparently Theo and she are siblings." I bared my teeth in a feral smile. "She tried to help me get loose, but he knocked her unconscious."

Despite my best intentions, the beach landscape was wavering as fatigue set in. I didn't know how long I could remain here.

He stepped closer, his hands coming up to grasp my arm. There was some expression on his face, one I couldn't quite read that spoke of pain and fear and something else. Something I refused to see. I wasn't ready for such an emotion from him. If I'd ever be ready.

"You need to get away from her. I know she's your friend, but once the change is on her she won't recognize you." His words were intense and hushed as if he could impart his desperation through them alone. I nodded. I knew that. She'd told me as much. "Run. Run as fast as you can. Don't look back, and don't stop for anything. We're coming for you. Just hold on."

The word 'run' echoed in my head as I came alive with a gasp, the last of the sun's light fading from the sky. Damn it, that hadn't been wise—napping when I needed to be escaping. With one hand free, I was able to divest myself from the rest of my bonds in moments, using some of the increased strength being a vampire gave me.

I gained my feet just as the sun began sinking below the horizon, turning the world a golden orange as it went.

Caroline stirred, a groan announcing her return to consciousness.

"Caroline," I said, taking a step in her direction and stopping.

"Aileen." Caroline's words were groggy as she sat up, coming up short as the collar and silver chain jerked. "What's this?"

"Don't touch it," I warned, moments too late as her hands closed around the chain. She yelped and whined, letting go of the chain—her palms bright red and blistered.

Awareness returned to her eyes as she looked around with dawning horror. Her eyes flickered, the color of her wolf shining through for a moment before returning to Caroline's normal blue. She looked up at the sky, fear on her face.

"You need to kill me," she said, her voice a few decibels lower than it should be.

I shook my head in denial, then kept shaking it. There were many things I could do, many levels I could sink to in the interest of surviving. Some horrible, some necessary. That was not one of them. I could not kill my best friend—not even if it meant saving my own life.

"Aileen, please," she pleaded. "I'm not going to be able to stop myself."

"No, no, I'm not doing that," I said, backing away.

She strained against her collar, her face a mask of rage for one moment before the old Caroline gained control. "How do you think I'll feel waking up after the change covered in your blood?"

Horrible. Terrified. Full of self-loathing.

"Same way I'll feel if I kill you."

"You're my best friend, and I'm begging you to do this. I don't want to kill you," Caroline said, her voice breaking.

"And I don't want to kill you," I said, taking another step back.

"Then go. Run and don't let me catch you," Caroline roared, hair sprouting along her hands and face.

"But—" I took another step closer, every fiber of my being telling me I should help free her first. It went against the grain to leave her attached by a fucking collar and leash to a tree—as if she was a dog to chain up.

"Leave!" she shouted, her breath coming in pants. "I'll be fine. This won't hold me for long."

Lisa groaned as she came to consciousness, her head lifting as she looked around the woods with an alert gaze. Her eyes fell on Caroline. "Oh, fuck."

She started to struggle against the chain, thrashing to get free. "Don't go. You need to help me. Her wolf will kill me."

She had a point. There wasn't a lot of love lost between the two. I started for her, not wanting to leave her tied up and waiting for death.

Caroline's voice brought me up short. "Aileen, forget her. Run. She's pack. I won't hurt her—probably. I will hurt you. My wolf already yearns for the hunt so it can feast on your blood."

That was a rosy picture. It finally got me to back away on slow steps, my eyes holding hers. "Don't die."

Her smile was a little toothier than normal. "You too."

I turned and jetted off into the surrounding woods, not pausing even when I heard a spine-chilling howl lift to the fast darkening sky. Shadows thickened on the ground, following me like reaching hands as I raced through the twilight, cursing at the weakness pulling at my limbs. My body had been through too much recently— the werewolf bite, then getting knocked unconscious, followed by an afternoon of prolonged sunbathing. Even bathing in the blood of two of the most powerful vampires of the city wasn't enough to give any pep to my step at this point.

Keeping upright and moving took my entire willpower, forcing me to dig deep for the unrelenting survivor I hid at the core of me—the one willing to do almost anything it took to live another day. She was the one who had gotten me through some of the most hellish experiences of my life. I let her guide my thoughts, wiping anything but the next step from my mind. Each step was like slogging through quicksand. My mind was urging me to move faster, but my body could just not answer.

The moon was fully up by now, lighting the world and making it as easy to see as if it had been noon. Even a human would have no trouble on a night like this. I'd have no chance against a werewolf's heightened senses.

How much longer did I have until Caroline lost her battle and shifted? That chain wouldn't hold her long before it snapped, and I'd seen her move. Fast and deadly. There was no chance I would outrun her, not unless I stumbled across a fighter jet or its equivalent. That meant I needed to be smart. Fleeing blindly in a panic was just going to get me killed faster. I needed a plan. Unfortunately, I didn't have one yet, which was why I kept moving, my mind turning over possibilities as my feet took me up another hill.

It was a common misconception that Ohio was entirely flat. Granted, the majority of it was—especially up North—but there were areas of the state that were decidedly less so. The biggest example of this was Hocking Hills, located in the southeastern part. I've hiked there many times, exploring Old Man's cave, the waterfalls and the hollers that riddled the area. I doubted Theo had taken the time to drive us two hours south to that area. Furthermore, the ravines I navigated weren't as deep and lacked the unique rock formations that made Hocking Hills famous.

No, if I had to guess, we were in the northeastern part of the city. Maybe near Hoover Dam or Alum Creek. Both areas were wooded and known for the modest hills and ravines I was stumbling over. Orienting myself with the moon and North Star, I pointed my feet south. If nothing else, maybe I'd stumble across a road and be able to catch a ride before Caroline caught up.

There was a rustle of movement in the trees, and I froze, looking around me as I waited for an attack. When it didn't come, I moved carefully forward, trying to keep my movements as quiet as possible, my gaze alert. I broke into another jog. One thing being a bike messenger all these years had given me was decent stamina. Running might be a little different than riding a bike, but at least I hadn't lost all my cardio when I left the military.

My foot caught on a dead branch, and I pitched forward down a sharp incline, my shoulder bouncing off a rock before my knee slammed into a tree as I tumbled, collecting bumps and bruises along the way. I fell into empty air then hit the ground several feet down with a thump, coming to a halt as I reached the bottom. I lay there a moment, blinking up at the dark trees standing sentinel over me.

Dampness seeped into my pants, and I sat up with a silent groan. My legs had landed in water, while the rest of me was still on dry ground. I rotated my shoulder, grimacing at the stab of pain. My knee wasn't much better. My healing abilities had already been maxed out because of the sun, so both hurts lingered when normally my body would have started healing them by now.

I looked up at the hill I'd fallen down. It looked every bit as high as it had felt during my trip down, making me glad I hadn't broken my neck in my headfirst tumble. There was a cliff of rock above me, which explained the fall through empty air. I was at the bottom of a ravine that had a small creek running through it.

Near the top of the hill, my othersight picked up on a flicker of inky darkness broken by streaks of burnt umber. Caroline. I pressed myself to the ground, ignoring the mud that seeped through my clothes as I kept my eyes focused on where I'd seen the umber and dark. Suddenly my tumble seemed less like an inconvenience and more like a timely save.

Her light moved back and forth before she disappeared up and over the hill. I let out a tiny sigh of relief.

She wouldn't be gone long. When she realized she lost my scent, she'd have to circle back. Eventually, she would find her way down here. I needed to be gone before that happened.

First, though, I needed to do what I could to disguise my scent. It was already half done with all this mud clinging to my front and back. I dug my hands deep in the bank, pulling up mud and smearing it over my arms and legs, covering myself as best I could given the time constraints.

Finished, I climbed to my feet and hobbled along the creek, being careful to move quietly and quickly. My othersight flickered wildly, giving me odd glimpses of light trails. Some in colors I didn't have words for. Some showing shadows like wraiths across the ground. It was like trying to watch two movies at the same time. One normal and the other technicolor.

I blinked rapidly as my left eye showed me a yawning chasm while my normal eye just showed more of the same hill covered in years of dead leaves. Not having time to humor this new oddity of my eye, I stepped forward, reasonably sure that the yawning chasm wasn't really there, or at least not in the sense of the real world. Black ink blots detached like seaweed waving in some unseen ocean as they drifted toward me, only to shy away from touching me at the last moment.

A harsh growl came from my right, and I jerked back, forgetting this new world my eye was showing me. A wolf's eyes gleamed at me from the dark, its head lowered. Caroline. I backed up a step. She advanced before skirting to the side. I turned with her as she circled me, not coming closer. Every time she veered too close to the chasm she would hop back before continuing her slinking walk.

I watched for several seconds, amazed that she hadn't already killed me, even as she snarled and whined in confusion. She wouldn't pass the chasm. How was this possible? How was she seeing the same thing I was? Could it be the wolf? It was the only thing I could think of, the only thing different.

Another growl came from my right, and a much smaller wolf crept into view, its head lowered, and teeth bared, as it eyed me like I was juicy steak it wanted to eat. Lisa. It passed the chasm like it wasn't even there, taking no notice of the thing that kept Caroline at bay.

"Oh crap," I whispered. What worked on one didn't work on the other.

The wolf crouched, the slight bunching of its muscles all the warning I had before it sprang—its leap carrying it through the air. I dropped, rolling under it in a burst of speed fueled by adrenaline and fear. It landed across the clearing, close to Caroline, spinning as it darted back toward me.

Caroline's wolf swiped out a paw, knocking it several feet to the side. A yelp escaped Lisa, and she scrambled to her feet even as Caroline leapt, landing on her, teeth buried in the smaller wolf's throat.

While they were ripping and tearing at each other, I darted away, taking advantage of their distraction in the hopes they'd keep each other occupied.

There were twin howls as I disappeared over the hill and then the snapping of branches as they chased after me. I flew across the ground, reaching for more speed with each stride. Behind me came the sound of pursuit as they gave up on stealth in favor of running me to ground.

Lisa's wolf appeared next to me. I veered sharply to avoid the snapping teeth. Caroline bounded up on my other side, leaping at my throat as I ducked and rolled, hitting the ground on my bad shoulder, then popping to my feet and taking off again. I darted around a tree, weaving through them as the two snarled and snapped at my heels.

My thighs burned as I sprinted uphill. I came to a crashing stop as a cliff appeared, my arms pinwheeling before I grabbed a tree. I stared at the sharp drop, panting.

There was a snap of branches behind me as the two wolves slunk into view. They'd been herding me. That was clear now. With the cliff at my back, I had nowhere to go.

I stepped away from the tree and the cliff's edge, holding my hands out in front of me. "Caroline, I know you're in there. You don't want to do this."

I had little hope that talking to her would help, but I was desperate, and this was the only option left.

My plea had no effect on her as she circled one way and Lisa circled the other. I kept my eyes on Caroline. She was the bigger threat.

"Do you remember how we met?" I asked, my voice high. "We were in elementary school, and I liked Jimmy Grey. You told me I was an idiot for trying to get his attention, and then you dyed his hair green when you caught him talking trash about me to his friends."

The wolf didn't pause as it crept closer, its eyes focused on me with single-minded intensity. It was a massive animal. Majestic and beautiful. At another time, when my life wasn't in danger, I would have been tempted to capture its beauty on camera. Now, I just wanted her as far from me as possible.

"Caroline, don't. You need to control your instincts," I warned, backing up. One foot slipped over the edge; I caught myself from pitching backward and stumbled forward, falling to my knees in the process.

Caroline was there, her fangs snapping at my throat. I jerked back as she towered over me. Her eyes had intelligence in them, but it was hard to tell if it was the kind of intelligence that was slightly crazy or if my friend was in the driving seat.

I held very still as her growl faded, and she dipped her head to snuffle at me. She whined before growling again.

Lisa darted forward, catching my arm and sinking her teeth in before jerking her head and almost wrenching my arm off. I cried out, claws tipping my fingers as I raked them down her face, catching one eye under them. She yelped and let go. Caroline body checked her, forcing the smaller wolf away from me.

With my othersight, I could see the umber streaks were snarled and tangled at the base of her chest. They called to me, whispering of their wrongness—like a song where one note was off-key, throwing everything else off balance. I had no other time to consider them before Caroline was on me, her teeth in my shoulder as she shook her head fiercely.

I screamed, punching and raking at her with my claws to no effect. Her blood dripped down, mixing with my own. Somehow, my hand landed on that snarled knot, and I did something in my panic and terror—that something born of desperation and a will to survive. I wasn't sure how, or if I could do the same something again. The tangle unknotted, just a little bit—the inky blackness and burnt umber separating just slightly and seeming to work together instead of apart.

I punched her in the head one last time before my arm fell to my side, blood coated my neck and chest. "Caroline, I love you," I managed to whisper.

Her teeth gentled on my shoulder, and I slipped to the ground as she took a step back. She nudged me where I lay unmoving, a whimper in her throat. She nudged me harder.

Before she could do more, a smaller wolf barreled into her, snapping and snarling. Caroline snapped back, drawing blood and using her larger mass to hold her own. Lisa was no slouch, using speed to attack. Caroline snarled, her head darting down, her teeth closing around the smaller wolf's leg and jerking. There was a yelp, and then Lisa limped off, disappearing into the forest.

Caroline padded back, nudging me with her head before licking at my shoulder a couple of times then moving to my other wounds. The cold that had been spreading, a product of her demon taint, began retreating under her ministration. Having given each wound her attention, she lay down next to me, setting her head on the unwounded part of my stomach. Her ears tilted forward, and she laid her tail over my feet as if she was trying to keep them warm.

I didn't know what had happened to cause her to change from ruthless slayer of vampires to something close to man's best companion, but I was too tired and wounded to try to fight my way free. Instead, I held still and hoped that she remained Caroline.

We stayed like that for a long time as my body fought to heal itself. I remained conscious as pain throbbed in the individual wounds, the skin just beginning to knit together, the blood slowing and stopping.

There was a pop of air, and then Liam appeared at the edge of the forest. Caroline's ears twitched, and she lifted her head, her lips peeling back from her teeth. Her chest vibrated with a nearly silent growl. Liam moved closer, his feet whispering over the ground—his face a dark, murderous mask as he took in my blood coated body.

His eyes turned to Caroline, death on his face and his fangs down. His blue eyes burned with fire, the skin on his face thinning and letting some of the monster within peer out. I realized with a start that he thought I was dead, and she was feasting on my body.

"Liam, I'm fine," I croaked. "She's protecting me from Lisa."

I chanced laying a hand on her back and sitting up. She swung her head, forcing me back down, the movement sending shards of pain through my shoulder. I gritted my teeth against the groan of pain, knowing it wouldn't help matters.

When the haze faded and I could focus again, I realized Caroline was standing on all fours, straddling my body as she faced Liam, the fur on her back standing upright and her ears pinned back against her head.

I turned my head, noting that Liam wasn't the only vampire standing there. Several of the enforcers were at his back, including Eric and Anton. A wolf I recognized as Brax appeared out of the woods like a ghost. I blinked and realized there were several wolves at his back, like silent sentries as they ringed the two of us in a half circle, the cliff at our back, cutting off any possibility of retreat.

"Stay down, Aileen," Liam ordered when he saw me try to sit up again, his focus entirely on the wolf over me.

"She's not a threat," I said. Not entirely true. She'd always be a threat, that was the nature of the wolf, but I didn't get the sense that she was an immediate danger to my survival.

"The blood coating your body would say otherwise," he returned in a cool voice.

Fair enough, and normally I would agree.

"That happened earlier tonight. I'm practically healed now," I said.

He didn't answer, advancing on her with steady steps, Brax mirroring him from a few feet away. Caroline's head swung between the two, unsure which one presented the bigger threat.

"Ready?" Liam asked.

Brax chuffed.

Liam sprang at us, his body a blur of speed. Caroline whirled toward him with a snarl. Brax hit her from the side, his body weight knocking her off me, the two of them going over the cliff.

"Caroline!" I screamed, rolling over on my stomach to crawl to the edge.

T.A. White

CHAPTER TWENTY

LIAM WAS BESIDE me in the next moment, his arms scooping me up and quelling my struggles.

"She isn't dead," he said in a low voice in my ear. "That fall wouldn't be enough to hurt either one of them."

"How do you know?"

He chuckled. "I've thrown the alpha off much higher objects during the course of our acquaintance."

"Caroline's barely been a wolf for a few months. She won't have his healing," I returned as I tried to wriggle out of his arms. His grip tightened, and he dropped his head to run his nose along the side of my face, breathing deeply at the same time. He dipped his head further until he could reach the wound in my shoulder, his tongue darted out in a move much like the wolf's as he licked it once before straightening.

"No, hers is better. A consequence of her taint," he said, sounding unworried as he resumed walking at a pace that had the trees blurring around me. "They'll fight it out until the moon sets, at which point she'll be taken into custody. You can see her then."

I let my head fall back, looking up at his face. "What will happen to her?"

His eyes met mine. "That has still not been decided."

I set my forehead on his shoulder and closed my eyes. I'd survived, but it didn't feel like I'd won anything since Caroline's fate was still up in the air.

We reached a road that had several cars parked along it, including several black Escalades I assumed belonged to the vampires. Liam carried me to one car, barely pausing as Eric appeared to open the door for us. Setting me inside, Liam climbed up beside me as Eric shut the door, sealing us alone in the car.

Liam wasted no time, divesting me of my shirt so he could get a better look at my wounds. His hands were clinical as they pushed and prodded the tears in my skin, which still sluggishly seeped blood.

"I never did thank you for saving my life after the werewolf bite," I said. "Even if I could have done without the coffin full of blood."

His lips firmed. "I wasn't going to let you die so easily. The blood bath was the best way to keep you alive. The wolf's bite had spread and almost killed you by the

204

time Brax returned and was able to pull some of its poison from you." He gave me a meaningful glance when I opened my mouth to argue. Brax might have returned, but I suspected it was my trick with the tree that saved my life.

His eyes held a warning, as if telling me to keep my mouth shut about being able to see magic. For now, I'd listen. Mostly, because I was too tired to do otherwise.

"You need more blood," he said in a decisive voice before I could say anything else, rolling up his sleeve.

I turned my head away when he held his wrist up to my lips. I know he'd lost way more blood than me in the last twenty-four hours, and though weak, I wasn't at death's threshold. "I'm fine."

"Aileen," he snapped.

The door on the other side of me opened, and Thomas climbed in, pulling it shut behind him and taking a seat beside me. He looked at the two of us, noting the frustrated expression on Liam's face and the mulish one on mine. He guessed the cause in moments. "You either take blood from Liam, or you take blood from me. Your choice."

My expression turned even more stubborn as he quirked an eyebrow at me, making it clear he wasn't going to budge on this. I had a sudden vision of being held down with one of them forcing my mouth open as the other dripped blood into it and knew that I would be on the losing end of any struggle. Faced with drinking under my own volition or being forced into it, I took the path that would at least leave me with some modicum of dignity.

Liam was smart enough not to let a smile cross his face when I turned to him, though there was a certain smug light in his eyes that made me want to throat punch him. He tugged me so that I was leaning back against his chest and facing Thomas, one of Liam's arms a snug band around my chest while he held the other to my lips.

"Drink, Aileen," he rumbled in my ear.

My fangs snapped down and I sank them into his skin, relishing the soft pop as they pierced his flesh, then the dark taste of his blood as it coated my tongue—better than chocolate, more decadent than the most delicious of desserts, aged to perfection and dancing across my senses with a maestro's expertise. My eyes slid shut as heat suffused my core, spreading with a lulling fire throughout my body, waking up parts of me that had long been ignored.

There was a heavy groan in my ear, one echoed by my moan moments later. I could feel him harden against my back where I pressed against him. I wiggled back, relishing the power it gave me when he muttered a curse in another language, the arm around my waist briefly tightening.

"That's enough, acushla." His voice was a tickle against my neck as he gently pulled his wrist away.

I opened my eyes as his thumb caressed my bare stomach in a gentle movement, sweeping back and forth as I returned to myself. Thomas watched us with an enigmatic gaze, his chin propped on his hand and his fingers tapping at his lips. The lassitude that had taken over my limbs was slow to fade. It was like I was a lion gorged on a good meal, nothing seemed too important.

"This is an interesting development," Thomas finally said to Liam over my head.

My guard snapped down, and I stiffened and would have drawn away if Liam hadn't held me close, his warm embrace suddenly turning tight.

Whatever gaze they exchanged must have spoken volumes because Thomas didn't make any further comments, his gaze dropping to mine.

"Now that I see the yearling is safe and fed, I think it's time to take care of that other matter," he said, his face a polite mask.

"Theo," I said. It wasn't much of a guess. I could think of no other reason for Thomas to be here.

One side of his lips quirked up in answer.

Damn.

"He's probably close," I said. "He planned to kill Caroline after she'd taken care of me and collapsed into a coma after her shift back."

He wouldn't want to be far away, but he also couldn't be too close without risking her turning her focus to him.

"Yes, there's a cabin not far from here that his master used to own," Thomas said in an amused voice.

"Makoto is a hacker," Liam said in answer to my unvoiced question. "When pointed in the right direction, he was able to uncover a lot of very interesting information."

Eric got into the driver's seat, Anton by his side in the passenger seat. It was odd to see someone other than Nathan in that spot. Anton didn't turn to address any of us, staring forward with a fixed expression.

"What do you plan to do with Theo when you find him?" I asked, looking away from the enforcers as we began to move.

Thomas's face turned amused. "What do you think I have planned?"

"I don't know. That's why I'm asking," I said in a measured voice. My fear was that Thomas would do exactly as Theo wanted, turn him into a vampire. If he did that, I very much suspected Theo would bide his time until he could act against Thomas. Eventually, he would come after me, and I would never be safe.

"What do you want to have happen to him?" Thomas asked, his head tilting in question.

I wanted him dead. He'd killed multiple people, and he'd planned mine and Caroline's deaths, not to mention almost sacrificed his sister when she tried to help us. He was a psychotic killer. Making him a vampire wouldn't change that. It would just make him a more efficient killer.

I didn't know if Thomas would see it my way. Though the relation was long ago, Theo was Thomas's descendant. How would I feel two hundred years from now if I was in Thomas's shoes and it was Jenna's great, great grandson facing judgment? Would I still feel an attachment to that long-ago family?

Liam's hands tightened briefly in warning around my waist.

"He's Steven's creation," I finally said. "And he's responsible for at least two deaths that I know of, though I suspect you'll find many more that can be lain at his feet."

"And?" Thomas arched an eyebrow.

Vampires didn't have the same attachment to life I had. At his age, Thomas alone was probably responsible for more deaths than I could count.

"He tried to kill me," I said, lifting my chin. "I want him dealt with in a very permanent way."

A part of me broke at that request. I wasn't the sort to solve my problems with violence, and basically asking for someone's death went against the human part of me I tried to cling to. I saw no alternative. Next time Theo might not be content to plot against just me. He might go after Jenna or her daughter. I couldn't risk my family, and if it meant sacrificing some of my humanity to ensure their safety, so be it. Every soldier knows they might have to sacrifice a life in defense of their country.

"What will you give me for this outcome?" Thomas asked, an anticipatory expression on his face.

I opened my mouth and then closed it, meeting his stare with one of my own. That was what Liam had been trying to warn me about. That's what all his questions had been leading toward. Tricky, tricky vampire.

"Nothing," I said with a note of finality.

Anton's head turned slightly before he directed his attention forward.

"Nothing?" Thomas looked amused. "You're not very good at bargaining."

I arched one eyebrow, not allowing his words to shake me. "It's in your best interest for you to take care of the matter permanently."

"Oh?" His lips curved.

"Yes, your enemy did a very good job convincing him you were the problem. Theo has a very developed victim complex, and in his eyes, you're the source of all the wrong in his world. How long do you think it will be before he starts plotting against you?" Answer: Immediately. "I know vampires are very long-lived. It may be centuries before he sets his plans in motion. I bet you never even see it coming because he will have utterly convinced you of his loyalty."

"You don't have much faith that I can sway him to my side," Thomas returned, a half-smile on his face.

I snorted. "Please, I've seen your methods of persuasion. They need a lot of work."

That surprised a soft chuckle out of him.

"Whatever he might have been, whoever he could have been, died as soon as Steven got hold of him," I said, my expression serious. "He tried to sacrifice his own sister for his plans. This isn't someone you can ever trust. You'll need to watch your back around him for all of eternity and never show him any weakness. Is that really the kind of person you want on your side?"

He made a 'hmm' sound and turned away, not answering my question. My lips tightened. Fine. If I needed to find a way to end the threat Theo presented, I would.

"Also, you give him what he wants, and you can kiss goodbye any chance of ever persuading me to your side," I added as an afterthought, letting him see how serious I was. For whatever reason, Thomas still thought he could win my loyalty. It might not be much, but the possibility of my endorsement was all I had to bargain with.

He didn't respond beyond a thoughtful glance my way.

We turned onto a dirt road, the car jostling on the uneven path. A cabin sat between the trees up ahead, rundown and looking like it was one stiff wind from falling apart. It was the type of place that would have been right at home in a slasher film.

The Escalade came to a halt, and Eric and Anton got out of the car, the doors slamming at the same time they appeared on the porch. I started to shift so I could get out when Liam's arms tightened around me.

"Let them handle it," he said in a soft voice.

I settled, seeing the logic in that. Though his super blood had energized me, helping the wounds heal at double the speed they had before, I was still tired, hurting, and mentally exhausted. If he wanted his enforcers to do all the heavy lifting, I wasn't going to argue.

Moments later, Eric appeared in the doorway with Anton behind him, dragging Theo with a firm grip around the neck. The human in his hands was bloodied and bruised, one eye turning black, and his cheek swollen—his arm bent at a weird angle.

Thomas shoved out of the car.

"Why don't you wait here?" Liam suggested when I tried to follow.

"It was me he tried to kill. I want to see what happens to him," I said. If Thomas granted him mercy, if they let him escape unscathed, I wanted to know—one way or another.

Anton threw Theo to the ground at Thomas's feet, the human flopping down in an ungraceful heap.

"I'm disappointed great, grandnephew," Thomas said in an amiable voice. "If you wanted my attention, you only needed to ask."

Theo lifted a tear stained face from the ground. "He broke my arm."

Thomas lifted an eyebrow at Anton who gazed back at him with a stone-faced expression, no hint of remorse on it. "Did he now? Well, you can't really blame him. You did kill his companion."

"That wasn't my fault. Lisa was only supposed to scare her, but she fell and hurt herself. Lisa lost control."

"Liar," I said, stepping forward. Vengeance beating in my chest. Red tinged the world around me as I felt my vampire side take over. That side wanted to rip out his intestines and make him watch as I knitted a quilt out of them—a human intestine quilt, bloody and awful.

Liam caught me and pulled me back, murmuring soothing words into my hair.

"It's not true," Theo said when Thomas glanced back at me. Desperation tinged his voice. "It was an accident. I was hoping to help you by exposing Caroline for the menace she is."

"By starting a war?" Thomas asked, his voice silky. I shivered at the predator I heard there, one that I knew lay within me too.

Theo shook his head. "No, we were just trying to show where Aileen's loyalties lay, and how she would betray you for her friend. I was trying to help. Perhaps I went about it in the wrong way, but I've only ever wanted your esteem."

I hissed, the sound that of a pissed off mountain lion. This little ass. He was trying to lay the blame on me.

Thomas considered him, his thoughts hidden behind the genial mask he wore. "Why didn't you come to me when you first realized you were my descendant? You must know descendants are given first priority for the kiss."

Theo blinked and looked taken aback, some of the smugness wiped from his face. "I was afraid you wouldn't believe me. You must know that Steven raised me." He got a crafty look on his face. "He had a hand in Aileen's arrival in your world as well. I can tell you about it if you'd like."

My eyes widened and my mouth dropped open. Liam's arms became steel traps. "Don't move," he rasped in my ear. "Wait."

I settled down, meeting Thomas's gaze as calmly as I could, given Theo's little lie. Thomas studied me with an unwavering expression. It was a mystery how much stock he was putting in his grand nephew's words. I stood my ground and straightened my shoulders. If this meant my death, I was going to do it standing, unafraid.

"I believe you are owed a blood debt, Anton. Do what you will with him," Thomas said, his eyes never leaving mine.

Anton's fangs snicked down, a feral expression taking hold. Gone was the emotionless warrior, in his place was wrath given form.

"What?" Theo's eyes widened with real fear, and he struggled to his feet. He didn't make it further than his knees before Anton stomped down hard down on one leg. The crack of a bone reached me as Theo let out a high, thin wail.

Thomas looked back at him, unruffled, his expression unchanging except for a sly amusement that tugged at the corners of his eyes. "I am not such a fool as to believe the lies of one such as you. I'm glad my brother is long dead. He would weep to know such a pathetic specimen came from his line." Thomas looked at Anton. "You have until sunrise. Make sure he doesn't see the light of the morning sun."

Anton inclined his head in a formal bow. Thomas acknowledged it with a flick of his fingers before turning his back on Theo as he started screaming for mercy.

"Let's go. You don't need to see this next part." Liam didn't wait for my agreement, turning me and guiding me to the car, his hold firm.

Theo's screams followed us, the kind that I would hear in my nightmares, the kind that would haunt me for years to come. That piece of humanity I thought I was willing to part with, I wanted it back, even knowing it was too late now.

We got into the car, Thomas climbing into the front passenger seat as Eric took the driver's seat. We didn't say anything as we drove off, leaving Anton and his victim in the clearing.

"You were right about him," Thomas said as he stared out the window.

I turned my head to look at him but didn't say anything.

"He would have betrayed me in the end." I didn't know if the words were meant for me or for himself. "There was no other choice."

I took that to mean the decision regarding Theo's life had been a hard-fought one—up in the air until Thomas spoke with him. I went back to staring out the window as the car sped down the twisting road. I didn't know how I felt about that, or if I had any right to feel anything.

It was over. I had survived. That would have to be enough for now.

*

Two days after the full moon, I followed Sondra into the basement of Lou's Bar, my footsteps echoing harshly on the stairs as we descended. I'd slept for most of that time, exhausted from my trials. My sleep hadn't been peaceful, instead interrupted by the voices of the dead. Even though I'd managed to save Caroline, I felt like I'd lost a large piece of myself by leaving Theo to die. It was an irrational feeling, but then feelings often were.

Events after Caroline's fall from the cliff had unfolded exactly as Liam predicted. The wolves had chased Caroline to ground and battled each other the entire night, until Caroline collapsed into her post-shift coma shortly after sunrise. Once they'd come back to themselves, Caroline had been taken into custody

The only thing left to do was recover, gather our strength, and find a more palatable solution for Caroline's dilemma.

I reached the bottom of the stairs, noticing the silver cages that rimmed the perimeter of the room. Only two of them were occupied. Caroline sat on the hard ground, facing the stairs as she looked out from behind the bars with a dead expression on her face. Lisa glared from a cage across from her.

I stopped at the sight of Caroline, momentarily off balance. Except for a few bruises that already looked weeks old, she looked unharmed. Physically, at least. Mentally and emotionally she looked bereft, as if she had lost that spark that made her Caroline.

"What did you do to her?" I hissed in a low voice at Sondra.

"Nothing. She's been like that since she woke up in here." Sondra looked upset about that fact. "She's not eating or drinking. She refuses to talk to any of us. I hoped you could get through to her."

So, that's why they let me down here with minimal argument when I showed up at Lou's. I thought I'd have to call in a few dozen favors to get this chance, but they'd shocked me by being reasonable for once.

Sondra watched her with sad, regretful eyes. "I don't understand this. Her wolf seemed to accept us toward the end."

"Perhaps it has something to do with being locked in another cage." My voice was acerbic.

She didn't respond to that.

"What do you plan to do with her?" I asked. "Last we spoke, you and Brax were entertaining the idea of putting her down."

Sondra looked unsettled, her gaze going to Caroline. "That's over now. I don't know what happened that night, but her wolf has settled. She's not experiencing the unstable shifts that were a side effect of the demon taint. Her bite has also become less deadly. Now that her wolf sees him as her alpha, Brax is able to exert some control over her. It has bought us some breathing room."

That was very good news. Thomas had been most interested to learn about the wolf whose bite was lethal to all. Such a weapon in his hands would have meant bad things for any who opposed him. With that out of the equation, it meant Caroline could be a normal werewolf.

It did beg the question of whether any of Caroline's stabilization stemmed from what I had done to the snarl of burnt umber and pitch-black webbing I'd seen in Caroline's chest when she attacked me. Even now, it lay pliant and smooth, the strands of magic looking almost harmonious. Whatever I had done that night seemed to remain.

Caroline's eyes shifted to me. "Have you come to break me out?"

I stepped forward and stuffed my hands in my pockets. "Not exactly."

"Figures," she snorted.

"You're not eating?" I asked, lifting an eyebrow. "That doesn't seem very bright."

She lifted her shoulder in a shrug. "Haven't been hungry."

"They tell me you're not talking either."

"Hasn't been much to talk about." Her voice was sullen and very un-Caroline like.

I paused before taking a seat in front of her cell. We sat in silence for several moments as we each regarded the other. What I saw sent worry crashing through me. She looked defeated and without hope. And angry—so angry.

"Enough of this shit," I told her. "You're a werewolf. That sucks. You have to obey an alpha. That sucks too, believe me I know. What other option do you have?"

The look she slanted my way was full of wrath. "That's rich coming from someone who refuses to complete the century's service and won't let the vampires train her. I know you're planning to move back into your apartment. Must be nice."

"Is that it? That's why you're acting like a three-year-old? Because I never fulfilled my contract?"

She shrugged one shoulder and gave me a look that said, "if the shoe fits".

I growled. "You look at me, and tell me you're not a danger to others. Then maybe we'll talk."

She looked away.

"You damn near killed me, not just once, but twice. Brax and his wolves managed to put off their transformation for over two hours on the full moon. How long did you last?" It did not feel good confronting her with these truths. "Caroline, you're barely keeping it together. Listen to them. Let them help you. They're not your enemies."

"Like the vampires aren't yours?" She met my eyes with a stubborn gaze of her own.

I turned my head slightly, knowing that Liam was just upstairs out of sight, no doubt listening to everything that was being said. I'd been surprised when I'd arrived to find him and Eric having drinks at the bar with the wolves watching them for any sign of aggression.

I sighed, feeling like a hypocrite. How was I to help her when I'd bucked the system at every stage, unwilling to consign my life to another's control ever again? I rubbed my forehead as we sat in silence.

"Unless you're here to get me out, you might as well go. We have nothing to talk about." She looked away from me, trying to shut me out.

"Why are you so angry with me?" I asked. "Really?"

She had been from the get go. Beyond reason.

"You know why," she said, some of her wolf making itself known in her voice.

"Do I? Enlighten me."

She was silent for a long time. I began to give up. If she didn't want to talk, there wasn't much I could do. I started to turn away.

"You left," she said, suddenly standing by the bars. "You left me behind, and you never even thought twice."

I inhaled a sharp breath, feeling stung by the accusation. "I joined the military. I didn't exactly leave you behind, and you told me not to come back anyways."

"It certainly felt like you left me behind. You didn't even tell me before you did it. You just showed up with the papers and said you had to report to basic in two days. I told you everything." Her voice was tight with emotion. "You knew about my mom, my family issues. I shared every dark secret with you. Yet, you shared so very little."

Her words felt like little shards of ice. I had never thought she cared, let alone would notice my absence. She never asked me about my life. I was always the tag along. She was always the brains. The brain doesn't ask what the arms and legs want, it just expects them to comply.

"You were so driven. You knew exactly where you were going and how you were going to get there," I told her. "I felt lost and thought joining would help me find my way."

"Why didn't you tell me that?" she asked.

I lifted one shoulder. "I didn't want you to think less of me."

"Well, I did anyway." She folded her arms and looked away.

That was the truth.

"Then, you came back, but you didn't. Not really. You had this secret—one you kept for years." She met my eyes with angry ones of her own. "How would you feel if our situations were reversed, and I had frozen you out while keeping this massive secret that could change everything?"

Furious. Hurt. Everything in between.

"I did it to protect you," I said.

"Look how that ended." She looked sad as she stared back at me.

There weren't words to defend myself with. She was right, but so was I.

We were quiet for a long moment. I didn't know how to fix what was broken, or even if I should. Still, I wanted our friendship back.

"I didn't mean you harm," I told her. "Is there any way you can forgive me?"

Her face crumpled. "We're friends—even when we hate each other."

My laugh was a little watery.

"What if I made you a deal?" I asked, clearing my throat and bringing us back to the matter at hand. "I'll be more open to establishing a relationship with the vampires if you learn what you need to know from the wolves."

Her head snapped back to me, her eyes surprised. My mouth was turned down as I stared back at her with a grumpy frown. Yeah, I'd said it. It was a major concession, something I wasn't really known for.

"It's still not fair," she said, looking like she was considering it. "My life is entirely controlled by them."

"I'm not joining a clan," I said in a flat voice.

She lifted her chin. "You have to receive training from them like I do the wolves."

I took a deep breath and blew it out with a disgusted sigh. "Fine."

"Every day."

"No. Once a week."

"Twice a week." Her expression let me know she meant it, that that was as far as she'd compromise.

"Fine." Her lips twitched, and then stilled at my next words. "You have to stay part of the pack, and you can't run again."

"Aileen, they want me to quit my job." Her expression was slightly shamed as her eyes fell from mine. "You know what that means to me."

I did know. Sondra had informed me before bringing me down here. They didn't think she was stable enough to be around humans, especially ones on the brink of adulthood with all the hormonal behavior that brought. Caroline defined herself by her work. She'd come so far in life that giving up her goals would feel like a major blow.

"If it makes you feel better, I got fired because of all this," I said with a sly grin when she gave me an exasperated look and rolled her eyes. There really was no comparison between the two, since my job was one I'd fallen into while hers was a career. "It's not forever, you know. Prove you can control yourself, and I'm sure they'll lift the restriction."

"And if they don't?"

"Then we fuck their shit up." I arched an eyebrow, feeling relief when she nodded. I grinned before standing. "I'll tell them you're ready for food."

I turned toward the steps.

"You'll be back, right?" Caroline's voice was insecure.

I looked over my shoulder and gave her my best daredevil grin. "Try to stop me. We'll both make this work. Together."

She nodded. Her eyes were still sad, but she didn't look like she was beaten. It was something. More than when I'd walked down here.

I paused before I headed up the stairs, turning to Sondra. "What will happen to Lisa?"

She looked at the other wolf with distaste. Lisa lifted her chin and gave us a snooty look. "That hasn't been decided yet. She did kill two people, plotted against a fellow pack member, and conspired with an enemy."

I hesitated, not sure it was my place to say anything, let alone whether it was wise of me to. Lisa had been painted with the same brush as her brother. While I got the sense that the woman had wanted to get away from him and his schemes, she had waited until the last possible moment.

"If it helps, she did try to free me," I said, my conscious getting the better of me. "Even knowing it would have repercussions for her. I got the sense from Theo that the companions weren't entirely her fault."

Sondra considered that. "I will let Brax know, and he will factor that into his decision."

I nodded then walked up the steps with grim purpose. That was all I could do for now—all I was willing to do. Everything else regarding Lisa was in Brax's hands.

Liam leaned against the wall in the hall next to the basement, his arms folded over his chest as he watched me with an appreciative gaze. My steps faltered as I noticed him.

There were a lot of questions I had for him. This wasn't the best place to ask them with prying ears all around, but I needed to know.

"Why do you keep helping me?" I asked. He'd had plenty of opportunity to wipe his hands of me and my problems. "Sondra told me you're the reason they were finally able to track us down."

The waking dream I'd had of him by the beach and ocean had been real—the mark he'd forced on me creating a link he could follow. I may have done most of the heavy lifting in saving myself, but he and the wolves' timely arrival had gone a long way to helping the situation.

He studied me with hooded eyes, his head tilting in consideration. "You fascinate me."

I blinked at him, nonplussed. "I fascinate you."

Not the answer I had been expecting.

He gave me a wicked smile. "In so many ways."

"Does that have anything to do with this?" I tapped the skin under my magic-seeing eye.

His eyes went to where I pointed and some of the amusement dropped from his face. "That's part of it. I won't lie. But, you're so much more than that. You have potential. I'd like to see that potential realized, in more ways than one."

Not exactly a romantic declaration, and it didn't allay any concerns that his interest in me might have more to do with his own alliances. I turned his words over in my head.

His gaze was intense as he continued, "For now, I think it's best to keep that piece of information to yourself. There are many in this world who would do anything to secure such a unique ability."

I nodded to show I understood. I'd thought as much. "By that, can I take it that you have no plans to share this with our not-so-mutual friend?"

His smile flashed. "I'll keep the news close to the vest for the moment."

I didn't like the thought of owing him. He was a vampire—one who probably had enough secrets in his closet to sink a ship. Owing him one thing might lead to a whole nest of problems that I didn't need.

While we did share an attraction, it wasn't one I entirely welcomed or even understood. His loyalties would always be to the vampires, and while I didn't view them in the same light as I once had, I still didn't trust them implicitly. I'm sure he felt the same way about me. It made any potential relationship between us a long shot. Not that I was all that sure he had designs on a relationship either.

"I hear we're going to be getting to know each other better," he said as I stepped past him.

I ground to a halt. Damn it. I knew he'd been listening.

"I said I'd get training. I never said who it would be from."

He straightened from the wall, his body brushing mine. "As your sire, Thomas will appoint a mentor. We've already agreed it will be me."

My head snapped towards him, he smiled with a smug expression and sauntered past me. "I'll expect you an hour after sunset on Monday."

"This is just temporary," I shouted after him. He lifted a hand in lazy acknowledgment. Just temporary until I learned what I needed to know and could convince Caroline of a better course of action.

Eric stepped past me, startling me. I hadn't known he was back here. He paused before turning. "The owner of the Book Haven's shadow side said he's looking for an assistant. Your friend is qualified and there are no humans to worry about in the night store."

I stared after him with an open mouth as he followed Liam on silent feet. The suggestion was a good one, and I kicked myself for not thinking of it before. The hint the book gave me a few nights ago made more sense now. It had been trying to tell me the solution to Caroline's problem all along. I just hadn't been listening. Even more shocking was that it had come from him, a man I could have sworn would prefer to drop me into a deep dark hole. It almost made me like the other vampire.

I'd talk to the shopkeeper before presenting it to Brax, but I was sure I could work out a deal for Caroline. With a solution in mind for her problems, I headed home. My real home. My room at the Gargoyle was luxurious with a shower and bed that would tempt a nun, but it wasn't home. After the week I'd had, I wanted to be surrounded by my own things in the home I'd created for myself.

*

"Where are my stairs?" I shouted at the foreman who'd been less than helpful since I arrived home.

The man was middle-aged and looked like he wanted to be anywhere but here right now. Possibly because I had intercepted him and the others as they were leaving for the night. It might also have been because I'd been shouting for the past five minutes, beside myself since I couldn't get up to my apartment without that staircase.

"I told you, lady, the former stairs violated building code. The landlord wanted it torn down and a new one built in its place." He chewed a piece of gum, looking like a cow with a piece of cud.

I took a deep breath through my nose. How would it look to Caroline if hours after I chastised her for her lack of control, I murdered an obnoxious construction worker? Don't kill the human, Aileen. You need him to construct the staircase since the old one was currently in pieces on the ground.

"How long is that going to take?" I snapped, tired and wanting to be home, curled in bed with a good book.

He shrugged. "A few weeks."

"Weeks?" My voice reached registers not meant for human ears. The foreman winced, and his crew looked over at us with an assortment of expressions ranging from humorous to scathing. "What am I supposed to do in the meantime?"

All of my clothes were up there. My computer. Everything. I needed to start looking for a new job. How was I supposed to do that when I couldn't access my apartment?

He shrugged. "Not my problem."

My jaw dropped open, and I took a threatening step towards him. "How 'bout I make it your problem?"

He rolled his eyes, obviously not finding me very threatening. "Look, lady, all of the residents were informed of this via letter. You got a complaint, take it up with your landlord."

I hadn't seen a letter. Furthermore, that still did not solve my problem.

The foreman turned his back, not waiting for me to say another word and stalked off, muttering about hysterical women. It took more self-control than I was proud of not to follow him and show him just how hysterical I could be. Instead, I turned and headed to the mailboxes for the building, determined to find the landlord's number and give him a piece of my mind. I'd missed a few days of mail with everything that was going on. It showed too, with the mailbox crammed full of paper.

Even though we were in the digital age, I sure got a lot of junk mail. I sorted through the stuff I could throw away and pulled out two pieces of mail that looked like they were important. The first was from my landlord and included a notice of sale saying that the new owner planned to make a few improvements to the current building and its parking lot. I looked around at the newly paved lot, understanding its presence now. The second was addressed to me and was a form letter stating that construction of the steps would begin on a certain date, and that I would need to arrange alternative accommodations. I checked the date, realizing that was tonight. The letter went on to say my rent would be prorated for those days that I was inconvenienced and unable to get into my apartment.

I skimmed the rest, which was just a lot of fancy lawyer talk. None of which told me what I was supposed to do in the meantime. My gaze caught on the name at the bottom of the letter. A name very familiar to me.

Thomas Bennet.

My hand dropped to my side as I took in the apartment and its brand-new parking lot with a horrified gaze. Everything was owned by Thomas. My sire was my new landlord.

DISCOVER MORE
BY T.A. WHITE

The Broken Lands Series
Pathfinder's Way – Book One
Mist's Edge – Book Two

The Dragon-Ridden Chronicles
Dragon-Ridden – Book One
Of Bone and Ruin – Book Two
Shifting Seas - Novella

The Aileen Travers Series
Shadow's Messenger – Book One
Midnight's Emissary – Book Two
Moonlight's Ambassador – Book Three

CONNECT WITH ME

Twitter: @tawhiteauthor
Facebook: https://www.facebook.com/tawhiteauthor/
Website: http://www.tawhiteauthor.com/
Blog: http://dragon-ridden.blogspot.com/

Click here to join the hoard and sign up for updates regarding new releases.

ABOUT THE AUTHOR

Writing is my first love. Even before I could read or put coherent sentences down on paper, I would beg the older kids to team up with me for the purpose of crafting ghost stories to share with our friends. This first writing partnership came to a tragic end when my coauthor decided to quit a day later, and I threw my cookies at her head. Today, I stick with solo writing, telling the stories that would otherwise keep me up at night. Most days (and nights) are spent feeding my tea addiction while defending the computer keyboard from my feline companion, Loki, who would like to try her paw at typing

EXCERPT FOR PATHFINDER'S WAY

The Trateri are about to learn a vital lesson of the Broken Lands. Deep in the remote expanse where anything can happen, it pays to be on a pathfinder's good side.

Nobody ventures beyond their village. Nobody sane that is. Monstrous creatures and deadly mysteries wait out here. Lucky for the people she serves, Shea's not exactly sane. As a pathfinder, it's her job to face what others fear and find the safest route through the wilderness. It's not an easy job, but she's the best at what she does.

When the people she serves betray her into servitude to the Trateri, a barbarian horde sweeping through the Lowlands intent on conquest, Shea relies on her wits and skill to escape, disguising herself as a boy to hide from the Warlord, a man as dangerous as he is compelling.

After being mistaken as a Trateri scout during her escape, Shea finds herself forced to choose between the life she led and the possibilities of a new one. Her decision might mean the difference between life and death. For danger looms on the horizon and a partnership with the Warlord may be the only thing preventing the destruction of everything she holds dear.

Chapter One

"For God's sake, woman, the village will still be there if we take an hour's break."

Shea rolled her eyes at the soaring mountains before her. This was the third rest stop the man had called for since setting out this morning.

"We must be half way there by now," he continued.

Maybe if they hadn't stopped several times already or if they had moved with a purpose, but as it stood the group had probably traveled less than two miles. Half of that nearly vertical. At this pace, it would take an extra half day to get back to Birdon Leaf.

And who would they blame for the delayed arrival?

Shea. Even though it wasn't her needing to stop on every other hill when they felt a muscle cramp or experienced shortness of breath. Since she was the pathfinder, it was obviously her fault.

She could hear it now.

The pathfinder sets the pace. The pathfinder chooses when to take breaks. Yada. Yada. Yada.

She hated running missions with villagers. They thought that since they'd gone on day trips outside their village barriers as children, they knew a thing or two about trail signs and the Highlands in general.

It was always, 'We should take this route. I think this route is faster. Why is it taking so long? These mountain passes are sooo steep.'

Never mind it was her that had walked these damn routes since the time she could toddle after the adults or that the paths they suggested would take them right through a beast's nest.

Nope. She was just a pathfinder. A female pathfinder. A female pathfinder who hadn't grown up in the same village as them. Obviously, she knew nothing of her craft.

The man yammered on about how they couldn't take another step. Any reasonable person could see how worn out they were. She wasn't the one carrying the gear or the trade goods.

Whine. Whine. Whine.

That's all she heard. Over the last several months, she'd perfected the art of tuning them out without missing pertinent information.

It was all in the pitch. Their voices tended to approach a higher frequency when they regressed to bitching about what couldn't be changed. As if she could make the switchbacks approaching the Garylow Mountain pass any less steep or treacherous.

"We'll take a rest once we reach the pass," she said for what seemed like a hundredth time.

They had begged for another break since about five minutes after the last one.

She had a deadline to meet. Sleep to catch. Most importantly, she didn't think she could last another half day with this lot.

"We're nowhere near that pass," the man raged.

The rest break obviously meant a lot to him.

"It's just over that ridge," Shea pointed above her.

Well, over that ridge and then another slight incline or two. It was just a small lie, really. If the man knew the truth, he'd probably sit down and refuse to take another step.

"That's nearly a half mile away." The man's face flushed red.

Really if he had enough energy to be angry, he had enough energy to walk.

"Quarter mile at most."

"We're tired. We've been walking for days. First to the trading outpost and then back. What does an hour's difference make?"

Shea sighed. Looked up at the blue, blue sky and the soaring pinnacles of rock then down at the loose shale and half trampled path they'd already traveled.

"You're right, an hour's rest won't make much difference." His face lit up. "However, you've already wasted two hours today on the last two breaks. You also wasted several hours yesterday, and the day before, and the day before that. We should have been back already."

She held up her hand when he opened his mouth.

"Now, we are getting up that pass. We need to be over it and down the mountain by nightfall. Otherwise you're going to have to fend off nightfliers. Do you want to fend off nightfliers when you could be sleeping? Or would you rather suck it up and get over that damn ridge?"

The man paled at the mention of nightfliers, a beast about three times the size of a bat that had a disturbing tendency of picking up its food and dropping it from a high altitude. It made it easier to get to the good parts on the inside.

"We'll wait to take the break." He turned and headed down to the last switchback where the rest of their party waited.

"Oh, and Kent." Shea's voice rose just loud enough for him to hear. "Please let them know that if anybody refuses to walk, I'll leave them here to fend for themselves. Nightfliers aren't the only things that roam this pass come nightfall."

He gave her a look full of loathing before heading down to his friends. Shea kept her snicker to herself. Good things never happened when they thought she was laughing at them.

Idiot. As if pathfinders would abandon their charges. If that was the case, she would have left this lot behind days ago. There were oaths preventing that kind of behavior.

What she wouldn't give to enjoy a little quiet time relaxing on the roof of her small home right about now.

They didn't make it back to the village until early the next morning. Shea brought up the rear as their group straggled past the wooden wall encircling the small village of Birdon Leaf.

The village was a place that time had forgotten. It looked the same as it had the day it was founded, and in fifty years or a hundred, it'd probably still be the same. Same families living in the same homes, built of wood and mud by their father's, father's, father. Most of the buildings in the village were single story and one room. The really well off might have a second room or a loft. Nothing changed here, and they liked it that way. Propose a new idea or way of doing something and they'd run you out of town.

They didn't like strangers, which was fine because most times strangers didn't like them.

They tolerated Shea because they needed the skills her guild taught to survive. Shea tolerated them because she had to.

Well, some days she didn't.

A small group of women and children waited to welcome the men.

A large boned woman with a hefty bosom and ash blond hair just beginning to gray flung her arms around a tall man with thinning hair.

"Where have you been? We expected you back yesterday morning." She smothered his face with kisses.

"You know we had to keep to the pathfinder's pace. The men didn't feel it would be right leaving her behind just because she couldn't keep up."

There it was. Her fault.

Anytime something went wrong it was due to the fact she was a woman. Even looking less feminine didn't help her. A taller than average girl with a thin layer of muscles stretching over her lean frame, Shea had hazel eyes framed by round cheeks, a stubborn mouth and a strong jaw-line she'd inherited from her father. Much to her consternation.

"What the guild was thinking assigning a woman to our village, I'll never know," the woman said in exasperation. "And such useless trail bait. They must have sent the laziest one they had."

Trail bait. Dirt pounder. Roamer. Hot footed. Shea had heard it all. So many words to describe one thing. Outsider.

Shea turned towards home. At least she would have a little peace and quiet for the next few days. She planned to hide out and not see or talk to anyone.

Just her and her maps. Maybe some cloud watching. And definitely some napping. Make that a lot of napping. She needed to recharge.

"Pathfinder! Pathfinder," a young voice called after her.

Shea turned and automatically smiled at the girl with the gamine grin and boundless enthusiasm racing after her. "Aimee, I've told you before you can call me Shea."

Aimee ducked her head and gave her a gap toothed smile. She was missing one of her front teeth. She must have lost it while Shea was outside the fence.

"Pathfinder Shea. You're back."

Shea nodded, amused at the obvious statement. Of all the villagers in this backwoods place, Aimee was her favorite. She was young enough that she didn't fear the wilds lying just beyond the safety of the barrier. All she saw was the adventure waiting out there. She reminded Shea of the novitiates that came every year to the Wayfarer's Keep in hopes of taking the Pathfinder's exam and becoming an apprentice.

"Um, did you see any cool beasts this time?" Aimee burst out. "Nightfliers, maybe? You said they liked to nest in the peaks around Garylow's pass. What about red backs?"

"Whoa, hold up. One question at a time." Shea took a piece of paper she'd torn from her journal last night in anticipation of this moment. "Here. I saw this one diving to catch breakfast yesterday morning."

Shea handed her a sketching of a peregrine falcon in mid dive. It was a natural animal, but to a girl raised in a village where all non-domesticated animals were considered 'beasts,' it would seem exotic. Shea had sketched it during one of the numerous breaks the men had taken.

"Pathfinder Shea," a woman said from behind them, disapproval coloring her voice. "The elders wish to speak to you."

Shea's smile disappeared as she schooled her face to a politeness she didn't really feel. Aimee hid the drawing in her skirts.

The woman's eyes shifted to Shea's companion. "Aimee, my girl, your mother's looking for you. I suggest you get on home."

Aimee bobbed in place, suitably chastened and followed as the woman swept away, but not before aiming a small smile in Shea's direction.

Shea lifted a hand and waved. Aimee had become something of Shea's shadow in the past few weeks. It was a welcome change, given how most of the villagers pretended she didn't exist or treated her with barely concealed hostility.

Shea looked woefully towards the tightly packed dirt trail leading to her little cottage. Her muscles ached and three days of grime and dirt coated her body.

She wanted a bath, a hot meal and then to sleep for twelve hours straight. She didn't want to deal with the grumpy, blame-wielding elders who no doubt wanted things they couldn't or shouldn't have. But if she didn't deal with them now, they would just show up and nag at her until she gave them her attention. They wanted something from her. Again. Better to deal with things now so she could have an uninterrupted rest later.

Her well-deserved break would have to wait

Her steps unhurried, she turned in the opposite direction of her bed. Even moving as slowly as she reasonably could, she quickly found herself in front of the town hall. It was also a pub and gathering place, basically anything the village needed it to be.

There were only two stone structures in the entire settlement. The town hall was the first and greatest, holding the distinction of being the only building large enough to shelter the entire village in the event of an attack. There was only one entrance, a heavy wooden door that could be barred from the inside. The thin slits in the upper levels kept attackers of both the four legged and two legged variety from slipping inside.

The building was the primary reason the founding families decided to settle here and was the village's one claim to wealth. The rest of the village, small though it was, had sprung up around it as a result.

For a place as backwards and isolated as Birdon Leaf, the town hall was a majestic building they couldn't hope to replicate. Even without the skills to maintain it, they were lucky. Some of the larger towns didn't have a structure this versatile that could act as both gathering place and shelter from danger.

Shea reached the doors and paused to brush the dirt from the back of her trousers and make sure her thin shirt was tucked in and her dark brown, leather jacket was lying straight.

Moonlight's Ambassador

Manufactured by Amazon.ca
Bolton, ON